CALAMITY

CALAMITY

CONSTANCE FAY

BRAMBLE

TOR PUBLISHING GROUP

NEW YORK

CALAMITY

Copyright © 2023 by Constance Fay

A Bramble Book
Published by Tom Doherty Associates / Tor Publishing Group
120 Broadway
New York, NY 10271

www.brambleromance.com

Bramble™ is a trademark of Macmillan Publishing Group, LLC.

The Library of Congress Cataloging-in-Publication Data
is available upon request.

ISBN 978-1-250-33041-3 (trade paperback)
ISBN 978-1-250-33042-0 (ebook)

Our books may be purchased in bulk for promotional, educational, or business use. Please contact your local bookseller or the Macmillan Corporate and Premium Sales Department at 1-800-221-7945, extension 5442, or by email at MacmillanSpecialMarkets@macmillan.com.

First Edition: 2023

Printed in the United States of America

0 9 8 7 6 5 4 3 2 1

To Carolyn Gillespie Fay and Jack Fay,
amazing people and supportive parents
who taught me to love stories,
and to treasure love.

Thank you for showing me it can be real.

CALAMITY

CHAPTER 1

The searchlight hits Ven's startled face at the same instant my chest hits the broad surface of the dune. I yank on my captain's ankle, tumbling him to the sand alongside me on the off chance that someone *didn't* notice a surprise person in the midst of what's supposed to be an unpopulated world. The searchlight pans back over the air above us.

"I don't think they saw us," Ven says just as a bolt of blaster light strikes the sand near our conjoined hands.

I scramble to my feet, unsteady in the light gravity and uncertain footing. "Oh, you think?"

Three more bolts hit as we crest the dune, both of us half falling when the sand slides from under our feet. He reaches back and catches my arm, yanking me up and over the peak to the dubious protection of the downslope. I duck lower while I skitter-skid down the smooth surface of the dune, darkness pressing close because when one is on a stealth surveillance mission, carrying a light is counterproductive. I have a pair of infrared glasses in my pocket somewhere, but I took them off when I was nearly blinded by the bright lights of the illegal grow operation.

"Guess we found out what was in the dead zone on the satellite and drone maps." I'm running so quickly that I have a hand to the side, scraping the steep slope of the dune for balance. My cheap body armor is stiff and awkward, making running more difficult than it should be. The dunes fade to a rocky plateau in front of us, pitted with stone chimneys and caves. The perfect place to hide from the pursuers I can already hear climbing the other side of the dune.

"Temperance, if you don't draw your blaster right this instant, I'm going to shoot you in the foot and leave you for them." Ven likes to call me by my full name. My mother did the same thing, to remind me of its meaning. My father shortened it to Temper because I have a bad one. Most people use Temper.

"If I unholster my blaster, I'm going to trip over the sand and accidentally shoot you in the back. Nobody wants that." It's a nice back. Better without holes.

We reach the bottom of the dune, sprinting headlong toward the nearest stone chimney, lit only by the light of dual crescent moons. Ven reaches back and captures my hand, pulling me forward. It would be romantic if it wasn't for the running-for-our-lives part.

One of the planet's many tumbling air-plants suddenly goes up in flames next to me. Like an idiot, I turn my head to look back. I don't know why I do it. Knowing what our pursuers look like won't do a thing to keep their blaster fire from killing me. It's about ten people, vibrant banishment tattoos glowing under their eyes. Their leader has a big blaster and Pierce-blond hair, illuminated by the light mounted on a neighboring weapon.

We reach the first pale stone chimney and put it between us and our pursuers, carefully winding our way between pits and narrow basalt towers. When we're far enough into the stone formations that they can't see us anymore, Ven gives me a boost to the hole in the side of one of the chimneys. I brace my legs inside and hold out a hand for him. He lets me haul him up after me. "Chimney" is the right word. It's a narrow tube, pressing us together. Chest to chest. Hip to hip.

Other things to other things.

"Do you really have an erection right now?" I hiss at him. Seems like inopportune timing.

His shrug displaces a thin rain of dust from within the walls of the chimney. It patters down at our feet. "You inspire me."

I laugh, nothing more than a puffed breath, forehead falling forward against his chest. I focus on keeping my breathing silent even though it feels like I inhaled about half the dune. As I catch my breath, Ven contacts the ship on his coms. Nothing much they can do now. We'll hunker down here and then sneak back; vid evidence captured to share with the Flores Family. Our job is just to scout the place, not to enforce whatever law the growers are breaking.

I don't even know what the stupid night-blooming flower in the vibrant green fields under the stark grow lights was, but you don't go to a ghost planet near the edge of charted territory to grow legal florals.

"They were all banished." Ven is fascinated by my own mark of banishment. It's the first thing he ever commented on, when we met. All banishment tattoos are the same aesthetically, a glowing line that drips from beneath the left eye, about two finger-widths long. His finger traces down the line on my cheek, tender. Both of us have helmets, but the face shields are back—it's too dark for them.

A shaft of moonlight from the hole above us illuminates his narrow face and sharp jaw. Ven's built like a fencer, long and lean. His hand drifts from my cheek to where a strand of my dark-red hair has escaped, coiling it between his fingers. I press upward on my toes, adrenaline still hammering in my veins, and his lips meet mine in a frantic hard kiss. It builds in intensity until I feel like I could float away.

Which is stupid because there are very likely still people pacing around this stony valley waiting for us to make a noise so that they can murder us. We can get away with whispers, between the thick rock walls and the wind whistling between the formations. Not more than that. I disentangle myself gently.

This thing between us isn't new. It's been simmering for about half a standard year. Sometimes boiling. Sometimes exploding. But always a secret from the others on board the *Quest*. According to Ven, fraternizing with the crew leads to feelings of unfairness. Better to keep it quiet.

Honestly, I was just happy to be getting laid. Now, it chafes. It's time for us to come clean. I want to tell Caro and Itzel, our engineer and biologist. Micah, the medic. Fuck, I even want to tell Itzel's intern, Oksana. I don't want Ven to be my secret anymore.

Ven traces a finger on my cheek one more time and takes the opportunity to state the obvious. "People aren't driven to frontier planets unless they've been kicked out of regular society. They're dangerous."

All the shooting was a good clue. I snort. "The reason they're here is probably the reason they were kicked out. They're farmers, not soldiers. Besides, regular society isn't all that safe. The Five Families are at each other's necks and the next Ten are just as bad."

"You were wasted with the Families, especially with Frederick." Even trapped in a stone pillar, whispering to avoid getting shot, Ven has a way of stabbing me right in the heart with kindness. Perhaps it's because my heart is so unused to defending against it.

It's maybe the shock from that kindness that makes me say what I do next. "We should tell the crew."

He blinks. Glances up at the night sky visible through the chimney above us. "I did just tell the crew. Sent an image of the flowers to whoever's awake. Maybe they can ID them."

A sly spike of discomfort worms its way down my spine. I quell it. He misunderstood. He's not trying to change the subject. That's just my brain trying to sabotage itself. "I don't mean about how we were chased by murderous farmers. I mean about us. We've been doing this long enough to know it's not just hormones and tight spaces. It's real. I'd like to try it outside storage closets and stolen moments. Not that I don't enjoy a storage closet here or there."

He shifts his weight slightly, hand slipping up my back, when the crunch of gravel outside makes its way through the whistle of the wind and the stone of the chimney. We freeze. More steps sound around us, and I flash through a vivid fantasy of them shooting blindly into the rock formations, hoping to startle us out. I hold my breath. Ven is absolutely motionless.

Something scrapes the rock on the other side of the chimney, like the barrel of a blaster being dragged over the basalt.

"Where did you guys find plankat nibarat flowers?" Oksana the intern's loud cheerful voice squeals out through my inner-ear coms, almost startling me into movement. I do twitch. Ven does, too. I also grimace because of *course* it would be plankat nibarat.

I'd rather it was drugs.

In the glory days of personal modifications, the one thing that never quite worked was intelligence boosting. Plankat nibarat was a sort of superfuel for fetal brain development and a medium fuel for adult brain enhancements. Nearly every one of the Fifteen Families had their hand in plankat refinement and some even experimented on their own.

Plankat does make geniuses. It just *also* makes paranoid sociopaths. One murdered his way through a whole satellite before he was finally captured. Shockingly, that wasn't as popular. After a few very public examples of what became known as plankat poisoning, the cultivation of the flower was banned, and any existing crops were destroyed.

If they were making synth out here, no one would care. Plankat is a different matter because plankat is banned *everywhere*. It's a danger to everyone. Plankat is one of the rare things that would drive a Family out of its comfortable territory.

Which means our pursuers *really* want to kill us. More footsteps approach. My palms grow sweaty.

"I haven't seen it outside the banned-biology section in school!

Could you get me a sample? Everyone would be so jealous if I could get an actual sample of plankat. The professor didn't even have one." Oksana keeps yammering, apparently having taken no cue from our silence.

Halfway through a midterm pleasure cruise, Oksana got dumped by her rich boyfriend and left at the nearest way station. She's trying to save enough credits to work her way home, too embarrassed to admit the situation to her family. Ven's been generous enough to take her under his wing, pointing out to Itzel that she always said she could use an intern.

"Hello? Are these coms working? If you're responding, I can't hear you." She blithely continues as the scrape of metal against stone comes from our other side. I shift my hand to my hip, drawing my blaster and pointing it up at the open space above, heart lodged firmly in my throat. A slight mutter and scuffling sound comes from the other end of the coms.

"Oh no, you're in danger. I didn't know you were in *danger*." Now she's whispering. I pinch my eyes shut. "Itzel says you're being chased, and I need to shut up because I'm distracting you because you need to lose them before you can come back here. Oh . . . She says I'm *still* distracting you. I didn't mean to dis—"

The coms cut out. Thanks to Itzel, I assume. Ven's chest moves against my own and I glance up to find that he's silently laughing. I shake my head. Not the time or place. It's not charming, it's dangerous.

He silently laughs harder.

The sound of footsteps on gravel retreats. They don't return. We continue to wait to be discovered or shot.

"My drones just passed over your location." Caro's calm voice comes over the coms sometime later. "They're currently searching the dunes to the south. There's a window for you to escape to us in the north if you do it fast."

"Good." I stretch upward to the hole above, fingers gripping the edges. "I'm starting to get a cramp in my leg."

Ven thumbs his coms off. "I could have rubbed it for you."

I raise a brow. "And what would you have wanted me to rub in return?"

He laughs out loud this time. We finally exit the narrow stone chimney and head north, leaving the basalt formations and setting out across rolling hills of sandy desert. The moonlight spills silver on the pale gray sand.

We almost make it to the ship.

"Shit. They have a drone of their own deployed. They're approaching your location. I missed it. Shit." Caro's voice sounds in the coms again. Less calm. I'd define her tone as seriously fucking concerned.

"How far out are they?" Ven asks as we start jogging faster, glancing over our shoulders.

"Don't jog. Run."

The sand slides under my boots, loose and silty, turning my attempted sprint to a stumble. We finally reach the last hill and there it is in the distance, our glorious hideous ship, a dark bulk against the dunes. Ven found it in a junk heap and named it *Quest*. It's not a good name but we're used to it. Ven loves the name because of some story he read as a child. The *Quest* is the closest thing I've had to a home in ten standard solar years, and I love every dented bulkhead like it's my own and I love its crew even more.

"There they are!" someone yells from behind us and the heat of a near-miss blaster shot traces over my hip.

As motivations go, it's a fantastic one. I tuck my chin down, lengthen my stride, and push as hard as I can for speed. Ven pulls ahead of me.

"Run faster! They're catching up and they have blasters. Really big ones!" Oksana's voice breaks through the coms yet again, continuing to offer the sort of top-notch advice that will get her hired on exactly zero future scouting crews. She then appears to respond to something that was said to her outside of the coms stream. We try not to clutter the airways. "What? You said I had to be quiet before. They're being chased now. Clearly the bad guys know where they are. I am being *supportive*. You can do it! Run faster!"

The *Quest's* lights come on and the sand stirs around the landing gear as the engines rev up.

It's all going so well until my foot plummets far deeper than a loose spot in the sand should allow. I crash down on my face, knee-deep in some sort of burrow or hole or maybe wherever the stupid air-plants that roll lazily around the surface of this desert originally grew. It should be easy to free myself, but my foot is caught. I shove at the sand ineffectually, trying to get a firm enough grip to pull through it but failing every time.

Ahead of me, Ven reaches the safety of the ship. He turns, probably expecting me right behind him. I'd love to meet expectations.

I give up tugging and dig around my ankle, shoving sand in the air. As I paw at the dirt, I look behind me. In the darkness, lit only by the crescent moons, it's difficult to count pursuers. Luckily for me, they were all banished, so I can go by the little glowing tattoos bobbing above the ground. Which means that all ten pursuers have crested the hill after us and are closing in on me.

I point my blaster back at them with my free hand, shoveling with the other, and squeeze off a volley of fire. I'm not even aiming. I'm just trying to slow them down. I look back at the ship to find Ven racing toward me, tension bracketing his mouth, eyes darting from me to our pursuers who are getting ever closer. As I frantically yank my ankle again, Ven skids to a halt at my side, reaching into the hole with a knife in his hand. He starts to saw at the thick knotty roots.

My foot breaks free with shattering force, still tangled in roots that don't seem to have an associated plant, but I don't even care because I'm back on my feet, and we're sprinting for the ship as fast as we can. A shot collides with the back of my armor, and two others with the helmet. The sizzle of energy dissipating dances over my skin.

My ankle hurts. Breathing hurts.

My heart, though, is so full it might burst. Ven came back for me. This isn't just a fling. It's real. He didn't get a chance to answer earlier, but of course we're going to go public with our relationship. This is more than sex.

We burst through the hatch, and it immediately swivels shut behind us. The ship vibrates as Caro launches. I lean against a bulkhead, panting for breath, and watch Ven, heart in my throat. A bead of sweat trickles down my neck.

He looks from the hatch to me, and I open my mouth to say everything I'm thinking. I've been his partner for years on the ship, it's time to be his partner in truth, in all things.

Oksana runs into the chamber and hurls herself into his arms, rich brown-blond hair nestled beneath his chin. Her voice quivers. "I was worried."

I start to laugh at the overdramatics when she grabs his cheeks between her hands and kisses him like he's going to war. Like he just came home. Like he's a bomb that she needs to diffuse with her tongue.

It doesn't look like a first kiss.

My mouth stays open, but all the words die in my throat.

His eyes find me, over her head, and they hold a kind of panic. Not the panic of someone who's surprised. The panic of someone who's found out. They dart back to her and his expression changes. He made up his mind. He kisses her back.

I feel like I'm intruding on a personal moment between the

man who I lo—*liked* and the woman-child who accidentally
exploded a rocking furnace in the fume hood the other day because she forgot it was on.

She finally breaks for air and a perfect crystalline tear tumbles
down her cheek. "I thought I'd never see you again. I don't care
about keeping it a secret anymore. I love you."

That was my line. There's a kind of dull buzzing between my
ears. My head goes light and airy. I suck in a slow breath.

I've never cried that beautifully in my life. I haven't done many
things as beautifully as Oksana. Compared to her willowy frame,
I'm short and solidly built with both an ass and nose that are slightly
too big for current fashion. She has smooth skin and so much hair
she could hide a weapon in its thickness. I have dark reddish hair
that can't even decide if it wants to be curly or straight and despite
the radiation-resistant mods that allow me to absorb the light from
suns of any spectrum without developing cancer, my pale skin is
still far too reactive for my own good.

A humiliated—not humiliated, *angry*—flush creeps up my cheeks
and I look down at the floor, swallowing hard. It's not embarrass-
ment. It's *not*. I can't believe I thought he was telling the truth.
That I thought he'd really care about me.

Who wants a banished lover who ties them down to only un-
charted space? This tattoo that so fascinates him is a closed door.
A small squeak that might have been a sob catches in my throat as
I stare at them.

He's still looking at me with those eyes that beg me to just play
it calm. To accept my lot and not make a mess of things.

Clearly, he doesn't know me at all. Making a mess is, like, my
best skill.

"What the fuck, Ven?"

Itzel and Micah appear in the entry to the hold, momentarily
frozen by the unexpected vitriol in my tone.

"What do you mean?" He's still desperately trying to play pretend.

"I mean, where do you get off sleeping with me and the intern at the same time?" I enunciate each word carefully, in case Oksana isn't paying full attention. Then I realize exactly what I implied and clarify. "Not the exact same time. Overlapping times. How long were you going to play us against each other? Telling me it would make the crew uncomfortable if everyone knew?"

"I have no idea what he'd mean by that. I'm certainly not deeply uncomfortable right now." Micah's sarcastic tone breaks through the wall of rage building in my head as he crouches near my ankle, poking at it. The ship's cams probably showed it getting stuck.

"I knew." Oksana's voice is quiet. Censuring, even. "He told me how you came on to him. He said he made a mistake."

A mistake that he kept making for the better part of six standard months. Also, I did *not* come on to him! My mouth drops open, too astounded to even get any words out. Like my rebuttal is a traffic clog in my throat. My finger just stabs angry points at Ven like that will get my position across.

It seems to. He looks terrified.

Micah gives me the all clear to get to my feet. Itzel's still staring at us, as fascinated as if we were a holo-show. I can't stand being in this space one more instant. I'm nearly out of the hold when I turn back to Ven and Oksana. "What's going to happen next? When Oksana finally goes back home? We all know she isn't going to be a professional scout."

And what was wrong with *me*? Sure, it's a pathetic question, but it's a real one. I've known Ven for years. We have chemistry. We have banter. I thought we had everything. Except I only had half of Ven. If that.

"He's going home with me." Oksana staunchly clutches his arm like he's a trophy. I'm suddenly disgusted with him. With them. With myself. I'm not going to fight over *Ven*. I need to take a moment. I need to breathe and think and maybe drink a metric fuck-ton of whatever liquor we have on board.

Ven looks anywhere but in my eyes. "I'm selling the *Quest*, Temperance. Don't make a scene, please."

Like I'm the one out of line, here. Maybe, just like my mother, he was also always trying to remind me to restrain myself. To be a little less than I am. I bite the inside of my cheek, hands curling into fists. Micah finally decides he's done with this whole scene. His shoulder pushes Ven into the doorway as he passes the captain.

My jaw sets. Fuck Ven and fuck maturity.

"I think I'm entitled to make a scene, Ven." When he starts to speak, I cut him off. "I also think you're desperate. No one's buying a ship as old and shitty as the *Quest*. Not with the new phydium engines coming any day now. And I know you don't have the kind of savings that can get two people across charted territory."

I know who does, though. Ish. I know what it takes to be a captain. Mostly. I've taken care of everything but the budgets, and how hard can that be?

By the time we get to Landsdown Way Station, I've consulted with the rest of the crew. Ven and Oksana get their tickets across charted territory.

I get the *Quest*.

For about half of what it's worth. Which is still double what I can afford. Worth it to never see Ven again.

CHAPTER 2

My savings weren't enough to cover the full purchase, which means a debt collector is waiting to seize the ship if I can't make payments. We need a big job to stay in the sky and to keep the crew together. We're specialized for planet scouting, which is a big payday when you can find it.

I have two things working against me.

One: everyone appears to be scared bugfuck of hiring me directly and pissing off my brother, the head of the Reed Family. Or, possibly, scared of the reputation of an untrustworthy traitor like me. Frederick made sure rumors spread throughout charted territory after my banishment. The most recent was that I tried to sabotage one of their satellites by selling the plans to a lower-tier family who planned an act of terrorism.

No one bothers to ask why I'd do something so mindlessly evil and stupid. They heard it on the streams, so it must be true.

Besides their issues with me is disadvantage two: it's a bad time to do business in general.

A couple standard months ago, an article went into the feed about new engines that could revolutionize space travel. The advancement would open uncharted space to everyone—not just generation ships. The problem is that these fancy new engines need fuel. Specifically, the insanely rare mineral phydium.

No one has it. Everyone wants it. And no one wants to make a move on any existing picked-over planet when there might be a better one right over the proverbial horizon once they figure out the resources.

Scouting vessels like the *Quest* are equipped with faster-than-light drives that allow us to explore farther than most, but if we want to get to the very edge of charted space, we have to go on the same long slog as everyone else. It isn't worth the money.

In my desire to screw Ven over, I may have just screwed myself. I now have a very expensive ship in a market with no expensive jobs.

I win?

The Five are the only ones who can pay enough, which is why, when I receive a summons from the Escajeda, I grudgingly—and by "grudgingly," I mean "very professionally"—make my way to the Escajeda Family's very expensive suite in Landsdown. It's luck, even if the high-ranking Families make me personally uncomfortable.

When I pound on the heavily embossed outer door of the Escajeda's rooms, I expect a snooty-faced servant of some kind to reprimand me over the external coms but, instead, the door slides open under my hand and I almost punch Ina Escajeda in her flawless face.

As a way to nonplus me, it's shockingly effective. I catch my hand and yank it back into my personal bubble, at a loss for words. Ina Escajeda is the wife of Armando. The other half of the empire. She's not the sort to answer doors. She's the sort to be featured in a fashion designer's holo-campaign—lean angular body sculpted just for artistic poses and sparkling brown eyes vibrant with manufactured emotions.

Because she's probably a sociopath. Families are like that.

Some might call her the second-in-command but that's only because she looks soft and gentle and comforting. She'll look that sweet up to and including the moment she pulls the dagger from between your ribs and licks the blade.

She probably doesn't *really* either stab people or lick the blade, but she does in my imagination.

"Temperance Reed," Ina says with a faint accent that is one hundred percent pretension. There are certainly many languages floating over the universe, but Family leadership all speak Standard, and they have for generations.

She's wearing a slim wrap dress in black and red that probably cost more than the *Quest*, paired with dangly black earrings and perfectly styled hair in the kind of updo that is impossible to achieve without a personal stylist. It makes me very aware of my own unfashionable hair, which is corralled in a braid—my only reliable hairstyle. My coveralls are two sizes too large because I bought in bulk and this way Caro, Itzel, and I can share. The cuffs are rolled so I don't step on them. It's like I'm playing dress-up as a planet-scouting captain.

The Reeds were in the Ten, one tier beneath the Five, but my parents focused my prebirth genetic manipulation on health, coloring, and physical utility. Most aesthetic mods are applied when one is fully grown. By then, Frederick was in charge of our coffers, and he didn't spare funds to create perfect skin and a whittled waist. In fetal development, the best they could do was ensure that I had the red hair, green eyes, and inconveniently pale skin of a Reed. I've heard that Pierce made their aesthetic genes dominant. Any child created by a Pierce parent will have distinctive blond hair and warm brown eyes.

I don't have time to linger over appearances . . . there are lives to ruin.

Specifically, my own.

"I received a message from the Escajeda." The head of a Family gets the name as a title. It gives the impression that there's a monolith-like presence that controls the Family through generations.

I wait, watching her, and she waits, watching me back. I wonder if she's going to stand there indefinitely. I stare at her until she presses her index finger against the tattoo on her ring finger. Must be a pressure link that will alert the Escajeda when she wants him. It's a shocking intimacy for someone of their status. Families are practiced at keeping their own at arm's length, and most spouses are conjoined more by contracts than love. Yet, he's allowed her under his skin.

I have a brief flash of Ven and Oksana, so coiled in each other it's hard to tell where one ends and the other begins. It's something special to let someone within your walls. Something I don't fully understand. My parents were like that. True partners in everything, not just Family business.

The round entryway behind Ina Escajeda has an elaborate gold-tiled mosaic floor, a surreal golden marble wall—it must be quarried within their territory because I've never seen anything like it before—and a floating chandelier made of crystal spheres. A dramatic arched doorway behind Ina leads to a dark-paneled wooden hall. That doorway also has reinforced bars just waiting to drop if someone breeches the entrance. Probably all those shiny gold floor tiles are angled just right to reflect security lasers all over the room until I'm diced into tiny cubes.

When the silence has stretched past awkward to comfortable and then all the way back to awkward again, Ina Escajeda abruptly turns and says, "Follow me."

I don't get sliced by a laser in the foyer and I make it under the bars and through the dark hallway without impalement. The hallway opens to an impressive formal sitting area decorated in shades of cream and gold, with splashes of dark burgundy. The Escajeda

sits in the center of a spotless cream sofa with gilt-framed paintings arranged behind him in a shape reminiscent of a throne. His
hair is a carbon-black sweep so artful it might as well be carved.
His face is the specific type of ageless that comes with ridiculous
amounts of money, cheekbones high and dark eyes intense. He's fit
for someone old enough to be my father, but that could be because
his clothes are expensively tailored in a classic style that hides im-
perfections. His chin is shaped like a butt.

Ina leads me to a chair opposite him and, when I take a seat, it's
so uncomfortable that it must be purposefully designed that way.
I smile like I enjoy springs piercing my back and snuggle into it.

Ina perches beside the Escajeda, barely on the sofa. It's like she's
always poised to attack. He really did marry a guard dog in a wig.
A whisper of sound draws my attention to a dark-red chair on the
Escajeda side of the room. I briefly completely forget what Ven
looks like. I forget what *anyone* else in charted territory looks like.
The man who is sprawled in the chair looks like he belongs on a
billboard instead of a meeting room. Or maybe an anatomy lab as
an example of the perfect male form.

Not all sliced up with his guts out or anything.

Maybe that. I haven't spoken to him yet.

The second Escajeda child, Arcadio. Second in line for the
throne after his sister and ahead of his four younger brothers. Besides being the second-tier offspring, we don't have much in common. If I hadn't been banished, I might know him personally.

Arcadio shares his father's black hair, although his is slightly
mussed—like he's run his hand through it in frustration recently—
and a dark shadow of unshaven beard lines his jaw. He probably
shares his father's butt-chin, although it's hard to tell beneath the
beard. His eyes are black as the void. His features are chiseled. His
body exceedingly capable. He's stunning in the same way that a
star is—staring at him for too long could cause damage.

My stomach clenches and I wipe my hands on my coveralls. My ego is usually pretty healthy, but after Ven scampered off with Oksana, I'm feeling stale.

The whole Escajeda clan is far too beautiful. I rarely trust the artfully pretty, although I sure do like looking at them. It's a tool, and anyone smart enough to be in a Family knows to use it against you.

I turn my attention from the son to his father. "I received your message."

"We have an opportunity to explore, and we understand that you are between jobs at this moment." Certain Families speak using the imperial "we." It's an affectation I've never enjoyed but I suppose they're entitled to it.

"What possible opportunity would serve both of our purposes?"

"Herschel Two."

Is this the beginning of a guessing game where I'm forced to drag every bit of information out of him? "What about Herschel Two?"

A hologram pops up on the long table between us. That's fine craftsmanship because the table looks like a genuine antique. The planet spins over the fine-grained wood and, for a moment, I get lost in trying to figure out how the projection works instead of watching the planet itself.

"If anything we say leaves this room, you won't have to worry about your new debt. Your ramshackle ship will explode from an unforeseen mechanical error, and we'll ensure that your crew is on board when it happens." His eye contact does not waver, and a shiver of discomfort skitters its way up my back. That was either a lucky shot or a low blow considering how my parents died. I stare back. Maybe I win if he blinks first. Instead, he continues, assuming I'm suitably intimidated—which I am.

"Our spectrometric probes continuously map the chemical composition of unclaimed planets because, although we have many established mining outposts, new materials frequently gain popularity. Recent scans indicated Herschel Two may possess phydium deposits beneath the surface." I nearly drop the small tchotchke that I've been fiddling with off the corner of the holo-table. Phydium. What everyone wants and no one has. The key that unlocks the universe. It's mildly terrifying to imagine the Escajeda with that key in his pocket.

"Why me? You've always contracted with Nylla and Hovis and their twelve-person crew if your personal Family crew was otherwise occupied."

"A smaller team is advantageous for our goals. You can go unnoticed. If other Families know we are scouting Herschel Two, they will either send their own scouts or move on the planet outright. We have no desire to start a land war. It would be better if this planet is acquired in silence. Our crew is otherwise occupied with an investment in the Haxon sector. Nylla and Hovis are prestigious. People keep track of their jobs."

Apparently, my crew is shitty and obscure enough that no one bothers with what we do. I'll update our promotional material accordingly. Who knew it was such an advantage? It all makes sense, but something about it still doesn't ring as the complete truth. For one thing, why the Escajeda himself is meeting with me along with his wife and son. He has a station manager for this sort of task, I'm sure.

It also won't be as simple as he anticipates. I poke at a northern region on the spinning hologram before giving him the bad news. "Herschel Two has a settlement of the banished. Some religious order. Which means that region is protected from acquisition by the Safe Haven Accords. You can't acquire the whole planet." About twenty standard years ago, a group of banished people protested to the Family council about an acquisition that gobbled up some of the rare territory they could claim.

Normally, that wouldn't have provided successful results, but one of the banished happened to be an ex-Nakatomi. It was enough to remind a few members of the council that one bad week could make the difference between being on the council and being in that seized territory. The accords state that no one may acquire a segment of territory that has been settled by a group of over one hundred.

A muscle twitches in the Escajeda's jaw. "That is our concern, not yours. We are confident that the regions of interest are outside territory used by the settlers."

That's fair, I suppose. Also, he just threatened to blow up my ship, so perhaps this isn't the time to press him on following the law on colonization. At this point, I can't even run away from him without using his own credits to do it. "Do you have any reason to believe they're dangerous?"

He waves a hand dismissively. "That's what I'm paying you for."

"And what *are* you paying us?" I'm not worried about the planet. It's been surveyed a dozen times. There are streams of data about it that are far more useful than whatever he can tell me. Beyond pinpointing a region of interest, I can find what I need on my own and I don't want his slant on the information. Honestly, I don't want to spend one more moment in this carefully manicured room being watched by the Escajeda, his attack-dog wife, and his silent son who may as well be a statue. I don't even know why Arcadio is here. Did the room not have enough pretty people in it? Is his sister unavailable? Have his legs fallen asleep, and he can't stand up?

The Escajeda winces. I've been tacky, talking about money. It's never tacky when the wealthy do it, but it's grasping when people like me do. "For your expediency and your discretion, I'll pay one and a half times market rate."

This time I do drop the tchotchke. It rolls under the table with a resounding thunk and I silently wish that nothing broke. Then again, this man is throwing around such high pay rates that maybe he doesn't care. Maybe I could trip over this priceless holo-table on my way out and he wouldn't even blink. I didn't even have to negotiate for it. I could do a lot with those credits. The sheer quantity makes me suspicious, but you know what they say about the desperate and the suspicious; you can be one or the other, you can't be both.

"One and a half of market value. Half down." I add that last bit to clarify.

He nods, which seems too easy until he continues. "Silence is imperative. We must be confident that neither you nor anyone on your crew shares information on the phydium. If anything leaks, we will act accordingly. Don't assume there's anywhere you could go that we can't find you."

"Of course we won't share confidential information." We're professionals, after all. Even if we aren't of the caliber of Nylla and Hovis. "But we can't be held responsible for everyone who knows about this. People in your employ know. What if they talk?"

"No one in my Family will talk."

That's not the same thing. I start to argue again but he talks over me.

"This is time sensitive, as you might imagine. We require your mission to be completed in one standard month."

I don't have anything to drop this time. His time limit is ludicrous. No wonder he's willing to pay a lot. We won't find anything in that little time, and he won't have to pay the second half. Or, if we do find something, he can find a way to worm out of his contract due to a travel delay. "It will take at least six standard days to reach Herschel Two. Six to return. That does not leave enough time to scout an entire planet. It's unrealistic."

"We will provide a specific region." His face is impassive, like a carved statue of power in human form.

"And if I don't find anything in this region, you want me to leave other areas unscouted?" I want him to say the words.

"I expect you to complete your mission."

That's not an answer. Frederick modeled his operational style after the Escajeda, which means I know his tricks. The thing with working for Families is that the little guy doesn't have a leg to stand on. If they decide not to pay, you can appeal to the Inter-Family council—who will ignore you. Families love not paying for things if they can manage it. That's part of how they keep their wealth. Working for them offers big paydays if you make them very happy, but as with all things that are high-reward, they come with risk.

Even half of a payment is enough to get me out the door of the station, which buys time and intact limbs. Maybe time to fly as far as we can from anyone with the last name Escajeda. Better to be a thief than to be exploded. So, even if he's trying to screw me over, I have to go with it. I nod my understanding.

"I'll forward the pertinent information to your cache. One more thing." His voice is dry, like this just slipped his mind. Nothing slips his mind. This is yet another manipulation. One that's being captured on the contractual camera. I could refuse, but then he could withdraw the whole offer. We need those credits. Enough to put up with his unreasonable threats and timelines.

I turn, bracing for the worst but not even knowing what the worst is.

"Your team has no security."

"You wanted a small crew. It's a predominantly empty planet. Settlers can be avoided. Two of our team members are trained to double as security." I'm seeing the hook now and trying to dodge it even if I'm not sure where it's going to stick.

"The deal is contingent on one addition to your crew to maintain security."

It's not an unreasonable request under the circumstances.

Clearly, he's been monitoring Herschel Two closely. Perhaps he's seen something I haven't. Extra security isn't a problem. I can bring Victor and Victory in, if I need to. The twins used to be crew, but they left about a year ago to take up contract work. Pays better than scouting. Although this trip might just be worth it to them. "I'll recruit qualified applicants before departure. Same pay rate for the new crew members."

"No need for that. I have the perfect candidate." His voice is oily.

"I couldn't possibly take one of your security team from you." It's a weak effort. The deal is done. I can try to negotiate more, but I've already received all the allowances I can expect. I'm trapped with whatever spy he sticks to me, and he knows it. He's already threatened to chase us to the ends of charted space and blow up our ship—with us in it.

"It won't be a member of his security team." It's a new voice, deep with the requisite hint of Escajeda accent. The statue speaks. Arcadio leans forward, elbows on knees. "We need assurances that, if you find phydium, you don't claim you didn't and then sell the information to the highest bidder. Only Family can guarantee that."

Well, shit. That makes perfect sense and I hate every syllable of it. This is worse than a random guard-spy, it's a spoiled princeling. Security-team members have high mortality rates. If it was a spy, I could maybe let them fall into a crevasse and give Escajeda the paycheck back. Harder to do that with one of the man's sons. Yes, hc looks like he could bench-press a spaceship, but that's aesthetics. I don't know if he has any utility. Even if he does, it will come with an ego the size of the way station.

He's a Family man. They're all the same.

"Is he qualified?" I direct the question to the Escajeda, partially because he's the ultimate authority in the room and partially to needle the son and see how he reacts. He doesn't. I guess he's either not that bright or very controlled.

The Escajeda's mouth twitches. A slight vibration reverberates from the interface tattoo at my wrist. I activate my datapad. Arcadio's qualifications. Any child of the Five, or even the Ten, has combat training. It's protection against abduction if nothing else. Arcadio Escajeda isn't any child of the Five. Apparently, he is his father's general. Ranking off the charts in endurance—which my brain tries to take a detour on until I steer back in the right direction—strength, and tactics. He's in charge of security for his whole Family, which means I don't stand a chance in a black hole of claiming he's unqualified.

I want to protest but it's clear from his presence in the room that this was the Escajeda's plan all along.

The Escajeda holds out a hand, thrusting it through the hologram of Herschel Two, and I take it. His grip is hard but controlled. He's not squeezing but creating a cage around my hand. His is softer than I expected and very warm. It's sort of like holding a slab of meat fresh out of the oven. With that shake, I've sold my soul to get my soul back.

"I'll accompany you to the docks now. If we leave tomorrow, I must assess the state of the ship to make my own preparations," Arcadio says smoothly, as though I have nothing better to do with my time.

It's the competent answer, so I should be happy, but it sets my teeth on edge even more than they were already. It's probably the delivery that bothers me the most, a deep baritone voice with the confidence of someone who's never been told no and the commanding inflection of someone who expects to be heard. I'm also bothered by the way his father waited until our deal was almost done to slip him in.

His father watches him with pride.

I remember the first time my father looked at me that way. I was in the training arena, sparring with Frederick, who was five years older than I was. The size difference between us was significant. He was strong, but I was sneaky, and I pinned him. My father beamed with pride.

Later that day, Frederick caught me in the library and broke my leg. He threatened that, if I ever told anyone, he'd break my best friend Kari's leg in retaliation. I learned quickly that, with Frederick in my life, I didn't want to attract too much parental admiration. As it happened, ten years later, I attracted Frederick's undivided focus anyway, and someone else paid the price.

Arguably, everyone else paid the price.

"Follow me," I grit through my teeth as we exit the opulent suite.

CHAPTER 3

■ ■ ■ ■ ■ ■ ■ ■ ■ ■ ■ ■ ■ ■

"This body armor is a disgrace. The rest of your ship is equipped sufficiently, but for some reason your personal-protection equipment is a joke." Arcadio Escajeda pokes at my armor with one stiff finger as we walk toward the helm. He's been spending the first hours of our journey performing inventory of our armaments and—shockingly—has found them lacking. Lacking enough that he needs to bring the whole suit up and wave it in front of me as though I don't know my own armor.

Sure, my armor is a little outdated. My helmet doesn't match the rest because I got shot too many times and had to replace the suit. Helmets are expensive, so I kept the old one.

"Credits don't grow on space stations. I had to spend our deposit on fuel and food." And repaying debts. "You're welcome."

"There's a gap between helmet and collar. The circuit won't complete. That means no heads-up display or night vision—not that that would be a problem for you. That sliver of exposed skin is a huge vulnerability. You might as well not wear armor at all."

He apparently assumes I'm an idiot and don't understand how armor works. He also assumes I have night-vision mods. Most Family-raised people do. I don't. Yet another of those little perks that Frederick decided I didn't need. But I'm not in the mood to share even more weak spots. "Look, as a Five Family member, maybe you deal with a lot of highly trained snipers. I get shot at, but it's mostly by idiots who barely know how to hold a blaster. If

I'm dumb enough to make a target of my neck, I deserve to get shot in it."

His coveralls are a black so dark that they must never have been laundered before. All blacks become gray after being placed in the ship laundry. Just that little hint of wealth is enough to make me intensely dislike him. "You need to—"

"I don't need to do anything besides scout the territory. And speaking of that . . ." We arrive in the helm where the rest of the crew waits for the briefing. This will be the first one that I've run as captain.

I pull up a holo of Herschel Two on the corner unit. It isn't as fancy as the Escajeda's. A section on the southern quadrant keeps shorting out. Caro helpfully smacks the side of the unit and the projected image smooths. Clearly, the *Quest* was a fantastic investment.

"Herschel Two." Itzel shakes her head as we study the inhospitable surface of the planet. "Everyone assumed it was useless desert territory. There's one vaguely habitable region in the north that wouldn't require aquatic featuring but there are so many volcanos and cliffs that it would cost more credits than any Family has to flatten it out enough for buildings. What could the Escajeda possibly want with it?"

"Escajedas mine, they don't build." Caro walks around the unit, studying the planet from all sides even though the projection lazily rotates. "But plenty of people who aren't us have scouted it before and deemed it worthless. That's why they don't quibble about the cult that's set up on the surface. You know a Family would try to push them out if there was any value."

"It's a cult?" Micah rubs his chin with one broad hand. "I thought it was just a religious order."

Everyone who isn't an Escajeda avoids looking at Itzel. If one is generous, the monastery of the Dark Mother of the Void, where she was raised, could be considered a religious order. The kind that religiously loves a murder-goddess. Time for me to make a convenient interjection. "Let's not parse the fine details of religious preference. Herschel Two *was* considered useless for habitation up until recent Escajeda scans indicated the presence of phydium beneath the surface of the planet. Still useless for habitation, but now it's the sort of thing that could make a fortune. Another fortune."

Everyone now avoids looking at Arcadio. Probably all thinking what I'm thinking, which is that the last thing his Family needs is one more advantage.

"If they've detected phydium, what do they need us for?" Micah traces a hand through the holo, disrupting the light.

"Phydium graphical peaks are very similar to ulonium. They can't get better information without sending a team to the planet's surface." Above the planet, I project the signatures of the two minerals.

"My father's intelligence has outlined this area of interest." Arcadio activates the holo and one region of the northern hemisphere lights up. It's suspiciously close to the cult's settlement.

Of course it is. Fucking Families and their maneuvering.

That said, I really like remaining unexploded, and I have no doubt that the Escajeda will follow through on his threat if I renege. Maybe his son will do it for him. I haven't told the crew about the threat. They won't work with Arcadio if they know, and I need them to work well together.

If only *I* could work well with him. Between the fact that his father threatened to kill me and that Arcadio himself is airbrushed holo perfection, I'm constantly braced for the worst. His presence is forebodingly burly and masculine in a very specific way that makes me want to poke him until he explodes. It probably says something unflattering about me that my first instinct upon feeling attraction for a man is to irritate him.

Then again, we've already established, vis-à-vis Ven, that my instincts are faulty.

. . . . .

The ship's been making a weird grinding noise since we launched from Landsdown. I'm not out to impress Escajeda, but I'd prefer that we didn't look quite so pathetic in front of him. I haven't even had a chance to fail at captaining yet.

"It's the normal kind of grinding. Not the bad kind," Caro reassures me while barely hiding a grimace as she reaches into a battery chamber in the engine room. Her hair has at least three styli stuck in it, and a collection of gold earrings lines the dark-brown skin of her ears. She's a little taller than I am, a little curvier, and a lot more cynical. Her identity appeared out of nowhere about ten years ago. Prior to that, no one had ever heard of Caro Osondu. I've gleaned a fraction of her history, but she clearly wants to keep it private, and I respect that.

"Normal grinding has never happened before," I point out.

"When are you renaming the ship? You know *Quest* is a terrible name, right? There's no charisma. We're a charismatic crew. We deserve a good name."

"Charisma" is one thing to call what we have. "I'm not renaming the ship. There's nothing wrong with *Quest*. I have enough problems. First and foremost, finding samples of the mineral that's going to put us out of business." Our faster-than-light engine won't be able to compete with phydium-powered engines.

"I wish we were twenty years in the future and the phydium problem was solved." Caro stares at the engine dreamily.

"Because our engines would be better?"

She looks at me like I'm crazy. "It's not just engines, Temper.

That's the first thing, the biggest. But it's anything that needs energy. Fuck. Phydium, if controlled by someone else, could completely put the Pierce Family out of business. It would revolutionize energy sources. Your blaster charge would last for thousands more shots at higher intensities. With more reliable power, it would be cheap to set up a new colony, to power terraforming engines, to clean oceans and atmospheres from the polluted core worlds. Anyone could do it, not just Families. It makes tools like this one"— she holds a sensor aloft—"far less likely to fail us. Because the solar panels for this piece of shit aren't quite in tune to the spectrum emitted by most suns and the recharger is spotty. Phydium doesn't just change space travel, it changes everything. You didn't think it only revolutionized ships, did you?"

"Noooo. Of course not." The article I read only mentioned space travel. I've been a little distracted by the whole "betrayal of my captain and potential love interest whom I only just decided to love and maybe didn't even really, but a betrayal is still a betrayal—oh, and also now I'm in debt and might be exploded" thing. "I definitely knew it had other purposes."

Caro glances at me sideways and I give a big, confident grin. She rolls her eyes. "Phydium changes how we live. I hope to my ancestors that whoever does find a deposit isn't part of a Family. Then again, anything that hurts Pierce sounds like a good idea."

She has a thing about Pierce. None of my business. She's not wrong. Whoever secures this mineral suddenly has a stranglehold on all commerce. No one should have that much power.

But they will.

"I wish we didn't have to take this run. I don't like the way the Escajedas do business, and I don't like the son on our ship."

She waves her hand loftily as if to say that's a silly quibble. "You're being sensitive because your boyfriend left the ship with the intern none of us wanted to take on in the first place. We're better off without her, certainly. Without him, too. Something new and pretty to look at won't hurt you."

"Ven saved my life after I was banished," I protest. "Twice. Well, more than twice, but the lifesaving bookended our working relationship."

"What's he done besides that?" She tosses an oil-smudged towel over her shoulder and digs deeper into a gap where a belt wraps around a rotor shaft. Or, where it should wrap around the shaft. It's shifted. "These piece-of-shit belts are slightly out of spec. No wonder they were so cheap. Sorry, I thought they were fine when I specced them for you. I'm serious, Temper. Ven drummed up business. Sometimes. More frequently it was word of mouth because the rest of us did a good job. On-planet, he held a blaster and looked dramatic. If we really needed help, we brought on Victor and Victory, and they did all the work."

I try to find the lie in what she said. I can't. The words escape before I properly think about whether or not I should share them. "He told me he was in love with me. A couple months ago, on Landsdown right after we had that hairy mission on Terraform Twenty-Five."

"He *what?*" She almost disembowels herself on a pipe she turns around so fast.

"Said he loved me. Kissed me like he thought I was—" I pause, searching for the word. I *know* the word but that doesn't mean that it isn't embarrassing to actually say it. I glance away from her, toward the doorway. "Like he thought I was precious."

She snorts, returning to the battery. "Oksana is precious. Shiny ornaments are precious. You're exceptional."

"'Exceptional' is a bit strong." I tuck a chunk of hair behind my ear and hand her a wrench when she makes a clutching motion in its direction. She's moved on from the belt to a clamp on a fuel line. "I'm an ex–rich girl with some fancy tech in my brain and a high pain threshold."

"You can be more than one thing." She looks over her shoulder at my face. "Okay, look at it this way. Why'd you wait to tell anyone? He professes his love, hands you himself on a platter, and you still keep it a secret? That doesn't sound like someone in love."

Sounds like *me* in love. I don't know what the fuck I'm doing. Never have. Not with emotional stuff.

"Who's in love?" Itzel wanders into the engine room, holding a bucket of algae destined as supplemental fuel. She uses the algae to eat excess lab compounds that require safe disposal. The algae digestion process renders most chemicals harmless. Her hooded coveralls shadow a pixie face with delicate features and wide dark eyes. The space-pale skin of her usually tan hands is nearly completely obscured by the intricate tattoos that declare her a former acolyte of the Dark Mother of the Void.

I fill her in on our conversation. She doesn't act like any of it is a surprise. "Ven had been sparking Oksana since she came aboard and started shedding her hair all over my lab."

"Sparking?" Caro asks before I can.

"I'm working on a new euphemism. The current ones are boring. 'Sparking' is nice, right? Like generating heat and power."

"That's very romantic," I allow. "I'm surprised it's not already been used."

She shrugs and hefts the bucket higher. "Then I'm bringing back an old euphemism. Don't get caught up in the technicalities."

I take her advice and return to the primary subject. "So, we nearly had complete overlap. Ugh. I feel so stupid. Wait, if you knew they were doing it, why didn't you tell us?"

"It was none of my business. If it makes you feel better, you were much better at keeping secrets than she was. She made up a little song about their happy future that she sang to herself in the lab. If I knew he was going after both of you, I'd have warned you." Itzel dumps the bucket in a tube near the wall. "Still, if you have to keep it a secret, it's not right. You're one of the most forthright people I've ever met."

"To paraphrase Caro, I can be more than one thing." Like a romantic mess. I can definitely be that thing. That isn't all, though.

It's not that I have a tender heart because Ven didn't wait for me and decided he could do better—it's *whom* he decided was better. "I don't know if I'm more hurt that he didn't stick around like he said or that someone like *Oksana* was a suitable replacement for me."

"He's a man, isn't he? They all like incompetent beauties because they seem so much more impressive by comparison. You ran circles around Ven on the regular, Temper. He isn't the type to handle that." Caro cranks the wrench hard and smacks the wall beside the control panel of the generator with one flat hand. A bright-green light flashes on.

"All men aren't like that," Itzel chastises. "Some are not so easily intimidated."

Caro cuts me a glance. "You ever meet one of those?"

"Ven *was* like that, though," Itzel continues before I can answer.

"He taught me everything I know about scouting," I protest. It's come around far enough that I feel like I need to remind them about his good points because I'm now aware of so many bad ones.

"And that's probably about when he lost interest." Caro wipes her hands off again and rinses out Itzel's bucket using one of the hoses in the wall. As little droplets splash, she continues to share her personal worldview. I've never known Caro to be intimate with anyone since she came on board, so I'm not sure where all this expertise comes from. Perhaps she's had a torrid affair or two but is simply fiercely private. "Once you got better than him, he didn't feel impressive anymore."

Itzel takes the bucket back. "I don't know that it's as bad as that, Caro. That's how *you* see men. Ven's nice—kind of dumb, but nice. Not for Temper, though. She's a lot."

That sums it up.

"I've sworn off men, anyway." I take the wrench back from Caro and slide it into its slot in the tool drawer.

"Was he bad in bed?" Caro studies me like I'm a bad engine. "Is that why you took so long to decide?"

"You know who *wouldn't* be bad? Or who would—in the most delicious way?" Itzel interrupts before I have a chance to defend Ven's honor. Kind of defend it. He wasn't bad. He just wasn't earth-shattering.

Caro points a finger through the ceiling and raises her eyebrows in response to Itzel's question.

Itzel nods emphatically. "He's like a space walk—takes your breath away."

Somehow, I don't think they're talking about Micah. "Escajeda is from a Family. They don't waste time with the commoners."

"Don't ruin the fantasy, Temper." Caro waves her hand at me again.

"Aren't all men awful and only after beautiful idiots?"

"And they can *also* be excellent kissers. You know what they say is the best way to get over someone?"

"To get *over* someone else!" Itzel holds up a finger.

Close enough.

I cross my arms over my chest and use my brand-new captain voice. "There will be no getting over an Escajeda. I'm not into threesomes and that man goes nowhere without his ego."

．　．　．　．　．

"Get out of my infirmary before I rip off your leg and beat you to death with it," Micah barks so loudly I hear it from the bunk area.

I'm briefly concerned that I might need to intervene, so I approach the door just in time to collide with Escajeda as he storms out of the infirmary. Our limbs tangle and my face smushes up against a chest that is unsurprisingly well-defined. One of his hands snakes around my waist and presses against the small of my back, keeping me from bouncing away.

The Escajeda Family genetic manipulation and mods may have created an imposing specimen on-planet or in a station, but he is a nightmare in a ship—taking up far too much space.

Once we recover our equilibrium—or he recovers his equilibrium and I internally smack myself in the head repeatedly because it suddenly got too tight inside my skin and my gut feels like I've been kicked in it—I realize that my fingers are clutching very impressive biceps and my lips have nearly made contact with the smooth corded muscle of his neck. His body is curled around mine and it feels far better than it ought to.

His hand on my waist tightens for a moment, and my eyes probably nearly bug out of my head as lust and professionalism battle to the death in my body.

Caro and Itzel are probably right. He'd be an excellent lover.

Where did *that* thought come from? Where did any of this come from? I am stronger than my hormones. I can*not* find anyone from a Family attractive. It's a recipe for disaster in nearly every conceivable way.

Luckily, he opens his mouth. "This place is chaos and there don't seem to be any rules. Did you make it a point to hire a whole ship full of sensitive criminals?"

"That's offensive." I want to take a big step back, but the hall isn't quite large enough for that. "Caro isn't a criminal."

He looks at me dubiously, as though something smells slightly of dung. "You weren't even loyal to your own Family. Don't pretend to be loyal to your crew."

It stings. I don't know why it should. I've been judged by better than him. I was judged by everyone in my own territory. A banishment is a harsh punishment, but sometimes people secretly reach out to the banished. They offer funds, or at least support.

I received no such offers. After what happened to her father, my best friend, Kari, refused to even speak to me. Frederick so effectively painted me as the villain that even people whom I'd known my entire life—who knew him his entire life—assumed the worst. No one seems to understand that Frederick is the one who betrayed our Family. I just betrayed *him*.

"Don't worry, you aren't a part of my crew, so my dubious loyalty doesn't extend to you," I snap.

A head of lettuce flies over my shoulder and Escajeda catches it in one hand, glancing behind me. Itzel calls from the galley, "I need someone to help chop veggies."

She absolutely does not. She's giving him a chance to be one of the crew. And he's going to turn her down because he thinks he's too good for us.

"Happy to help." Escajeda edges past me toward the biologist, tossing the lettuce casually with one hand. I snap my mouth closed. "Bet I can chop them finer."

"Oh really? Better put your credits on the table." Her delighted grin tells me she's already planning how to spend them.

I leave them to meal prep and duck into the lab, the door sliding shut behind me. Micah's sitting by a lab table that will double as a bed in case of medical emergencies. His usual sleeveless coveralls display well-defined arms, and his brows are pinched in their habitual scowl. The table is strewn with an array of medical supplies. Now that I'm captaining, he's taking over some of my old roles—supply inventory being one of them. Before, he was backup security for Ven when he wasn't gluing one of us back together.

Micah is a man of many hats. And now, a man of many bandages.

"Did a rat get loose in the lab?" I ask brightly, poking at a bright-orange gauze. "And did it steal all the normal gauze?"

"Orange is cheaper." He gives me a pointed eye at the word "cheaper." He's still using his cranky voice, so my effervescent presence must not be making a difference.

"What was our new security officer bothering you about?" The infirmary is small. Cabinets and built-in benches line the walls because the thing about a spaceship is that everything has to be secured. If something goes wrong and we lose gravity, having a room full of floating syringes could be problematic. Even more if you happen to be inside that room and the ship maneuvers hard to starboard.

Micah snorts, running a dark hand through his short black hair and disrupting the natural wave that gives him an almost boyish air—if he didn't look like he'd happily bite you in half. "Pretty Boy was worried about how we control our medications. Thinks we're going to inject opioids and then shoot a frag cannon for fun."

The only one of us who would do that is Itzel, and she wouldn't use opioids from the clinic, she'd find them on-planet, and only for experimental purposes. Mostly. I understand the question. I even appreciate it. The problem is, Escajeda shouldn't be striding through my ship making demands of the crew. Being rich and wellborn doesn't make him the captain, and medical supplies don't fall under the purview of security.

I barely have any authority over him and it's already slipping through my fingers.

I shove away from the table. I've held my tongue thus far. Well, I've kind of held it. I've *meant* to hold it. "Someone needs a reminder about his place on this ship."

And this time I won't touch him, so his impressive musculature won't distract me.

Micah's dry chuckle follows me to the door. "This is why I don't have any desire to be captain. Everyone's problems are yours. At least back in the day, you could make it Ven's problem."

I never did. I make everyone's problems my own anyway. It's like a gift. I'm halfway to the helm—which means I've taken roughly five steps—when the running lights in the hall flash from white to blue. We are being hailed by another vessel. No one ever hails you because they just want to tell you your ship is pretty.

When I reach the helm, Escajeda is already there, a scrap of lettuce stuck to his sleeve and his hand poised over the coms console like he's going to answer the hail. He really does think that he's captain here. I shoulder-check him out of my way and brace myself in front of the console just in case he tries to throw some of his weight back at me. He doesn't push back. Good. Maybe, just maybe, he understands priorities in the face of an external threat.

I activate the holo-field and a projected face pops up in front of me. Male, indeterminate height, with a slightly upturned nose and dark eyes. His mouth is a slat of irritation, probably because I took a moment to answer the hail, and no one likes to wait.

"Scouting Vessel *Quest*, speaking to—?" I'm trying to be professional, but Escajeda is crowding me again. Guess that answers my question about priorities in the face of an external threat. He's standing so close behind me that my projection in the other ship must have a misshapen lump of light looming over it. I throw an elbow into his gut to try to make him back up. He absorbs the blow but only retreats a hair.

"Scouting Vessel *Quest*, this is Nakatomi *Horizon*. You have infringed in Nakatomi-owned space. You have five standard minutes to vacate this space, or we have rights to defend our territory." He seems very proud of himself. I'd laugh except the scans show me that the Nakatomi *Horizon* is armed to the teeth and close enough that my shielding—impressive as it may be for a small vessel—isn't nearly enough.

I shove back harder against Escajeda while bringing up the detailed navigational readings. The last thing I need is for the Nakatomi Family to find the eldest son of their mortal enemy in a dingy little scouting vessel and decide that blowing us into tiny pieces is a fun way to spend the day.

The nav readings confirm what I thought. We aren't in Nakatomi space. We're close to Nakatomi space but not *in* it, which means this is a territory grab that they're trying on someone who knows better. Normally, I'd run because it's none of my business if Nakatomi wants to pull something over on the other Families. The problem is that deviating to the border where they're claiming Nakatomi space ends will add standard days to our schedule and put us perilously close to actual Flores space. Deviating around *that* will add a month to our trip and I don't know if we have the fuel to sustain that kind of a burn. I definitely don't have the money for more fuel, not until we get paid. And we won't get paid if we take a month.

"Nakatomi *Horizon*, this space is public transit. Nakatomi space starts at the gravity well of newly acquired planet Kohaishimi. *Quest* is well outside that range." Now they know I know.

Escajeda has finally stopped hovering at my back but instead, he's moving toward the weapons console. I flip my side of the ship-to-ship communicator to mute and turn around to address the fool.

"What do you think you're doing?" I hiss, like I still need to be quiet. Itzel runs into the helm and stands between us. Of all my crew, she's the least helpful in this situation.

She's great if you need to poke a plant or tame a creature. Shockingly good if you need violence—if you have time for the panic attacks and recriminations that come later. Not talented whatsoever at negotiations or intimidation. Caro and Micah, the two who are better at those, are probably nailing down everything on the ship just in case I need to maneuver.

"I'm activating our weapons system. The Nakatomi Family *attacks*. They don't negotiate." Escajeda speaks slowly like he needs to educate me about bad Families.

"It takes one to know one, I guess," I say, very maturely. "Of course, they attack when they think they can get away with it. They just don't realize they can't get away with it, yet. You fire on them, we're a bunch of tiny pieces of scrap metal punctuating a bunch of tinier pieces of frozen flesh. Or, if we luck out and destroy them before they retaliate, I've just declared war on a Family that is known for their weapons. Oh yeah, and top-tier spaceships—which means we *won't* get lucky and destroy them. Maybe you're well-connected enough to survive a war with the Nakatomis, but I sure as shit am not. Now keep your hands to yourself and let me de-escalate this son of a bitch."

And now, I have to stop paying attention to my on-ship problem because my off-ship problem is responding to my coms.

"Scouting Vessel *Quest*, your information is out-of-date. Nakatomi territory extends a milliparsec from the planet's gravity well in any direction. You have two standard minutes." Officious little priap. I wonder if he even knows he's lying. Escajeda is inching closer to the weapons console and we're two minutes away from crisis.

"Nakatomi *Horizon*, my information is current. Who do you think scouted the fucking planet for you? I'm still picking the pooling-tree sap out of the soles of my boots. I know exactly what's under that old-growth forest facing my ship right now." A trifle exaggerated. We scouted the planet a couple years ago. Ven got along with Nakatomi. Clearly better than I do.

"Scouting Vessel *Quest*, you have one minute to comply."

He's not going to see reason, which means I need to go into annihilation mode. I lean over the console and give him good hard eye contact, which is difficult because my camera isn't anywhere near where the holo's eyes are. "I'll spell out the threat that I just politely obscured. Nakatomi *Horizon*, your Family was interested in Kohaishimi because of deep reserves of weapons-purity gas beneath the forest on the northern hemisphere of the planet. One particularly large deposit is within range of my ship. With one shot, I can blow a crater in that planet so large you'll never recover your investment. I strongly recommend you reconsider your position because I guarantee, no matter what weapons you bear against me, I will get one shot off."

I go back on mute. "Escajeda, activate the shield and target the coordinates I forward to the console."

I send him the location with a swipe of my hand and don't bother to see if he's complying. Itzel straps herself into the chairs, something I should be doing but I'm so caught in the mythos of my own negotiation prowess that I don't bother. The next few seconds will tell all.

The ship is visible through the ports that line the front and ceiling of my helm. It's a sleek, vicious thing with a battery of cannons pointed at us. Somehow the mouths of those cannons are blacker than the space around the ship. I hold my breath, fingers clenched around the coms console, knuckles white. I might puke a little if they don't explode us in the next few seconds. The sound of a buckle clicks to the other side of the helm. Caro has come up to watch.

I flip the inner-ship coms to private. I've been broadcasting the whole exchange. "Micah, strap down, wherever you are. It might get turbulent in a moment."

"Better turbulent than absolute zero." The medic's wry tone rings through the coms.

I wait a few more heartbeats. I'm either about to be vindicated or embarrassed. Less important than alive or dead, but still, it matters. I don't want to look directly at him, but I tilt my head a little to the side to catch Escajeda in my peripheral vision. He's waiting, calm and collected, like he's ready to explode a planet every day. Like he's ready to be exploded every day.

It occurs to me that my upbringing was no pleasure, and I was only one of the Ten. What must it be like to be raised in the Five—with the Escajeda as a father?

Luckily for me, before I develop too much empathy, the cannons move away from us, one by one.

"Scouting Vessel *Quest*, we have verified position on our maps and found a glitch in our navigational calculations. You are free to pass."

Generous of them. I release my breath in a slow stream. "Nakatomi *Horizon*, message received. Be sure you investigate that glitch. I'd hate for you to accidentally harm any other passing ships."

That's snide bluster and we both know it. There isn't a glitch and the very next ship to pass, they'll try this again. That ship won't have any leverage, so they'll get out of the lanes and the Nakatomis will have advanced their territory with little more than a threat and a lie. Next time, they may not bother to give the vessel a chance to retreat.

For something so large, space can seem awfully tight.

"Keep the weapons targeted until we're out of their range," I tell Escajeda as I bump up our speed. My knees might just give out any moment. "How's everyone doing?"

Caro's already back to her datapad, the golden interface tattoos that bedeck her fingers flashing in the helm's light. "Still breathing."

Itzel blinks open her eyes. Her hands are on her lap, twisted into strange shapes. Our biologist is a mystery, even to herself. A pacifist assassin monk who parted ways with her death goddess but still wears the vestments of her order in her free time. In times of great stress, habit takes over and she spells out the scriptures using sign language or traces them on her skin.

"That was an impressive bluff." Escajeda's still poised at the weapon's console, looking at me like he sees something unexpected.

"Something you should know about me, Escajeda: I never bluff."

Which is a lie. I nearly always bluff, but today? Today I almost believe that I would have taken the shot.

CHAPTER 4

Herschel Two isn't special. From space, it's about as unspecial as a habitable planet can be. Warm reddish soil on a scale from tawny to sienna, threaded with chalky gray-white. Thin high clouds that look more like the glass of my view ports is dirty than planetary atmospheric activity. The surface is pockmarked with craters but also pimpled with volcanos. It's close to a weak reddish sun, but the surface is too rugged for traditional homesteaders to be on-planet. There are only a handful of places flat enough to put the *Quest* down safely. The one that Escajeda has insisted we focus on, in the supposedly phydium-rich region of the planet, is in the northern hemisphere, alongside the largest planetary volcano I've ever seen.

Scans identify it as a shield volcano. Less dramatic than some of the other kinds, but still dangerous if you happen to be nearby. It's reading as mostly dormant, although if you delve a bit deeper, there's activity. I plug in the coordinates, and we wait in the helm to watch the landing.

Micah whistles low and long next to me, arms crossed over his chest. "Never treated lava burns. This will be fun."

"We get burned by lava from that thing, you'll just be straining our ashes off the top," I point out.

"It's an impressive structure." Caro's thumbs are hooked in her pockets, and she carries a large pack on her back that contains a geo-mapping drone and will fold out to a platform, allowing the drone to dock and charge while we're on the move.

The ship vibrates as we enter the atmosphere. That grinding sound that's been coming and going returns and I'm worried that we'll fall apart, but we make it through the zone where we're a fireball on the outside without becoming a fireball on the inside, so it's a problem for tomorrow. Maybe tomorrow I can afford the fix.

The current rock in my boot saunters into the helm to join the rest of the crew. He's wearing more firepower than I've ever seen on one man, and he looks like he could single-handedly take on an army. I'm not ashamed to say that it works for me.

I have yet to find a physical aspect of him that doesn't work for me. It's just all the personality ones. Not when he's dealing with anyone else—he's actually *nice* to everyone else. He saves his dismissive condescension for me, in particular.

"You better watch out or a metal mite will make a snack out of you." I can't resist saying it. I shouldn't. I shouldn't talk to him any more than I have to. He isn't my friend. He isn't even my crew, not really.

Itzel snickers softly behind me.

Caro whispers, "Sounds like *you're* thinking of making a snack out of him."

Her comment was too quiet for him to hear, surely. I give her the look. The "we're supposed to be friends, how could you verbally betray me like that?" look. She grins back, completely unabashed.

Sure, I'd like to take a bite out of him. I'm not blind. Now that I've seen him handle a crisis with a steady calm, now that I've watched him play Naijong tower cards with Micah and lose with grace, now that I've watched him reach things from high places for Itzel, well, I'm slightly more tempted to follow through on that desire.

The thing that stops me is when I imagine the look on his face if I tried. He might be slumming it on my ship, but it's for a priceless resource that could revolutionize space travel. It's not for a tryst. And he's made it clear that he thinks I'm a Family traitor. Which, technically I am. My ego's already taken a few blows; I can't handle a rejection right now. Or, even worse, a grudging acceptance that we both regret later.

Oh, and I've recently sworn off men. I suppose that stops me, too.

A weight is lifting from his shoulders the farther we go from the way station. He had three whole facial expressions the other day and he's really relaxed into the crew. He even provided a supply of the spicy protein paste that's nearly impossible to find on the market. Supply chain often breaks down on the way out to Landsdown. It's about the last place that any distributor wants to go.

Any distributor who isn't working for an Escajeda, that is. Sometimes I feel like I've missed something in my assessment of him. I want to get under his skin to see what's really there, except what's really there is probably more of that unbridled Family pomposity that took over my brother when he came of age. Any kindness I've seen is probably merely manipulation.

"I'm prepared for any eventuality. Unlike you, I don't fly by the seat of my pants."

It's things like that. He delivers the dig with a completely impassive face like he doesn't even realize he's doing it.

"Thinking about the seat of my pants, Escajeda?" I say it before I properly think about it.

"Do you want me to be, Reed?" The corner of his mouth twitches up in a sharp smile.

Caro's snickering has become all-out laughter. We're going to have to talk about loyalty one of these days. Is it not too much to ask for one's crew to have her back when some outsider implies that she wants to ride him like a hover bike?

If Ven was looking for a pretty moron who was utterly dependent on him, I have no doubt that an Escajeda possesses as many if not more complex issues with his own masculinity.

"Never going to happen, Escajeda," I say, as though I'm some great prize.

I am to *myself*.

The ground's coming up fast now, cracked red soil under a butterscotch sky. It seems too fast, but landings are always like this. The planet rushes at you until you feel like you're about to throw up, and then suddenly, you're briefly weightless again as the ship delicately touches the rock. The landing struts deploy with a solid thunk and we're secure.

After running our usual tests, we open the hatch and venture out. The planet's atmospheric composition has been stored in the public stream for probably about a century, but I trust our instruments more. The atmosphere is breathable. These days, even the average person has Pierce Family algae injected directly into their blood. The algae produce oxygen when they photosynthesize. It opened up habitation options to even planets with technically inhospitable atmospheres. The long slope of the volcano rises behind me, dominating the sky. Some of those thin clouds snag on it as they pass.

Directly before us, a canyon drops off; striations of umber, gold, and bloody-red line its broken sides. Something pale and fibrous grows around the edge, trailing down its walls. Maybe a plant. Could be a fungus, although they usually prefer more water than this place has. Hopefully not psychedelic because my heart can't take another close call with Itzel. Two planets ago she sampled some sort of leaf and spent the entire mission stoned after one lick of its striated surface. She's already got a specimen jar out and is taking a clipping. I gingerly walk over, placing my boots carefully. A planet this dry and this broken, the soil's going to be uncertain.

There's a metaphor there applying to me that I don't want to approach head-on.

Escajeda has a blaster out and ready. A whir from behind me signals the drone lifting from Caro's launchpad. It'll map the canyons in more detail than we can get from a satellite. It will also land in open territory and take core samples. Phydium may or may not be present. If it's deep enough, the drone won't reach it, but a subterranean probe can be more effective than a surface or depth scan. Either way, we'll still want to crosshatch the territory from above before we explore below.

Hover bikes would make this much easier, but they're nightmares in sandy environments so, yet again, we're on foot. Besides, the Escajeda wanted us to keep our presence quiet if anyone's scanning the planet, and the energy signatures would attract attention.

"This is going to be hard to travel by foot." Micah peers over the edge. This is the point where Ven would normally lay out his plan for the territory, shooting blind as usual. I swallow a throat full of emotion. He has plenty of faults, but he'll always be the man who took a chance on a banished rich girl and who taught me everything I know about scouting.

Maybe not everything. I've learned that shooting blind is a great way to miss the target.

"I don't want to risk the canyons until we get at least one day's worth of terrain mapped." It will show us if there are any paths down or if we have to repel in and climb out. Climbing out will be brutal.

"You don't intend to physically investigate the area immediately?" Escajeda doesn't bother to keep the judgment from his tone as he scans the canyon.

"Is there an urgency that I'm unaware of?" I snap one of the plant leaves and smell its blood. "Safety in exploration is the priority. The drone scans offer information about how we can explore at the least risk to the crew. Our lives may not be that important to you, but they are to me."

"There is always urgency in Family business. When we made this deal, we didn't assume you'd be sitting back and watching drone scans. We could have done that ourselves." His jaw is hard and it's very clear that—if this was his command—he'd be charging heedlessly into the canyons. Maybe security experts have that in common. "The Escajeda Family doesn't sit around staring at their thumbs when they could be doing something useful."

"You're welcome to look at whatever appendage you'd like." He is just . . . insufferable. Then again, I'm not used to captaining. Maybe I *am* being overly cautious. Maybe this is different from the normal practice. When in doubt, bluff harder. "You hired us for our expertise. This is what expertise looks like. You don't like it, you're free to venture out on your own."

"This is how it's done," Micah interjects as we walk north along the edge of the canyon. "If you had a battle to fight, would you scope the territory first, or just run out into the field?"

It's quiet. No Escajeda retort. No rushing water in the canyon or rustling plants. No scuttle or flutter of animals. Our boots crunch in the gravel with a dead hollow sound. I blink at Micah. He's not the type to say anything he deems extraneous. I can't decide if it's heartwarming or insulting that he thought I needed support. Some of both, I suppose.

Caro puffs out a surprised gasp. Immediately, all of us have our weapons drawn and we're arrayed in a circle with her at the center. I glance over my shoulder because I'm facing a long climb up the volcano and no one's coming from that way. She's tapping at the side of her interface glasses and squinting, so I'm pretty sure that whatever startled her, it isn't here. I don't holster my weapon. Just in case.

"Cenotes," she says like that means something to me. Itzel

gasps with glee so apparently it does mean something, and Caro isn't having a stroke.

I glance out of the corner of my eye at Escajeda. He looks stoic as always so I can't tell if he doesn't know what it means either. I'm going to have to ask. "What or who is a cenote?"

"Essentially, it's underground water. Usually in a sinkhole or a cave. They have a very small opening to the sky," Itzel explains, fingers flying in the air over her datapad as she enters her shorthand notes. "They're often fascinating ecosystems because they may have developed independently depending on if they formed from rain or groundwater. I've always wanted to explore a cenote planet."

This place doesn't look like it gets much rain, but anything is possible. This hemisphere is in winter, which could be arid.

"The landscape is littered with them, too deep in the canyons for our sensors to find." Caro gazes through her glasses. "There must be an extensive underground water system."

"That'll fuck with mining," I say to Escajeda, but he shrugs like it isn't a concern. Maybe they've got safeguards, or maybe they just don't care about the safety of their miners. The process is never all automated because the hard truth is that people are cheaper than machines.

"Only if there actually is—" Escajeda starts.

"People," Micah interrupts. "Coming out of the canyon to the north."

People are the worst. It's always easier without people. This must be the cult/religious group.

"They're all wearing matching clothes . . . creepy." Itzel peers over my shoulder as I pass her, moving toward the front of the group. I wave Escajeda to take the rear in case this is a distraction.

"*We're* all wearing matching clothes." Caro gestures to our coveralls.

She's not wrong, but she's not right either. "Creepy" is a good word to describe these people. Their attire is indeed all matching in color, a sort of warm ivory tone with reddish splotches. That wouldn't be so remarkable, since this planet doesn't look like it offers much in the way of natural dyes. It's not just the color, though. The cuts are antiquated. Like, before-any-of-them-were-born antiquated. Their pants are loose, with a sort of placket over the front at a diagonal. Shirts are high-necked and long-sleeved. There's no tailoring or structure besides those collars. They don't look comfortable. They also share a hairstyle, an almost crest-like snarl that's as maintained as a topiary.

When Micah tries to step away, my hand on his arm arrests the movement. There's one more thing they all share: banishment tattoos. It's better that two of their own kind greet them. Micah's tattoo is a little older than mine, not quite as bright, but it's just as prominent. No one else on the crew is banished.

I do take the lead, though. Micah's not known for his diplomacy, and he doesn't possess a translator chip. As they approach, I take in more detail. They appear unarmed, although I can't quite imagine such a thing. A mixture of races, ages, and genders, although the women are walking in the rear—which could be how it worked out today but could also be a cultural trait that I don't love. They shouldn't have that feeling of sameness about them, but they do. I realize they're walking in step, like someone far away is conducting their movements. A chill skitters up my spine.

The one in front takes in our marks. Takes in the lack of marks on anyone else. He has the biggest hair and the biggest belly, which I take to mean that he's the leader. The hat principle can apply to hair. He folds his hands in a way that should look peaceful but on him seems a touch aggressive. "Greetings and welcome to the Valley of the Children."

Nope. I don't like that at all. He's speaking in Stupniketi, which is the primary language of the Chumak Family territory, but something about his cadence is off. Isolated groups do form linguistic quirks, but this feels more pretentious than that. Like he's trying to give weight to his words or like he's reading a text out loud. I haven't spent much time with the Chumaks—they're a minor Family in the Ten—but my translator chip recognizes the language. Recognizes it well enough to be confused with his delivery.

Also, generally speaking, any time a group of adults calls themselves "the Children," you've got trouble at hand.

"Thank you for your generous welcome," I reply in Standard. "To whom do I have the honor of speaking?"

A shorter member of the group scurries forward to stand just behind the leader. His hair isn't nearly as impressive. He uses Standard to respond. "You have the honor of addressing the most supreme Rashahan."

I don't know if that's a name or a title. I don't suppose I need to know except to confirm what Itzel said. They're creepy. A tally in the direction of cult versus religious order. Also, apparently the supreme Rashahan must be announced. I introduce myself but not the rest of the crew. Names have value and I don't want them to be used against us.

"We would welcome you and your woman's presence in our flock," the supreme Rashahan addresses Micah. Supreme pain in my ass, more like. "However, we cannot take the unmarked."

"She's not my woman," Micah protests.

"If anything, you're *her* man," Itzel helpfully points out, and then grins a gamine smile. "We're all of us her people."

"Not *him*." Caro shoots a look in Escajeda's direction. Itzel and Micah may have warmed up to him, but Caro—when she isn't teasing me—still regards him with the same vaguely hostile suspicion she reserves for everyone who isn't crew.

"We aren't here for your flock." I ignore the helpful interjections of my crew and demonstrate that prime diplomacy that makes me the last scout anyone wants to hire. "Herschel Two is unclaimed and we're here to scout the territory."

That sets off a little flutter among said flock.

"Have no fear." My personal Stupniketi isn't the best and I can't quite capture the cadence he's using, which means I sound stilted when I address them in what I assume is their own tongue. In this moment, it's more important that the flock understand what I'm saying than that my crew does. It won't let him twist my words to them, later. "There is more than enough planet to go around and, odds are, our client won't be acquiring it anyway. We can all agree that the resources here don't seem to be the sort to attract a Family."

Something flashes through Rashahan's eyes too quickly for me to place it, but I can guess what it is. We're standing conveniently close to a canyon. He's gauging whether this whole little problem goes away if we disappear. "If something unfortunate were to happen to us, of course, they'd just send another crew. One with more weapons and less-pleasant dispositions."

"In that case, let me extend my hospitality and hope that you do not need it for long." Rashahan's tone has turned cool. No longer trying to impress new converts but playing the proud host to impress the old converts standing behind him. One of them has moved his hands behind his waist. I'd bet credits that he has a weapon stashed there.

I allow a smile that says we're all on the same team here. We aren't remotely on the same team, but he seems the sort to respond better to a woman armed with softness than with a blaster. "It is greatly appreciated, Rashahan. My ship isn't a trade vessel, but we do have some items for trade if you or your flock has any need of hygienic and medical necessities. We also have a medic who can see to the needs of your . . . flock."

That part is the truth. It's convenient to carry trade items because traders are treated better than invaders. A flutter of excitement comes from the flock at the talk of trade. It's hard for the banished to keep stocked with medical basics and the small cosmetic luxuries. My research indicated that two cultists appear on Landsdown every few months to stock up on basic supplies and send probes into the streams for new members. Landsdown has some services, but not many, so I'm sure there are basic luxuries they lack. Rashahan sends them a quelling glare and then returns his gaze to me. "The Children provide for themselves. Kaiaiesto provides for the Children."

Well. Nothing I can say to that. Lots I can think to it. The first is wondering who or what the fuck Kaiaiesto is. "Is there anything we should be careful of? Regions prone to rockslides, venomous fauna, or toxic flora?"

He takes a while to respond. Probably deciding how much of his time to spend with this. Following that thought to the next. If we get injured, someone will come looking for us. That's even more people disrupting his flock. When he answers, it's like he's mad at me for putting him in the position to help us. "There is a large subterranean river beneath the canyon. At places, the ground is fragile, like thin ice over a lake."

It's good information and makes sense with what we know about the underground pools. We bid our farewells to the Children and pass each other carefully.

"They're going to be trouble," Escajeda states the obvious. Then again, he kept his mouth shut during our interaction with the Children so he's doing better than I expected.

"No shit." Micah says it for me, deep voice indignant. "He's keeping his people without medical supplies."

"Maybe they've been recently resupplied, and they don't need anything. Not everyone has a diabolical backstory." Itzel frowns at us in disappointment. She's often disappointed in our worldview.

"Itzel." I float around the edge of our group, blaster still out and watching both the volcano and the canyon for movement. "We live in the same universe, right? The only one of *us* who doesn't have a diabolical backstory is Caro. I imagine the creepy cult has some shadowy spots in their past. Or present."

"What makes you think I have a diabolical backstory?" Escajeda asks. He's still bringing up the rear, right where I put him. He's a solid anchor. Which is not helping to create the distance that I need from him. Why is competence such a turn-on?

"You're an Escajeda. You *must* have a diabolical backstory. I don't think there is a person born to the Five who doesn't have skeletons of one kind or another."

"The Escajeda Family is a fine, upstanding member of the Five. Everything we do is in the public eye. We have no secrets." Escajeda delivers that fantastic pile of bullshit with a straight face.

I'm ramping up to an explosion when I catch the quirk of his lips. A joke.

Maybe—just maybe—an Escajeda who can laugh at himself is worth investigating further. That twist of his mouth reveals a dimple so deep I want to run my finger over it. He catches me staring and makes a deep noise in his chest. His eyes turn speculative and then immediately frost over with his habitual disdain.

I look away. He's from a Family. A *Family*. Which means: so far beyond my social status that it would be like flirting with a star. I shouldn't need to remind myself.

"Of course, compared to the pure and pristine Reeds, who could measure up?" The lip quirk is gone but the glance he sends me is barbed.

"Don't ever refer to my brother's Family that way," I growl, lust momentarily suppressed in a drowning mess of regret and loss. What I'm asking doesn't even make sense. That's the name of Frederick's Family. It doesn't matter that it doesn't remotely reflect what my parents would have wanted.

Which leads down another dangerous path. If I'm so sure that a name does not make a person, why am I certain that Arcadio is a copy of the Escajeda?

CHAPTER 5

I wake up early for my watch. It's oddly quiet on the ship. Most systems are powered down to save energy, so only the dry rattle of the air circulation softly vibrates the walls of the *Quest*. It's almost soothing. If I didn't have so many worries knocking around my head, I might be able to fall back to sleep.

But I do, so I don't.

First and foremost is this contract with the Escajeda. Even with the need for secrecy, it doesn't make sense that he'd hire us instead of handling it in-house. I can't imagine another project more important for his personal scouting team to be working on than the most critical resource in charted territory. On the opposite but equally weird side, even with the importance of phydium, I don't understand why he'd send someone as important as a son to oversee his investment when I'm sure he has scads of toadies who'd love the opportunity to ingratiate themselves. And why give us the extra pay? It's the best deal I've ever received. There's got to be a hook but I can't see it. Which means it's going to bite me in the ass when I least expect it.

Not that I had another option besides broken knees and a repossessed spaceship. So, even if a hook is coming, my knees are intact, my ship is not only still in my possession but has a functioning humidifier, and we have something to do. Finding natural stores of phydium is the sort of thing that gives a crew a reputation, and work begets more work.

This is an opportunity, no matter the Escajeda's motivations.

I flip on the small light on the desk by my bunk and the room washes into view. My eyes are gritty, either because of the dry sandy air or the early hour. The humidifier keeps it habitable, not necessarily comfortable. I could only afford to buy Caro a temporary patch on the regulator, which buys us time on the old tech. None of us wants to push it too hard. The canteen on the desk still has a dribble of water left in it and I knock it back to clear my throat. No going back to sleep now. I might as well get up and take over watch. Let Escajeda get some extra rest.

I won't imagine what he looks like while asleep, those shields down. Vulnerable. That full lower lip released of its constant tension. Probably warm as a furnace.

I pull on my boots, turn off the light, and head toward the helm, where we camp out for watch. Mumbling comes from Caro and Itzel's door. Caro. Itzel punctuates the mumbles with a snuffling snore. I had to share a room with Caro on one scouting mission. Never again.

The red nighttime lights illuminate the latest makeshift mural on the walls. They didn't start as murals. Despite having any number of tech devices upon which she can take notes, Caro has a habit of sketching diagrams, equations, or process flows on whatever piece of bulkhead is available when inspiration strikes. Sometimes she doesn't use erasable markers because she's so caught in the moment. Many of our walls have been permanently stained. She claims that it helps her to see things written large.

Over time, Itzel has added embellishments. Delicately sketched vines twist around the hastily drawn schematic of an engine that I pass. In the gym, a cybernetic eye—I'm not even sure why Caro drew that one—has been turned into a fish with long trailing fins. In the mess, some sort of monstrous cephalopod reaches tentacles from an air duct to wrap around an equation for slingshot trajectory. A couple cycles ago, Micah went through them all and carefully changed the equations to be slightly wrong. We all bet how long it would take Caro to notice the old art had been altered. We barely had time to make the bets before she came in, waving one of her charcoal markers, yelling about how some priap had destroyed all her notes. She made Micah scrape away the offending edits with a razor blade until everything was correct again. Except small patches of bulkhead show razor marks and scuffs.

Each little scrape tells a story. Spaceship walls can be stark and cold. The *Quest* isn't cold, despite the cheap blue-tinged lighting. It reflects the personality of those who call it home. Something an Escajeda probably couldn't ever appreciate. The door to the helm is open, but when I enter the room, I find it empty. The seat is cold. Escajeda isn't on watch.

I can't believe I was just thinking tender thoughts about his lip. I spin to stomp out of the helm when he appears in the doorway, and I almost run into him. He doesn't step back, so neither do I. It's my ship. I'm not ceding ground. Apparently, he thinks that it's his money, so he isn't ceding ground, either. That means I get a fantastic close-up view of his sternum and he gets to admire the snarls at the top of my head. His coveralls are still perfectly black. Makes me want to spill something on him.

"Where were you?" There, that's polite of me. It's better than yelling at him for not being where he's supposed to be. I've never in my life been so physically attracted to someone who drives me so bugfuck insane.

"Getting stir-crazy. I went out and did a lap of the ship. Checked for footprints. Is that against the rules? Should I have knocked on your bunk and asked permission?" He stretches in the doorway, reaching up with one arm to clasp the top of the frame. It's an irritating way for him to invade my space even more without seeming like he's doing anything.

Or could be I'm reading too much into stiff muscles. My bunks are small and he's a big guy. He probably doesn't fit. Maybe I should have given him my old bunk. It's unfair to make him share with Micah while there's a whole unused bunk.

But I like having Micah keep an eye on him. Clearly, when no one does, he wanders off.

"Have you ever been on a ship that you didn't own?" I step forward a fraction of an inch because that's about as far as I *can* step forward without colliding with him. A collision feels like it would be disastrous. I already feel the heat emanating from his body and only supreme self-control keeps me from closing the distance. "You might be trained at actual security, but you certainly aren't trained at being a security officer who reports to a captain. If you were, you'd know how to follow orders or how to come to me with security recommendations instead of demanding changes from our medic or our engineer."

He starts to argue, and I raise my voice and speak over him. "And you'd know how to do all of that without getting resentful. If your father wanted *you* to scout a planet, he wouldn't have needed to hire me and my crew."

"It's amazing how effective stomping your foot and demanding to be in charge is. I hear all the best captains do it." His voice is mild and pleasant. His face is punchable. His chin is still shaped like a butt. Dark circles shadow his eyes and lines of tension bracket his mouth. Whatever he was doing, it wasn't taking a nap.

It concerns me that he looks so bad, because he's likely been trained from birth to hide his weaknesses. It concerns me more that he's caught on to the fact that I don't know what the fuck I'm doing as a captain. It magnifies all my existing defensiveness.

My fingers twitch with my desire to strangle him. "The best captains get rid of bad crew, but your daddy's money means I'm stuck with you."

"Is there a second in your life when you don't think about my father?"

"Is there a second in your life when *you* don't?" He can't pull that on me. I know how it is to be raised in a Family, to want to measure up to a legacy. There was a time when I wanted that more than anything else. Sometimes I still do. I curl my fists tighter to keep myself from jabbing a finger into his chest.

Something crosses his face too quickly for me to decipher it. Might be an emotion. Might be gas. Either way, he doesn't say anything, so I press my advantage. "Your father is the client. All evidence to the contrary, we're good at what we do. Maybe you are, too—it's rare for a Family to have an incompetent in their ranks. I'm trying to work with you, as well as I'm able."

"Constant insults are what 'trying to work with me' looks like? I don't know how I ever thought you'd be able to work with a team. You couldn't even work with your own Family. I know all about you, Temperance Reed, and you're a calamity waiting to happen. It's my job to mitigate the damage." He leans down so we're eye to eye. I glare into his near-black gaze, and he glares back into my own swampy green. There are little flecks of gold in that black. I wonder if they were detailed enough to engineer those in or if he just got lucky.

Clearly, if he really knows all about me, he'd know that I'm a calamity *already* happening.

"You don't know a thing about my Family, and I said, 'as well as I'm able.' I'm surprised you even heard any insults—I thought the chorus of your own ego was so loud you couldn't hear my voice. That's certainly how it seems considering I said, 'keep watch in the helm so if anyone from that creepy cult comes after us you can shoot them full of holes,' and what you heard was, 'take a walk and enjoy the night air.' If you've never scouted a planet before, let me fill you in. We get ambushed all the time, which is why we have a watch in the first place. It's not because I'm mean and don't want you to get your precious sleep."

His jaw clenches and I brace myself for another jibe, but it doesn't come. It's not because he has nothing to say. His lips are pressed together so hard it's like he's trying to choke on his own words. His breath feathers against my cheek. His perfectly straight nose is . . . I look again. It *isn't* perfectly straight. How marvelous. At some point, Arcadio Escajeda broke his nose—or someone broke it for him—and it didn't set right. I don't know why they didn't fix it properly, but I'm intrigued by the humanity of the imperfection. The hitch in the smooth slope transforms his patrician features into rugged masculinity.

I'm stricken with the sudden perverse impulse to lick his nose. Not because he's particularly lickable (although he is), but just to see what he'd do. Probably scream and run back to his suite to take a shower. It would be one way to shut him up and get the last word.

It would also be insanity. I dart my eyes away, horrified at myself. Perhaps I'm delirious. It's the only explanation.

"As you can see, I'm up and ready for a fight, so I'll take over your shift. Tomorrow night, I expect you to stay where you're put."

He opens his mouth like he has something to say. Closes it. Makes a noise that I would call a snarl if it came from an animal and stalks away. Good enough for me. I spend the rest of the night sitting in the helm with my boots up on the console and a cup of stim-water. By the time the sun rises behind the volcano and the rest of the crew joins me, my mood has not improved.

No one tried to kill us over the night, so it's another tally in the "win" column.

．　．　．　．　．

The canyons are a claustrophobic mess. It appears that, in the years the river wore away at the rock before it disappeared below the ground, it took a hard turn such that the canyon curves inward in a "C" shape with a precarious overhang shading the land below. No wonder satellites didn't detect human habitation. We make our way down in a portion of the canyon where the overhang has crumbled and dropped. It creates three sides of deteriorated canyon walls and one mouth that leads into the canyon. The drone mapped the path, but it didn't highlight how many patches of uncertain ground there are on the winding route from surface to floor of the canyon.

I nearly eat dirt about five times and only the fact that everyone else is stumbling around like drunks on ice makes me feel better about my lack of grace. My old fencing instructor must be spinning in his retirement.

When I finally hit the bottom, narrow and covered with more low off-white plants, I believe I'm past the danger zone. It's that kind of cocky thinking that leads to a fall, and I do—arms flailing and skidding the last few steps before I wind up on my ass. I sit on the ground for a breath, wondering if I can pretend that I did it on purpose.

The blast that explodes the rock wall where my head would have been if I was standing vindicates my clumsiness. Shards of dirt rain on my hair as I skitter on my side, scraping the hells out of my forearm as I unholster my own blaster and take cover behind a craggy boulder. Another five shots land around me, setting up puffs of dust and drilling holes in the stone. Caro lets out a noise like "eep" and ducks behind another boulder. Itzel joins her in silence, blaster already in hand. I'm glad Itzel is with her because Caro can't hit the broad side of a spaceship on the shooting range.

There are only two boulders nearby that offer cover, so Micah takes theirs, firing around the edge of the ruddy rock. That leaves three people crammed behind one medium-sized boulder and only me behind the large one. Escajeda looks like he's considering

being shot but eventually slips across the open space at the bottom
of the canyon and joins me. Usually, he's a pain in my ass, but just
at this moment, he's graceful as a predator and all those weapons
strapped to him look good.

"We're penned in here," Escajeda growls.

No shit. That's how three sides of canyon wall work. There's
no available retreat the way we came. We'll be blindingly vulnerable picking our way up the canyon wall. "The only way out is
through."

Which could basically be my non-Family motto.

"Who?" It's all I manage to get out before another volley of
blaster fire hits the canyon walls around us. Escajeda hisses and
ducks back, colliding with me. I grab a handful of his armored vest
to keep from ricocheting away and out of cover. Something warm
trickles over my knuckles and I feel around his arm until he jerks
it away. "How bad?"

"A graze. Stop sticking your fingers in it." He returns fire but
we're shooting blind, trapped behind this rock. "I caught a glimpse.
Doesn't look like the Children. Not wearing the stupid little outfits,
at least."

I drop to the ground, in a push-up position, and peer up the
canyon past his shins. A party of seven, wearing militaristic outfits
and face shields. There's another large boulder diagonally across
from us and it leads to a fall of rocks that offer shelter and a much
better angle. I pop back to my feet before they think to look down.

With a whistle, I snag Micah and Itzel's attention—Caro has
chosen this moment to mess with her datapad—and hold up seven
fingers. Micah nods and gestures up the wall, clearly asking if we
should retreat. Escajeda shakes his head. It's the response I was
going to give, and he *is* the head of security, so I let his direction
slide.

I make little finger guns at Micah, indicating that he should provide covering fire. Because this is a very complicated code, he stares blankly at me a moment before complying. I sprint from my rock to the one across the canyon. A hot flash slices along the top of my shoulder but I make it to the other side without any real damage. Luckily, my armored vest took some of the hit.

We all wore vests instead of full armor. It's ridiculous to wear full armor while scouting a planet that is reported as uninhabited except for a weird little cult. You can't move properly in armor—at least not if you have armor like I do. Plus, it's a desert planet. Armor is hot and dehydration is real.

Right now, it seems like it might have been a good idea to risk a little dehydration and wear the full armor.

Escajeda curses and a moment later he collides with me behind the rock. If I'd known he was following me, I would have made room, but he makes it well enough by crashing into my already bleeding back and smooshing me against the boulder. We really need to work out a rhythm as a crew.

"Am I, or am I not the head of security?" he growls in my ear, pressing me against the hard stone and gazing around the edge. It feels like he's smothering me with that hard body. His arms are braced on either side of my head, a wealth of muscle that would be fascinating at any time when I don't need to handle a literal firefight.

It takes a moment to realize that he believes that he's protecting me. He probably doesn't even trust me to hold a blaster correctly. I wriggle away, careful to stay behind the boulder. "Fine, dazzle me with your strategic competence."

He fires three shots and I hear a thump from the direction of the seven shooters. I take advantage of the moment to scope them out again. The armor has the look of the Nakatomi Family. Families are vain. They like a cohesive look. Nakatomis are known for warfare, so if someone's wearing top-of-the-line body armor, odds are high that they're a Nakatomi. If it has a dragon on the collar, like these do, odds are even higher.

When you're in a firefight in the bottom of a narrow canyon, the Nakatomis are the last Family you want facing you. Which leads to the next question: Why the hells are the Nakatomis on Herschel Two?

Escajeda fires two more shots and ducks down. No shots coming from Micah and Itzel's rock. Probably a bad angle.

"I'm going to stay here, be a big target, and shoot a lot. You're going to sneak along that rockfall until you're behind them." Escajeda nudges me toward the rockfall with a broad hand on my lower back. It's a decent plan. I'm feeling vaguely positive about our teamwork until he continues, "Maybe manage not to fall on your ass too many times. I can only be so loud."

I consider sticking my finger in his blaster wound. It would probably be unprofessional. Might be worth it anyway.

Showing exceptional emotional maturity, I allow him the last word and clamber along the fallen rocks, keeping as low as possible. My own blaster wound stings as I move. I scramble over a particularly large boulder and then hug close to the canyon wall as I worm my way between it and another large pile of fallen rocks. It's precarious but I'm trying as hard as I can not to fall and prove Escajeda right.

He stays true to his word and makes a lot of noise. He fires into the rock above the Nakatomis, causing debris to rain down, then shoots at them while they're distracted. Despite myself, I'm impressed with the strategy and the aim. I'm nearly level with them when I run out of rockfall. It's not ideal. I can't even blame Escajeda for sending me into a risky position because it really did look like the rockfall stretched farther from our previous angle. Either I take the surprise and fire upon them from here, or I run out and try to get cover behind them before they know what's going on. I have many skills—*some* skills—but stealth isn't one of them.

I wait until they're busy firing upon Escajeda and distract one with multiple shots to the upper body and drop another with a shot to the knee. Then I'm flattened to a rock that they're trying to shoot to dust. I frantically look to either side, palms sweating. There's no obvious escape. My hair sticks to my cheek in sweaty strands and dust catches at my throat. Escajeda has moved half-way up the rockslide while I distracted them and fires from the new location. He only draws the fire of half and the rest keep me pinned down.

I'm running low on clever ideas. We're down from seven to four but two each is plenty to keep us pinned. Micah and Itzel don't have a good angle. The last time someone surrendered to a Na-katomi, their empty ship floated to Prism Way Station completely open to space with a warning note spelled out in void-frozen blood in the helm.

The crunching sound of gravel under boots tells me that some-one is approaching the boulder that shelters me. I spin to my back and hold my blaster level at the space where they'll appear to am-bush me. Instead, someone grabs the collar of my armor and yanks me backward along the rough ground. I glance up for a split sec-ond before I focus back on the rocks. Escajeda. He's been grazed at least one more time in the arm he was hit in before. He looks mad.

I'm sure I look mad, too. Being shot at does that to a person. At least, I hope I look mad. That's better than looking scared shitless. "Any more great ideas?"

Escajeda yanks me to my feet, steadying my balance with one arm around my waist as we duck behind a slightly larger boulder. He glances up like he's thinking and suddenly, from the sky, comes the answer to our prayers. Caro's drone drops hard on one of the

Nakatomis. It spins around them, blades flying, crashing into helmets and armored shoulders, before they start firing on it. We both pop up with our blasters to take advantage of the distraction and they start to withdraw.

Micah's moved to the boulder where Escajeda and I initially took shelter, and he joins us in firing upon them. As they retreat, the Nakatomi crew continues to fire, and they tear a large hunk of earth from the canyon wall above us.

Escajeda lunges at me, shoving me to the ground and covering me with his body as the huge stone crashes to the center of the canyon floor. The ground ripples like a wave with the impact. His arm curls around my head, blocking my line of vision. He grunts out a breath as debris rains down around us and I try to get a better angle to see if the Nakatomis are going to shoot us where we lie.

"Stop squirming," he mutters, breath hot against my ear. His voice sounds pained, and suddenly I have a new concern. Maybe he was hurt. While trying to protect me. Which is some special insane Family nobility that has no place in scouting.

I twist up to confirm he's not crushed, patting my hands around his shoulders and back. Dust and armored fabric and hard planes of muscle. A little blood but nothing to indicate a mortal wound. Escajeda gazes down at me and, for a moment, we just breathe, eyes locked. It's the most I've ever liked him.

Probably because he isn't talking.

It's a very brief moment. He rolls off, and a cracking sound comes from the ground under the crashed boulder. The earth beneath us groans. I can feel my eyes go wide as my fingers curl in the dirt. The ground quivers like the ripples on a lake.

"Get back!" I scream at the rest of the crew.

The floor of the canyon gives way, opening in a dark chasm. I reach out to catch Escajeda but it's too late. He's already fallen and I'm tumbling behind him.

CHAPTER 6

Jagged rock walls kaleidoscope past me as I plummet, uncontrolled, into a chasm below the canyon. Wall. Sky. My own arm. Wall. Falling dirt. Darkness below. My leg crashes into a jutting formation and the force of the collision sends me off in a new direction, backflipping through the air. My mouth opens to make some sort of noise—I'm not even sure what—but I hit water face-first and instead of yelling I just swallow half a river.

I don't have time to be afraid. I don't have time to be anything. Water. Foam. Air. Water. More water. Bouncing off a wall. Water. I don't know what way is up. I'm surrounded by black water pressing into my face, my mouth. Trying to find its way to my lungs. Blindly panicked, I pick a direction, which turns out to be the correct one. I fight my way to the surface, flailing with my arms. I gulp a mouthful of air, spinning along with a current that's confusingly fast. The river sweeps me into darkness, away from the crater that cracked open above.

"Escajeda!" I yell, gasping for air. It's so dark, I can't see anything. My blaster is gone. My datapad. My armored vest absorbs water, dragging me down, and I strip it off as the current carries me. I can't hear over the sound of the river rushing, over rocks and my own heartbeat thundering in my ears. My other senses are too overwhelmed to give them a try. "Escajeda!"

Silence. He could be anywhere. Hanging off the rock wall. Ahead of me in the river. Stuck between two fallen rocks under water, slowly drowning to death. He tried to save me. Put his body between me and danger. I couldn't save him back.

It's a struggle to keep my head above the water. The walls run straight to the rushing water. After long spans of darkness, periodic cracks open in the ceiling of the cave, letting in splinters of light. It's enough to show me there aren't any nearby ledges. Only an endless stretch of darkness, smooth walls, and inky-black water.

A narrow shaft of light illuminates something floating in the water in front of me. I swim, adding my own momentum to the flow of the water until I collide with a body. I feel around it. Skin. Durable cloth. The familiar shape of an armored vest slowly taking on water. Not the body armor of the Nakatomis. I yank the floating body closer and, in the dim light of my banishment tattoo, can just barely make out Escajeda's bloody face.

There's a cut at his hairline, another slicing through an eyebrow. They don't appear serious, but head wounds are always messy. I try to wrestle his weight, but I can't fight the mass of the waterlogged vest. By touch, I fumble for the fasteners of his vest, awkwardly ripping it off while trying to keep him afloat. Once he's finally half naked, I link my arm under his biceps and over his chest, pulling his back against my torso so I can keep his head above the water.

He's heavy and it's an extra strain on the leg that hit the wall. An ache swells whenever I kick. I look for a distraction, any distraction from the pain that starts to slither up my nerves. His hair smells surprisingly good. The *Quest* has showers, but they aren't the kind with perfumed-soap dispensers. They're the kind with ionic decontamination that comes in jets of pressurized air. He's also warmer than I am, and it doesn't feel too bad to be pressed this closely against him. Not that I'd admit it, even if you held a blaster to my face. I try to float as much as I'm able and we ride the current for an indeterminate amount of time.

I don't think anyone else fell. They were farther back, in the

safe zone. I tell myself that over and over until I start to believe it.
If they're safe, they can track us by our ident chips. Hopefully the
Nakatomis took the opportunity to flee.

At long last, the current kicks us out into a cylinder of light. The
river widens into a large round lake with turquoise waters that are
lit from the hole above. I finally get a chance to use Caro's new
word: "cenote." The water must drain somewhere on the other
side, but I can't see it. The rock rises steeply in layers of pale and
dark red all around us and those spindly white plants dangle from
the hole above like tattered lace. A tree version of the white plants
rises against one of the rock walls, stretching over the water. Even
better, there's a small shore on either side of the crystalline lake.
It's not hospitable—no hammocks or cocktails to be seen—but it's
better than half-drowned in the water.

I drag Escajeda over to the edge and, with a heave, I get him
partially on land. Enough that he won't float away. His chest rises
and falls in a steady rhythm. I rest my hand against it briefly, as
though I need to reassure myself that he's alive.

He handled himself well with the Nakatomis. I can put up with
attitude if it comes with competence. He trusted me to contribute,
and he put himself at risk to give me the opportunity. He didn't
have to do either of those things. I gently feel around his body to see
if I find any more blood or lumps. Not much there. Well . . . some
stuff. Rather impressive stuff. I keep my diagnostic professional and
don't linger anywhere.

The two cuts on his head have stopped bleeding. His hands are
scraped but not seriously. That leaves the two blaster wounds in his
arm. Deeper than I'd like and still dribbling blood.

I feel around in my ear for my coms. Gone. Lost at some point
in the fall or the river along with my weapons. His is, too. In fact, I
don't have anything beyond my boots, pants, and compression bra.
That limits first-aid options. The only place to get a large swath of

fabric is from the legs of our pants. I can just imagine how he'll react knowing I already discarded and lost his armored vest, so I rip a long strip of the durable material from my own pants instead of his.

So now, I'm wearing a compression bra and tattered half pants. It's glamorous moments like this that drew me to the scouting profession.

Now that all the triage is done, I have time to linger over the view offered by my similarly half-dressed companion. Rich sunlight highlights warm tan skin. A broad chest narrows to abs that are rippled in a way I hadn't previously imagined humanly possible. His chest is lightly dusted with black hair and a narrow trail of it traces his abdomen as it makes its way below his waistband. Through massive effort, I don't consider anything *else* below his waistband.

It's not so impressive, anyway. His family probably paid a pretty penny for modded musculature. Genetic mods increase the ability to build muscle, but doctors can actually bulk up existing muscles if you like wasting your credits on something you could do yourself. I'd bet he's done both.

I mean to drag myself away after I bandage him, but I'm so tired. My eyelids droop and a fuzzy darkness gathers around the edges of my vision. I should be worrying about something. Several somethings. I just can't muster the energy to do so. I can't muster the energy to do anything. When I collapse, my cheek collides with a chest that is both muscular and slightly damp before everything goes black.

. . . . .

I wake up as pain shoots through my leg. I flail to a sitting position and yell because it just feels like the right thing to do. Escajeda is awake, crouching near my feet, poking at my ankle.

"What the flaming fuck are you doing?" I yelp, one hand grabbing his shoulder and the other in the sand.

"I'm trying to tell if your leg is broken. It isn't. Just a sprain." He tightens a fabric brace around my now bare ankle, and stars dance in front of my eyes.

That makes sense. I was so busy saving our lives and taking care of his wounds that I forgot to check on my own. That's when I realize that his pants are now as tattered as my own and a strip of fabric is looped over my shoulder where I took the blaster shot. It's chilly. Sun isn't coming into the cenote anymore and my compression bra wasn't made for warmth.

His skin is hot against my chilled hand. I yank it back like it's scalded. "How long—?"

"Have we been here? I'm not sure. The sun is setting. How long did we float before we came here?" It might be the longest he's ever spoken to me without an insult. Beyond the initial one of interrupting me.

Then again, "How long—" was probably the longest I've ever spoken to him without an insult. "It's hard to judge. I can't track time floating in the dark and both of our coms were lost at some point. Caro has our tracker signals, so they'll find us eventually." I tap on the little chip imbedded in the skin at the base of my neck. He has a matching one, inserted on the flight to Herschel Two. "The canyon and the depth of the cenote might delay matters."

He presses his lips together and looks up, like he can summon Caro's drone with only his attention on the sky.

"How's your arm?"

He glances down at the haphazard bandage before looking at his lack of clothing and quirking his lips. "In better shape than my clothing. Couldn't resist the chance to see some skin?"

He can't possibly be flirting with me after near-drowning. I'm reading something into this that isn't there. Some sort of heretofore unknown sprained-ankle delirium.

If someone asked me a year ago what I'd do if I found anyone from a Family unconscious and injured, my answer would have been "finish the job." I'd have been 40 percent joking. This particular Family scion is different, though. He was good in a fight. He thought *I* was the sort of person who needed protection. I helped him, and he returned the favor.

He was a partner, and he might be worthy of something more than overt hostility.

A tiny part of me that's been burned so many times it's smaller than an atom unfurls a warm sparking arm.

The sky above grows darker, losing its warm-yellow glow and slipping into deep violet and then black. The water of the cenote laps on the sand. The chill deepens. I shiver, wishing that I'd managed to keep hold of the vests.

"You think that tree has any branches dry enough to catch fire?" I ask Escajeda, since a string of his footprints indicate that he investigated the bottom of the cenote while I was unconscious.

"I thought everything washed out of your pockets. Your eyes might shoot pretty flames when you're angry, but I don't think they're literal enough to help us."

"Can't you ever just answer a question? There are more ways to start a fire than with modern tools. Unless you'd rather be cold out of spite." I try to shove my way up to standing but wobble when weight hits my ankle.

Why would he say my eyes are pretty? What does he hope to get out of it?

"Look who's talking about spite." His hands on my shoulders push me back down to a sitting position and he walks over to the tree, wading in ankle-deep water part of the way. The branches make a snapping sound as he breaks them off and, when he returns to me, it's with an arm full of tinder, collected from the dry branches near the top.

I collect it from him and create a little scaffold to keep the fire off the sand. A sharp rock splits one of the branches lengthwise and I scrape it in a trough. Crushed leaves go into the trough, and I finish my preparation with two sticks of equal size, one curved. One of my bootlaces loops around the curved stick, and I now have a bow-and-drill fire starter.

Escajeda watches with fascination, as though I'm performing an arcane ritual. "How do you know how to do this?"

Most of my scouting skills were learned on the job. Ven taught me the best strategy for rock climbing. Itzel showed me how to detect quicksand. Caro taught me how to swim. This, though, came from before I met any of them.

"After my parents died, Nati—my tutor—used to take Kari, his daughter and my best friend, and me to the closest habitable moon on our birthdays. Instead of staying in one of the Reed habitats, we camped under trees so tall that they seemed to touch the stars. He taught us how to navigate by the night sky—which isn't as helpful as one might believe because the thing about scouting is that the night sky is different with each new planet—and he taught us how to start fires without tools."

His brows furrow like he doesn't know what to do with that information. "You were an heiress."

I burst out laughing. Mostly because even when I was an heiress, I didn't exactly lead a charmed life. "It didn't matter that I was an heiress. Nati believed in self-sufficiency over any other virtue. Which was lucky for me because it's about the only virtue I possess."

With a grunt, I move to my knees for the right leverage. He catches my shoulder when I briefly lose balance. I don't shove his surprisingly calloused hand off. Instead, I move the curved bow like a saw, spinning the straight stick in the leaves with more speed than I could manage with my hands alone.

This kind of fire-starting is labor intensive and doesn't always work. I saw until my hands hurt and the faintest sliver of bitter smoke rises from the leaves. "Can you smell the smoke?"

"I can." He's still supporting half my weight, my shoulder pressed against his chest, hip against his thigh. It's hard to swallow, all of a sudden, unless I focus all my attention on the fire.

"If you breathe gently on the leaves when you smell the smoke, you'll feed the spark and we'll get a flame." And maybe he'll put a little distance between us to do it. In the press of the darkness, with only the sounds of the water lapping against the sand and his breath in my ear, I'm finding it difficult to remember exactly who he is and exactly why the direction of my thoughts is a terrible idea. Not that he'd ever entertain them. Families don't dally with commoners. I'm probably safer from intimacy here, with him, than I would be with anyone else.

Not that anyone's been banging down my doors with offers.

The scent of smoke wreaths between us. "If I let you go, are you going to fall over?"

"Your throbbing masculine presence isn't that powerful," I scoff.

A flash of white teeth in the darkness. "I was talking about your ankle. Interesting that your mind went to my masculine presence. Throbbing, is it?"

Oh shit. Got caught there, didn't I? "I assume you're always thinking about your own masculine presence. That's how it works for scions."

"Hmm." The sound rumbles from his throat like a purr. Like he knows he caught me and now he wants to bat me around for a while.

His silhouette is visible in the faint light thrown from my banishment tattoo as he crouches on the ground near the bow and follows instructions. It must be a miracle.

It takes a while, working in tandem, but finally, a tiny flicker of flame appears. We feed it like a baby bird until it grows, and I laugh like a lunatic when a fire finally dances on the beach near the weathered cenote walls. Escajeda looks at me like I'm just as insane as I sound, but even his lips quirk into a smile.

That small spark within me flares again, a flush of warmth that works its way to my face. My laugh dies in my throat. It's weakness and he'll take advantage of it if he sees it, so I go on the offensive before he can notice. "Why are there Nakatomis on Herschel?"

The smile drops and he redirects his gaze to the fire. "Why do people scout any territory? Because they think there's value in it for them."

What a delightful nonanswer. The Family is showing in him. "I assumed your father would be more competent in keeping your Family's interests obscured. Now, we find your mortal enemies not only exploring the planet but armed to the teeth. Seems like you have a leak."

"I know you think my Family is behind every dastardly move in charted space but everyone in the Five has equally dirty hands. The Nakatomis have their fingers in more pies than all the rest combined."

The territory grab in the airspace around Kohaishimi initially read as normal Family bluffing. Why pay for goods you can steal, after all? I'm aware of my tunnel vision about the Escajeda Family in particular. I think they're the worst of the bunch—because they've allied with Frederick, whom even Ven understood was 80 percent hot air and 20 percent serpent—and there hasn't been any evidence that my assumption is incorrect. That doesn't mean that other Families are good.

"Your assumption is that the Nakatomi Family is after phydium?

Discovered through their own probe scans?" It's my hypothesis, but it feels like I'm missing something. Some piece of the puzzle that doesn't quite fit.

"That assumption makes the most sense." I'm not sure if he just has a habit of speaking like that or if he's deliberately trying to avoid the conversation.

"We both agree it makes the most sense. That's not what I was getting at. Why do *you* think they're here?" The light from our fire throws dancing shadows on the walls of the cenote. Dark spokes stretch behind the tree and black water licks at the sand. It's almost comforting beyond the chill that still permeates the air despite the flames.

He pauses for a long time before responding. "If they're here, they must be after phydium. I can't see anything else to recommend this place."

I lean back against the wall in a huff, irritated that he agreed with me because I still feel like there's something I'm missing.

His black hair casts shadows on his forehead, and he doesn't look at me when he speaks. Even so, his rough voice rubs against my skin like velvet. He sounds exhausted. "Why didn't you ever petition the Inter-Family council to ask for your banishment to be partially lifted? It's what anyone else in your position would have requested. They might not have been able to get you back into Reed territory, but they can open up the rest of the settled territories to you."

I open my mouth, but nothing comes out. It honestly never occurred to me. The average banished person doesn't have the option, but I was well enough known that I probably could have received a review. They can't remove the tattoo, but they can change the color of the ink. The white glow indicates that I'm banished from everywhere. If I was banished from Reed space, the ink would glow green. Micah's is yellow. He's only banned from Pierce space.

My banishment has been inconvenient, but it never bothered me as much as you might expect. Something that would probably be confounding to anyone else. Honestly, it saved me from Frederick's mess. It put me out of his reach. The only thing I regret is that I couldn't do the right thing for my Family and try to cancel out some of his influence.

My immediate reaction is to tell Escajeda to fuck off because it's none of his business.

"Fuck off."

Satisfying, but there's something about the way the darkness nestles close, the way the fire licks at our skin and the unrecognizable stars glimmer down, that feels like we're set apart in time. He's still an Escajeda and I'm still a . . . nothing . . . but here, battered and hungry in the bottom of a canyon, we're also people and maybe I can ignore the rest of it—just for the moment.

Or maybe I just *want* to ignore it, no matter the consequences.

"The banishment is a fair consequence." I settle on that response. The air smells wet down here. Dank. "If I'd succeeded, things would be different, but I failed."

"What did you do? It never went public."

A complicated question with a simple answer. "I disagreed. There's more to it, of course. Frederick was and probably still is a sadistic priap but that's what it comes down to. Frederick changed the business model we operated under for generations. The AI my parents developed in our lunar labs, and the programming we produced was always conceptualized and developed in-Family. We had these labs—amazing places—where scientists just . . . experimented. There were a lot of failures, as you might imagine, but there were enough successes. Enough to bring us to the Ten, which is more than most ever get. We believed in doing it ourselves, not buying ideas from others."

I shift my weight, staring into the fire because I don't want to look at him and see the judgment that must be in his face. My parents were idealists. That's not how business is done anymore, I've heard it again and again. An antiquated model. "When they died, Frederick wasted no time in decommissioning those labs and selling them for parts. Then, when our tech started to get outdated, he targeted the Hossepians. I'm sure you haven't heard of them. They were a little-f family with one big idea—a special kind of bio-compatible material that allowed chips to be implanted in a new location and modified postimplantation.

"He ruined them. Enacted sanctions, blocked vessels from their territory, cloud-seeded their agricultural planet until it flooded and destroyed the crops. I don't know for sure, but I think he paid someone to tinker with their space station, so the air cut out." I swallow, the fire so bright that I still see it when my eyes are closed. "When they were desperate, he swooped in and acquired all their intellectual property for a steal. He did it again to the Khanhs, the Dukes. Maybe my parents were too far on the internal side—but his strategy was so extreme that he destroyed us. We didn't make *anything* anymore. We just bought things after we ruined their inventors."

Escajeda doesn't say a word. This was a mistake. Why would I ever believe that the son of a Family would understand my side of it?

"When he started it with the Wolf family, I couldn't take it. I slipped them enough intel to counteract his plan to steal their investors. I also told them who in their family was really on my brother's payroll. By that time, I was being watched, so I used Nati—my tutor—to share the information. I thought of it as diplomacy, right? Building a connection because you can't only make enemies. I

thought that I could swoop in and make a deal with them behind
Frederick's back. Maybe show him that we could do business without devouring the people involved."

I was young enough and naive enough to believe that might
actually work. I lapse into silence, waiting for a laugh or at least a
snort. Waiting for anything, but the man beside me doesn't move
at all. His head is still tilted back, eyes closed. Perhaps I put him
to sleep.

"What happened?"

Perhaps not.

"Frederick found out. He killed Nati, for treason. They had a
rushed sham trial, attended only by my brother's cronies. I certainly wasn't allowed to speak for him. Frederick told me it was a
lesson for me. Like Nati didn't matter at all. Like he wasn't Frederick's tutor also. Like his daughter wasn't my best friend. Like he
was a toy that could be taken away when I misbehaved. Frederick
gave me a chance to stay in the Family. I refused."

"Good. You didn't belong there." Escajeda's voice is a low
rumble.

"I'm sure you're right. I'm not the type to succeed in a Family."
I think I keep the hurt out of the words. Probably.

It hadn't been much of a chance. I thought he would kill me
that night. Maybe I even expected it a little. Frederick is an unstable explosive of a man. He had his hand around my neck, vein
throbbing in his forehead and eyes so wild that they practically
howled. Then he dropped me on the floor at his feet and walked
away.

He never looked back. Just wrote me off like a bad investment.

He could have done the same to Nati. I confessed immediately.
Frederick knew the leak came from me. He wanted to make a
point. It didn't matter to him that Nati had been one of our mother's
childhood friends. That his exquisite blown-glass chandelier still

hovers in the receiving hall of the Reed station, right over where Nati's body was displayed for a month as a warning to anyone else who might seek to ally with me or betray my brother.

Frederick killed a brilliant artist and father to send a message. He succeeded. Kari only spoke to me one more time—when she told me that I was responsible for her father's death and that the Family would be better off without me.

There may be a reason why I have difficulty getting close to people.

Arcadio moves at last, turning to face me, and I can't help meeting his gaze. The firelight reflects from his eyes. His voice is carefully flat. Serious. "I mean good that you refused. Your brother is an unstable warhead and at least half of my impression of you was based on having met him."

"Your Family allies with him." The words are out of my mouth before I think of editing myself.

An eyebrow cocks. "I think we've established that it is possible to not be our Families."

"Not if you want to stay in them," I mutter, looking away again. I didn't expect him to understand, and I can't help trying to read some scheme into his words. I can't see how he'd benefit, but life has led me to look for a hidden blade.

"It helps that I won't inherit, and no one expects me to conform." The smile is audible in his voice although it hasn't broken through to his face. "None of us brothers will."

"Do you think you'd be a bad heir?"

"Too devastatingly attractive, I'm afraid. No one would ever get anything done spending all day ogling me."

Considering I've been noticing a real reduction in my own personal efficiency due to ogling, I can sadly attest that he's telling the truth. "I think you confused yourself with someone else. Besides, it seems like you toe the Family line. You looked pretty conformist when I met with your Family. Do you guys stage the room for maximum intimidation?"

"Maybe you're easily intimidated." The smile's broken through to his eyes now, almost as warm as the fire.

I smack him in the chest. I *don't* notice that it's well muscled and still bare.

One dark brow arches at me. "You only get one hit before I retaliate."

It's like he doesn't know me at all. I hit him again.

At least, I try. Quick as a flash, he captures my wrist, yanks, and suddenly I'm straddling his lap, sitting directly on hard-muscled thighs. My free hand clasps his shoulder for balance. My mouth drops open into a perfect circle, so stunned that every single thought tumbles out of my head and all I can hear is a hollow echo that sounds halfway between eager encouragement and abject terror.

He's called my bluff and suddenly I realize that, despite what I claimed after the Nakatomi ship almost shot us into pieces, I'm all talk and no action.

Escajeda makes a *tsk*ing sound but does not release my wrist. "I told you, you only get one."

Technically, I only *got* one. The second didn't make contact. I flick his ear with my free hand.

His rich dark eyes widen and then narrow. The firelight splays across his face, painting its planes with warmth. His jaw is tense. It's always tense.

Shadows play around his lips. I'm transfixed by their subtle flexing. The tease as the corner turns up, all masculine satisfaction. He caught me watching. So I flick his ear again.

In another swift motion, he tugs me forward until I'm flush against his torso, thighs cradling the hard frame of his hips. My breath escapes me in a gasp because clearly, he's not afraid to escalate.

Usually, people are afraid.

My nose brushes against his cheek. My lips graze ever so lightly against the corner of his mouth when I breathe. His hand splays over the small of my back, scalding as a burn. My heart clogs my throat, stopping any words that might want to escape, which is a blessing because the only word that springs to mind is *"more."*

We stay frozen, wrapped in each other, for an eternal moment. Long enough for me to memorize the feeling of his muscles going rigid beneath my fingers. Long enough for me to mentally recite the million ways this is a horrible idea. Long enough for me to forget every single one of them.

He turns his head just a fraction, perfectly aligning our mouths. If I so much as breathe hard, our lips will touch. I forget how to breathe at all. I'm still mystified as to how I got here, how this evening transitioned from insults to honesty to . . . play.

It's been ages since I played with someone.

He's so far out of my league that we're playing different games. I'm not supposed to be tempted. Not supposed to want to close that minuscule distance where our breath mingles and see what he tastes like.

I can't read anything in his face, but this close, I feel the pumping beat of his heart against the palm of my hand that, somehow, has found its way to his chest. That throbbing masculine presence we previously discussed is pressing so close to where I want it that, if I move just a fraction more, I'll be there.

If I go there, I might never want to go back.

Horrifying.

When I move, I don't even know if it's to close the distance or to flee. I press down wrong on my bad ankle and gasp out a pained breath. Escajeda blinks like a spell has been broken, shaking his head slightly. He releases my wrist and sets me back on the ground, bending to look at my offending limb.

"I shouldn't have done that."

There are a million reasons why—I enumerated and forgot them earlier, but it still hurts to hear. I can't look away from his lips. I have to look away from his lips or I'll seem desperate.

I don't argue. The moment is broken and it's for the best. He's the client, or close enough. He's from a Family, which means that anything with me would be nothing more than a dalliance, and I have no interest in being the mistress to a scion.

Which is getting so far ahead of myself that I can barely see me back there in my own dust.

"The notorious Family traitor." Escajeda's voice is a low brush on my oversensitized nerves. He snorts. "You aren't the calamity I expected."

His shoulder is still brushing against my own. I don't lean away from it. As the night closes in around us, I shiver and he wraps one big arm around my shoulders, pulling me closer. The dancing light of the fire casts the same glow across us both.

"You aren't either."

. . . .

CHAPTER 7

"I can do it." I stare up at the smooth rock wall of the cenote, a wash of red color in the morning light. It doesn't have many hand-holds and I have a sprained ankle. I absolutely *can't* do it. "It'll be fine."

Escajeda shoots me a dubious look. I return fire with cocky optimism.

It's probably less effective than I hope because I'm *not* cockily optimistic. I'm pridefully pessimistic, which is never a good combi-nation. It is, however, one I'm very familiar with. I can handle the climb because I must. No guarantees Caro's drone will be lucky enough to get the right angle on this cenote to sense our tracking chips. Escajeda could climb out on his own to get help—he even offered to do so this morning when the first light bloomed laven-der in the sky—but that would imply I need his help, which I very much do not.

He gestures toward the sun-drenched wall and grins like he can't wait to watch me fall.

I hope he chokes on that grin. Much as I choked on the stew of my own hormones all night while he slept the sleep of the bliss-fully unaware. The rock is rough under my fingers as I wedge them into a long horizontal crack about the height of my head. I hop my good leg up to a tiny outcropping. I've committed to the idiocy now.

It continues for a long time. I make progress, arm over arm, hopping my leg for support, but not as much or as quickly as I'd like. With only one good leg, more of the work is going to my arms. They're shaking, my fingers cramping. If I fall, I'll either die or be hurt worse than I already am. When I come to another crack in the smooth cenote wall, I'm getting so weak that I forego caution and ram the foot of my sprained ankle into the opening, just to take pressure off the other limbs.

It works, in a way.

The sparks of pain that shoot across my eyes are enough to make me forget about the weakness in my arms or the quivering in my good leg. They aren't quite enough to loosen my grip and send me tumbling back down into the water or beach below, but it's close. I cling to the rock wall like a particularly anguished lichen, wondering if humans ever evolved wings instantaneously or if I could be the first, purely fabricated from force of will.

No miracles occur, so I have to commit to continuing the climb or falling.

"Giving up yet?" Escajeda's just under me, looking up. No sweat on his brow.

"I don't give up," I grunt and reach up for another handhold. When I wrench my foot out of the wall, pain quivers through my body and my grasp loosens. I slip, just barely managing to regain a grip.

I'm not going to make it.

The thought is crystal in its clarity. Whenever I stop for breath, my muscles take on more strain. There are no handy little ledges, just a smooth, pale rock face that isn't getting any more climbable. I'm not sure I can even make the climb back down. My pride has signed a bill that my body can't pay.

Escajeda clicks his tongue against the back of his teeth. A rustle comes from beneath me. "Move away from the wall."

"Um." Not sure how I can do that. My arms are only so long and right now, they're spent to their max. "What are you going to do?"

He grumbles something under his breath. "Would you really rather fall to your death than trust me?"

I might rather fall than trust him. It's close. An experienced captain probably wouldn't be in this position in the first place. With quivering arms, I grip as strongly as I can and push outward, good leg wedged onto a foothold and bad dangling straight.

Escajeda climbs right up in front of me, wedging himself between me and the cenote wall. "Put your arms around my neck and try to loop your legs around my waist."

I don't do it right away. That pride comes sweeping back, overpowering all other weakness. "I'll be fine."

"You won't be fine. You're breaths away from falling and it would be embarrassing to have managed to climb so far on three limbs only to fail because you're afraid to touch me." He tilts his head around and eyes me. "Maybe only one breath away from falling."

He's not wrong. That's even worse. With a grimace, I loop one arm around his neck, waiting for him to shift under my weight. He doesn't, so I go for the other arm and the legs. "I'm not afraid to touch you."

It sounds petulant, even to me. Then again, I know it absolutely *is* petulant.

"Sure, you are. You're afraid you'll like it too much." He starts climbing again. Those lab-made muscles are earning their keep because it seems almost effortless.

"I've never liked them medically created. Some people earn what they have." His ear's right by my mouth and when I speak it's almost like a whisper. If he imagined I'd be whispering sweet nothings, he woefully misunderstood me. Even if I was tempted, which I'm not—I'm *not*—I'm not the sweet-nothing type.

Besides, he said last night was a mistake.

A laugh rolls through him and I can feel it reverberating into me. It's too much intimacy and, I hate to admit, it feels good. "Someone tell you my parents tinkered with my genes? They sold you an empty cargo if they did. You've experienced my Family. Do you think they'd ever admit their own genetic structure had room for improvement? I may have money and opportunity, but I wasn't altered on that level. None of us were. Nice to know you think I look like a perfect specimen, though. Talk like that could inflate an ego."

"Yours inflates much more, it might pop. I'd love to be around to see that."

"Nice way to talk to a man who's saving your life." He grips a piece of wall that looks almost flat to me and uses that to ascend even farther. If he's not genetically manipulated, he must have spent his entire life in physical training. And my bar is high. Frederick and I trained in hand-to-hand combat and endurance no less than twice a day, every day. Families don't like weakness.

"I saved your life yesterday. This is just your attempt to even the odds." I adjust my hold. *Not* to allow my palm to rest against his flexing chest. He's almost at the top, long limbs eating up the rock face of the wall. A moment later, we crest the top of the cenote and find ourselves below even taller canyon walls strewn liberally with veiny pale plants. I hop off his back and make it one pace away when I realize I can't easily locomote up here, either, unless I feel like crawling.

The plant life isn't strong enough to make crutches. When I look back at Escajeda, he's staring at me expectantly, arms out. "I can carry you like a princess."

I snap my teeth at him but limp back until I'm close enough to throw an arm over his shoulder. "If you ever tell anyone about this, I'll ventilate your bunk to space."

"I wouldn't dream of it, your majesty." He supports my weight and I hobble next to him. His hand is large on my waist. I try very hard not to think about how comforting it feels.

. . . . .

We haven't made it far when I spot the first pinkish-red outfit, crowned with a crest of hair. Whoever it is ducks down low and skitters away, taking shelter behind the rocks.

"Did you clock that?"

"They're a cult. Cults aren't great at stealth. They like their members to be very visible in case they ever try to escape." His voice feathers in my hair and I resist the impulse to wipe at my head. The canyon is deep here, but wide. The walls switchback and undulate as they rise. The light that angles in is warm. It would be a lovely place if I wasn't stumbling through it, leaning on Arcadio Escajeda. "One popped up on the border of Escajeda space a couple years ago. A woman who convinced her followers they were all a portion of a quasar-based psychic goddess. Of course, the leader was the biggest portion and spoke directly for the goddess. They wouldn't disband. Force or coercion would do nothing to solve the problem. They killed anyone who tried to get out."

I walk beside him, trying to avoid his support because I'm not some kind of helpless princess, but also putting as little weight on my ankle as possible because I can practically hear Micah's scolding in my head, telling me that I'm making things worse. Escajeda's low voice is a welcome distraction. "My brother Pablo was in school then and one of his classmates joined. Despite everything the rest of us tried, the group grew more and more entrenched. My little brother figured out the solution. He suggested that we shine a light on the cult. We made false promotional material for the cult that subtly highlighted how ridiculous they were and advertised in that specific region. Cults thrive on being outsiders—persecuted by the masses. By making it a purported favorite of the Escajedas, he robbed them of their power."

"He sounds insightful." I brush a hanging white plant out of the way. Yet another highly competent Escajeda.

"He is. He has a way of finding opportunities in the impossible." He trails into silence. Something tells me that isn't the whole of the story. He clearly isn't in the mood to share whatever caused the lull in the conversation. For once, I'm not in the mood to poke.

"You think the Children's attention is good news or bad?" I change the subject while looking around. I thought we'd have been found by now. Maybe Caro's drone was damaged in the fight. Maybe the Nakatomis continued the shoot-out after Escajeda and I fell into the river.

"Nothing on this fucking planet has been good yet." It's the first time I've really heard him swear and I'm oddly proud that we've managed to bring him to this in so few days.

"I thought the sunset was quite nice last night," I say, just to needle him.

"Have you seen any life-forms besides those vines and the tree?" He changes the subject rather than take my bait. I'm going to have to try harder.

Or maybe not. The last time he rose to my bait, things spiraled out of control quickly. "No. With the water so hard to get to, surface plants or animals must be very hardy. Maybe subterranean?"

"The cult's trade records at Landsdown are fairly minimal. Implies the plants are edible."

It could. Or the plants are all that is left on the surface because anything edible has already been picked off. "You want to take the first bite? If you don't die by tomorrow, I'll give one a shot."

Before he gets a chance to respond, the leader of the Children appears from a crevasse in the canyon wall, flanked again by a contingent of his henchmen. The supreme Rashahan seems to be wearing the same thing as the last time I saw him, but so am I. I can't judge. Not on that, at least. On the almost predatory glee that coats his face when he sees us, I can absolutely judge. Fuuuuck. A wide grin spreads his cheeks. "Scout Temperance and her fellow scout . . ."

He wants to know Escajeda's name. I didn't give it for a reason, but I wonder if Escajeda is egotistical enough that he wants to be recognized. He merely smiles pleasantly at Rashahan. I balance myself so that he can do his security-expert thing if he must without worrying about dragging me along.

I give Rashahan a sweet smile. "This is Scott." Escajeda's muscles tense under my hand but I toss him an equally beatific grin. "Scout Scott."

He makes that sort of rumbly sound that evidences displeasure but it's quiet enough Rashahan won't hear.

"We came across the signs of your battle late yesterday. I am pleased to see you survived the ordeal. The rest of your crew retreated by then, so we didn't have the opportunity to offer aid." At least he didn't find their bodies. That's positive. He's still speaking to any male standing next to me before he addresses me, which is less positive. "We will have to extend the offer directly to you. Your camp is nearly another day's journey. Our medical aid and table are at your disposal."

"We're happy to accept your generous offer."

Rashahan darts a glance in my direction and then redirects his attention to Escajeda. It stays there for the rest of the interaction. Could be the most Supreme knows who Arcadio's Family really is and sees some use in him. Or Escajeda's just the only man present and therefore more interesting. Considering how Rashahan reacted when Micah stood by my side, it's the man thing.

Usually, people who think like that have problems with their own man thing.

We move under a deep overhang where they've set up camp. There are some rough huts made from dirt bricks, fused to the canyon wall. Some members, either the newest or the least important, live in tents.

There are a lot of tents. How did this man convince so many banished to live in a hole on one of the least-interesting planets in charted space?

Escajeda and I are walked into a large tent that has a folding cot covered in a waterproof tan fabric and a tool chest that's been repurposed for rudimentary medical supplies. A harried and frail-looking woman shuffles in behind us. Her banishment tattoo is shallow. Old. The glow has nearly faded. If you haven't done something incredibly bad, sometimes they give you that kind of banishment, so it wears out just before you are elderly—allowing you to return to the loving arms of the Families for your golden years.

"I'm Temperance, what is your name?"

She glances up at me, then darts a look at Rashahan, who lingers inside the tent as though he has nothing better to do. That wide smile is still plastered on his face, but it grows a bit stiffer.

"This is Child Modesty." Rashahan says it like he's making a polite introduction, but Modesty's nervousness tells me that she is not supposed to speak. "All of the Children take on virtue names when they leave their old life behind."

Well, shit. Here I come with my own built-in virtue name. None of that virtue, but I'm not sure cults really care about that sort of thing.

"Thank you for your assistance, Child Modesty. We have a medic of our own who is very talented, if you would ever like to share stories with him." Her cold fingers tighten briefly on my wrist. If I can link her with Micah, she might get a chance to trade supplies in secret.

She slathers something on my blaster shot. It doesn't come from a medical-looking package, just an unmarked metal tub. Escajeda gets the same treatment, so if it is poisonous, we'll go down together. At least they have some semiclean material to rebind the wounds.

"We will host you for dinner." Rashahan makes a sweeping gesture toward the tent flap as Modesty stores her supplies, such as they are.

The Children gather around a massive fallen-rock table. It makes me think of an altar. It's long and narrow and the supreme Rashahan takes his place at its head. Escajeda is placed at his right hand, and I am placed one seat down. Two of the younger female Children sit across from us and then the whole half of the table is populated by men with women clustered at the far end. I guess it's an honor that I'm sitting up with Rashahan's favorite cult bunnies.

They are introduced to me as Charity and Generosity. Generosity must have been late to arrive to get saddled with a name like that. I guess she could shorten it to Gen. Or Sity. Charity's original hair color is nearly white, but it appears she's applied mud to achieve the crest shape that some of the others have done through snarls. I'm not sure if this implies a greater or a reduced sense of commitment. Generosity has a lovely face, scattered with freckles, and her mark of banishment is as stark as her bones are delicate. There's something a little bit off about it, but sometimes local medics aren't properly experienced in banishment. Dark circles sweep beneath her bronze eyes, making the tattoo look all the brighter.

Rashahan stands and I expect a toast; instead he starts talking and just doesn't stop. It's like he's in a talking contest and wants to take the universal record.

At first, it's hard to piece it together. He's using big words in ways that don't make sense, but they fly by so quickly you assume you misheard him. My translator chip is still learning his particular twist on the dialect, so I miss one word every handful.

"You have all been harmed. Victimized. Abused. Thrown away by a system that feeds on humanity and discards the -----. But is that enough for them, brothers and sisters? Is that cruelty enough?"

A chorus of "no"s comes from the gathering while I'm still trying to figure out what the word my translator glitched on is. Escajeda is close enough that the heat of his arm brushes against my own. It's anchoring.

"Not for them. Not for the Families who keep picking at the scraps! Who want to burn you until there's nothing left. We are living on the verge of violence, and it would take one tiny pressure—light as a ----- feather—to send us tumbling over the precipice. But some of you, some of you good people have things from that past you won't release! Anchors that tie you to your history. The chains the Families made and bound you with that you've grown to love."

"Release the chain!" the man sitting next to me exclaims fervently. "Throw it back at the Families. Wrap it around their neck until they choke."

"Yes, Child Candor! One day they will come for us, and we shall be ready. You must release the burdens imposed by them if you ever truly desire freedom. If you ever ----- a place at our table. If you want to be the salt that ravages their earth. Because the day is coming, my Children. The day is coming where they will reach into our circle, our flock, and cast it asunder unless we rise. Unless we wrap our fingers around their necks and squeeze back in the same way our own bodies have been squeezed, milked, for everything they can provide. They will wipe us from existence without a thought because we are their greatest threat—the enlightened few."

You know, normal predinner stuff.

The words wash over me with almost as much force as the river did. There's something about his voice that blends in until it almost sounds normal, and you stop listening until one phrase pops the bubble and then you're suddenly back in it. Also, I'm fairly certain that, in a list of Family threats, the Children don't rank in the top million. Maybe billion. No one is threatened by them because everyone has forgotten they exist.

That narrative doesn't help him, though. Like Pablo's friend's cult, this one thrives on being on the periphery. Rashahan can't keep his flock separate from the rest of the civilized worlds if he doesn't have them angry and scared. He's created a common enemy.

Escajeda's hand drops to my knee under the table, his fingers firm. Normally I'd slap it off but it's not a presumptuous touch. It's camaraderie.

As Rashahan continues to drone on, a couple of less-popular Children come out of a slot canyon near the table and deliver two long platters of food. One holds a selection of tiny slices of overcooked meat. The other has the pale plants, as charred as the meat.

The arrival of food cues the conclusion to Rashahan's speech. The following silence is heavy. Everyone in the group is given one slice of meat and unlimited plants. I was reticent to eat the plants before, but everyone seems to be enthusiastic about them, so I assume they aren't poisonous. Escajeda and I—as well as Charity and Generosity—are afforded two chunks of meat. Rashahan's plate remains empty.

"Do you want any?" I gesture at the tray. Are we expected to feed him?

"The supreme Rashahan has evolved beyond the needs of the body," Candor, next to me, finally breaks his silence to brag.

Sounds to me like the supreme Rashahan is full of shit.

"What animals have you found on this planet?" I gesture to the meat. Might as well take advantage of this and do some scouting.

Candor is done talking to me but the Rashahan answers. "For years, upon our arrival, we utilized a molecular printer for nutrition. We saw no evidence of animal life. Then, a year ago, the printer malfunctioned. Some of the flock doubted our provenance on this planet, but we were provided for by the Creator."

"The . . . Creator?" Escajeda asks this, which is good because it was my next question—after my initial question that still hasn't been answered. Nearly every religion followed by humans involves a creator or two—but I don't know if theirs is one of the garden variety or a special model that serves Rashahan's purposes.

"We crouch at his feet," everyone at the table says in unison. A shudder runs down my back. I don't enjoy an unexpected call-and-response.

Rashahan nods sagely. "Kaiaiesto. He who births worlds in fire and rock. Lava tubes run beneath the surface of the planet. A colony of reptiles had settled in the tubes that circle Kaiaiesto. When our need was greatest, they appeared in the canyon. We have penned off a farm of them."

Kaiaiesto must be the volcano. Awfully location-focused for a worship system followed by immigrants. I shovel my two lizard-bits onto Escajeda's plate. There *might* be lizards, but I can't get the gaunt, gamey look of the Children out of my head whenever I look at the stringy meat. I've never eaten human flesh before, and on the off chance he's lying, I'd like to keep it that way. Escajeda doesn't appear to have the same compunctions as I do and happily goes to town on the fibrous protein.

Across from us, Generosity eats her maybe-people-meat and ignores the plants. Maybe that spark in her eyes was insanity.

Or prions.

She catches my eye and shakes her head minutely. Not sure how to decipher that. The pale plants are spongy and water-filled, nearly popping on my tongue when I bite into them. Their flavor is mildly bitter but fresh, despite the char that's crusted the outside. I wonder what Rashahan's really eating. No one evolves beyond the needs of the body but plenty of people like him use that excuse to avoid eating in front of their followers. Because they're eating something much better, usually. Rashahan certainly hasn't missed any meals by the look of him. I'd bet nearly every credit in my account that one of these little side passages is filled with real food.

Then again, my account's nearly empty.

Rashahan takes advantage of the fact that he's not eating to give us another sermon about their noble purpose under the slopes of Kaiaiesto and about how everyone wants to destroy the Children. About how they must strike first. The fact that no one has any interest in hunting them down is beside the point.

I hope they never find out Escajeda's name, though. This is not a Family-friendly place.

My eyelids are growing heavy, a sort of fuzzy numbness staticking around the edges of my vision. It's a bad place to get sleepy. I never just fall asleep when surrounded by the enemy. I pry my eyes open and glance around the table to see if anyone else noticed. They didn't, but that's because everyone's heads are drooping. Their eyes are glassy and vacant. Escajeda sneezes three times in quick succession.

"The . . . plants . . ." I manage to say. They've done something to the food. Drugged it, maybe. Drugged *everyone* except the supreme Rashahan, who's looking at Escajeda and me like we've just been gift wrapped for his pleasure.

Shit.

CHAPTER 8

■ ■ ■ ■ ■ ■ ■ ■ ■ ■ ■ ■ ■ ■ ■

"What is your name?" Rashahan leans over the table, murky gray eyes locked on me. It's a strange opening gambit considering he already knows my name. My thoughts are sticky.

"Temperance." My voice is slurred and it's like the name is pulled out of me against my will. I blink as hard as I can, vision swimming.

He clicks his tongue in impatient distaste and snaps his fingers. I hate it when people snap at me. "I know that, girl. What is your Family name?"

My first impulse is just to speak—immediately speak—and the desire is almost blinding, but there are two answers, and the momentary confusion allows me to pick the least harmful one. "Lost when banished."

A sun rises in his eyes. "So, you are Temperance alone. A virtue."

Gross. I feel drunk. Woozy. My tongue is too big for my mouth. I realize Escajeda's hand is still on my knee, and I poke it with a stiff finger.

"What are you—?" Escajeda stumbles over the words and then loses his train of thought. He lifts his hand and stares at it like it isn't his.

"And what is your name, fallen man? Certainly not scout Scott?" Rashahan shifts his focus to Escajeda. Fallen man? Where did he fall? We both fell into the river. Maybe that.

"Arcadio Dimitri Escajeda." He doesn't try to withhold it. Doesn't even hesitate. I hesitated. I think.

We're so screwed.

"Arcadio Escajeda." Rashahan draws out the name like it has a hundred letters. Like he can taste it. I can taste chalk and dust and the bitter herbaceous edge of the plants. "Son of the Escajeda. What are your reasons to be on this planet?"

He's addressing both of us now and, again, I don't mind telling him the truth because I already did. Mostly. "We are a scouting party. Here to map and catalogue the planet for our pliant. No. Our fliant." My brain rolls sluggishly, and words slip around it. "Client. Our client."

"And yours?" This is directed at Escajeda.

Escajeda stares back. The muscles in his neck are tense, like he's trying to move and is frozen. I'm impressed at his resiliency because I want to talk, and the question isn't even for me. Maybe he didn't eat as many of the plants as I did. He could have used some of that same discretion earlier when it came time to reveal his name.

"What is your purpose on this planet?" Rashahan spells it out with more emphasis, leaning closer to Escajeda.

"To spy on me," I blurt, while Escajeda says, "To serve my Family's interests."

It's like Rashahan reached down my throat and yanked the words out.

Rashahan returns to his full height. It's not that impressive. Taller than I am. Shorter than Escajeda. Doesn't mean much. Some trees are shorter than Escajeda. "And the mysterious client?"

Since Escajeda kept his mouth shut for a while, I try to match his discipline. I fail. "The Escajeda."

My head dips toward the table. I snap it back up, eyes locked on the plants on my plate. I should have just eaten the people meat. Maybe people meat. No one else is reacting to this. They're all staring into space. Fuck. If this is what they eat all the time, this is how they're so easily controlled.

"Do you really have a medic?"

The question is so unexpected that I don't even have a chance to withhold an answer before it's already out. "Yes. He is very talented."

"Everything you told me, except this imbecile's name, is the *truth*?" Rashahan explodes. Maybe he bought his own mythos and thinks someone really is after him. Or maybe he just wants his followers to think that. They're all bumbling around like I am, though, so I doubt they're an appreciative audience.

I blink muzzily at him. That is a hard question. I don't remember everything I told him. What even is the truth? If something is more than 50 percent true, is it true?

"What aren't you saying?" He leans in and spears me with intense brown eyes.

"He's so insanely attractive I think he was born in a lab." Did I say that? That's not possible. Maybe Escajeda threw his voice, and it sounded exactly like me.

"She's far more distracting than she should be." Escajeda almost talks over me. What a priap. He can't even let me speak on my own when I'm being interrogated on truth-plants.

How distracting *should* I be?

"Did you come here for us?" Rashahan is speaking louder now. Almost yelling.

"No," Escajeda and I answer in unison. I realize my hand is on Escajeda's leg now. Part bracing for balance, part reaching for connection. I should take it back. Any moment now. His broad thigh is warm under my palm. I shouldn't rely on him. Ven was reliable and even Ven left.

"Are you hunting the Children?" Rashahan actually *is* yelling now. A blood vessel throbs in his forehead and little flecks of spit arc over the table.

He already asked this, but the answer is still dragged from my throat. "No. Didn't even know about Children. Well, I knew about children . . . like . . . baby humans. Not about capital-C Children."

The crunch of footsteps sounds from behind us, but I can't look away from him. I curl my nails into Escajeda's pants. Rashahan is pacing at the head of the table, face ruddy and sweaty. "Who told you about—?"

"Move away from them!" The voice is dizzying. Everything is dizzying but the voice especially because it's Caro's. I flop my head in the direction of the sound and there she is, resplendent in patched dirty green coveralls with one blaster clutched between both hands. I duck low. Even in my current state, I know that an armed Caro is dangerous. She's as likely to hit me as anyone else. We usually don't even let her carry a blaster.

She's flanked by Micah and Itzel, no less resplendent, but I can't make my eyes focus that far with any consistency. I wave cheerily from my position nearly prone on the table. That seems polite. Escajeda paws at my hand, lowering it back to my side, and I turn to glare at him. He should keep his hands to himself.

Oops.

I retrieve my other hand from his leg. It's more difficult than it should be.

"You look like shit, Captain," Micah greets me.

"My ankle is sprained, and we found a cenote and now we've been poisoned," I inform them. Once the truth pump is opened, it's hard to close.

"Dosed," Escajeda corrects me. What a priaphead. "I carried her up a cliff. She was helpless. Like a kitten or a child. She also sat on my—"

"It's so good to see you!" I yelp loudly over his words.

"Step away from the table, Captain. You, too . . ." Caro pauses, not sure what to call Escajeda. That jig is already up, though.

Escajeda and I scoot away from the table, pushing off our clumsy sitting-rocks.

"We're going to retrieve our people from this . . . whatever this is." Caro waves us over. She looks like a goddess with the backlighting of Micah's blaster and her bold, strong stance. Itzel helps me hobble to my engineer and my medic. Escajeda follows us. Itzel and Micah have extra blasters, but they don't offer them to us.

Probably a sound decision.

Rashahan watches like a coiled lizard. Something about this feels more dangerous than it was before when he was screaming. This scene, with drawn weapons and aggression, this is what he wanted all along. He wants us to be a threat because it builds his story. As drugged as these people are, they might forget our coerced answers—they won't forget the standoff. More dramatic than a confession and hazy enough for Rashahan to manipulate. This is the opposite of Pablo Escajeda's magnificent solution. We're safe now, but we're in more danger than we've been since hitting the planet. His eyes follow Micah's movement, focused on his banishment tattoo.

The climb out of the canyon is painful. Maybe I *am* helpless and weak like a kitten or child. Everyone needs to hold their weapons, and now that I have a tiny bit of food in me—and a large amount of drugs—my pride is strong enough to keep me propelled forward.

Once we get back to the ship, Micah shoves both Escajeda and me into the infirmary before we can even eat anything better than truth-plants. I reach plaintively for one of the protein-paste packs but it's too late. As the most injured, I'm first. Escajeda, who did manage to snag one of the packs, eats it while watching Micah poke at my leg. The best part is that our ship has painkillers so, for the first time in over a day, the pain finally starts to recede. I flop back limply on the table and stare at the ceiling while the medic works on my leg.

"Of course you had to try to walk on it and swim with it," Micah grumbles at me and at no one. This is his bedside manner. Angry. He prods at the leg with a tool. A projection on the wall shows my ankle bones. "Couldn't just wait around for us to rescue you? In a state of emergency, you're not supposed to wander. You know who taught me that? *You*. It's like Escajeda over there is infecting you with his idiocy."

"Wasn't sure about the drone after the fight," I point out. That was somewhat lucid. The effects of the plants must be wearing off.

"I wasn't just going to wait around for you to get off your ass and find us. Disaster seems to follow your captain. She's a calamity," is Escajeda's much-less-diplomatic response. He keeps calling me that. He's still alive, isn't he? He should say thank you, not throw around insults.

"Caro's the one who gets off her ass to find you. I'm the one who decides whether or not to use painkillers when I fix your wounds, and she's *our* calamity. Sit up."

I blink. Oh, that last part was for me. Also, if I was hoping for an impassioned defense from Micah, I am clearly destined to be disappointed. I sit up and Micah pulls aside the bandages to take a look at my shoulder. This time I don't get the happy numbing juice so maybe both parts were for me. Whatever he uses to clean off the sludge that the Children used on the wound stings. "Fuck, Micah, I'm not the one who told you to get off your ass."

He favors me with a small smile. "Not deep enough to merit the good drugs. The leg is another matter. You have two choices there. The first is to do a natural heal. We can keep that relatively painless, but you won't be doing much running. Second is the fun option. For me. Much less fun for you. We do a fast phagocyte wash of the wound. That will feel like someone's spraying a fire hose of lava in your leg no matter what painkillers I use. Then, we'll put the blastclast machine on you, set on the rapid-growth cycle. The setting will be shorter than for a break . . . it's only repairing tissue in this case, not bone. That will feel like lightning instead of lava and drugs will work a little bit. Moral of the story is, you won't get much sleep tonight, but you'll be running again by tomorrow."

"Second option." I'm not leading my first scouting mission as a captain from a bed in the ship.

"Not so fast, I'm not done with the warnings yet. With option one, you have a perfect recovery. With option two, the tissue may not ever be the same as it was. You'll be more likely to resprain it. You're also more likely to get malformed bones from the blastclast. Fast is rarely best."

"I don't have months to heal, Micah. We've already been in a firefight, cave-in, and standoff and it's only been two days. Granted, this planet has longer-than-average days—but not that long. Option two gets me going as soon as I can to help everyone else."

"You sound almost coherent. Those plants must have worn off."

"*You* sound almost coherent. Did your personality wear off?"

"I'll let that slide because you're about to be in pain and you're probably cranky about that. Stay on the table."

I'm trying to hop off. Hoping I can spend my convalescence in my bunk. Public showings of vulnerability aren't my style.

Micah injects something into my leg, just above the ankle, and my eyes roll back in my head. It's not pain like before. It's hot and present and *moving*.

"Wanted to go to bunk," I manage to grunt. If I open my mouth more, I'll moan. That's why I wanted to go to my bunk.

"I know you wanted to go to your bunk. You're like a sick animal that wants to hide so no one can see its weakness. Unfortunately for

you, I *have* to see your weakness in case something goes wrong."
Micah pats my head like I'm a horse that can't be tamed. I bare my
teeth at him, and he grins down at me. This isn't our first adventure with speed-healing. Every time I try to make the argument
for privacy. Every time, he ignores it. Medical competence is so
aggravating.

I roll my eyes toward Escajeda. I don't want him here. I don't
want him to see me weak. I also don't want to look too deeply into
why that is.

Micah purposefully misunderstands. He turns to Escajeda.
"If you're done sitting there looking pretty, I need a second set of
hands for this. Hold her leg immobile. If she twitches it around,
the machine may target the wrong thing."

I expect Escajeda to protest. It's outside his realm of responsibility on the ship and Micah didn't exactly couch it politely. He
doesn't argue. Instead, two large warm hands wrap around my leg,
one on my calf and one on my foot, completely trapping the zone
that currently feels like it's on fire.

"Good. While you're holding her still, I'll take care of you.
Luckily, someone ripped most of your clothes off, which makes
it easier." The familiar sounds of the clinic intrude into my pain.
Packaging tears around surgical instruments. The wet plop of ointment scooped out of a jar. The shifting weight of footfalls from the
hallway outside as Itzel or Caro watch.

I focus on breathing, on the reddish light of the back of my eyelids. I focus on the pain because it drowns everything.

Everything except the feeling of those two hands holding me
fast, not so much as twitching when Escajeda sucks in a breath of
discomfort at whatever Micah is doing to him.

Whoever called it fast has a lot of nerve. Days, weeks, maybe
moments later, I realize that it's fading. I'm aware of the sounds
again. The smaller pain where the edge of the table digs into my

fingers as I clutch it. I open them and am briefly blinded by the lights above. Escajeda is gone. Micah's still there, by the table, dark eyes watching me with something akin to sympathy. It wipes away when he catches me watching him back.

Like I said, he knows me well.

"I sent him away when you were too lost in it to move." He readies the blastclast machine, adjusting the size of the aperture so it will fit my foot and leg. "Didn't need to, though, you didn't make a peep. If you want him to think you're a cyborg in female form, you're doing a bang-up job."

That doesn't sound so bad. Cyborgs are strong. One does not fuck with a cyborg. Nor does one call a cyborg a disaster.

"You might consider letting him know you're a human in female form instead." His voice is carefully mild, which is simply bizarre coming from Micah, who doesn't bother with such things as the feelings of others. "He isn't so bad."

I don't want people to think I'm human. Who would want that? Humans are filled with soft, squishy vulnerable bits. Humans are fragile and breakable and *flawed*. Me most of all. Someone like Arcadio Escajeda, the son of a Family, doesn't deal with humans . . . in business or otherwise. Families see two options: strength or weakness. There's only one right way to be.

"You don't know what it's like to be in a Family," I mutter.

"Thank any deity that will hear me." Micah laughs as he slides the blastclast device over my leg. The dark sleeve doesn't look like much, but I feel the moment it activates. He was right, it's like lightning. He reaches for an IV that they hooked up to me at some point and injects something. Just past it, tucked in a narrow sliver of wall beneath a cabinet and above a desk, is one of Caro's schematics of a sensor, hastily outlined in charcoal marker. Itzel has turned the surface of the sensor into a trampoline and two figures, Itzel and myself if I'm interpreting correctly, leap on it while Micah stands at the side with arms crossed. Way up above the drawing, another figure is tucked beneath the cabinet, dangling down with one hand outstretched to catch ours. Ven.

When I get up, I'm going to take some solvent to him.

When Micah finally retakes his seat, he points at his banishment tattoo. "I never told you how I got this, did I?"

"You didn't." I never asked, either. Banishment is private.

Micah leans back in his seat, watching the wall behind my head. Someone cooled this room down and the air chills my face. It's a welcome distraction to the electricity thrumming through my leg. "My family was one of the Fifty. I see your face and I know—no one calls them that. No one except the other families competing for the right to enter the upper tiers of society. You think the Five or the Ten are vicious, you don't know the Fifty. Within the Fifty, there are tech families and bio families. Mostly because no one can afford both, so they have to pick one or the other."

"Tech or bio, meaning mods? Chips versus tissue?" I cling to the subject as a distraction. It's better than talking about how showing weakness is a good thing.

"Exactly. It's a polar divide. Tech families don't associate with bio and the same goes the other way. Advantages to each, of course. Bio tends to be healthier for a person. Less traumatic. You can do half of the bio work before birth and make a child that's faster, stronger. You're never going to biologically modify a child to have laser hands. For some people, that's better than smarter, faster, or stronger. My family, they were tech. You broke a leg, they'd hack it off and give you a new automated one."

I think of the chip in my head, the one designed by my Family that translates for me. The one that learns from exposure, so I'll never be without language for long. Something happens to that chip, I'm probably not smart enough to do it on my own. If my Family had genetically modified me to have an enlarged language center in my brain, maybe I would. But the brain mod might have done something else to me at the same time. "Either way seems dangerous."

"Since when has danger ever stood in the way of advancement? Anyhow, we made medical tech. I liked the biomods. Because I couldn't experiment publicly without being caught, I experimented on myself. First thing I did was figure out how to detect disease by scent. Handy skill to have, that, has some unexpected benefits. Night vision was next. Then reflexes."

"Thought you fought too well to just be a medic," I mutter. "You saved us a lot of credits that way . . . we didn't need to hire extra security for most jobs. We only needed Victor and Victory for the big jobs."

"No one's 'just' one thing on the frontiers. I was a lot of things pre-banishment, and I've been even more after. Few of them were legal. I didn't reveal to anyone what I was learning. Until I did. A kid came in. Not even a relative, just a kid from a nearby outpost who was dying from Glancy's Syndrome. That's when the radiation biomods are rejected by the body and it starts taking in more radiation instead of blocking it. Fool parents had gone budget to one of the other tech families for a treatment and were hoping tech could fix it. Problem was, it can't. Not even those clever little nanos. Bio could. I fixed him. Didn't tell them what I was doing. I foolishly thought it wouldn't matter. Who cares what saves a life, right?"

"Wrong." Should be right but it isn't. People love getting in their own way.

"Yeah, wrong. Anyway, that's the horrible truth. I got excised for saving a life. That's not what they called it, of course. I'd experimented with foreign science without approval—even from the family. Medical malpractice." He shakes his head disgustedly. "I could have asked permission before I did it. I just couldn't handle looking at their faces while they said 'no.'"

"As dirty secrets go, that's pretty weak." I try out a smile. "I was hoping for something much tawdrier. Just so we're clear, you should use whatever methods you can get your hands on to keep me alive. I'm not picky."

"I said it was how I got banished. I never said it was my dirty secret. I'll hold on to that a little longer." The levity drops from his face for a moment before flashing back on. "And we all know you're not picky. Escajeda's armor was torn off and your hand was in his lap at the cult's nest. Plus, you sat on his . . . something."

"I was drugged and in pain." I go for dignified. Probably miss it by a parsec.

"That's what you tell yourself, Captain. That's what you tell yourself."

CHAPTER 9

When Micah finally decides I'm not going to try to sprint to my bunk or have a reaction to the blastclast machine, he leaves the infirmary to search out his own supper. That doesn't mean that I'm finally alone to suffer the pain in peace, though, because Escajeda—*Escajeda*, of all people—cruises in right after my medic leaves. He looks healthy and hearty, with a spring in his step, wearing another pair of those perfectly black coveralls.

I almost forgive him for looking so hale because he has a packet of protein paste for me that has the distinct red label of the spicy mixture. Protein paste only comes in four varieties: nothing, salty, sweet, or spicy. I never had much of a sweet tooth and salty would just make me drink more of the water we need to hoard. Plus, I like spicy. Maybe the burn in my tongue will let me forget the pain everywhere else. Or maybe not. I snatch the packet out of his hands and squeeze some into my mouth. Much better than those plants.

"You think the meat was people who tried to leave the cult?" It's the last coherent thought I remember from our time with the Children.

He raises his eyebrows and takes a moment to consider it while he pulls a chair out from under the table. When he sits, he blocks my view of Ven in the trampoline sketch. Good. "You've got a twisted mind, Reed. I don't know. Maybe. Clearly safer to eat than those plants."

"Why do you call me Reed?" It's been irking me. I don't know if he's taunting me like his father did, or if he's actually forgotten. "It's not my name anymore."

"Why do you call me Escajeda? That's my father's name. Mine is Arcadio. I won't ever be the Escajeda. Even if something happens to my father, that's my sister—not me."

I asked an easy question and he's not answering it. I feel the conversation teetering on the precipice of disaster and decide to give it one final shove. "I call you that to remind myself of who you are."

"I'm not my parents. And they're not the Escajeda—not really." He runs a hand through that dark hair and then leans forward on his elbows like he's decided something. "My father is the Escajeda— the one everyone knows about. His father before him was the Escajeda. Neither of them was the *real* Escajeda. The real Escajeda was my grandmother, and her name was Vasilisa Peña. I can see you trying to place that and no, she wasn't from any kind of Family you know about. The one smart thing the original Escajeda ever did was to marry a no-one who ran his empire more efficiently and ruthlessly than he could have ever imagined. The reason everyone quails at the name Escajeda has nothing to do with any actual Escajedas. It was a Peña. But, at the time, my grandfather's name was older—more prominent—so his name won."

I'm not entirely sure where he's going with this. "I'm not entirely sure where you're going with this."

"Names are lies we use to distance ourselves. Not just here, everywhere." He shakes his head as though that's mystifying. Leans back on the cabinet and plays around with a medical tool. I don't know what kind. A poker. He sounds tired. "You assume it's important to me, but it isn't. The Escajedas aren't real. If they took my name away, I wouldn't care because her name is the one that matters, and no one can steal that because no one knows it."

He's speaking from a place of privilege that he can't even recognize. "It's not just the name. It's what it represents. A sense of duty and responsibility that isn't obliterated when your social status is."

"I know. I thought you were the one who wouldn't understand loyalty or obligation. You were a notorious Family traitor. The full story of what happened never went public, you know. In the streams, you were the woman who tried to sell out her brother and he implied it was over something flighty or evil. Combined with the unexplained death of someone close to you—" He lets his thought trail off.

I'm not surprised. I saw the press. Frederick couldn't decide if I was having a torrid affair with the Wolf patriarch or if I was too stupid to know what I was doing—easily bribed by jewelry or some other bauble. It would have been embarrassing if I had any emotions left to feel at that time. What hurt was that all of my own people believed him. Or, at least, were too afraid to speak up. It hurt that Kari believed him.

Although, her father's death is my fault. There's no arguing that. So, in her case, I don't suppose it matters whether or not my motivations were good. I don't blame Escajeda for assuming the worst of me.

After all, didn't I assume the worst of him?

"I remember my eleventh birthday. I was still too young to overtly participate in the Reed business, but I wanted to. I wanted to go to work with my mother and see what she did every day. She took me to a territory hearing. You know the kind. Regional leadership airs their grievances to the Family. When we went home, she had me write up a plan for how to serve the needs of that particular moon better. That was my birthday present, being able to contribute to the Family." She also bought me my first formal Family uniform that day. Made of fine iskien wool woven in the

Enjiers sector of Flores territory. Fabric like that costs nearly as much as the *Quest* and will probably last longer. Luxuries like that were so common that I didn't even blink at them.

Most of us living on the edges get our clothing from fabric recyclers. Cloth is cheap and probably on its fourth or fifth form by the time it gets to the border way stations. I desperately miss nice things like that uniform. Like Escajeda's spotless coveralls, which slough off dust and launder perfectly.

"Perhaps she was training you to be a good captain."

I never thought of it like that. There's a lot about running a Family corporation that lends itself to captaining a ship. Prioritization, planning, plotting, nebulous ethics, fierce loyalty to those in your crew. You'd think I'd be better at being a captain, then. So far, my leadership has led to everyone being shot at.

Escajeda's mouth curves into a vaguely wistful smile.

"My father did something similar, you know. He believes in keeping as much of his industry within the Family as possible. My sister was always clearly going to be the heir—she has the patience for the diplomacy and the ruthlessness to protect our interests. After that was resolved, he tried to find an appropriate niche for each of us brothers. I was always the best fighter and, as I got older, I learned to be strategic. My skills already leaned toward security by the time he took me to one of our lunar mining operations and asked what I'd do to improve their efficacy."

"What did you say?"

He chuckles under his breath. "Defense. The moon was near the edge of our territory and pirates hit it every month or so. I suggested we implement an orbiting missile-defense system that could identify Escajeda craft and attack any others. My father was already planning on implementing it, so my plan wasn't novel, but it showed where my skills focused."

"Your brothers?" I don't know much about the youngest Escajedas.

This draws an actual chuckle, but the corners of his mouth crumple the tiniest amount before he speaks. Something's gone down with his brothers recently, I can tell by the way he speaks about them: pride tinged with regret. Whatever it is, the Escajeda must have kept it out of the feeds. "Jorge didn't show up at all, Jamie tried to stage a coup—they're the twins. Antony created a new activity flow for the mine that increased efficiency. Pablo realized their accounting system was a mess. Reorganized the whole thing and found out that the local governor had been skimming resources."

I want to press but it's none of my business. I've been so caught up in what it is like to be an ex-Reed, I never really considered what living as a current-Escajeda would be like.

We have a lot in common. Which is something I never thought I'd say. When he stands to leave, he brushes my hair back from my face, his touch light and almost gentle. The heat in his eyes is anything but.

After he leaves, it isn't long before Caro and Itzel burst in.

"Are you okay?" is the first thing Itzel asks.

"What did you sit on?" is the first thing Caro does.

I make a lewd gesture, suggesting what *she* can sit on.

"I would have thought your disposition would have improved in that case." She deliberately misunderstands. "Oh. Unless he wasn't any good. Was he not any good?"

He wasn't good. He was something else. Some dizzying combination of intense and electrifying.

"That didn't happen," I clarify, lest he think I'm spreading rumors among my crew. "He's the son of a Family. I don't get off on uneven power dynamics. Something I understand even if he doesn't."

"I think you have that wrong." Itzel's voice is soft. She sits down on the seat Escajeda abandoned, absently takes a marker from the inside of her sleeve, and adds Caro to the trampoline sketch. Caro bats at her hand to distract her but Itzel pushes the engineer's chair away with her foot. "He understands it. Just doesn't want to. You want to, but don't quite understand."

My mind tries to wrap itself around that and fails.

"So . . . he *wanted* you to sit on it." Caro nods sagely.

The blastclast lightning is at home in my leg, dancing from point to point, an electric symphony. I stare at the lights on the ceiling until they make my eyes water.

"I sat *near* it," I allow.

"How exactly did that come about? It was giving him mouth-to-mouth, wasn't it? I hear that crotch-to-crotch is also a very effective method." Caro laughs at herself but Itzel nods as though it makes perfect sense.

"None of your business," I say as primly as I can—which isn't all that prim because this may be the first time in my life that I've attempted the state.

"Well, now she'll never stop pestering you about it," Itzel says like I'm an idiot. I might be. "You know how Caro is about a secret. Except her own, of course."

Caro's eyelids flicker and she snatches the marker from Itzel. Even I see it for the distraction it is, but I don't have the mental energy to drill deeper.

When I fall back into the discomfort of the blastclast machine, it may be a respite from their questioning. I can almost imagine things stitching themselves together in my ankle, one short sharp spike of electricity for each fiber of each tendon repairing and re-attaching. It's awful but reassuring in a way. Pain isn't so bad if you know it won't kill you.

Caro and Itzel have given up on me and are talking to each

other when I next open my eyes. They've moved on to Itzel's quest for her birth parents. It's been going on as long as I've known her.

Eventually, they leave. I'm not very entertaining tonight. Being slowly electrocuted isn't exactly a mood upper. Not too long thereafter, Micah comes back. He pokes around the display of the blastclast machine and takes my vitals. For my perseverance, I am rewarded.

"You might be far enough along for the good drugs to work." Micah adds something to the IV before disappearing into the hallway. When he comes back, he has my pillow and a blanket from my bed. "Take a load off, Captain. We'll still be here when you wake up."

. . . . .

When I wake up, I'm not sure how much time has passed, but the blastclast machine on my leg is lying limply, all its flashy running lights deactivated. I wriggle my toes and no sharp bark of pain accompanies the gesture. That experiment went so well, I slide off the table, bare feet pressed against the cold metal floors of the infirmary. No pain.

The illumination in the hallway is dim—only the running lights that line the path from cargo to helm. That means it's night, or at least it's what we're calling night. So long as we can align to daylight exploration, we try to keep roughly on standard time. It's easier that way. Herschel Two has longer days than standard, but we can still make it work.

Snores and mumbling come from Itzel and Caro's bunk. I linger outside Micah and Escajeda's bunk. No sound at all. When I make it to the helm, Escajeda slouches in my chair, head tipped slightly back, but eyes open on the dark desert outside.

The night sky is a deep, velvety purple. The ground is crimson under the light of the three distant moons. When they're in alignment and full, they must be bright enough to throw shadows. The volcano looms large to the side, a long smooth slope that seems to go forever.

It is silent and peaceful. For the first time in a long time, I'm almost relaxed. He's here. He didn't creep off somewhere. I puff out a relieved sigh.

"How long was I out?"

He tilts his head further and eyes me. "Not very. Looked like you needed it. Likely you spent so long roused by my—how did you put it?—throbbing masculine presence that you didn't sleep much in the cenote."

"If it was actively throbbing, I suppose it kept you up all night," I respond with sugar-sweetness.

"Any number of things kept me up all night. That was just one of them."

It felt pretty throbbing while I was straddling his lap. I spin the navigation chair to face him and sit down, gingerly setting my foot on the console. "Any action tonight?"

Action. Bad choice of words. Or good. No. Bad. Definitely bad.

He raises an eyebrow but doesn't acknowledge my blunder. "Quiet. No Nakatomi or cult activity."

"How is your arm?" He's still in his black coveralls, which is a shame. I was sort of hoping the pants-only thing would catch on. The man should wander around half naked all the time. Maybe all naked. No one would get anything done, but it would be a glorious waste of time.

I assume. It would be so disappointing if he has a grossly malformed penis.

"Micah glued my arm back together. I assume it was more medically complicated than that, but essentially."

I chuckle under my breath. My own shoulder is also patched with a thin seam of glue. When I move my foot, I accidentally knock one of Caro's styli off the edge of the console. I reach for it at the same time Escajeda does. Our hands collide on the floor, my fingers tangled with his as we both grasp the tool. I freeze, eyes locked beyond our clasped hands. The cuff of his coveralls is flecked with grains of sand.

He might be here now, but at some point, he went back outside.

Maybe for nothing. Maybe Itzel asked him to collect some of the strange truth-plants. Maybe he felt like pissing over the edge of the canyon. Or, maybe, he left his watch yet again for a mysterious purpose.

I want to trust him. Especially after we reached our peace in the cenote. I want to think that he's worthy of *my* trust. But he's still lying to me. Maybe. Maybe he's hunting for phydium. Hoping he can find it before any of the rest of us do. Whatever he's doing, it isn't keeping me and my crew safe when we're vulnerable.

I pull my fingers from his. Place the stylus back on the console. Redirect my attention outside, comfortable camaraderie forgotten. He doesn't try to reclaim the moment. I think of all the things that Ven left unsaid. All the subtext that I edited over with the text of my heart, not the text of my mind.

I can't make that mistake again. I can't trust someone just because I *want* to trust him.

The sun peeks over the horizon, the soil vibrant and warm. A breeze stirs up a wave of golden dust that almost sparkles as it flutters down the glowing side of the volcano, over the stretch of warm earth, and down the dark, jagged crack of the canyon. In the helm, silence stretches between us.

CHAPTER 10

The volcano, Kaiaiesto, dominates the landscape in front of us. I can't handle returning to the canyon so soon after the chain of disasters we experienced within it. As long as we're moving *somewhere*, Escajeda seems satisfied. There is other land to explore on Herschel Two and the surface offers better visibility in case the Nakatomi scouting crew is still lurking in this region.

"The primary drone was damaged when I rammed it into that tall Nakatomi. I've had our lightweight drone out ever since then." Caro notices me scanning the horizon, hand on my blaster. The rest of the crew fans out around us, scanning the area for any sign of phydium. Itzel pauses to take a swig of water before returning to her samples.

"They were much better armed than your usual scouting crew." I drag my gaze away and study the woman walking beside me. Caro has her hair wrapped up in a turban patterned with splotches of vibrant neon colors and her eyes have returned to her datapad. It's a wonder she doesn't trip over rocks more often. "Who do you know that scouts in full body armor and helmets? It gets in the way of anything related to scouting. What were they afraid of? The Children don't appear well armed. We are, but we've passed other crews plenty of times. You shoot the shit when you see another scouting crew—you don't shoot the shit *out of* the other scouting crew."

She hums under her breath in agreement. "I did some research. The Nakatomi Family has been acting up in all sectors. Territory grabs like we saw on the way here. Encroaching on smaller Families. They're the new Escajedas, except Pretty Boy's family at least knows how to keep plausible deniability."

"It's the problem with the kind of specialization that the Families practice." I've spent a lot of time thinking about what causes a Family to go wrong. Besides everything. No one starts out intending to be evil. They think they're doing right until it calcifies into something else. "Nakatomis control the gunships, which, to them, means they can control everything. Doesn't matter that the Escajedas mine the materials used to make the ships—Nakatomis can just shoot them until they hand the materials over. Nakatomis want a newer and better power source? Well, then they'll threaten to shoot the Pierce Family. On the other hand, if the Chandra Family wants something, they can withhold medical treatment—or offer it. Flores can spatter propaganda throughout the universe. Everyone owns something essential. It was supposed to be a failsafe but, instead, it's a temptation to corruption."

"Anyone ever tell you that you have a bleak outlook on life?" She enters some data point with a flick of her wrist and spares the time to shoot me a glance.

"Only all the time. It's one of my defining personality traits. Doesn't mean I'm wrong."

"Doesn't mean you're right, either. Always seeing the dark side means that, more often than not, you stay in the dark."

"Pithy. It's not like you're a sunny optimist, Caro."

"I'm a scientist. I see probabilities. Sometimes, a good thing is probable. Not in your worldview, though. You prepare for the worst and then everything lives up to expectations."

I open my mouth.

"And then, when someone says something you don't like, you go on the defensive and attack until they retreat."

I close my mouth.

"That said, you're good at what you do, dedicated to your people, and funny on occasion, so we can all look past the attitude."

"I *knew* everyone liked me for my personality."

"At least you managed to sunny-side *that*." She snickers. "I just wonder if Arcadio has figured out that every time you snap, it means you're feeling all squishy and vulnerable. Probably. It's only Family people who are quite that defensive."

Just about time to bring this conversation to a close. My squishy vulnerable parts are my own business.

"What do you miss most about being one of them?" Itzel's clearly been eavesdropping. Which makes sense. Sample collection doesn't require much attention. Micah might also be eavesdropping but, more likely, he just doesn't care. Escajeda is marching forward like we're slowing him down with our pesky scientific methods. "There must have been good things."

There were. So many that I don't often think about them because I might start feeling sorry for myself, and nothing good comes of that. I open the door in my memory a tiny crack. "Private chefs and fresh root vegetables—the things that are too wasteful to grow on a ship or a station. I was never hungry, and I was never bored. The Reed station had a whole level that was a manicured garden, complete with waterfall and river. It can't compare with the vistas we've seen but . . . something about it felt like home. There was a little bower that had nesting birds. So wasteful for a station—so fucking ostentatious. I named them all and they ate out of my hands."

My only fear was Frederick, which meant that, when he was off-station, I wasn't afraid of anything at all. Wealth is the only thing that buys that kind of comfort. "I miss learning. I never got to continue my education after my first year of university. Believing that, one day, I'd have the power to change people's lives for the better. Having the resources to make that a possibility. Fashion. Nothing we can buy can compare so I don't bother anymore. Custom dresses in exquisite fabric. I had one dress that glowed like an aurora. Another that looked like a fire in the sunset."

"Were there very fancy parties?" Itzel again, in a voice like we're telling deep secrets. Her upbringing was so frugal, she looks at indulgence with equal parts horror and entrancement.

"The fanciest. With tiny little cakes and candy light as clouds. Music and dancing—which was wasted on me, you know my lack of basic grace. Ardot—the cloudier the better."

Ardot root liquor is beyond my reach, deep in Reed territory and, thus, off-limits. The last little part of the Reed Family I can almost touch. It tastes awful. I miss it terribly. That's plenty of time reminiscing about the past. Escajeda has been listening in for a while now and I don't want him to see that part of me.

"Pulling up anything interesting?" I redirect. We haven't found more than a trace of phydium on the planet. We haven't found ulonium either, which is the mineral that reads most similarly on a spectrometer. Essentially, each element reacts to light just a little bit differently, which means that, when you illuminate a sample with specific wavelengths of light, you can tell exactly what it's composed of. The devices output a chart composed of peaks, and different compounds may produce similar peaks, especially if the test is conducted from a distance.

The Escajeda's probe found something, but a beam emitted from space covers a broad area on the surface of a planet and we clearly haven't sampled the exact right region to find what we're looking for.

"No." Caro sniffs and notates more data.

Itzel ranges up front in a zigzag pattern. Every so often, she pauses to dig into the soil to take a sample. The little glass tubes go in loops around her belt. There's a chip in the stopper of each tube that is geolocated to the exact spot of its retrieval. Escajeda roams up ahead of her, taking the lead.

It's quiet on the surface. No wind whistling through the canyon walls, no soft static rush from the river below the ground.

"It's getting late," I call to the group after over a half day of uneventful exploration. With hover bikes a losing proposition on this planet and our all-terrain vehicle pawned at Landsdown for supplemental credits, this exploration is going slowly. I feel the clock ticking in my mind; so little time until the Escajeda's deal runs out. Arcadio's looking worse every day, so clearly the stress is impacting him as well. "Time to turn around and head back."

"We need to get closer to the top," Escajeda protests, continuing forward, face intent on a sensor in his hand. Must be Family tech, because he won't let me near it.

"Sure. We can do that." I'm using my mild voice. I never use my mild voice unless I'm calling someone an idiot and the crew knows that. Caro snickers from beside me. "Except, we know there are enemy combatants on-surface. It's not a night I fancy sleeping on the ground without cover. Especially not so close to where we saw them."

"We're wasting time." He spits the words, clearly frustrated by something.

I puff out a frustrated breath of my own. I swear, this man is more obstinate than anyone I've ever met. "Itzel, have we found any indication of phydium in the soil?"

She shakes her head but gives me a dirty look. Itzel doesn't like being used to make a point.

"Caro, have we found any indication of phydium in our satellite or drone scans of this region? Or any region, for that matter?" I turn to the woman beside me who's still nose-deep in her datapad.

"No. No phydium," she replies, and I turn to Escajeda to continue making my point, but Caro continues. "But there's something weird here. We expect heat activity . . . it's a volcano, after all, and not a dead one. Some structure, too—lava tubes. You mentioned that the Children told you about lizards that lived in them."

"But?"

"But there's something weird. That's all I can say. I'm seeing the tubes. I'm seeing the heat. It's expected. It's just strange. A little too clean."

"The lava tube is clean?" Micah asks, as we pull together into a tighter knot. Well, my crew pulls together in a tighter knot. Escajeda is a string thrown out at the edge.

"The array of them. The spacing. I can't exactly explain it, it's just . . . off."

As Escajeda starts perking up, I shake my head. Time to nip this in the bud. "All the more reason not to camp on top of it without more research."

The sun is low in the sky when we approach the *Quest*, and its shadow stretches long until it drops into the canyon. A smaller shadow creeps out from beneath one of the landing struts. Human-shaped, but too far away to see much more than that.

"Micah, what do you see?" Now that I know he's got some sort of vision mod, might as well take advantage. My blaster's filling my hand and we've split into our combat diamond shape. Escajeda in the lead, me and Micah to the sides, Itzel covering our tail, and Caro in the middle.

Escajeda answers instead of Micah. "Nakatomi. There's another behind the rear strut."

He has a high-intensity rifle with him today, in addition to the blaster strapped to his thigh, and he's gazing down the scope. Either his scope is modded or his vision is, too. Probably the vision. Micah nods.

"Only two of them?" I ask.

Caro zooms her drone in a wide arc. "Two heat signatures

and . . ." Now she's at her datapad. "No sign the ship has been breached. Someone tried the passcode keypad but got hit by the deterrent."

"The deterrent?" Escajeda asks under his breath.

"She programmed it to deliver a fifty-thousand-volt electric shock if the wrong code is entered." Itzel's voice is a bit muffled, turned the other way as it is.

"What if you accidentally enter it wrong?"

"This seems like a tomorrow conversation," I interject. We're still far enough away that they haven't heard us unless they have mods, but that distance is closing fast. "Any sign that the stunned one is still on the ground?"

Escajeda and Micah both shake their heads.

Maybe more of them were here earlier and they carried away the injured party. Or the armor protected them, and they got back up. Either way, we have two heat signatures lurking around my ship. Two to four is a better ratio than we had in the canyon, but we don't have any cover and they do. They might not be able to get inside due to the code, but they could potentially damage the *Quest* if they see us coming and get desperate.

"They're going to see us soon and experience implies that they will engage rather than retreat. We don't have many advantages. The soil here is too unsteady to shoot one of the ship's cannons unless it's a last resort, plus, they are presently under the ship. When they take aim, I need one of you with night vision to tell Caro immediately. Caro, you'll remote activate the ship, which will provide a distraction to buy us a little time."

"This wouldn't be a problem if you had an undercarriage particle gun," Caro says in her wheedling voice.

"I can't afford an undercarriage particle gun. Maybe someday after we get paid, but that falls near the end of the list of necessities. We have to stay in the sky."

"Just saying."

"Well, stop saying. Escajeda, you think you can approach from another trajectory?" We're a bigger target if we're all together.

He doesn't answer my question. Instead, he raises his rifle, breathes out a slow breath, and fires. Once. Twice. Both Nakatomis fall.

That's another way to take care of our problem.

I'm not used to high-classed firearms. None of our rifles would be capable of that accuracy and, probably, none of us would be capable of making the shot if they were. There's a reason the Escajedas are on top, and it's not just their mining empire. He ignored my suggestion, but his way was better. No one on my crew needed to be at risk and I nearly made an oversight because I underestimated him. No one likes to be wrong.

"Or you could do that."

"That was a *nice* shot." Micah, whom I previously thought was impervious to friendliness, sounds like he might want to start a fan club.

When we get to the ship, the Nakatomis are still there. One dead, one not long for the world. I should feel bad about that, but people don't try to break into your ship if they have good intentions. I leave the live one for Escajeda. Like a gift to thank him for solving the problem. The dead one is still dressed in body armor, visor down except the visor window is broken where Escajeda's shot penetrated. "Is this their armor's primary point of vulnerability?"

He shrugs. "I use armor-piercing in a rifle like this as a habit, but the face mask is nearly always an effective shot."

Good to know. "Itzel, look away."

"Why?"

"I know how you get about the sanctity of the dead and I'm about to shoot this body a lot to see if there are weak points in the armor."

"Ugh, and you don't think I'd like to look away from that, too?" Caro activates the opening sequence on the keypad.

Itzel makes a gagging noise and follows her into the ship, calling out behind her, "You shoot him, you have to bury him later."

I study the large body. Dumping him into the canyon is like a burial, no? "Honestly, Caro? I thought you'd be curious."

"I sure as hells am." Micah steps up alongside me. Trust him to be just as intrigued by damaging a body as by fixing one up.

Escajeda is trying to question the other one, but he shot them in the face, too. It gets in the way of talking. Honestly, I'm surprised they're breathing at all.

Oh. They aren't anymore.

I look down at the body splayed before me and grimace. I take no pleasure in this. It was a person, after all. One with a family. But it was also an enemy and I need to know if they have any weaknesses.

I shoot the body once in the torso. A burn mark on the suit, nothing else. I thumb the setting of my blaster all the way up and try again. The burn mark penetrates deeper. Micah reaches into his pack and takes out a tool to plumb the hole. Still no full penetration. At the narrow joints, at full power, the tool comes back red at the tip. The neck. The knee. Hip. Not the groin, though. The groin is well protected. People spend a lot of time thinking about that when designing armor.

At full power, a blaster's charge doesn't last long. There's a reason we usually set it about halfway up the intensity. That and it's really inconvenient to shoot a hole in the side of a spaceship. I click my tongue against the back of my teeth in frustration. "We need to invest in better weapons."

Micah nods. Escajeda has wandered over to stand by us. I glance at his rifle and realize something. "That thing throws projectiles, doesn't it? How old is it?"

I'm so used to seeing the usual light-based weaponry that something as antiquated as old-fashioned ammunition didn't even cross my mind.

"Not old. Something new we've worked on internally. The Nakatomis have invested heavily in light-based firepower. It's efficient, commonly adopted, and doesn't require large stocks of ammunition. They've also invested in a wide range of body armor intended to offer protection against light-based weapons. That's a lot easier than you'd think because all it requires is reflectivity at the correct wavelengths. All uncertainty in a light-based battle comes down to that. It's why ship-based shielding can be done so effectively. Actual projectiles are more challenging to block, so we decided to exploit the weakness in the current trends."

"If you run out of . . ." The word escapes me for a moment. It's been a long time since I learned my history. "Bullets? Bullcts. What then?"

He shrugs. Unconcerned. "Same thing that happens when you run out of charge. Don't worry about it. I have a lot of bullets. And cartridges. And shells. All far more effective than that little light show you keep in your holster."

I don't even know what those last two are—I assume some kind of superbullet. Here is another example of how single-Family specialties weaken our system. Nakatomi has built an empire from creating weapons and defenses against those same weapons and has apparently produced quite the weak spot in the process.

Competence is attractive and he's been very competent the past few minutes. I need a distraction and fast or I might try to climb him like a tree.

Again.

The thought of him reminding me that it's a bad idea sufficiently douses my lust.

Micah and Escajeda drag the two bodies to the canyon, gossiping about weapon tech and bodily damage like schoolkids.

It isn't quite time for dinner, and I've never been the type to nap. Unspent adrenaline still courses through my body from our almost-battle. I climb down to the lower deck. Caro clanks away at something in the engine room. The soft thuds and louder curses offer a comfortable accompaniment to the air circulators and other ship noises.

I go straight to the fitness area. It's equipped with a sparring ring, a heavy bag to punch, a small climbing wall, a resistance setup embedded in one of the walls, and several cardiovascular machines. A rack of blunted weapons, all looped into place, lines the sparring ring. I start on the climbing wall.

My ankle held up today. Micah's work always lasts. I chart a course up the wall using the medium-sized hand- and footholds. The impact bag hovers beneath me, ready to catch me if I fall. At some point, Caro leaves the engine room and walks by the open door to the armory. She peeks in and shakes her head at me before going to the upper deck.

"I see you're afraid of having to rely on me to climb again." Escajeda's voice startles me so much that I almost fall off the wall.

"Now that you're here, I can practice punching someone in the face," I say as I hop down, landing softly on the impact bag. My breath is rough. It's only then that I realize what I just offered. "I know you get all sensitive about being hit."

The smile that uncurls across his face is slow and anticipatory. "Are you saying you'd like to spar, Temper?"

CHAPTER 11

"Think you can take me, Arcadio?" I offer his first name in exchange for his use of mine.

I'm not so dumb that I don't see the many ways in which I am at the disadvantage in this proposed fight, but I can't miss the opportunity to see the kind of training that they give Escajedas.

And to get my hands on him again.

He smiles a real smile, not that sardonic twist of the lips he usually uses. It hits me right in the gut. That smile is a deadly weapon. It's like a sunrise—intense and natural. Something awakens in my belly that I choose to tell myself is hunger because this is about fighting, not sex. He's keeping secrets from us. No matter what else, no matter that moment of honesty when I was recovering or the moment of *almost* in the cenote, he doesn't trust me with the truth.

I return his smile with a glare.

He takes his time with a slow perusal of my sweaty body. "I'm not sure if you're up to it now. Maybe you need a break."

It's a juvenile attempt but it elicits an equally juvenile response from me. "Afraid?"

He gestures to the sparring ring and the weapons rack. "After you. Since you're already tired, I'll let you pick a weapon."

He probably expects me to argue about fairness or something ridiculous like that. Instead, I lightly jog past him, scoop up a bo staff, and turn, already swinging for his head. He ducks the blow and reaches for the staff. I spin it out of his reach and sweep low, aiming for the ankles. My sparring staff is wood, but a flexible kind. It wouldn't do any damage, but it helps increase my reach and mitigate his.

He leaps over the sweep of the bo and dives in close, behind the staff.

I fold my arms and sink an elbow into his gut as I turn, twisting the staff behind his ankles and shoving forward with my shoulder. He puffs out a breath as he loses balance, probably not expecting so much aggression, although I can't imagine why.

I sweep up with the staff, encouraging the fall. He tumbles but snags the front of my coveralls with one long-fingered hand, bringing me down with him.

It's exactly the position I didn't want to be in. Or I do. No. I definitely do not.

My staff is trapped under his body. Our legs are tangled. I have very little advantage if we're wrestling unless I break the rules—and biting or hair pulling during a sparring match is frowned upon. I try to roll out of reach, kicking out at his knee when I do. I make contact but it doesn't do as much to slow him down as I wanted it to. He follows me, crawling agilely across the mat, a smile still flickering on the edges of his lips. It occurs to me that this might be the first time I've ever seen him enjoy himself.

I catch the smile on my own face too late to hide it. Maybe I'm enjoying myself, too. I kick again, catching the side of his abdomen. Then I get greedy and go for a third shot. He captures my ankle and yanks me closer, trying to grapple. I slide across the mat toward him but manage to slither out of his reach when he's adjusting his grip.

I'm absolutely going to lose if we stay on the floor.

I'm absolutely going to lose *anyway*, but I'd prefer if it was less embarrassing. I'm supposed to be this badass ex-Family scouting captain. A cyborg, like Micah says. I roll to my feet and throw a quick series of blows at his head and torso as he rises. He blocks most of them using forearm trapping or simple shielding, but I make contact a few times. I'm about halfway through the combination when I finally realize that he isn't exactly fighting back and hasn't been this whole time. He's defending, but he's never gone on the offense.

I don't *want* him to punch me in the face, but I'm a little offended that he hasn't even tried.

"Why aren't you fighting?" I spit out, as I swing a right hook at his temple. He blocks with his forearm, which gives me an opening on that side to front-kick his kneecap. He puts his weight into the leg—just enough to protect the joint.

"Wouldn't be fair." That infuriating smile again. His dark eyes are laughing but it's a soft laughter, not the razor edge I'm used to from him. "You hiked all day after a speed-repair."

"What, so you'll just sit back learning all my moves and I don't get to learn any of yours?" I follow the front kick with a double uppercut to the abdomen, which he mostly absorbs by a quick turn, catching my fists with his obliques instead of his stomach.

Laughter undercuts his comment. "You have moves? I'm still waiting to see one."

I snarl and go after him in a flurry of kicks and punches that finally have him retreating across the mat. He blocks most but not all of them, and I'm wickedly pleased to see the sheen of sweat on his brow and the slight flare of his nostril when a particularly hard blow hits. I'd pull my blows but that would be an insult.

Now I'm smiling, too, and not even bothering to try to hide it. I go for a strike pattern that I learned from a very young age, hitting with the hard outer edges of my bladed hands. Neck. My opposite arm crosses to the same side as the neck strike but hits the ribs. The other side of the neck. The soft skin near the waist. Not so soft in this case.

It's pure muscle memory and my arms lash out in a dervish until, finally, he's done trying to deflect my blows and he changes his goal.

Before I realize that the rules have changed—my rules are that I'm allowed to hit him until he cries, and he's not supposed to do anything in return—my arms are twisted behind my back and we're chest to chest. I give an experimental twist. Nope. I'm well and fully trapped. When I glare up at him, he's already looking down at me, dimple flashing in his cheek. I stomp on his instep. The smile morphs into a wince but returns within a moment.

I test his grip with my wrists, trying to figure out how to take him by surprise. It's going to take more than the right angle because his big hands have handily captured me. As my haze of anger starts to recede, I become more aware of how we're standing. Pressed close together. My breasts are flat against him and the friction that my exploratory movements are causing is activating a completely different part of my nervous system.

He still smells good. I breathe out, suddenly at a loss for what to do next. Every time I'm around him, I feel like the piston in an engine, shooting violently from one emotion to the next: caution, trust, disappointment, hope, panic, attraction.

I still want to strangle him, that never goes away . . . it's just my body is suddenly open to any number of more exciting alternatives. I lock my eyes on his sternum. I'm not going to look up and let him see me all flushed skin and dilated pupils. I'm going to get myself under control. He takes a deep breath and suddenly now he's rubbing against *me*.

I do a quick catalogue of our position to try to see if there's a way to escape with my pride intact and that catalogue alerts me to something that I missed in all my humiliating reactions to our proximity. There appears to be a metal bar of some sort wedged against my stomach and it's growing. Against my better judgment, I squirm again. Yup. Definitely growing.

I look up, preparing to gloat, feeling like all my imagined power has suddenly returned, but I get lost in his dark black gaze before I can properly torment him. He adjusts his hold on my arms and the action presses us even closer together.

"What do you think you're doing?" My voice is embarrassingly raspy.

"Wondering what you'll do if I kiss you." If my voice is raspy, his is like being dragged down a dirt road. Rough. Abrasive. Damned out of line.

"Dare you."

Do I know that there isn't anything I can say more likely to guarantee his action? Maybe. Do I regret it? No. Regrets are for tomorrow and I'm sure I'll have plenty of them. Right now, his head's descending, eyes shuttering shut, and I'm still torn between giving him a violent head-butt to win and seeing what's going to happen. Curiosity wins out and, when his lips hit mine, something within me ignites like he is a lit fuse and I'm an explosive.

There is no easing into this kiss. No long breathless pause like in the cenote. No soft request followed by deliberate action. It's wild and hard and, when his tongue slides into my mouth, I meet it with my own. At some point, he lets go of my wrists and I wrap one hand around the back of his neck and one in his hair, holding his head in place so that I can angle it just right. His teeth catch my lower lip with a sharp nip, and I pinch his earlobe with my fingertips in retaliation as I pull away, breathing hard. His hair is tousled, cheeks flushed.

He looks like he's been slapped.

He kisses like a storm and I'm happy to drown in it. He makes a guttural sound in the back of his throat and ducks his head again.

I rise to meet it, hands roaming over his shoulders, back, waist. Anywhere that I can sink my fingertips into hard muscle. His palm flattens between my shoulder blades, holding us pressed together, and the other tangles in my hair, angling my head as his thumb strokes along the line of my jaw. His beard scrapes on my skin in a way that's so good. I dig my nails in where I'm clutching his waist, like I want to burrow beneath his skin. My heartbeat thunders in my ears, loud enough to drown out any second thoughts that may be swimming around my skull.

The hand between my shoulder blades encourages me upward.

I ignore the gentleness of the hand and leap up, wrapping my legs around his waist, and he takes five swift steps to a corner sheltered by a weapons rack and a storage unit. He presses my back to the bulkhead. Much better alignment this way. I want this man. Not forever—that's not in the cards for either of us—but for now. I can allow myself that much. His fingers slip over my waist, my ass, tracing hot paths over my thighs as they venture to the juncture between them. One slides directly over my core, and he swallows my gasp in his kiss.

"I've been wanting to do this for days." His voice sounds like he just woke up, lust-drugged and thick.

"You stopped," I can't help but argue.

"You never started." He nips a fiery path up my jaw. "Also, you were injured."

"Excuses, excuses." I'm hungry for skin against my own, so I tug on his shirt, hauling it over his broad back, but get flummoxed halfway up because his arms need to move for the shirt to come off, but his nimble fingers have found the exact right spot to work, stroking over the fabric of my coveralls in a way that I never before considered could be erotic. I don't want them anywhere else. He growls under his breath and sets my feet on the floor long enough to shrug out of his shirt and unzip my coveralls. The long slow slide of the zipper ramps up every ounce of adrenaline in my body.

Some people may be patient lovers. It is not one of my particular talents. Deciding to take matters into my own hands, I . . . take matters into my own hands.

His fitness pants are lightweight, the fabric doing very little to disguise how much he wants to be here. There's a special gift in that aspect of humanity—the inability to hide true desire if one feels it. He wants me, of this much I have no doubt, and a heady power thrums through my body. I close my fingers over him, stroking my thumb across the broad head through the soft fabric.

He's large, my fingers can't quite wrap around him. I expected it—he carries himself that way—but I start to wonder about the mechanics of us fitting together.

"Do you want this to be over before it starts?" Arcadio takes my hand in his and presses his lips into my palm. It's a chaste gesture but his eyes are bottomless black pools that I could get lost in. The emotion that lingers, deep down within them, could be described as longing. It may be reflecting my own back at me.

"You think it's going to start anytime soon?" I reclaim my hand and drag my fingers down over his abdomen. His muscles quiver under my touch, power barely restrained.

"I'm trying not to fall on you like a rabid animal. Demonstrate some refinement." He runs his thumbs over my nipples once. Again. Lowers his head to take one into his mouth.

Once I blink away the stars from my vision, I manage, "Oh. Yes. Women always spend a lot of time bragging about their lover's *refinement*. And, with a lady as couth as myself, I see how you could view that as a high priority."

I grab his package to show how much I value refinement. He moves so fast I'm dizzy. Suddenly, I'm back up against the bulkhead, pressed flat to the metal. I tug his head toward me and lick a hot line along his jaw and down the side of his neck, stopping to sink my teeth lightly into his shoulder as his fingers return to their clever work at the juncture of my thighs, this time tugging aside my underwear and pressing directly against my flesh. They smoothly slide through wet heat, curling just right. An intensity grows, uncertainty and fear and attraction so strong it's near blinding, all twisting inside me and building in a growing crescendo.

He presses one long thick finger within me as his thumb continues its devilish work, and it's enough to push me over the edge when he works the two together. I lose myself for a moment, waves of pleasure crashing to shore, near-drowning in intensity.

"Fuck. Arcadio." Those are the only words to come to mind. I don't know if it's an exclamation or a demand.

He nuzzles his face against my neck, tracing a trail of scalding kisses down the sensitive skin. It's like all my nerves have been activated, like the sexual version of a fast phagocyte wash shooting tingles throughout my entire body. The heat of his body, the heady clean scent of his skin, the rough trace of calloused fingers against my flesh is encompassing. Overwhelming. I reach for him again, but he steps away.

"This one was for you."

I blink but my brain hasn't fully returned to itself yet and the words don't make sense. "What?"

"You clearly won our sparring match. I was helpless in your hands."

That's not exactly how I remember it.

He approaches again, ducking his head for one long slow agonizing kiss that threatens to weaken my knees even more than they already are. "When we go further than this, we're going to have more privacy than a tight corner of your armory."

"When?" Brain's still not working. He slowly rezips my coveralls.

He returns for a lingering brush of the lips. "When. Not if. We *will* be revisiting this conversation."

I swallow, everything catching up and crashing down all at once. "I'll prepare an impassioned rebuttal."

My heart pounds so loudly that it threatens to drown out my voice. Not loud enough to drown out Caro when she yells out from the galley, "Time for dinner!"

. . . . .

When Escajeda goes on watch, I'm waiting. Not for the *when*. There may be no *when*. Not unless tonight proves him to be trustworthy. The armory was a mistake. Maybe. A fucking amazing mistake that I'm attempting to erase from my recollection, lest I accidentally repeat it. Just the feeling of those shoulders, the smooth slide of his lips, the urgency of—

Erasing.

No, what I'm waiting for is to see what he does. Perhaps a little too late considering I was just wrapped around him like a vine, but our interlude in the armory increased my fear. I cannot get involved with someone who keeps secrets from me.

Again, I mean. I can't get involved with someone who keep secrets from me *again*.

The tiny Escajeda on the holo walks into the helm and relieves Micah from duty. Micah glances up at the camera and winks at me as he leaves the helm, his back to Escajeda, who is already looking out through the windows.

I told Micah about my plan earlier, after dinner when I assumed the swelling in my lips and the rough scrape of beard against my skin had probably gone down. The laughter in his eyes said it hadn't. Still, he didn't say anything except that he'd be happy to keep watch while I track Escajeda on his nightly adventures. I put odds of Escajeda staying in place tonight at roughly half a percent.

I want him to be trustworthy—all evidence to the contrary. He's good crew. Handles security well. Hasn't questioned any of my commands lately and he stopped telling everyone else what to do after I talked to him. Also, that thing with his fingers that I've already erased. He's a priap sometimes but if I couldn't work with those, I'd never work at all.

Let's be honest, *I'm* one of those.

I know better. Escajeda might be everything that I said, but he's still going to disappoint any expectations I may have of him. That's how it works. I believe in people's potential, but people are never much interested in living up to their potential.

Or, at least, not living up to my view of what it is.

So I'm not surprised when he leaves the helm moments after Micah retreats to his bunk. At least he locks the keypad on the gangplank. Once he's off the ship, I leave my bunk, tapping lightly on Micah's door to let him know that I'm on the move. I have a small drone, about the size of my thumb, that I can use to track him, but two of the moons are bright enough that I can still see him in the distance when I creep out of the ship. The lack of cover makes him easy to follow, although—if he turns around—it will make it harder for me to hide. I've seen him shoot and I don't want to be mistaken for a Nakatomi.

I thought he might be working with them—before he shot two of them. Thought maybe the Escajeda–Nakatomi Cold War was just for show and the two were secret allies. It wouldn't be the first time something like that happened. But I don't think he'd take out two allies with a very traceable weapon. Pulse guns or blasters are hard to trace—light is light. It disappears on contact and it's possible for different wavelengths and intensities to leave similar damage in flesh. Projectiles, on the other hand, are easy to iden-tify. That's part of why they went out of style.

So, not working with the Nakatomis, but up to something none-theless.

I have no idea what he's really doing but his nightly cavorting and his caginess when Rashahan asked his purpose on the planet both imply that, whatever it is, it's not only scouting for phydium.

I'm well aware the Nakatomis may be out tonight—set on revenge for their two fallen comrades. I send the drone high and to conduct a running scan of heat signatures in our vicinity. Escajeda follows our trail from earlier in the day, starting up the slope of Kaiaiesto. Before the climb grows steep, he breaks off into an arc, periodically scanning the ground with some handheld piece of equipment. Thin sparse patches of pale plant life, like waist-high cobwebs coated in thorns, are scattered around this elevation. When I walk too close, one of the thorns pops off and springs at me, tangling in my hip pocket. I stagger away and get hit in the ass with about five more from the plant behind me. Fucking things spit thorns.

I couldn't be exploring a planet made of cloud candy and soft cuddly creatures, could I? Just once.

Keeping a leery distance from the shrubs, I drift forward again, after Escajeda. He seems to find something of interest beneath his feet and paces back down the slope of the volcano, this time following a careful path, double-checking the device in his hand until he gets to the canyon. It's farther than we journeyed to enter the canyon on the day we first fought the Nakatomis. When he reaches the edge of the cliff, he peers over the break. His shoulders hunch like he's carrying the weight of the world and his hand wipes over his mouth. He looks like shit.

"You could save me some time and jump." I don't bother to mask the irritation in my voice as I approach him from behind.

"You could save me a return trek to the ship and push me," he volleys back, not bothering to turn. He sounds tired.

"So, this is where you go when you're supposed to be protecting my crew. Following underground structures. I know they're not phydium deposits because you started your path in an area we crosshatched. I'll be curious to hear your next lie." I cross my arms over my chest.

It's hard to swallow. I feel like someone has my throat in a clench. When I imagined this moment, I didn't picture the crushing disappointment of certainty. A tiny part of me held out hope that he didn't have ulterior motives.

He turns, finally, assessing me with those near-black eyes. They grow even blacker when he kisses. Which is something I'm still not thinking about. His gaze snags on my mouth before he jerks it up to meet my own. "I told them you'd figure it out."

"'Them' meaning your parents?"

"They suggested that I not confirm even if you did." He seems to consider something and a minute tension in his face relaxes. "Despite what you think, I'm not my father's creature. I know enough to judge whether someone can be trusted. And I can't do this on my own."

I'm nonplussed. Completely out of pluss. I was preparing for a big scene, not capitulation. It gives him the opportunity to continue.

"Phydium was an excuse to get on-planet. A public reason for a scouting mission that no one would question—if they bothered to look in the first place."

"And the real mission?" I take a wild stab. "Something to do with the Nakatomi Family?"

He's silent for a long moment and then nods. His shoulders lower as though he's dropped a heavy weight. "We suspect they're using the planet unofficially. They have no ownership, but Nakatomi vessels have been seen around Herschel Two more frequently than normal transport would justify. More than a scouting party. Heavily armed. Focused in the area around the volcano. Too deep under to track."

"I'm not an idiot. I figured that—"

"My brother, Pablo, was sent to investigate. My father thought he needed more field experience—less time in an office." He cuts me off and my mouth snaps shut. I hadn't figured *that* out. "We lost his signal shortly after he landed. Nothing since. The Family can't go public with his disappearance because he was spying on Nakatomi activities."

His brother. The Nakatomis have his brother. No wonder he's been so impatient. No wonder he's gone out on his own every chance he had. Why didn't he tell us? We'd have helped him, if he'd just trusted us.

If he trusted me.

"You're here because it looks weak for the Escajeda to misplace a son. What was your plan, exactly? Find him in the night, spirit him away from a cohort of Nakatomi soldiers, and hide him under your bunk, hoping I don't notice I have a new stowaway?" I'm unable to keep my mouth shut. Something bubbling deep in my gut pushes the words out. My mind is still spiraling through all the ramifications of this new complication.

Some of the tension leaches from his face like we can finally be friends. "I'm here to rescue him but I couldn't show up with a full Escajeda ship or we'd risk a war that no one wants. I couldn't tell you unless I was sure you could be trusted. You were a Family traitor, and he is my *brother*. Why wouldn't you sell us out to the highest bidder? We have a ship in stealth mode parked on one of the moons to cart him away when I found him."

I understand his position. Really, I do, although I wish he'd stop calling me a Family traitor. His brother is in danger. We do anything for our kin. Well, not *me*, specifically, but most of us. The problem is that he put us in more danger than I even considered.

"You brought my crew into immense inter-Family conflict without warning. You continued this charade, including leaving us unprotected at night, so you could search in secret because it might make your family look bad if we knew the truth. Don't tell me that ship was for him. It was for *both* of you. You were planning on leaving with him when he was rescued. Leaving us behind to face the Nakatomi anger that we had no idea was heading our way."

Why does this keep happening to me? Why am I so messed up that I only develop affection for a man immediately before he betrays me?

He doesn't say anything, so I keep going. "What have you learned in this critical exploration? Something of great value, I hope."

He huffs out a breath and takes a step or two away from the edge of the crevasse, perhaps sensing my mood. A mollusk could sense my mood. "The weird lava tubes aren't all lava tubes. Some of them are tunnels."

"We already knew that. The cult told us about the tunneling lizards." I pause. Perform a mental head-slap. "People tunnels. You mean people tunnels. How do you know that?"

"They're too perfectly shaped. The one that branches off from where we explored earlier turned at a perfect right angle. That was the first clue." Escajeda hands me his scanner. "The Nakatomi Family is building an infrastructure beneath Kaiaiesto."

CHAPTER 12

■ ■ ■ ■ ■ ■ ■ ■ ■ ■ ■ ■ ■ ■ ■ ■ ■ ■ ■

I make Escajeda tell the crew the story the next morning. He
doesn't want to, but I point out that if he doesn't, I *will* and my
rendition of the truth will be out of his control.

"You were put in a terrible position, between your loyalty to
your family and our crew." Itzel gently rests her hand against his
forearm as though she's comforting him. Comforting the one who
lied to us and then left us undefended. She's a morning person,
and the hot stim-water steams around her face in a beatific halo.

Caro pierces him with a harder gaze. "Does this mean we don't
get paid? The contract was for scouting under the pretense that we
got phydium."

"I'll ensure that he pays what he owes," Escajeda placates.

"You won't have to." I run my hands over the surface of the table.
"I reviewed the wording on the contract. It was for a scouting
mission. Metrics of success or failure were never defined. So long
as we either find phydium or fully scout as we were hired to do, we
have upheld our end of the contract. My concern is if the Escajeda
claims that his son—as his representative—had the true mission.
And refuses to pay unless the rescue is also executed successfully."

"If we rescue Pablo, he'll pay for the mission, I'm sure." Itzel
looks at each of us. "What kind of father wouldn't do whatever he
had to in order to rescue his son?"

I let that truly naive statement stew in its own juices for a moment, hoping someone else gives her the bad news. I can't be the
only negative influence in Itzel's life. This is why the Escajeda

added a time limit. He wanted us to get close to Pablo quickly to allow Arcadio to rescue him, escape, and leave us caught in the cross fire. Even if we lived, it would probably take a while to get off-planet and we'd have to fly past Nakatomi territory on the way. He hoped we'd be taken out by their enemy, and he wouldn't have to pay. If we come back alive, he's got the other hook of the phydium that we wouldn't have had time to look for, what with all the shooting.

It's exactly what Frederick would have done.

"The fuck he will," Caro spits. "The Five don't get to power like they have by politely paying their bills. They get it by screwing the little guy. We could bring back his son shiny and new and the Escajeda will try to find a way to worm out of his responsibilities."

I cut a glance to Arcadio. Maybe I've misjudged his father. Maybe he realized the impossible position he put us in and—since I've been pouting about my hurt feelings instead of actually asking pertinent questions—he has some sort of guarantee that our little lives were considered when this plan was formed.

He looks upset instead of angry, which tells me that Caro's view is correct.

"What you're saying is, no matter which job we do, the Escajeda might say we did the wrong one." Micah wipes a hand over his face.

"We're talking about my brother's life," Escajeda snaps. He's leaning on the table, shoulders tight with tension. "I apologize for inconveniencing you, but I won't apologize for my priorities. I had it all in hand. You weren't going to be vulnerable. We weren't going to leave you. My father might have made a plan but that didn't mean I intended to follow it."

"Maybe if you'd told us your actual mission, we'd have found him already because we'd be looking for a person instead of a mineral!" Am I yelling? It feels like I'm yelling. I know that I'm being selfish here, but I thought he was different. He isn't. Just one more man who can't tell the whole truth because it inconveniences him to do so.

Yes, the fact that he did it to save a life instead of to get laid makes him better than Ven. "Better than Ven" is a low bar. I simply wish that, just once, a man's motivations will be all about me instead of any other mitigating factor.

Which is childish and, what's more, irrelevant. When Escajeda spoke about Pablo he practically glowed with pride, and it wasn't just the light on his smooth skin. His youngest brother is clearly dear to him. And now, Pablo Escajeda is in the Nakatomi Family's clutches.

It's time for me to get over my baser impulses and be a decent human. Arcadio is not his father any more than I am my brother. I'll believe that he did have a plan for us until it's proven otherwise.

Caro glances between me and Escajeda, clearly reading the subtext, as she continues. "How are we going to complete two missions and cover our bases?"

"You three will continue to scout for phydium, primarily via drone now that we know militant Nakatomis with something to hide are patrolling the area." I point at Caro, Itzel, and Micah. "Escajeda will continue his personal search to discern their plans. If the Nakatomis even have his brother. He *could* be with the Children."

Escajeda grimaces before he asks, "And what will you be doing?"

"I'll be with you every step of the way." I paste a sweet smile on my face.

"I *will* guarantee that my father pays you what you're owed." Escajeda runs his fingers through his hair. He sounds exhausted. Which he probably is, considering he spends half his nights doing double-scouting. That's not even considering the emotional stress he's under.

He's a good brother. Probably even a good man.

Maybe just not good for me.

. . . . .

My body armor is a size too large. It's heavy, which isn't a problem, but it's also uncomfortable, which is. By the time Escajeda and I get to the edge of the canyon, where I confronted him the night before, I'm worried that I'm going to get blisters. Compared to his sleek and stylish armor and face shield, mine looks clunky and out-of-date. It's the infamous suit where my helmet doesn't attach to the armor. There's a slim line around my neck that's vulnerable and Escajeda's eyes went straight to that sliver of flesh when I met him in the cargo hold. He didn't say anything, which is why I didn't eviscerate him.

Finally, as though the canyon's edge is our honesty place, he looks over and I can tell he can't hold in the words anymore. "You're going to get angry at me for saying this again, but you need new armor."

No shit. "I'm not going to get angry at you for stating the obvious, Escajeda."

"It's a glaring vulnerability."

Maybe I was wrong because I already feel defensive anger intensifying to a boil. Always better angry than vulnerable. "We can't all afford the best-of-the-best armor. It was this or no helmet at all."

"You're as vulnerable as if you had no helmet at all." His voice sounds frustrated, which can't be right because I'm the angry one. He unrolls a sturdy-looking black rope from around his waist and affixes it to a large boulder.

"Not everyone aims as well as you do, Escajeda." I take in the minute tightening of his features when I call him Escajeda. When I called him Arcadio, right before that moment that I'm actively forgetting, he lit up like someone had given him a prize.

"You can't even move properly." He gestures as I slip the rope through the descender on my harness. Maybe I am a little stiff. The too-big plates jab into my armpit and crotch and keep my arms from resting directly against my body. "Why does your crew let you walk around in substandard armor? Caro, at least, can afford better."

"It's not Caro's job to buy me armor." The tight grip on my anger slips a little. "It's not the crew's job to provide me with things. It's the other way around. If Caro wants to buy her own armor, she can. If she bought armor for me, I wouldn't accept it."

He spits out something under his breath that I can barely hear and tosses the end of the rope into the canyon. "It's not a slight for someone else to take care of you. I know you know that because you seem to spend all your attention taking care of them. It's why you followed me last night. Why you spent more credits than you had to buy your old captain out—to keep their home intact. You do it every day. But you don't allow them to return the favor. You're so worried about owing someone, about being linked through debts and affection, that you shove them all away as hard as you can with both hands when they try to reach for you."

My throat is clogged with anger. A big ball of it just roiling one breath away. He's wrong. I wasn't only keeping their home intact. It was more selfish than that. I couldn't handle losing another home of my own—losing more people. I couldn't handle more people who choose to never speak to me again. "You don't know anything about me, Escajeda. Or my crew."

But as I step over the edge and repel into the canyon, I'm not angry at what he said.

I'm angry because he shouldn't be this insightful after he proved to be a liar, and something soft and deep within me feels just as vulnerable as that strip of skin around my neck.

By the time Escajeda reaches the entrance to the lava tube, I've reined in my reaction and explored the edge of the formation. The ceiling of the tube is taller than I am, slightly shorter than Escajeda. It's nearly twice that wide—an awkward oval like a stretched mouth that plumbs deep into the earth.

"Is this the first tube entrance you've found in your nightly explorations?" Back to business. I check the power level on my blaster to ensure it is maxed out as he unloops the rope from his descender. At standard power, the battery offers maybe a thousand shots when new, decreasing with the age of the battery. At maxed power, it's down to under a hundred in a new battery—no clue how many in my dusty old tech.

"The first easily accessible one. There's another close to the Children's territory, but I didn't want them to sneak up behind me while the Nakatomis were doing the same from the front."

"I think your name took Rashahan by surprise. That implies he isn't the one with your brother."

He nods, fiddling with the harness. "I can't see them being competent enough to hold him for long, even if they ambushed him. Pablo is young, but he's an Escajeda."

"Can he handle himself—truly?"

My real question is unspoken: is Pablo Escajeda already dead? It's certainly possible. It's suicide for the Nakatomis to be caught with him, so if they captured him spying, they might want to destroy the evidence. Scions of Families are trained to expect abduction and manipulate it to their favor. Which works very well unless another Family abducts you. The Nakatomis will know all his tricks.

"Pablo's smart. Maybe the smartest person I've ever met."

Escajeda sounds thoughtful. Also rude. He's met *me*. "But he isn't battle-hardened. He's never even worked security in one of our holdings. The twins broke my parents of that little gem of an idea after they staged a coup. Pablo's an accountant. If he can keep his wits about him, he can think circles around them. Certainly, convince them to keep him alive."

"Do you think he can keep his wits about him?" It's an important question, albeit one I feel like shit for asking. If this is a body retrieval, I'm not risking my crew. Not even for all of the Escajeda's money. He protects his Family, I protect mine.

Escajeda lapses into silence, and when he clears his throat, the sound is thick. "I don't know. He's never experienced anything like this. He's not a kid, but he might as well be. He was so eager to prove himself a true Escajeda, or at least my father was eager to make him prove himself. I don't think he ever considered what would happen if he got caught." Another pause, and then even quieter. "He doesn't handle pain well."

Something stabs straight into my heart and tries to explode it. They train us for that. Or, I should say, train *them* for that. Being in a Family is being in danger. It's anticipated that, at some point in your life, you may be tortured. You're taught to handle that, too. The lessons are not pleasant. You can only learn through practice. Frederick was very good at it. Perhaps because he's so single-mindedly focused, or perhaps because he's always been an island within himself.

I'm good at it, too. He is my brother, after all. He oversaw my training.

I reach out and clasp Arcadio's hand before I think about it. The gloves of our armor insulate the contact, keeping the heat of his skin from mine. "I won't tell you it's going to be okay. You're smart enough to know the odds. I will tell you that my crew and I are damned good at looking for items of rare value, and we usually find what we're looking for. We could be allies, Arcadio. Not adversaries."

We could be "partners" is the word that I leave unspoken. The request I won't ever make because somehow my mushy emotions forgot the vast difference between our stations, but my brain hasn't.

His fingers squeeze mine briefly before he lets go and steps back. "We all have our orders. I couldn't tell you. I wanted to."

I smile ruefully. "That's where you're wrong. You follow the orders because you want to, and that's fine, but don't believe that everyone lives that way. Some of us only answer to ourselves."

Escajeda grumbles and sets off into the darkness, confident in the gloom. I step in a divot in the tunnel floor and stumble forward, just barely catching myself. "I don't have night vision mods. Could you slow down a little? I can't see a thing."

His footsteps stop. I hurry to catch up. A bit too much because I collide with him after about ten steps and bounce back, nearly falling before his hand catches my elbow. "Why don't *you* have night-vision mods? They're standard for the Fifteen."

"Once he inherited, Frederick only budgeted one of any mod. The deal was, we'd fight for them. I lost." It was one of the last fights we had before my betrayal was discovered. I still remember the day. Nati warned me not to, but I thought I had what it took to beat Frederick.

I was just past twenty. They can't do eye mods until your vision has settled, which doesn't happen until the early twenties. At twenty-five, Frederick probably weighed nearly twice what I did and had a much longer reach. My cheekbone, collarbone, and one of the bones in my left forearm were victim to Frederick's "lesson." I think I broke one of his nails when he hit me too hard. I did manage to burst an eardrum.

In retrospect, it might have saved my life. I still looked pathetic for my banishment. An execution would have made Frederick look like a bully. Which he is, but he's smart enough to dodge the accusation.

Silence greets my statement and I stare into the darkness, wondering if Escajeda has wandered off. The ghost of a touch wafts in the air near my face. Like he's hovering his hand, unsure what to do. In the dark, I'm not sure what he's doing either, but a sharp movement is involved. The sound of a helmet being fiddled with. "He made you fight him for it? Frederick is a behemoth. You're very capable but you're half his size."

I clear my throat around a thick gob of something sharper than phlegm.

That hand hovering over my head makes contact. A rough thumb smooths its way over my cheekbone, almost like he knows it was once broken. Warm lips press softly against my forehead, just under the cap of my helmet where the faceplate is raised, and I blink in the dark, sure I imagined it. I want to lean into him. Or slap out at him, furious to be caught in a moment of vulnerability.

He clasps my hand in his own before continuing forward at a more measured pace. His fingers are warm and firm. Solid. I don't know how far we venture into the tube but, after a while, Escajeda stops. I catch myself before I collide with him again. I can't hear anything dangerous, so I whisper. "What is it?"

The pressure of a finger rests against my helmet and my headlamp flashes in the dark of the tunnel. Escajeda looks away from the bright light. I blink hard, dark-adapted eyes awash with sensory input. A gigantic metal wall blocks the entire span of the lava tube, a massive, heavy door set in the middle with knobby thick hinges and a sliding grate in the center at eye level. It's currently in the shut position. I set my hand flat on the door. Distant vibrations run through it and my fingers curl against the metal. The Nakatomi crest arches above the door. What priaps. They're so confident in their superiority that they labeled their secret project with their own crest. I suppose they didn't assume anyone else would be randomly strolling around a lava tube on a useless planet, but still.

"You're right," I say, although it pains me to do so. "Clearly the Nakatomis are trying to make a move."

Escajeda hides small bits of spyware around the door, and we leave the lava tube. We've just stepped out into the wash of the reddish sun and I'm preparing to make the climb to the surface when my interface tattoo vibrates angrily as a series of messages finally reaches me.

I tap the activation pressure point on my wrist and the messages play in my coms unit. My palms grow sweaty. A furrow forms between Escajeda's brows and he looks at me in askance.

"We were right about the Children being a threat. And now we know why they were asking about a medic. They took Micah."

CHAPTER 13

▪ ▪ ▪ ▪ ▪ ▪ ▪ ▪ ▪ ▪ ▪ ▪ ▪ ▪ ▪

We meet Caro and Itzel in the canyon, near the narrow mouth of another cenote. This one opens like a vase beneath us, a thin window to a wide dark cave below, filled with cerulean water. Itzel has a wicked scrape on her forehead and a puffy black bruise forming in the tanned skin under her eye. Caro's lip is split and she holds her right hand like it's injured.

"They came out of nowhere." Itzel's fingers flex and open around a blaster. "I didn't even get a chance to draw my blaster before one hit me in the head with some kind of club. By the time I woke up, they were gone."

"I got my blaster out, but one of the men twisted it out of my hand." Caro's deep angry flush is visible even against her dark skin. "I should have practiced more. I need to practice more. You guys have to stop protecting me. When things like this happen, I need to be prepared."

That sounds like a reason to protect her *more*. Caro's probably the most important person on the crew, but for some reason, she seems to believe that her value is contingent on her ability to shoot stuff. Problem is, she has no aim. Practice hasn't helped.

The midday sun is past, but it isn't setting quite yet. The shadows within the canyon are long; just a sunlit spark rims the edge of the rock far above us. I don't want to hunt the Children in the dark, in their territory. Or with the Nakatomi Family out patrolling.

"Do you have his tracker signal? Did you approach their last known location?" I ask Caro, since she led the crew to our rescue only a few days ago.

"We tracked it to a lava tube just past this cenote. Once they went underground, we lost him."

I don't ask if they followed him. Itzel would have, but not with Caro in tow. Not without more weapons. Even now, I can see her eyes drifting in the direction Caro pointed, like once she has passed the engineer off for protection, she can float away and take matters into her own hands. I give her a sharp shake of my head and then ask Caro one follow-up question.

"Do you have any of the swarm with you?"

The swarm is a group of small drones that share a sort of rudimentary hive mind. They aren't full AI, exactly, but they aren't dumb either. They're small and skittery enough that the Children may overlook them at a glance.

She dredges around in the pockets of her pack and unearths two small drones. They're delicately articulated insectile things, with spindly legs that end in little grappling-hook-style feet and clear wings that unfold from a sensor-coated carapace. Each drone is about the size of my thumb down to the first knuckle. I weigh our options.

"Itzel, you take lead, scout the tunnel in your sneakiest manner. Caro, you fly the drones around Itzel unless they're making too much noise in that small area—signal her if they are, Itzel. I want to keep Itzel in view, so if they're noisy, we might need to use their creeper feature and have them crawl along the walls. It will be slower but also safer." My real concern is who should go second. It should be our next best and, much as it hurts, that's not me.

"We'll follow. If he's easy to extract, we'll grab him and run. If not, we'll scout the area and form a better plan." They wanted Micah, which implies they need medical care, but they scorned our medical supplies, so it must be specialized.

I brace myself for Escajeda's complaint that this isn't his purpose here. That his brother is the priority, and his brother isn't in the Children's tunnel. It doesn't come and I'm buoyed with relief.

Itzel shucks her body armor, revealing a tight black synthetic bodysuit beneath it. That kind of suit prevents chafing from the armor but also will enable her smooth movement. Body armor isn't designed for stealth and Itzel moves like a shadow without it. I'm not worried about her being ambushed when she's in the zone. She's death on the wind when she's in the zone. The problem is after.

Itzel fights her nature every day, wanting to be something she isn't. Something she can't be with this job. Scouting isn't a career for happy people. It's a career for deeply fucked-up or desperate people who have something to prove. People like me. Not people like Itzel. She straps her blaster back to her thigh and slips two knives into sheaths that rest flat against her forearms.

I catch her by the arm as she turns in the direction of the lava tube and sketch a shape on her left shoulder blade using my index finger. A different shape on the right. Back at the monastery, the monks did this before a mission. It's a sort of spiritual protection. I don't practice her faith but it's important that someone cares enough to do this for her.

The tattoos that line her fingers are nearly as dark as the bodysuit. There are all kinds of rumors about the tattoos that bedeck the monks of the Dark Mother of the Void. One says that they add a feature to their tattoos for each life they take. Itzel's are so densely intricate that it's hard to find a sliver of skin. I hope, for her sake, that particular rumor is not true.

She presses her forehead flat against mine in thanks and then moves away without a whisper of noise. When she passes Arcadio, his fingers bend into one of her scriptures and she pauses in her tracks. A tremulous smile quivers over her lips. "How do you know it?"

"I watched you when the Nakatomi ship threatened us. It seemed meaningful."

Her smile shines like the sun after a storm and she presses her forehead against his, too. Emotion sticks in my throat. Even then, he was watching us. Noting what was important. He didn't need to do that if he was using us.

When Itzel leaves, Caro turns to Arcadio. "Turns out, you aren't such a priap after all."

From our engineer, that's high praise.

"We're going to get him back." When I speak to Caro, my eyes catch Escajeda's. We're going to retrieve *both* of our lost men.

We follow Itzel into the lava tube. It closes around us like a hungry mouth, and once again, darkness presses close around me. If I had known how critical night vision would be, I might have fought Frederick harder that day so long ago.

Itzel rejoins us, silent as a whisper at the exact same time Micah's angry voice echoes down the lava tube.

"Oh, I can take it out for you. With a pulse blast to the face. They don't make them to be removed, you simplistic idiots." That's our Micah . . . the bedside manner of a blender. His voice sounds strong and stable. They haven't hurt him seriously, then.

"Found him," Itzel whispers. The smile is evident in her tone. Something in my shoulders unclenches.

Up ahead, the tube opens into a large round chamber. I guess the lava pooled there for a while before moving on, or maybe adjacent tubes combined in some way. The unnatural structures we detected from above are deeper within the volcano, connecting to natural tubes. Warm firelight dances on the rock walls but it doesn't reach us, far back in the dark. A slight fissure in the wall provides a hint of cover, and all four of us cluster within. Itzel traces a map on the ground with her finger while Caro illuminates it with a dull red light that shouldn't be visible from far away.

"It's not the whole group, not yet, but it seems like the cult wants him to remove their banishment tattoos, so it will be eventually. Micah's over here." She draws an "X" in the left side of the circle with a string that travels to the wall. "They've chained him by the neck to a metal hook set in the wall. He has a tray of medical supplies right next to him, even scalpels, but one of Rashahan's stooges has Micah's blaster. There's a woman in a chair within reach of Micah's chain. Looks scared shitless. Maybe also angry shitless. My guess is she's the experimental subject. Someone who pissed Rashahan off recently."

"How many Children?" Escajeda points down at the map. "And where are they in the chamber?"

Itzel draws four circles. One near Micah, one in the middle of the chamber, and two more near the far wall. She pauses and then draws another, very close to Micah, and points to it. "The woman. I don't know if she counts as a Child or not. Another thing you should know, they're better armed than a Five shuttle flying through enemy territory. This whole place appears to be Rashahan's weapons bunker. Blaster shot goes wild, something's probably going to explode."

"It's never a peaceful, happy cult," I mutter under my breath. "Do they look comfortable enough with Micah's blaster that you think they realize firing in that room turns it into a death trap?"

Itzel shrugs. "They look plenty stupid to me."

"Only one armed at present? Is his weapon pointed directly at Micah or just in hand?" I peer around the rockfall, in the direction of the light. No sounds of approaching footsteps. Lots of sounds of Micah continuing to berate the Children.

He's right, too. Only a fool thinks a banishment tattoo can be removed. They wouldn't be very effective if they could. The glowing ink goes all the way down to the bone in the tattoos like mine. They also scarify it enough when they create the tattoo that it won't ever heal right, no matter what kind of doctor works on it. You want to excise a whole cheek, you could probably eliminate the tattoo, but your face would be so fucked up everyone would know what you did.

Maybe one of the shorter-term banishments could be removed, but it would take so long to heal that you'd be at a draw timewise. Probably Families have something that does a better job but it isn't a tech they share. The few banishments I've ever heard of that have been lifted involved changing the color of the glowing ink. The tattoo doesn't go away, it just changes hue—and contains regulated nanos that provide authenticity of the recension.

Itzel draws a little blaster by one of the circles and draws a large shelflike shape along the back wall that she labels WEAPONS. "No, the weapon isn't pointed at Micah, but it is in the man's hand. Rashahan isn't in the room, but the people who are were all near the head of the table when we rescued you at dinner are. The woman, too."

So, it's Generosity or Charity. In a place of pride just a few nights ago. How far the well-placed have fallen.

"What do you think, security expert? How do we get him out unharmed?"

Escajeda turns to Itzel. Her muscles are tense as a predator's. She's ready. "Just how good are you? Can you get in the room with no one seeing you?"

"I can get in the room. It's possible Micah can provide a distraction. He certainly is right now."

Escajeda takes that at face value, without questioning her. He's slipped into being an active member of the crew rather than a thread unraveling.

"Good. You get between them and the weapons and keep them from arming themselves by any means necessary. I'll take out the man with Micah's blaster. We can take advantage of the distraction to rush the others. If you turn your blasters to low intensity, they'll injure flesh but won't damage the weapons or risk explosion. It might be hard to get a kill shot, but incapacitation should be possible."

"Why don't we have Itzel take out the man with Micah's blaster? He's the immediate danger." Caro points at the circle with the blaster.

"Because he's easy to snipe. The real danger is the other three and the rest of the weapons."

I don't fancy killing them because killing means the Children will be more likely to come at us with deadly force later. Also, it's wrong. That part should bother me, too. That's logic, though. They put a chain around Micah's neck. They hurt my crew. There's nothing logical about what I want to do to them now. "We have to be careful about the head count."

Escajeda pulls something out of his right hip pocket and holds it up in the air between us. In the low dim light, I can't make it out and I take it from his hand. Fabric. Torn at the edges. I trace my fingers over the raised shape in the center. It's familiar but I can't quite—"Is this the Nakatomi dragon?"

He nods. "Taken from the uniforms of the two who tried to ambush us at the ship."

Brilliant. I can't decide whether I admire or am horrified by the twisted way his mind works. Two birds with one Nakatomi crest. Since Rashahan is on the lookout for a big enemy, why not give him ours and let them batter it out between themselves? It might intensify his feeling of being attacked by Families, but I can't think of a reason why that should matter to me. They've all targeted us. They're welcome to kill each other.

"Do it." I nod, slipping the patch back into his hand before adjusting the sensitivity on my blaster yet again. "I'll get Micah. Caro, those drones have any capability beyond surveillance?"

Caro's grin is sharp and nasty. "One of the imaging capabilities

involves a megaintensity light strobe. Any color you want. Once Itzel gets in position, I can provide a distraction. You'll hear a high-
pitched whine. That's a good time to shut your eyes and turn away
from the center of the room."

The plan's as good as any we've ever had. Better than some.

Which isn't a great metric because we're generally shit at plans.

I nod. "Every piece helps. Stay behind the rockfall to avoid any
cross fire. If this goes weightless, we might need you to tow us out
somehow."

"No pressure," Caro mutters under her breath and returns to
her datapad.

"It's your op," I tell Escajeda. "You call the shots."

He looks at me with a gaze so intense that he clearly understands what that means and directs Itzel to do her thing and get
into place. Her fingers twist in the scriptures as she creeps down
the tunnel. I hate seeing it. I hate putting her in a position to stain
her skin with more blood and ink. The fact that she's volunteering
and it's our best option doesn't mean it's better. It just means that
I failed as a captain.

Luckily, I'm used to operating from a place of disappointment.

Escajeda and I press ourselves flat against the curved wall of the
lava tube. When I try to move in front of him, he hooks the back
of my body armor and tugs me back behind him, pointing to the
gap in my armor. I point at Micah and raise my eyebrows tellingly.
While Escajeda takes his shot at the armed man, I'm supposed to
be rescuing my medic.

He pushes down the face shield on my armor and turns around,
still in front of me. As I peer around him, he lifts a rifle against his
shoulder and peers down the scope, lining up a shot on the pacing
Child. It's the man who was sitting by the two bunnies at dinner. I
think his name might have been Justice.

I can't fully see into the large chamber, with Escajeda blocking part of the view and the Children's dim torchlight not doing much to combat the darkness. A large shelving system is carved out of the smooth wall of the chamber. It is about three-quarters filled with blasters, rifles, frag grenades, and knives. Open racks on the side of the earthen shelves contain full suits of body armor. There's even a small pile of Nomian shield bracelets—wrist cuffs that create a panel of intense light when they detect a blast in their proximity. If I survive this, I'm stealing one. I can't afford any armor that techy.

Which leads me to wonder how Rashahan and his followers— people who wear ill-fitting and dated clothing and have the medical facility of a primitive civilization—have an armory like this. Clearly, he's tithing *something* from his flock. He talked about people refusing to let go of their past at dinner. Perhaps this is what he meant. More donated credits lead to more weapons. It also implies he has bigger plans than lingering in the canyon.

When a cult has an armory and a grudge, it's the beginning of the end.

A Child paces into view. A shadow twists behind him and—if I didn't know Itzel was creeping into position by the shelves, I wouldn't realize she was there at all. I tap Escajeda's arm in case he hasn't noticed. Caro has, because a tight metallic scream blooms from the center of the chamber, echoing eerily around the smooth walls and down the tunnels. I tuck my face behind Escajeda's back and squeeze my eyes shut. Even then, the blinding light threatens to overwhelm my senses. Caro whistles, signaling the end of the flare, and we open our eyes. I duck in front of Escajeda, keeping low as he takes Justice out with a clean precise shot that pierces an eye.

"A little warning would have been fucking nice!" Micah growls, yanking on the chains. The woman in the medical chair is Generosity. She's struggling, squinty-eyed and tight-jawed.

A wet gurgle comes from Itzel's corner and another blaster

whine indicates Escajeda's shifting aim. When I reach Micah, he takes a swing at me. I duck the wild fist. "It's me, Micah."

Apparently augmented eyes are extrasensitive, but he drops his arm and lets me study the collar around his neck. It's an Elepenro slave collar. A particularly nasty invention that will deliver a violent bolt of energy if the person it's keyed to activates it. A small physical fail-safe keyhole rests above his spine with a fingerprint scanner next to it. "What digit was used to activate the collar?"

"Doesn't matter which one. It was Rashahan and he isn't here." Micah's nose is swollen and crooked and dried-blood flakes speckle his lip.

Just our luck. "I can get this off you in the ship, but not before that. Caro might be able to create an interference field around the collar for the trip back. He probably can't activate it from afar."

The sound of fists against flesh comes from the other side of the chamber. I turn to Generosity. "Why are you here?"

Her jaw is sharp as if she's chewing glass. It's at odds with her words and I file the disparity away for future analysis. "Where's Charity? I need to find Charity."

That seems like a misplaced priority at this exact moment—although if they did this to her, I don't know what they're doing to Charity. Generosity's wrists and ankles are secured to the chair with thin metal wire. A ring of sharp red blood lines one wrist. Well, fuck. I'm going to have to rescue her, too.

"Don't kill the girl yet," I yell, on the off chance that anyone is actually listening to me at this moment.

Micah comes first. The chain that connects his collar to the wall is sturdy. Too sturdy to take out with a blaster shot. They've affixed it to the panel in the wall with an equally strong loop. I tell Micah to hold still and run around the bowl of the room, past the limp bloody body of a Child. Past another that Itzel has just dispatched with one of her knives, a curtain of blood sheeting down his throat and pooling in the floor of the cave. Escajeda's final victim is a boneless heap by the weapons racks. A large piece of metal rebar leans on the wall by the rest of the weaponry. I don't know if it's intended for building material or fighting staffs, but it will give me sufficient leverage.

Escajeda paces between the downed Children, ensuring their deaths with a final shot to the head. He bends to the one I just passed and wraps the dead man's fist around the scrap of Nakatomi emblem, as though the man ripped it off his attacker.

When I get back to Micah, I wedge the rebar in the loop on the wall and push as hard as I can. The metal squeals as it bends. My boots slip on the floor, and with another grunt, I secure my stance and try again. Finally, with a groan, the chain releases from the wall and I stumble forward. Micah coils the metal links, looping it over his shoulder as I set the rebar down. "Can you handle that on the trip out?"

The look he sends me is scornful.

Generosity is next. A pair of Caro's wire cutters take care of her thin bindings. In their own way, they're nastier than Micah's collar. If she struggles at all, they'll keep cutting and eventually she'll sever a limb.

When we're done, we study the wall of weapons.

"We have to take them," I say, wondering how we're going to manage it. "Nakatomis wouldn't kill everyone but leave their weapons to be used against them later."

Escajeda shakes his head. "Nakatomis have their own weapons and don't need others. They'd destroy them. Especially if the goal was to block the tunnels."

It's a good point. "Can you spare one of the swarm?"

Caro nods.

We pile the weapons in the mouth of the far tunnel on the opposite side of the round chamber. The armor goes behind them.

I pocket most of the Nomian light-shield bracelets, leaving only a few in the front of the stack of weaponry. The frag grenades are affixed to the sides of the lava tube, with a few on the top of the weaponry. The small drone hovers in the open space, preparing to deliver one small bolt of energy to a frag grenade once we're a safe distance away. The resulting explosion should be enough to collapse the tube and destroy all the weapons.

There is one last suit of armor on the rack. "We forgot one."

Escajeda shakes his head. "That one's yours. It has a helmet that attaches and everything. It might even fit, unlike that monstrosity you're wearing."

"Take it, Temper." Caro has her arm around Itzel. My biologist is on the comedown from the kill. "You need something decent."

Itzel's voice is still clear but she's wiping her hands against her bodysuit. "You insist on putting all your credits in the ship—which, thanks—but you never spend it on anything for you."

That puts me in my place. I hope tomorrow is less about other people schooling me and I might get some of my own back. I slip into the new suit. It fits like a glove. Smooth and liquid. Like I'm not wearing anything at all. Like I could do anything. Which means to say, how body armor is *supposed* to fit.

I assign Caro and Itzel to support Generosity—by which I mean guard. She can't go back to the cult. Not until we're off the planet. If I had any faith left in humanity, I'd believe there's no way she'd go back to people who tied her to a chair and tried to force a doctor to experiment upon her.

She'll try to return before tomorrow night. It will be a nightmare keeping her in the ship—even if for her own good. But the second she goes back, she's telling the Children that the ambush was us instead of the Nakatomis, and then, assuming they have another storehouse—which I'm betting they do—they'll come for us.

My mind chews over that problem as we make our retreat

through the lava tube. When we reach the open air of the canyon, Caro activates the drone on its last mission. The shock wave is enough to shake the pale plants that cluster around the mouth of the tunnel.

CHAPTER 14

When we get back to the ship, Caro scans the collar and I retrieve my lockpicks from the secret compartment in my second pair of boots. Which maybe should become my first pair of boots for the duration of our experience on Herschel Two. Generally speaking, if you're in a position to need lockpicks, you're also in a position where you don't want anyone to know you have them.

I had a few misspent years in the beginning of my banishment—prior to joining Ven's crew. At a certain point of high-tech advancement, low-tech is actually more secure. A combination scanner is a hell of a lot easier to run than a set of lockpicks. So, I learned, because if someone put a mechanical lock on something, you can bet it was worth stealing.

The smallest tension wrench fits snugly in the bottom of the lock that rests over the back of Micah's neck, and I carefully select the right pick shape, settling on one with a double curve at the tip.

"My head isn't going to explode if you fuck this up, is it?" Micah is keeping very still, hands curled over the edge of the table.

"Probably not." Caro offers the encouraging answer while holding her datapad in the air near his head. "I've still got the signal dampener on, in case Rashahan decides to trigger it. It might also prevent a tampering alarm from within the collar."

"These collars aren't made for easy hacking," I point out as I get to work, applying pressure to the tension wrench before I slide the pick above it, feeling the bump as each pin is passed. "Our other option is to take a saw to it, and given its proximity to your neck, I assumed you'd be averse to that."

It's been a while since I had a real lock to pick and I spend the first few moments reacquainting myself with the feel of a mechanism, the pressure on the tension wrench, and the delicate manipulation of the pins. It's easy to get lost in the focus of a task like this, and eventually, I do, until the tension wrench swings around and the collar cracks in half, dropping into Micah's lap.

He throws the vile thing across the room like it's a snake. It dents the bulkhead near the door with a tiny divot. Fantastic; now I can remember my medic being captured and collared for as long as I have the ship. Probably Itzel will turn it into yet another charming doodle. Maybe featuring a dented Child. I walk over and retrieve it, holding the collar between two fingers as I study it. "Can either of you think of a use for this that isn't abhorrent?"

They shake their heads. I can't either. The scavenger in me doesn't like to discard something that might have utility, but shock collars are a step too far. I toss the collar to Caro. "Can you break it up for parts?"

She nods and, that problem solved, I search out Itzel. She's in her bunk with Generosity and very clearly only just holding her shit together. Her hands are so twisted in the signed scriptures that I can practically read them myself. I free her of the cult bunny and escort Generosity to the infirmary so Micah can assess any signs of long-lasting damage or malnutrition—as well as the nasty cuts on her wrists. Once she's under new supervision, I return to Itzel.

She shares the space with Caro but there's no confusing their bunks. Caro is on the bottom. The shelves surrounding her sleeping space are fitted with hooks and tabs to hold a selection of hand tools and datalinks. Her bedding is pale blue, and the wall is coated with more smeared sketches from when she woke up in the middle of the night with an idea and had to get it out before she could sleep again.

Itzel's top bunk is spare and empty. Her bedding is black and tucked in so tight that it's hard to figure out how she gets into bed at all. The small trunk built in at the foot of her bunk has nothing atop its magnetic upper panel, but I suspect it's where she keeps her personal store of weapons. My armory might have weaponry, but everyone brought their own and no one is keen on sharing.

Her walls are empty and blank of the charming sketches that she uses to bedeck the rest of the ship. Her bunk feels hollow and, as I look at the dark void of her eyes, I figure odds are high it reflects the emotions of the woman who calls it her own.

"You okay?" I ask, because I can't think of anything better. She's clearly not okay. Never is after a kill, but the question will hopefully get the ball rolling.

"Sure."

In the brief span of time when I shepherded Generosity to the infirmary, Itzel has removed both daggers from their sheaths on her forearms and is now scrubbing their blades with a smudged gray cloth. She's clearly done the same to her hands because they're clean, with the exception of a tiny flake of blood on her right index fingernail. The skin by her eyes is pulled tight with tension.

"Want to talk about it?" Sometimes she does, sometimes she doesn't. She only ever talks if she's asked. Itzel is polite in her breakdowns.

"No." Another sweep of that gray cloth along the blade.

I've offered to never put her in a situation like this again. I even mean it. I'll protect her as much as Caro if she wants it, but she doesn't really want it. She's good at wet work and she knows that sometimes she must do it to keep the rest of us safe. As a rule, monks are selfless, even to their detriment. When they expelled her from the monastery, I suspect they were trying to save her from herself, but it came too late.

"Want something to eat?"

A tight shake of her head. A looser quiver of the hand that cleans the blade.

It's going to be one of those nights. Sometimes she talks. Sometimes she cries. Sometimes she goes off on her own—but that's not an option here. "Want to hit something really hard?"

That finally gets a tiny nod. She carefully stores the daggers in the chest at the foot of her bed with the same care as if they were fragile porcelain and I leave the room while she changes into her workout gear. I would do the same, but I'm still breaking in the new body armor. It's been a long time since I had something new, just for myself. I'm loath to take it off.

Escajeda is already in the armory, running on the treadmill at a ground-devouring pace, wearing a black sleeveless shirt and loose fitness pants. Sweat shines on his collarbones and shoulders. He looks far too good, and I have a blinding sensory flash to the last time he and I faced off in this room.

When he gazes across the floor at me, his eyes are dark, and his smile is a sly invitation. A promise of more of the same.

He's wormed his way under my skin somehow, like a splinter you still feel even after you rip it out. I understand the sacrifices we make for our families, how they can drive you to the point of singular obsession.

I slip the pads on my hands and allow Itzel to whale away at me until we're both sweaty and loose-limbed. She's a tiny thing, but each blow reverberates through my arms with the authority of training and precision. I've never seen someone with more natural talent for violence than Itzel.

By the time I'm about to drop, she isn't smiling yet, but the tightness in her face has eased. When I step back, Arcadio takes my place, clearly sensing that Itzel isn't done even though I certainly am. My legs may not hold me much longer and that's not because I was force-healed, it's because Itzel fights like a monster.

And also because we had a very physically active day, and given my druthers, I'd already be in my bunk asleep instead of doing more fitness. No wonder Arcadio looks like he does. He's the sort of person who voluntarily hits the treadmill after spending the day hiking all over the planet. Insanity.

I leave them in the armory with a small smile on my face. He may not know it yet, but he's already part of the crew, even if just for now. Today proves that, had it come down to it, he wouldn't have abandoned us once he found Pablo. That worry lifted from my shoulders leaves me feeling almost weightless. I venture to the bunk across from my own, wiping sweat from my face with the back of a hand. Short term, it will serve for Generosity. In the helm, I adjust the locking sequence on that bunk's door and coms Micah to let him know where he can deposit her.

. . . . .

I eventually fall asleep watching the holo-feed from the helm, ensuring that Escajeda stays on watch this time. We're prioritizing his search, which means he has backup when he does it with us. After today, we'll focus all our resources on Pablo—leaving scanning for the drones. Hopefully maps will be enough to appease the Escajeda.

Some indeterminate time later, a light rapping on my bunk door wakes me. I groggily pull myself from my bunk and stumble to the door, hoping it isn't an emergency. It slides open to show Escajeda looming in the hall, leaning against the frame. He's looking down, staring at something intently, which is the moment I realize that I am wearing a loose shirt and I am not wearing pants.

"You aren't wearing pants." He states the obvious.

"It might surprise you that I don't sleep in my coveralls. Or body armor." I'm slowly pulling my thoughts together. Micah has watch after Escajeda. I'm after Micah. Either I slept through an alarm and Arcadio is doing me a favor, or something is wrong. "What happened?"

When he finally drags his eyes from my legs, he takes in the concern on my face. "Nothing. I wanted to talk."

Talk. That's never good. Unless this has nothing to do with me and he's so worried about his brother that he can't think straight. Keeping that secret would have been isolating. Men are weird like that. Usually when *they* want comfort, they pretend their goal is to comfort *you*. Not that I'm an expert. "Please tell me you don't have another big secret to reveal. My nerves can't take it."

"Nothing like that. I wanted to offer to answer any questions. If you have them. I would like to attempt a fresh start." He looks over my shoulder and suddenly he's through the door and halfway across the small room, backing me toward the bunk. My sleep-muddled mind is still a few steps behind, and I don't pull together a protest until he reaches behind me and pulls something from my bunk. My datapad, screen active, to the now-Micah-occupied helm.

"Checking up on me, Temper?" He's distractingly close, breath ruffling the hair on the top of my head, warmth seeping from his body into the narrow space between us.

"I had to know if this new trend of honesty extended to keeping your watch. It was a first."

Rather than seeming offended, he chuckles, the sound rolling over me like warm, sticky honey. Something twisted in my spine relaxes and then recoils even tighter. "What do I get for keeping my word?"

"For doing your job, you mean?" I ask, trying as hard as possible to keep a sudden breathlessness out of my voice. I'm moderately successful. "You get to *not* have my boot wedged so far up your ass that you can taste the animal that the leather came from."

His arm goes up to catch the frame above my bed, leaning even more into my space. I don't back up because if I do, I'll be in my bed. Not that the idea doesn't have merit but I'm pretty sure we wouldn't fit. A flush of heat works from my chest up to my face. I don't know if he notices, but he smiles like he does. "It sounds like your recollection of our last sparring match is incorrect."

"I don't need to beat you in a fight. I'm the boss and you'll do what I want regardless."

He ducks his head down until we're eye to eye, so close I can see the golden flecks within the black. "What do you want, Temper?"

I flash back to another time when we were in the same position and I was tempted to lick his nose, just to see what he'd do. So I do it. I run the tip of my tongue all the way up the smooth line, only slightly marred by the previous break. He jerks his head back, eyes unreadable.

"Did you just *lick* me?"

"I thought about it before," I confess, internally blaming the sleep-fog that's still drifting away for all the crazy. "I thought it might be the only effective way to shut you up and make you run off to clean your face."

Then he's a whole lot closer, chest brushing against my own, hand wrapped around the small of my back with his thumb slowly stroking my spine. His mouth hovers around my ear and when he speaks in his low rumble, I can feel his hot breath feathering my skin. "If you ever thought that, you seriously misjudged my reaction to being licked by a beautiful woman."

My thoughts snag on being called beautiful and then snag again because he's licking me back, his tongue delicately tracing the shell of my ear, canine dragging over the lobe. My breath stutters and my fingers curl in the front of his shirt.

I blink, wondering if I'm still asleep, dreaming an incredibly improbable dream. This is a terrible idea. One of the worst I've ever had.

For reasons that escape me at the moment.

Oh, right. If he's doing this because he just wants a connection and is worried about his brother, I'll personally feel like shit tomorrow. Also, he probably will, too, since he won't have talked about what he actually needed to. I hope he appreciates this sacrifice because if I were a worse person, I'd simply climb him like a ladder and let this whole thing play out. "If Pablo was so unprepared, why did your father send him?"

He freezes, still as a statue, breath against my temple. The muscles under my fingers tense. Great job, Temper, mood effectively killed. "My father has old-fashioned beliefs about strength. He expects all his children to be able to do everything, even if he acknowledges they have individual talents. It's ridiculous. My brother doesn't *need* to be a field scout. It's inane to send an accountant to spy on the most well-armed Family there is. If I'd have been present instead of on mission in—well, somewhere else—I'd have never let him do it."

"Let him?" I catch on those words. It's rare for a second born to have that kind of assumed power. I allow him to gloss over where his supersecret mission was. For now.

He sighs. "I would have volunteered, instead. That's what we usually do, Estella and the twins and me. We know that Pablo and my other brother aren't front-liners. They're thinkers—and thank Kaiaiesto or whatever creator you feel like thanking because my Family needs some thinkers. So we do what we can to watch out for them. I don't go quite as hard on them while sparring. Estella doesn't allow the pain-threshold training to go as high as it did with the rest of us."

He drops his head until his forehead rests against my own. "He wasn't supposed to be in this position. He was supposed to be safe in some satellite calculating profit margins."

"Your father pushed him to go?"

"And he wanted to. You know how it is, whatever your siblings do better, you think is valued more than your own contribution. He wanted to prove himself because he knew we were babying him." His voice gets empty. The darkness of my bunk wraps around us like a second embrace. "He didn't know how *much* we babied him, though. He thought he was ready and it's our fault that he believed it. Maybe if we'd really pushed him, he would have risen to the occasion."

I feel better about killing the moment earlier. The guilt is almost palpable in his voice. I rub my palms up his back slowly. "Maybe if Frederick had a real childhood, he wouldn't be the isolated bully he became. I'm sure he took the fact that my parents spent more time with me personally—even though he refused to join us for Family events because he was so used to being alone that he felt uncomfortable in groups that weren't under his thumb. Maybe we could have made him more kind. Or maybe he would have always been the way he is now. Put ten children in that scenario, all ten turn out differently. You had the same education that Pablo did, and you probably won't be revolutionizing your Family accounting structure. Causing him unnecessary pain to toughen him up only makes him tough, it doesn't make him *capable*. He had a job he was good at. He didn't need another."

"It isn't that simple."

"It is." I tilt my head up and brush my lips over his. Once. Twice. He spins us and presses me against the one open bulkhead of my tiny bunk. The cold metal of the ship is a stark juxtaposition to the hot hard wall of him. "Do you have any idea how much I wished to have a brother who cared enough to look out for me? A brother who protected instead of terrorized? Maybe you weren't a perfect brother, but you did your best and you are here, now. You'll do better the next time."

"If I get a next time."

I flick his ear like I did back in the cenote and he rears back, staring at me like I just bit him. "Stop sulking. You'll get a next time. We are fantastic at our jobs, and you are a trick-shot-capable, strategic, sickeningly handsome security expert. Your brother is stronger than you think he is because even if you protected him physically, he still has his smarts." He starts to argue, and I talk over him. "And you'll believe that until we find him because believing anything else does absolutely no good."

"My handsomeness sickens you?"

I shift a little against the bulkhead and the movement rubs my chest against his own. He pinches his eyes shut like he's trying to master a reaction. A spark of an oddly savage glee sizzles in my core. I enjoy making this man squirm. "Yes, I'm absolutely nauseated right now, can't you tell?"

He hooks the fabric of my shirt and tugs it forward, pressing my torso closer to him, something I wouldn't have thought possible. He ducks his head down and nips the tip of my nose. I scrunch my nose, tempted to wipe it, but my hands are performing an exploration of their own, rippling over the muscled "V" above the waistband of the low-slung pants, tracing up over his back.

"Hmm." He makes that rumbly contemplative sound that I enjoy so much. "You do seem repulsed."

I raise an eyebrow as a smile curves my lips. "Apparently that does it for you."

"I'm putty in the hands of a woman who is disgusted by me. That first time you told me to fuck off ensured I'd always be yours."

"All it takes is telling you to fuck off?" I can't stop the grin the curls my lips. "Little did I know, I've been whispering your version of sweet nothings ever since you came aboard."

"You absolutely have, you beautiful calamity."

It stings. Even though it isn't the first time. If I ever wanted to project an image of competence and authority, I've clearly completely lost the thread. "Why do you keep calling me that?"

He nuzzles a path of fire along the side of my neck. "Because you're like a force of nature. You're a typhoon. A solar flare. A volcano. You bend things to your will and walk away untouched."

"And bring a rain of ruin to everything I touch?"

"Only the bad things. To anger you is to court calamity. I should know."

I should not be smiling. What kind of woman melts when a handsome man calls her a disaster?

My kind, I guess.

"And then I discovered that you obsess about my throbbing masculine presence."

"You're never going to let me live that down, are you?"

"No." He shakes his head, pressing his hips gently against me. "Never. I can't. Because I'm so obsessed with your throbbing feminine presence."

My feminine presence is throbbing at this exact moment. Warmth spools throughout my entire body, boiling at my core. "You should talk more about that."

He chuckles. Runs his hands slowly up the curve of my waist, over my ribs and back down. With each pass, his hands creep forward. I might purr. "Your hair looks like a sunset. Your face is the most expressive I've ever seen. Your ass is . . . out of this world. But . . . for me . . . it's that mouth, always waiting to say exactly what it thinks. Other things about that mouth, too."

"Other things?" I'm not even sure what he's saying anymore.

I'm a thread strung tight between his fingers, vibrating with his movement.

"Hmm." The sound is a rumbled scrape over each and every one of my nerve endings. "The color of the lips, the shape. The way you purse them when you're deep in thought. Like a kiss could answer any question lodged in your brain."

Right now, it feels like it just might. "I'm very deep in thought at the moment. Drowning in it, in fact."

The corner of his mouth curls like a cat's tail. "I'm always happy to rescue a damsel in distress."

He lowers his mouth until his lips almost reach mine. I can't resist. "The distress is in my pants."

"You aren't wearing any pants."

"Maybe that's why I'm distressed." My lips brush against his as I speak. My tongue darts out to trace the seam, to nip at the full fleshiness of his lower lip.

One broad hand traces down my back, cupping my butt as his fingers pass over it, and trail directly over my core. "Hmm. Yes, you feel distressed. Maybe I can help."

I'm absolutely positive of the fact.

He tosses me back on my bunk so quickly I gasp out all my breath before I bounce on the thin mattress and almost crash into the bulkhead just beyond. My legs dangle off the side of the bed, bare toes almost touching the floor. "I don't think you'll fit."

There are two possible places he won't fit . . . one of them being my bunk. The long slow blink he gives indicates that he's already jumped ahead to the other one. But then he smiles sticky and thick as syrup. "I don't need to fit."

He steps toward the edge of the bed, looming over me as his thighs wedge between my legs. Then, when I'm again about to question the logistics, he drops to his knees between my legs, grabbing my ass and hauling it directly to the edge of the mattress. My mouth goes completely dry, and if he likes me talking, he's going to have some complaints about the next few moments.

His hands creep up to my hips and ease my extraordinarily sexy plain black boy shorts down, eyes locked on me like I'm his absolute favorite dessert. Except people who look like Arcadio probably don't have a favorite dessert. Maybe he's looking at me like I'm his favorite vegetable.

If so, he must fucking adore lettuce.

"Beautiful." He rumbles before nudging my thighs farther apart. He leans over me, delivering a long drugging kiss. Trailing his lips down my jaw, my neck, my collarbone. Then, as if by a miracle, my shirt has disappeared and reappears, landing on my desk in a crumpled ball.

I'm briefly bothered by lying splayed before him like some sort of naked vegetable buffet, but then he continues kissing his way down my torso, licking a fiery path up the crest of a breast until he reaches the nipple, which he teases into a sharp point, and when I can barely handle it anymore, nips gently with glossy white teeth. My breath catches in my throat.

He continues his path south. The curve of my stomach. The top of my thigh.

Wait. My thigh?

Why is he wasting time on my thighs when there's somewhere else in the neighborhood that desperately wants a visit? I run my hands through thick black hair, trace down over broad shoulders, and try to shove him into a better position.

He doesn't move.

"You need an anatomy lesson if you think that's going to get the job done." I gasp because I just might be on fire, and he could put it out if he just moved a little bit to the side.

"Patience."

"No. It's Temperance. Patience is probably out in that canyon eating truth-plants and people meat."

Those teeth take another sharp nip of my inner thigh and I bite back a yelp at the fiery flare that plumbs through my body. "Let's not talk about Patience."

"You brought her up."

"And clearly, you've never met. You don't have even passing familiarity with that virtue." His breath fans out over me. I curl my hands into his hair yet again, lost in the tactile fall of it against my skin.

"None. None at all. Stop torturing me."

"Maybe I like torturing you."

Maybe I like it, too. A little gasp squeaks out as he moves closer to the sweet spot. Presses a kiss where my thigh meets my groin. He licks one hot strip up the center of me and I almost combust. He licks again. A third time, and then his mouth latches over my core and his tongue plays as though he's learning a new language.

My back bows, fingers clenching in his hair. The bunk lights appear to be malfunctioning, little specks of firework fly over my vision, flickering and dying as every nerve in my body comes alive and stands at attention. The rough fabric of my sheets scrapes over my flesh. The hard frame of the bunk presses against my calves. Beads of sweat trace the valley between my breasts, and through it all, he does not relent.

I might kill him if he does.

My body shudders, nearly out of control, and he picks up the tempo, tongue flicking and one broad finger snakes its way within me. I shatter like broken glass. Simply come to pieces as he plays me like an instrument.

When I return to my body, the grin he gives me is like he's the first person to discover sex and, thus, is the best at it. He might be right. I mumble something unintelligible.

He'll never let me live it down if he knows how good that was. I'm pretty sure I can't hide it.

"That's been two for me and none for you." There, those are actual words.

"A man doesn't like to assume."

Bullshit. This man makes assumptions about everything ten steps ahead. It's part of what I enjoy about him. "Assume that if you don't get yourself naked by the time I regain the use of my legs, I'll do it myself."

He licks the shell of my ear before returning to my mouth, hot and skilled and just a little bit out of control. And then, like a miracle, he follows my suggestion and shucks those lovely lightweight exercise pants to reveal a spectacular erection.

Also legs and stuff.

They're nice.

Let's get back to the erection.

His dick is like a work of art: wide and long, a bead of fluid pearling the tip. Slight upward curve. Beautiful, which I'll never tell him because, for some reason, men don't like to hear that word describing them. I manage to get to my feet, advancing until I can lean against him, licking my own trail up his chest to his chin and finally his lips.

I wrap my fingers around him, velvet on steel, and pump a time or two, experimentally. Before I can get any further, he catches me under the arms, lifting until our heads are level and kisses me even more senseless than I already am. I wrap my legs around his waist, reveling in the feeling of all that hot, hard, smooth skin against my own. His chest hair lightly abrades my nipples. I rub against him, thrilling in the sensation. His hot breath sends shivers over my ear. "Are you—?"

"Yes. Nanos. No babies or diseases for me. Are you?" I can't even remember why I ever thought this would be a bad idea. It's probably the best idea I've ever had.

I'm a genius.

A genius who is hungry for another orgasm.

"I am." He replies with the magic words. I tighten my legs around his waist, rubbing against him uncontrollably. I want him. I want this.

I anchor one arm over his shoulders and reach down with the other, wrapping it around him again. I work my fingers up and down until he captures my hand in his own and poises himself at my entrance, rubbing his tip back and forth in my folds.

"You feel amazing." He nudges his way within me as he speaks, and for a moment, I lose track of words. I pant in pleasure, dig my nails into his shoulders. He snaps his hips up, thrusting fully within me. His eyes are dark and dazed. I love the expression on his face, the strength of his body around me.

I suck in a breath, overwhelmed by the feeling. Not just the physical sensation either. The *feelings*. This just started and already I'm halfway to drowning in him. Exposed and vulnerable and *needing*.

He'll go back to his Family when we're done with the mission. This will be a passing adventure, complete with a fling. It's more than a fling with me. I should know because I almost exclusively have flings. I ought to protect myself. Should build some distance.

I don't want to. I've rarely in my life made the smart choice and I'm not going to start now. I'm going to forget the future and enjoy the present with everything I have. Caro and Itzel and Micah will be here when it's over. I won't be alone.

And I'll have had this. I'm already halfway back to the precipice, teetering near the edge. "You feel amazing, too. You'd feel even more amazing if you were moving faster."

"I don't want to hurt you." The words hiss from his mouth, like he's clenching his jaw.

"Have our interactions ever made you think that I am in any way fragile?" Psychologically, maybe, but not physically. I use my legs around his hips to lift and let myself drop down on him.

He slams up to meet me. The dam has burst, all technique, all artifice set aside, and I wouldn't have it any other way. Nothing has ever felt this good. I am surrounded by him, by the masculine tones of his scent, his skin, the rumble of pleasure in his voice. I turn molten, liquid and scorching with pleasure. He pistons into me, smooth and rhythmic until I crash over the edge, starbursts exploding behind my eyes. When I open my mouth to shout my pleasure, his lips slam down on my own and muffle the cries and his thrusts become erratic.

Finally, he makes one last deep push and it's a good thing we're already kissing because I'm there to muffle his own groan of pleasure. We freeze there, leaning against the bulkhead of my bunk, sharing breath as we come down from the heights.

"That was . . . something," I say when I finally am back inside my body instead of spinning crazily through the ether. "Fantastic."

I start to uncoil myself from around his body but his hard hand wraps around my thigh, holding it in place. His other hand is flat on my back, stable, and Arcadio smiles that deadly grin, teeth flashing white against the beard. "There's a long time until your watch. We're just getting started."

CHAPTER 15

There is no basking in the afterglow. Especially not after I made such a big deal about people being on watch. Instead, I go to my shift, nerves on fire, and spend a while staring into the black, hoping that no Nakatomis show up, and trying not to think about what just happened. Then I return to my bunk, which is triggering on nearly every sensory level there is, and stare at the ceiling doing nothing *except* thinking about what just happened.

None of the thinking is of any use, just the panicked pacing of a creature locked in a small cage who wants to escape but isn't sure what that even looks like. Nothing is clear, except if I spent a day twisted up about how great a kisser he was, I have no idea what's in store for me now because—if he's a great kisser, he's a *fantastic* everything else.

I am so fucked. Both ways.

I'm finally about to fall asleep when an ear-shattering scream comes from Ven's old bunk. I'm out of my bunk and across the hall, blaster in hand, in an instant.

"Generosity!" I pound on the door.

The scream cuts off like she was choked.

"Generosity," I try again. "Everything all right?"

If it's not all right, I'm going to have to return to the helm to unlock her door. Considering I'm the only one with access to the bunk, I'm fairly certain no one is in there murdering her as we speak.

"I'm fine." Her voice is level, emotionless, and hoarse.

All righty. "Do you need assistance?"

"I'm fine."

"Is 'I'm fine' code for 'There's a blaster to my neck, please rescue me?'"

"I'm fine, Temper."

I haven't ever heard anyone say "I'm fine" more than I do. Sounds like she means it as much as I usually do, which means not at all. "I guess . . . yell if you need me."

"I won't need you."

She doesn't yell again.

. . . . .

Judging by how she looks in the morning, it's because she didn't sleep. We all sit in the mess to eat our breakfast and plan the next day. Because the previous day was particularly harrowing, Caro cooked a real-food breakfast instead of our usual protein paste. Biscuits and dried meats and beans from the hydroponic garden. Even some fresh sliced tomatoes.

Generosity devours them like she's never seen food before. Micah's scanner found her to be undernourished but in remarkably good shape despite it. She refused to let him do a physical examination, and he deemed the medscan sufficient, not knowing exactly what kind of trauma she's dealing with.

Itzel is composed but a little droopy. Caro keeps up a steady stream of conversation to try to drown out the awkward silence everyone else is contributing. Arcadio's knee presses against mine in a way I would have found irksome yesterday and I find startlingly intimate today. I try very hard not to look at his face because I'm afraid I'll blush if I do. Probably the whole crew is staring and wondering why their captain is being so fucking *weird*.

All that goes by the wayside when Generosity—or whatever her real, pre-cult name is—shoves aside her food and stands up, wiping her palms on the spare coveralls Caro gave her. Without all that shit in her hair, she's a blonde with a braid about as thick as my wrist. A smattering of freckles accentuates the bridge of her nose, and she has a tiny gap between her front teeth. She studiously avoids eye contact with all of us with the same discipline I'm applying to Escajeda, but her jaw is set and stubborn.

Arcadio. I can't think of his talented lips and call him Escajeda at the same time.

Micah leans back in his chair. At face value, he's lazily relaxed but he's actually bracing his weight to respond quickly. He modulates his voice to be as soothing as it ever is, which, for someone as perpetually cranky as Micah, undershoots calm and lands somewhere around mildly irritated as he studies our unwilling guest. "Where do you think you're going?"

Golden-brown eyes dart to him, then away. Her lips tighten and her jaw clenches as she studies the bright-orange bandages that ring her wrists. "I—" Her eyes flicker between us all, light as a flying insect but unwilling to land until she hits me. Then it collides with the force of a spaceship touching down—careful, but heavy. "Thank you for what you did. It was . . . kind. But I think you misunderstood."

Micah nods as though this all makes sense. "You volunteered, then?"

She pauses, jaw goes even harder. It's like she's angry at herself for being where she is right now. When her voice comes out, it's stiff. "Yes. I volunteered."

"Lie." Micah says it flatly. Also . . . obviously.

She glares obdurately at him. "Fine. I have unfinished business."

Which is a damned weird thing for a member of a cult to say. I learn forward. "Unfinished business?"

"People I'm responsible for. Who need me. Who will be punished if I'm gone. So I have to go back." She grimaces like breakfast is trying to crawl its way back up her throat. "Maybe apologize."

The way she says the word "apologize" is like it is particularly thick leather that she's trying to chew through. I knew she'd try to go back. I'm not sure I fully conceptualized that it might be to *apologize* for having the temerity to be upset at being tied up and tortured. Rashahan provided Micah with tools but not painkillers. It's even more confusing because this woman clearly doesn't actually *want* to go back.

"If you're afraid of a reprisal, you shouldn't be." Micah cuts to the meat of it with his usual aplomb. "They assume you are either dead or taken by the Nakatomi Family. Either way, no one will be punished because you're gone."

She shakes her head, like she hasn't even heard what he said but denies it anyway. Itzel has silently slunk from her own position on the bench by the table and is now blocking the passageway that leads to the cargo bay and the outside. She leans against the bulkhead and uses one of her daggers to peel the skin off a small citrus fruit we grew in the hydroponic garden. Caro looks around the room, like she's hoping someone will kill the tension. Arcadio eats his beans like there isn't a cultist at the table who would rather hang out with a cult than with people as demonstrably fun and interesting as we are. His knee is still pressed against mine.

Not that I notice it.

The downside of being captain is that I get to give her the bad news. "You can't go back. Not now. When we freed you—no, don't interrupt, we *did* free you—and Micah, we burned any goodwill they might have for us, and the only way we survive doing that is by framing the Nakatomis, who, to be fair, absolutely would have slaughtered everyone in that cave for fun just because the Children got too close to whatever it is the Family is working on. If you still want to go back to the Children when we are ready to leave Herschel Two, we'll leave you to them."

"I won't tell them. You don't know this, but I'm shockingly good at keeping secrets."

I shake my head. Micah's eyebrow raises and he looks at her like she's a puzzle box and he wants to find out what's inside. I hope with every tiny scrap of optimism I possess—which is maybe a quarter of a scrap—that we can convince her to see reason. She stares at me for a long time, jaw working like she's chewing on her rebuttal and it tastes bitter. Something I don't quite recognize flits through her eyes. There and gone.

When she agrees, it's too easy. She's going to try to run the second our backs are turned. Micah catches my eye and gives a tiny nod. He'll keep an eye on her. I make it easier on him.

"Micah, stay on the ship. Keep an eye on Generosity and keep both of yourselves away from any other prying eyes since you're supposed to be dead or captured. Caro, set the drones up on an automated low-altitude crosshatch for phydium. While they run, you and Itzel will join Arcadio and myself on the Nakatomi hunt."

I return to my bunk, dress in my shiny new combat armor, holster a blaster, slide a knife into the sheath on the thigh of the armor, wear the boots that hide my lockpicks, and then head down to the armory. At full power, my blaster barely penetrates their armor. It might cause discomfort, but it won't help me win a fight.

I heft a pulse launcher and place it over my shoulder, so it rests along my spine. With a quick manipulation of the strap, it will swing under my arm and throw a wall of energy at an adversary. It's not made to penetrate armor. It's made to push it.

When I rejoin the others in the cargo bay, I see Arcadio has had the same idea—although his pulse launcher is more modern than my own. His eyes clock my launcher, and he smiles, like we have our own secret deadly-weapons joke. Great minds consider similar mayhem or something.

I wish we'd had time to linger after last night. What would it be like to wake up beside him? Warm, I bet. Considering my bunk, probably also crampy.

Worth it, though. I don't know if this was a one-night thing or if it's the start of something more. I know which one I want. I also know it's foolish to want what I want.

Caro pulls a thin stylus out of her hair and uses it to sweep something from her datapad to a nearby holo-port, and a three-dimensional map of Kaiaiesto and the subsurface formations cascades into being. "I talked with Arcadio about the results of his surveying and my own." The subterranean river that slides beneath the canyon twists out and collides with the mouth of several lava tubes before it curls deep, nearly touching a tube that reaches the central core of the volcano. Several violent fissures crack the inside of the mountain, unresolvable because they blend with a blur that coats the center of the hologram, the area directly beneath the volcano, almost like a fog.

"Was the drone malfunctioning?" Itzel leans closer to the hologram.

"You get deep enough, the magma fucks with the image. Even the heat from it can mess up the scan, which is why we have these regions." She points the stylus at the edges of the blur where some slight formations are visible but wavy and then moves the pointer to a different tube. "This is the one we blew up yesterday. The one that runs almost parallel to it is the one you and Arcadio explored. This third tube is the one that opens in the Children's territory. Generosity has informed me that its use is reserved for Rashahan and his inner circle."

"We don't have to worry about that tube anyway." Arcadio

points at a distortion in the smooth line of the tunnel. "It appears to have been collapsed at some point. The fact that the Nakatomis haven't destroyed the Children yet is another indication. If Children were infringing on their territory, there wouldn't be Children anymore."

"So, the three tubes closest to us aren't good options for a sneak attack. Unless we wait outside the door in the middle tube to ambush them." It just can't ever be easy.

"Our best chance for an unattended entrance is here." Caro points at another tube to the south. "We haven't seen any action around it, but the scan shows it running very close to the blocked-off Nakatomi tube with one point of intersection after the iron door."

"What's the catch?"

"The mouth of the tube is caved in. But it runs directly alongside the river in that region and the layer of earth between the two is quite thin. If we swim under it, we should be able to break through that way."

That sounds awful. Maybe no one will shoot at us, but we might all drown. I'm not sure if that is a fair trade. I wince, gesturing for Caro to zoom the hologram around the region of interest. "You say the earth is thin. If it's so thin, how are we going to walk on it without it collapsing?"

"Thin in geological terms. It will support our weight even if we all jump up and down."

"How are we breaking through it without alerting them to an explosion?"

"There is regular seismic activity. I can time the blast so any signal is confusing." Caro pats the pack on her shoulders gently. "The submersible can be controlled from the surface, via swarm signal points."

"Swarm signal points?" Arcadio leans down next to me to look at the zoomed holo. His shoulder brushes against my own. I almost put a hand on it to steady my weight but catch myself. If there's any way to keep the rest of the crew from realizing what happened last night, I'll try it. Caro seems oblivious but that's probably because she's been focused on this puzzle.

If we survive this mission, I really need to give them a raise. Let Caro hit that casino floor for a month. Let Itzel do whatever she does on-station, which seems to be any willing person who will have her, male or female. Let Micah lose himself in dark corners with notorious ex-gang members who seem to be his only other friends.

Or maybe get us all some therapy, because when I lay it out like that, even our downtime is filled with unhealthy coping mechanisms.

"A dotted line of swarm drones that relay the signal to the submersible. It allows us to keep some distance, so we aren't there when the earth gives way." Caro lights up a pattern near the mouth on one of the lava tubes.

I sigh. "I miss the days when we were just searching for phydium. Regular scouting doesn't involve explosions."

"What missions were you on?" Caro finalizes an entry, wipes the hologram, and folds the datapad before slipping it in a cargo pocket of her pants. "The only time when things didn't explode was when there was no one to cause problems. Even then, about half the time, something blew up."

Perhaps I've colored my recollections to be much more pleasant than they actually are. If you think about scouting much, you'd never do it. Unless that's your only option. It wasn't mine, though. There are other things for the banished to do.

For instance, I could have joined a cult, like Generosity.

CHAPTER 16

. . . .

The swim to the punctured tube wall is uneventful. Itzel and Caro go first, sending little purple flares on the trail of swarm drones floating in the river to mark the path. While we wait for the two of them to space out, Arcadio gives my hand a slight squeeze underwater. I ruin the sweet moment by flailing around because I assume it's some sort of heretofore unknown river eel trying to kill me.

It's sad that my initial assumption is death by eel instead of gestures of affection.

Once he's done laughing and I'm done floundering, I splash him. I can even see to aim through the glow of the drone. When he draws back his arm to splash me back, I duck under, grab his ankle, and yank down. Even in the water, I don't move him much. When he pulls me up with a hand hooked under each arm, I expect another splash. His lips crash into mine in a short hard kiss.

"My turn to make the swim." I kiss him back and break away. The distance is short enough to not require oxygen and a regulator, which should make it less terrifying but actually makes it more. The purple pulses are easy enough to follow, but the thick darkness everywhere else presses in on my temples, my eyes, my lungs. I push forward in smooth strokes, grateful for this new armor that allows efficiency of movement and doesn't drag me down to the bottom of the river. Just when the lack of oxygen hits, I arrive at the last swarm drone, this one green-lit, marking the equally dark hole above.

I gulp in air when I break through the surface, very grateful that Caro taught me to swim and insisted that I practice whenever I could. Most space-based people can't swim. It's not like stations are wasteful enough to have large pools of water for people to dirty up. Someone grabs my wrists and anchors them as I pull myself out of the river. When I finally flop on solid ground, I'm grateful to be back on land even if the land in question is a closed-off tunnel under the earth. "That was a little longer than you led me to believe."

"You made it. Whining is unbecoming of a captain. This behavior goes public, you'll lose your credibility." Caro flips my face shield down and night vision flares to life around me. The lava tube looks like a lava tube. Bigger than the ones we've been in before. I might be able to park the Quest in this tube if it opened onto the land. Itzel collects samples from the inside of the tube wall. Caro crouches in front of me, her own face shield down. I know it's her because Caro has a more solid build than Itzel. And because Caro wouldn't care about samples in the wall.

"You don't scare me. It wouldn't exactly be a headline to have another bad story about me in the press."

She makes a *tsk*ing noise with her tongue on the back of her teeth. When she speaks, her voice filters through my coms earpiece audio—a little icon in the corner of my faceplate screen indicates we're in a private channel. "Good point. I don't think the Flores Family would publish a normal gossip piece about you. Unless something truly scandalous happened . . . like, say, hooking up with an Escajeda while on a top-secret mission."

The air rushes out of my mouth in an exhalation loud enough that it doesn't matter that the mask covers my face. Her soft laughter breaks through her own mask. "The Quest is basically constructed of tissue paper. The walls are thin. There was a lot of . . . banging . . . coming from your bunk. And the strangest sounds. When Generosity started screaming, I assumed it was you."

I must look as appalled as I feel because she laughs harder.

"Your secret's safe with me. But it won't be safe with anyone else if they get a gander at the two of you when you're together. You could cut the tension with a plasma blade, and the looks he sends you? Almost as hot as one."

"That's not all that's hot as a plasma blade," I grudgingly admit. "It's temporary, Caro. Don't make a big deal out of it."

"Doesn't seem like you want it to be temporary. You're glowing. I've never seen you glow. Certainly not with Ven. You were uncertain about him for a reason. Because it wasn't right. Don't wreck this because you jumped to conclusions."

They're my favorite thing to jump to.

"He's from a Family, Caro. That doesn't work. I should know, I used to be in one. They aren't for keeping. Not for someone like me."

"Maybe. Maybe not. You'll never know unless you try."

She's never been in a Family, so she can't know what the pressure is like to marry an equal. Fuck, even to date one. You are your associations, and no one wants to be associated with a ragtag scouting crew barely out of poverty on the edge of nowhere. Or that same crew's notoriously banished captain. Our lives don't mix. I literally legally cannot go home with him because the vast majority of Escajeda territory is off-limits to me.

Maybe if I was still a Reed. If I was the sort of person who made a difference—who influenced the future like people in Families do. When you scout, you have a job, but you don't have a *purpose*. Growing up, I knew that people would rely on me for their livelihood even if I wasn't the heir. I knew that I was responsible for safeguarding them. For building the tech. For guiding the future of our Family and even the direction of all Families. The expectations were limitless.

Currently they are limitless in that no one has any expectations whatsoever.

I'm saved from having to reply by said Escajeda bursting forth from the river behind me. He levers himself easily up into the tunnel. Caro's private-channel icon vanishes, and the group channel activates, linking the four of us in audio as well as shared faceplate metrics. Caro indicated the path ahead with a thin white line overlaid on the ground. An overall schematic of the tubes and Kaiaiesto is in the top left corner of my faceplate with a small green dot indicating our location.

Itzel feels around the edges of the lava tube, deft fingers poking in the crevices. "There's some form of biological life growing in the tunnel walls. Like an anemone but more mobile. If a slug and an anemone had a baby. Blends in smoothly with the hardened magma on the walls but, when I apply pressure, it's soft and spongy."

I reach around her and press on the wall. My gloves reduce sensation, but my ring finger slides into something fleshy and wet, about the size of the bottom of a drinking glass. Gross.

It sucks gently on my finger until I yank it away. Even grosser. I'm adding lava tubes lined with squishy mouths to my list of "never again" geological formations.

"Are they going to be a problem?" I ask her, wiping my glove off on my thigh.

"They're fascinating!" Itzel says, scraping two into a tube on her belt. She stretches for a particularly large one high on the wall that appears to be growing pieces of rock on its surface. When she can't quite reach, Arcadio offers her a boost, holding her aloft as she retrieves the squishy thing. She absently pats him on the top of the head when done and he lowers her to the ground, looking bemused.

"I think you're confusing 'fascinating' with 'icky.'" A lot of things are fascinating. Brand-new weapons systems. Discovering another person's secrets. Taking in a sunrise on a new horizon.

Not this.

We make our way down the tube, silently. After a bit, Caro sends a signal through our faceplates indicating the point where our lava tube runs closest to the neighboring one, and we pause for her to direct a high-powered laser at the tunnel wall. She outlines a small doorway, steps back, and points to Arcadio. He kicks out the loose block of hardened magma and we pause for a moment, listening in the dark for the sound of running Nakatomi boots. None come, so Caro sends a few of the smallest of the swarm drones to map out the space in stealth mode.

While they map, Caro cuts two slits in the block and thins it so that we can easily put it back into place to create the impression of a solid wall, albeit with a tiny peephole. Once we're all on the Nakatomi side, Arcadio and I heft the scrap through the hole into our original tube and set the camouflaged door into position. As we step back, his hand trails over the small of my back.

Itzel's voice is a whisper on the coms, tinny as the privacy shielding impacts the audio. "No anemone here."

"We aren't here for anemone, we're here for Escajeda's brother," Caro whispers back. "If there were anemone, the Nakatomis have probably killed them all."

Itzel pauses for a long time and then finally answers. "That other tube was an isolated ecosystem, right by the river. It must have developed in seclusion." She gasps. "We cut it open and now it's exposed to everything else."

I'm saved having to respond by the first mapping result from the swarm. It's a more detailed map than what our satellites produced. The schematic in the corner of my faceplate sharpens in detail. An energy signature comes from about twenty paces down the tube. Probably a motion sensor. It likely won't pick up anything as small as the drones. Motion sensors don't register bugs because if they did, they'd be pretty fucking useless. You can't maintain security if some gnat keeps activating your defenses.

Caro takes the lead, datapad out as she remote-scans the bank of small sensors embedded in the tunnel wall. A muffled snort weaves through the coms. She taps out a command and pushes it out of her datapad toward the sensors. They blink off for a second, just long enough for us to pass underneath them.

"Standard Nakatomi tech," she explains her disdain. "They didn't even bother to etherwall it. It looks like the crew here is very confident they won't be found. Chikao Nakatomi would shit fuel pellets if he saw how lax their security is."

Arcadio chuckles. I smile in the privacy of my helmet. He likes my crew. Which he should; my crew is fabulous. His voice in the coms sounds like a smile. "You don't assign basic workers to a clandestine mission if you can't afford to lose them. They'll have competent leaders, maybe scientists, but they don't expect any resistance beyond the cult, which means they probably don't have many soldiers."

There's a moment of silence where I assume all of us consider the fact that the Escajeda sent Arcadio and his brother on a clandestine mission—which means he considers his sons expendable. Also us.

Caro signals that it's safe to continue and we sneak down the tube. Unlike a usual cave, which is a consistent cool-wet temperature, it gets warmer the deeper we go. At the point I notice the first trickles of sweat creeping their way beneath my body armor, Caro sends a solid red light to the corner of our displays. If it were flashing, it would mean immediate danger. Solid, it just means potential danger. A view from the drones takes over part of my face shield.

This tube ends just ahead of us, and it opens into a massive fissure. It's essentially a cavern in the midst of the mountain, lined with jagged rock but finished by Nakatomi portable buildings and a leveled floor. A three-story structure follows the shape of the fissure, made with memory metal. A sheet of the material can be folded, crumpled, or rolled like fabric, but when exposed to a certain wavelength of light in the blue region, it will spring back to its initial shape and stay there until it's deactivated by another light source.

You might think that's a flaw, because natural light contains blue light, but the intensity combined with the wavelength is key. It takes a lot to lock and unlock memory metal. The intensity must be ramped up at a very specific rate and then activated by leaping to the activation wattage. No one's building a skyscraper out of the stuff, because one terrorist having a cranky day could destroy the whole building, but memory metal is very useful for situations like this, when you need a structure for convenience and don't antici-pate a threat.

A lot of frontiers people and scouts use it because it's a great way to make a portable yet solid building. I'd love some, but one sheet is probably more expensive than the entire *Quest*.

Most things are more expensive than the entire *Quest*. I really should rename it. I don't like the reminder of Ven that hangs over all of us.

Smaller portable structures perch on the fissure walls like tree houses, connected by metal walkways. The far end of the fissure is barely visible around the central building, but it seems to open on an even larger space, crosshatched with metal beams. Several moderately sized utility vehicles sit on a makeshift road at the base of the fissure, laden with cargo mysteriously concealed under heavy tarps. There's something in that distant chamber, but I don't have an angle for it.

"They have an evil-mastermind volcano-base," I breathe out in wonder. "That is so . . . *neat*."

The view switches to another drone, deeper in the fissure, pointing down at the top of the largest building. It's edged with thin metal railings that end in wicked points. Two people sit on the roof in portable camp chairs. Both wear dark-blue uniforms with the Nakatomi-dragon crest on the lapels. Both drink from aluminum bottles of fermented alcohol stamped with a fish on the side.

The drone sneaks closer and begins to capture their audio. They speak in Akentimogo, a language common in the core of Nakatomi territory. Nakatomis pay to keep it out of most translators, so odds are fairly high that I'm the only one who recognizes what they're saying. Well . . . me and Arcadio. I doubt the Escajedas skimp on translations. Now that I think about it, he probably has the exact same Reed translator that I do.

"You think he knows we're up there?" The man, I call him Hero because he looks like he thinks he is one, peers over one of the railings cautiously. I translate for the others in a low voice.

"I think he barely realizes where *he* is, much less where we are. That type won't remember you at all unless you personally inconvenience him. Then he'll make it his life's mission to ruin you." The woman makes a sour face. I call her Serpent because she looks like she could be one. I mean that as a compliment.

"You sound like a bitter ex." Hero laughs a little too loud for this to be a clandestine meeting and Serpent's censuring glance tells me she agrees.

"Laugh all you want. You don't want to attract his attention. You don't want to be in his circle of trust." Serpent stands and folds her chair with a definitive click. "You'd be naive to think that just because he appears to be on our side now, he's an ally. That one will take any path to the top he can, and he isn't a Nakatomi. He isn't *your* ticket to advancement."

With that, she leaves the roof, and her colleague finishes his drink and cools his heels up there just long enough to let her descend before he leaves.

"There's someone in charge here—in some capacity—who isn't a Nakatomi," I pass on to the rest of the group. "They don't trust him. More than that, they're afraid of him."

"It's got to be a Pierce. They've been allies for at least thirty years." Arcadio is close behind me, doing that looming space-invading thing that he does. I've started to suspect that it's his way of covering my back, something that is both ludicrous and oddly endearing. "It makes sense. They could provide the energy—and they're excellent at covering things up. There have been rumors for years that they perform illegal human experimentation in their labs—trying to make mods that do things the Chandras won't even touch."

Those growers on the last planet were banished but had Pierce coloring—the kind they genetically build in. It's very possible they used banished citizens for plausible deniability in plankat farming, looking for the secret to building brains without damaging them. I deeply hope not.

"So, not only do we have a top-secret volcano-base, but we also have two-fifths of the Five plotting together in said top-secret volcano-base." I state the obvious just in case anyone wasn't aware exactly how deep the shit surrounding us is.

"Why would they both take over a volcano on a planet only settled by a weird cult?" Caro points out as she controls the drones via hand mapping, tapping and twisting her fingers in the air in a language that even my translator chip can't hack. "What's the benefit to them? Ohhh, unless there actually *is* phydium somewhere."

I shake my head. "If there was phydium nearby, Itzel's sensors would have found it by now. She took all sorts of samples. This is something else. The Nakatomis are expanding under the radar, as you pointed out. Maybe they teamed up with the Pierce Family for a larger plan—which has to be done in secret if it's something as big as this seems."

Everyone knows they're allies, but there's a big difference between allies and collaborators. When two Families in the Five get close, the other three team up against them. Those two get dissipated and two of the Ten rise to take their place. It's what everyone in the Ten waits for. Greed always wins out and no house in the Five lasts very long.

The Chandra and the Flores Families have been around the longest. Chandra because they stay out of everyone's business and keep to their lane. No one wants to go after the people who control their medicine. Flores because they meddle with *everyone*, but they control most media outlets, so they also control the narrative. Each of them has been around about four generations. Escajeda next at two and a half. Nakatomi and Pierce are both at around one and a half. It's a transition period where they've each been helmed by the visionary who brought them to the Five and now that visionary is passing responsibility to the chosen officers of the next generation.

"Good point, except my samples were on the surface. I have no idea whether or not there's phydium down *here*. Could Pierce be using the volcano for energy in a different way?" Itzel creeps forward to the edge of the lava tube, low to the ground as she studies the construction in the fissure. It's a fair assumption. Energy is Pierce's personal monopoly.

Caro shakes her head, probably realizes that doesn't translate via helmet coms, and then says, "Maybe, but besides being big, this volcano isn't very special. I'm not sure what it could do for them that millions of others in the universe don't do. Or why it would need to be a secret. I think this particular volcano was chosen for camouflage. Even if someone scans the planet, the magma disrupts the instrumentation and hides whatever's happening."

"Bringing us back to the main question: what are the Nakatomis planning that requires camouflage?" I follow Itzel, moving down to my belly near the mouth of the lava tube. This tube opens about one-third of the way up the fissure wall, putting us above the makeshift road but below the rooftop the drones spied upon. Caro and Escajeda join us. Escajeda's elbow just brushes against my own.

"Your armor is close enough to Nakatomi-style that it will pass cursory inspection." Caro indicates two patrolling officers down below. "Except for the crest. Nakatomis love a decorative crest embellishment."

I adjust the bandolier around my shoulders, and it blocks the area on my armor where their crests rest. "I'm going down. The rest of you, try to gather as much information as possible with the drones and stay hidden in the tubes. If we're taken, it's probably a safer bet to get the fuck out, set the *Quest* on a programmed course for Landsdown, and as soon as you're in range, hail the Escajeda and tell him what's going on."

They nod so earnestly that I know they're lying.

"Great plan, except I'll be going with you. My armor is as close a match as your own." Arcadio's voice brooks no argument and I find that I don't even want to snap back. I want him with me. I barely recognize myself. Usually, I'd retort just for the sake of being contrary.

"That's fine. Caro and Itzel, I'm serious. Flee if you need to. They're not going to kill us. Not right away at least." They won't kill *Arcadio*. He's worth even more than his brother. Me, they'll probably huck into the volcano just to shut me up. It's been suggested as a possibility before.

I can't see through the face shields and Itzel and Caro's body language gives nothing away but they both agree and that's the best I can do.

The descent isn't as challenging as I thought it would be. There are enough handholds in the rock that we can scramble down unnoticed. Once we're on the road, Arcadio and I slip into the posture of patrolling soldiers, weapons carefully blocking our crest-free armor. His arm just brushes mine. A little closer than two patrolling soldiers usually walk, but authenticity is overrated. Sometimes soldiers spark each other, to use Itzel's parlance. No one even blinks as we pass. Caro was right; they aren't sparing their best and brightest for this endeavor.

"I haven't seen any Pierces." I keep my voice as low as possible. Arcadio hums an assent.

If they're partners in this project, where are they? Nakatomi uniform after Nakatomi uniform passes us, but no shocks of Pierce-blond hair disrupt the black. Pierces are blond, tan-skinned, and brown-eyed. They tend to be tall and rawboned. Generosity looks more like a Pierce than anyone I've seen in this volcano.

Our patrol leads us close to the central building and we take advantage of a rockfall and the slope of the wall to press against the headquarters. Voices filter through the thin, portable metal walls. I recognize one of them. It itches in a corner of my mind, but I can't quite place it. I have heard nearly everyone in a primary Five Family speak at one point in time or another, either before my banishment or on the streams. I glance toward Arcadio to see if he recognizes it before I remember that I can't see his face through the armor. He gestures at the thin panel of windows above us and offers me a boost.

As he lifts me, I catch the edge of the conversation.

". . . Missile lock has been optimized but is still restricted by planetary rotation. It limits high-profile target opportunities." A voice I don't recognize. When I get high enough, I see several people at the front of a room, presenting a holo to the others. Scientists or engineers, then. Meaning, the others are the bosses.

"We need better targeting. Is widening the caldera a possibility?" This from a Nakatomi leaning back in her chair, legs crossed with sharp precision in a sleek mercury-colored dress that could not be less appropriate for the venue. Kaori. The heir apparent for this next generation's handoff.

Arcadio got it wrong; they *are* risking the big guns. Apparently, literally big guns if the schematic on the holo is right.

The Nakatomi Family is building a massive weapon inside Kaiaiesto. One powerful enough to shoot space-based targets. Maybe very distant ones. Kaori plays with a stylus as she leans forward, blocking the other person on the receiving end of the presentation. I can't quite make them out. Male. Bigger than Kaori although that wouldn't be hard. She's a delicate little thing.

In the seediest parts of the most disreputable way stations, they call her the spider. No one needs bulk when they have venom. In the nicest parts of the way stations, they call her ma'am and do their best to get out of her way.

"Potentially, but a change in the form of the caldera may alert anyone pointing satellites our way," the scientist replies, gesturing around the top of the hologram. "The Escajedas specifically are paying attention to Herschel Two. They wouldn't miss a change like that."

"If we move quickly enough, the Escajedas won't be a problem for any of us anymore. Pablo's usefulness has diminished. I expected an Escajeda warship on a rescue mission in time for the grand unveiling. Nothing. Clearly, we should have captured the daughter." That familiar voice comes again. It's itching at my brain. Kaori leans back and it hits me like a punch to the face. I'm winded. I rear back from the window and only Arcadio's quick reflexes keep me from falling back to the ground. He fumbles with my weight for a moment and then lowers me.

"What happened?" His rough voice is a whisper through the coms. His fingers are tight on my shoulders like he's afraid I'll swoon or go screaming off into the deepest part of the volcano.

I might.

"It's not the Pierce Family." My voice shakes no matter how I try to steady it. "It's Frederick."

CHAPTER 17

■ ■ ■ ■ ■ ■ ■ ■ ■ ■ ■ ■ ■ ■ ■

It's him. I can't believe it's him. A wave of heat washes over me, collecting like swamp air at the back of my neck. Like a fist clutching
me there, pinning me down. The breath catches in my throat, sticky
as a cobweb. I never thought I'd see him again. The one benefit to
a banishment is that this particular man is supposed to be out of my
life forever.

A million memories vie for supremacy.

The triumphant smile on his face as he broke my leg. The
barely restrained glee on his face when he told me our parents
were dead. His expression the day he escorted me from my cell to
the receiving hall, where Nati's body was splayed beneath Nati's
greatest artistic feat, the chandelier's light starkly illuminating every
single thing that Frederick did to my only adult friend.

Frederick had carefully placed velvet-roped stanchions around
Nati's body in a grotesque star shape—preserving the horror for
anyone to see.

That's Frederick, a combination of brutal, dramatic, and fussy.
I didn't even recognize his voice anymore. Every time he comes
on the streams, I turn them off. I've suppressed everything about
Frederick I possibly can, but I can't suppress the actual man just a
wall away. My heartbeat roars in my ears, faster than it should, and
I realize that Arcadio is speaking.

"—working with my Family?" Of course. He's concerned that
his own Family, supposed allies of my brother, has secretly been
working on a megaweapon behind his back.

"No." I gasp the word like I'm catching my breath. I am. The wave of heat dies a quick and violent death and suddenly I'm bitterly cold. I quickly explain the weapon in the schematics. "He is working on his own. They said they couldn't expand the caldera because your Family was watching. They are afraid of you finding out too early. Once they found your brother spying on them, they abducted him to lure your Family here—to test the weapon. My guess is, your father severed the partnership with Frederick but hasn't gone public yet. My brother holds a grudge like most people hold their loved ones."

Arcadio rubs his hands up and down my arms, snaring my gloved hands at the end of one downstroke. I force a smile even though he can't see it. This is not the time for a breakdown. "It's fine. I'm fine. It took me by surprise, is all. Boost me again. We need to know more."

Arcadio takes me at my word. This time, rather than cupping my butt—which I greatly enjoyed—he sets said butt on his shoulder and loops his arm over my thighs. His low tone reverberates through the coms. "You *seem* superfine."

"Priap." The small sliver of normalcy that he offers is a balm on my nerves. It's like he understands that I need the familiarity of something to push against.

The meeting is still ongoing. Clearly no one psychically sensed a meltdown happening on the other side of the wall. I hook my toes behind Arcadio's back and return to listening at the window vent.

"When will it be ready to test?" Kaori asks the scientists as she impatiently taps the stylus against her datapad.

One of the scientists beams, pleased to have a good answer to deliver. "It is ready for testing now. Our sensory satellites tell us that a prime target—although unfortunately not an Escajeda vessel—is presently in the shipping lanes. The planet's rotation will be optimal for targeting in slightly over two days."

They sweep their hand, sending the precise information into her datapad.

"Once we've done the test, the ruse is up, and we can do whatever we want to the caldera." Frederick flips through something on his own datapad. His face hasn't lost its punchability—far worse than Arcadio's ever was. "Let them try to approach the planet. Between the southern hemisphere coverage and this system, combined with the expansion near Kohaishimi, your Family owns the shipping lanes that feed this whole branch of the galaxy, smothering travel to any known phydium deposits that have been mapped near the edges of space until such a time as you feel like harvesting them.

"Target an Escajeda property first. They'll be your biggest competitors unless you distract them."

Kaori sends him a look that could give a chill to the vacuum of space. "You have been a valuable contributor. Not a partner. Do not assume you can speak for Nakatomi's priorities."

Frederick's brows rise in surprise and immediately lower in fury.

They seem to be wrapping up in the meeting room and I tap Arcadio's helmet to indicate that it's time for me to come down. He takes his time lowering me, and I'm not sure if he's doing it for his own benefit or as a pleasant distraction for me. It *is* a pleasant distraction, so I tolerate it. And by "tolerate," I mean "greatly enjoy."

I relay the information to Arcadio. I wish I could see his expression through the armor's face shield. At the same time, I'm happy he can't see mine. I'm no good at hiding emotions and I probably look something on the scale between scared shitless and bugfuck infuriated. I want a hug and a full bottle of ardot and to climb into my ship and fly away forever. None of those are particularly attractive desires. Whatever this thing between us is, it's new enough that I want to pretend to be far more composed a person than I actually am. "He's gunning for your Family. Your father needs to know. Kaori doesn't seem sold on the plan, or at least not on the part where Frederick contributes to the plan."

His soft huff of acknowledgment filters through the coms. "As much as I want to continue the search for Pablo, we have to get a message out."

We wait until no one is around to make our exit from the shadowed alcove. Another purposeful walk finds us at the base of the lava tube, and Arcadio boosts me to the mouth. After a move that would have made one of my old gymnastics teachers proud, I hoist myself into the tunnel and turn to offer Arcadio assistance with his own ascent. He tackles it nimbly, leaping up the wall with the grace of a feline while barely touching the wall.

"What the fuck was that?" I hiss as we move into the relative safety of the lava tube. "Are you showing off? In the midst of a dangerous and secret mission? Inside a volcano-weapon base?"

Mostly, I just like saying the words "volcano-weapon base." How often in your life do you get to say that? It's especially riveting when you're using it to distract yourself from a personal crisis that could encompass you in mere moments.

"Not thinking about your brother now, are you?" I can't see his face, but I can tell he's smiling that dumb, cocky Escajeda smile. The one that flashes white against the dark beard. The lingering darkness in his eyes says that he's trying to keep himself from worrying about his brother as much as he's trying to keep me from worrying about mine.

"We need to talk about your methods of distraction."

"I seem to recall some methods that were particularly successful last night." He says the words as the green icon of the group coms flash on. Just in time to hear that little confession. Caro already knows, of course, but Itzel might not have.

"What methods were those, Escajeda?" Caro's voice has barbs, but there's a smile in it.

"Yes, were there moves? I always like to learn new sparking moves." Itzel slips into the exchange like it was choreographed.

Arcadio sounds curious. "Sparking?"

"Don't ask. Itzel, if he tells you all his tricks, you'll use them to steal lovers away from him," I point out. As though she needs any help. They take one look at those nimble tattooed fingers and the sweetness of her smile and abandon all common sense.

She makes a gleeful sound of agreement but then taps her finger on her chin. "I don't know, Temper, could I steal you?"

"What makes you think I'm his lover?"

She snorts when she laughs. I'll never live this down.

"Time to leave." I redirect the conversation to the here and now and our imminent risk. They can ask Arcadio for pointers another time.

It's an uneventful trip down the lava tube, which is why the two Nakatomis coming through the heavy iron door take us by surprise. Arcadio crouches by the wall, preparing to open the rock door we created, and suddenly we're face-to-face with the enemy.

They stop and stare. We stop and stare. I respond at the same time as the first Nakatomi, swinging the large pulse launcher under my arm and firing in the same motion. They fly back into the tube wall. Arcadio does the same with the other soldier.

An alarm blares.

The night vision in my helmet highlights the smooth walls as we flee toward the distant tube mouth. No time to retreat to our previous point of entry. Even though I'm running for my life, I recognize that this is an easier trip than the previous one I made with Arcadio. I'm no longer clutching a belt like a supplicant child, dependent on another to guide me. I'm in the lead, clearly discerning my path.

Night vision really is fantastic.

Caro left the swarm behind, a subtle wireless trail stretching behind us into the volcano on the backs of tiny drones. She beams the early signs of pursuit onto our face shields. A group of Nakatomi blips enter the tunnel, with five that move faster than others. "Hover bikes," she pants, breathless, over the coms.

Hover bikes are bad tools for scouting a desert planet. The hovering mechanism can be clogged with sand or confused by rough terrain. They're ideal tools for the smooth perfection of a lava tube and they're fast as hells. They have a chance to catch us before we clear the tube, and running before them in such a narrow space makes us perfect targets. I put on another burst of speed, rejoicing in armored joints that align with my own, supporting my movements rather than hindering them.

The bikes are nearly within targeting distance when we hit the mouth of the tube. I lead the others into the canyon, keeping my eyes open for cover or the Children. I don't see them, but I hear signs of the cult. A recording plays, somewhere far enough away that I can make out a voice but not the words it says. The sound echoes through the narrow slot of the canyon, reedy as it bounces off the smoothly curved rock walls. It rises and falls in a passionate verse, compelling and alien. My translator tries to make sense of the echo, to fit it into a preformed shape. The garble of words it feeds me are barely recognizable as language.

"Love is not . . . weapon . . . Fight . . . fight love . . . grueling . . . take it all. Take it like they made it themselves. . . . Betrayal . . . stole our children . . . lives . . . souls . . . Can't go back . . . won't let us. Fight . . . fight love . . ."

My helmet picks up a different audio signal, coming from Arcadio. At first, I think this is another near-miraculous power of my new armor, until I realize Caro has intercepted a transmission and is beaming the signal over to me.

"*Satellite XSPR8, relay signal: the spider has made a nest. I repeat, the spider has made a nest.*" Arcadio's low voice pauses, like he's considering something. "*She's feathered it with a Reed and armed it with a stinger.*"

Considering he probably didn't have a code word already planned for Frederick, it's a valiant effort. On the other hand, odds are very high his Family will assume that *I'm* the Reed in question.

The air-thin whine of the hover bikes bursts into the canyon behind us, around the curve of the serpentine canyon wall, offering only enough time to duck into a side passage and continue our headlong sprint toward the *Quest*. Although they hover, the bikes are probably too heavy for the pulse launcher to be much good. I pull out my blaster and ready the replacement battery.

The audio from the Children is louder, distorted by the canyon but driving in its intensity. Rashahan alternates languages in his messaging, targeting each of his followers—his flock—individually in their home tongue. He always returns to that same message, with a twist of special Herschellian dialect that must be unique to the Children. My translator chip processes it, stumbling over the words, and eventually it deduces the pattern, smoothing at just the moment that I want to tune it out, more focused on the danger of Nakatomi soldiers on hover bikes followed by what I assume to be platoon of incompetents on foot.

The first bike curls around the corner behind us, sleek as a warship. It's one of the new models with side paneling and a cabin, more protected than the naked-style hover bikes I'm used to. It's a cavalry mount, not a toy.

The windshields are tinted so dark that the shape of the drivers is just barely visible—hunched shadows. Small swivel-mounted cannons are fixtured near bright headlights that flicker in such a way that I suspect they're alternating light sources between visible and infrared.

One of the cannons takes a chunk out of the rock in front of me. We round another corner and find ourselves face-to-face with a group of Children sitting at their table, Rashahan standing at its head.

"Duck!" I yell as we look for cover, leaping behind a small rock-fall. Two Children run into a side tunnel.

The hover bikes open fire, chipping away at the rocks, and we return fire ourselves, a show of light and sparks that flashes over the sleek-fancy chassis and does very little else. Until Arcadio takes a shot with one of his projectile weapons. It hits with a solid crack, punching a hole in the chassis and torquing the bike slightly to the side. Three more shots and three more holes but he hasn't hit anything vital yet.

The Children have gone silent. Hopefully hiding behind their table. The only sounds are light-cannons shattering rock, the eerie engine whine, and the steady stream of profanity coming from Caro as she digs into her bag and fails to find whatever it is she wants.

But then another sound cuts through the din. A banshee-screech and a streak of fire and suddenly the first hover bike explodes in midair, raining shards of twisted metal, glass, and blood-specked meat on us. The force of the blast shoves me backward into Itzel, shoves Arcadio into the wall, and flattens all of us just in time for another screech and another explosion. Caro yelps an outraged squeal.

I blink, stunned and half-deaf. Did Arcadio's call bring reinforcements in so short a time?

A rough hand starts feeling its way up my legs and I kick it away, but it returns, gently prodding until it reaches my hips, my waist. "Stop trying to feel me up, Arcadio. I'm fine."

"Then get up." His clipped voice finally breaks through the ringing numbness that followed the blast as his hand wraps around my own and hoists me to my feet. A Child stands at the head of the table, near Rashahan, supporting a gigantic pulse launcher on one shoulder. Little scraps of hover bike litter the bottom of the canyon. Some shards are even wedged in the walls. Arcadio tugs at my arm. "I got the message out. This is going to be the perfect distraction for us to go back in and look for Pablo."

CHAPTER 18

. . . .

"Do you want to get dead?" I yank my arm out of his grip and capture Arcadio's wrist, intending to drag him backward. Mostly I just jerk at his very stationary body. "They're offering a distraction because everyone's going to be trying to kill each other. I doubt anyone will care if we're in the cross fire. We need to get better weapons, to send more detailed intelligence, and make a plan. A good one. Not like our normal plans."

He bares his teeth like he wants to bite something but finally lets me pull him away from the skirmish. We flee down a twisted narrow gully while the Children distract the last Nakatomi hover bike. The cult lets us go unhindered, focused on their newly created battle with the Nakatomis. Or, more specifically, on the battle with the Nakatomis that we completely fabricated.

"That answers our questions about whether or not they have a backup armory." I pant for breath as we climb the narrow switch-back trail from the floor of the canyon to the mesa above. To the *Quest.*

"In the tunnel reserved for Rashahan and his inner circle, most likely. Keeping the best weapons for his personal use." Arcadio's behind me but, through the coms, it sounds like he's whispering sweet nothings in my ears.

"Probably also cake." Itzel still has some bounce in her step as she ascends in the lead. "If I were a cult leader, I'd keep all the good food for myself while they eat the creepy truth-vines and lizard meat."

Speaking of lizard meat. "We've been knee-deep in lava tubes for the past few days and haven't seen any lizards. It's looking more and more like you ate people meat, Arcadio."

A soft scuff of body armor comes from behind me. Perhaps a shrug. Or a full-body shudder. For my own sake, I'm going to hope it's the shudder. When he replies, his tone is dry. "Better than the interrogation-vines."

"Is it better? Really?"

When we crest the top of the canyon and venture out on the cracked warm soil of Herschel Two, the familiar squat shape of the *Quest* is crouched in the distance. No one lurking under its chassis. Home, perched somewhere so alien. Caro coms an update to Micah now that we aren't beneath walls of earth. A thin white trail in the dusty yellow sky highlights the descent of another ship, targeting landfall near us.

"Is that your people?" I ask Arcadio, for the first time in my life hoping someone is an Escajeda.

The black helmet bobs in a nod.

My adrenaline is still spiking, leaving me jittery and suspicious, ready for a fight that may be over. It seems like our escape was too easy, but we've been so fucking unlucky that maybe we're finally due a stroke of good luck—if learning that the planet is poised to become an interstellar weapon wielded by two of the least scrupulous people I know can be counted as any kind of luck but abysmal.

That little white streak grows bigger and bigger as the ship approaches. Arcadio speeds up to a jog and, not wanting to split the party even more, I pick up the pace as well.

I'm still reeling from the shock of Frederick. Even now, it reverberates through my bones like fracturing ice on a windy lake. Like that same chilled wind is whispering his name over and over in the hollow space at the back of my head. I've feared him my entire life.

The one thing our encounters have in common is that he always wins.

As though my thought ushers it to reality, the whine of more hover bikes tears over the canyon walls right behind us. Well, shit. They crest the edge of the canyon like a wave, washing the dry earth with shadow and sleek metal. We break into a faster sprint as the sound of priming weapons rings in the air.

The first shot has the misfortune of blowing all the way through the sensitive knee joint in the back of my armor and blowing *part* of the way through the sensitive knee joint in the back of my flesh.

I catch the hiccupping yelp in the back of my throat and tumble to the hard cracked dirt as silently as possible. The crew—noble idiots, most of them—will try to rescue me if they hear me fall. It will get them killed. As it is, I have a brief window of opportunity to master the pain and cover their retreat.

I ignore the blood heating my leg, sticky and stiff in the armor, and spin to my back, angling the pulse launcher until, still blocked by my body, it's pointed in their direction. It might not have enough power to disrupt a hover bike on its own, but they're flying in a tight formation—showing off now that they've picked the weakest creature from the pack. I still have teeth and they're about to find out.

As a distraction, I crank the intensity on my blaster and make a pretty light show, hitting windshields and chassis and watching the high-intensity light pulses reflect from one surface to another. A quick glance tells me that Arcadio, Caro, and Itzel have nearly reached the safety of the ship and its weapons—some of which are effective planet-side. When the hover bikes are close enough to smell the exhaust, I thrust up the pulse launcher, sand cascading from its smooth barrel, and fire.

The pulse hits the first bike with a direct impact, shoving it back into the second and destabilizing them into a small floating pileup. While the other bikes swerve to avoid the destruction, I pulse a few more of them, less effectively, and then grab double handfuls of sand, throwing them toward the intake of two more of the bikes. One powers through it but the other, which got a more solid hit, sounds like it's gargling gravel for a moment and then, without any warning, thuds to the ground. They *really* aren't ideal vessels for travel on undeveloped planets. At least I know one thing that Frederick and his cronies don't.

The sand distracts the last bike from pursuing the rest of my crew, but not enough to save me. I try another pulse blast and another handful of sand to no effect because the two bikes I didn't hurt initially won't get close enough for me to strike. I spoiled all my tricks and these drivers, at least, are smart enough to learn. They're soon joined by the two other bikes that my first pulse blast disrupted, in a tight little square, cannons pointed directly at me, and I know that there's no going back. The incapacitated bike opens like a mollusk and a lean elegant figure in a Nakatomi uniform unfolds themselves from within, blaster out. Either they're about to compete for the prize in the "who can put the most holes in Temper" contest, or I'm about to become a prisoner in a war that no one outside this planet knows is happening.

The white plume of the descending Escajeda ship has reached the planet. The *Quest* hums in the distance as it powers up. They will have realized I'm not there by now, will have decided the ship is their best defense. I hope they have, at least.

One of the bikes peels away, leaving me surrounded by three others and in no better position to defend myself than before. It fires on my sweet baby ship in three precise blasts and smoke curls from the *Quest*'s hull. They disabled something. The firing continues but one of the bikes swerves to block my view.

"Get to your feet." The harsh, discordant voice could belong to an AI or could be filtered through the external speakers of the bikes. Considering they shot my feet out from under me, I conclude it can't be an AI because one of those initials means "intelligence."

"I can't. Priap. You shot me." There, that was diplomatic. I should get an award of some sort. The pool of red in the sand beneath me is bigger than I'd like. Any pool of blood would be bigger than I'd like. There isn't even enough structure in the armor to apply pressure to the wound, so the autotriage is applying it to my thigh instead. This is why smart armor isn't the same as human smart. It's decided the best bet for longevity is for me to lose my leg.

I disagree.

It's all I can do to keep from crying. Luckily, I'm a strong, unsuccessful woman and I can keep my tears in my eyes when I'm faced with the much larger concern of the ring of cannons pointed at my head. A disgusted snort comes from the standing soldier, like I let them shoot me in the leg just to irritate them.

"Matsuo. Tie her to the back of your bike." The command comes from the first bike. Clearly the squadron leader.

Why haven't they killed me? I would certainly have killed them if our roles were reversed. One of the bikes settles to the ground in a gentle puff of dust and the cockpit slides up, revealing Matsuo, who appears to be halfway through adolescence. His uniform is a size too small, but the one tiny medal pinned to the collar is so lovingly shined that it's clear he takes great pride in serving his Family.

He awkwardly bends to retrieve me with the help of the other soldier. I could shoot *them*. I'd probably even succeed at this range. They'd shoot me right back is the problem, and I'm just enough of a starry-eyed optimist to believe that, somehow, I may still make it out of this alive if I play my cards right.

Matsuo and his compatriot struggle with my weight, which I would find offensive in any other situation, and finally succeed in draping me over the back of the hover bike like roadkill and binding my hands to my feet beneath the chassis.

The boy soldier divests me of my blaster and pulse launcher, handing them to the other soldier. He misses the blade in the forearm sheath and the lockpicks in my boots. I'm glad that I decided to wear these boots today.

A roar in the distance signals a ship taking off. It's the Escajeda ship, not the *Quest*. That fourth bike is still circling the *Quest*, probing its weaknesses. Since my ship hasn't fired back, the bike must have disabled the weapons system before Caro could bring it online.

Or maybe they all got in the Escajeda ship. Maybe they're jammed into that tiny cabin and on their way to hail some sort of help. Maybe I bought them enough time.

Matsuo hops back in his protective shield, the bike shudders and quivers beneath me as it rises, and the Nakatomi bikes turn in the air, collecting their injured parties as we soar back to the canyon and the tunnels within it.

In the distance, the Escajeda ship continues its ascent, a slipstream splash of white against the tawny gold of the sky. At least someone will know what happened here. If anyone can blow the Nakatomis off the map, it will be the Escajedas.

I watch it like a talisman of hope. The hull glints as the sun's light reflects from it and I bare my teeth in a grin, pretending that it's a wink just for me.

The hover bikes approach the canyon, changing their mechanism to descend. The chassis beneath me jerks and then rumbles with a new frequency. My leg screams in pain; the adrenaline that numbed it finally starts to retreat as the cold reality of the future sets in. My sweaty palms twist in the gloves, trying to wrest free of the ropes.

But that ship, in the distance, is nearing the top of the clouds, the freedom of space. As the bike begins its descent into the dark channel of the canyon, I breathe a sigh of relief. They're going to make it.

That beautiful winking ship explodes in a ball of flame and a massive spiral of spent water vapor just as the hover bike plunges into the canyon.

CHAPTER 19

■ ■ ■ ■ ■ ■ ■ ■ ■ ■ ■ ■ ■ ■ ■ ■

Good news: I'm still alive.

Bad news: Everything else. Literally everything.

I make a list of the bad news because there's nothing else to do except cower in pain and terror. Item one: the Nakatomis have had the forethought to create a form of prison within the volcano and I'm presently ensconced behind iron bars on one side and rock-solid cooled magma on three others. As I was dragged bleeding to the cell, I passed a very thin man with very dark hair who is, no doubt, Pablo Escajeda. Item two: I'm separated from my crew. Even if they weren't in the exploded shuttle—and I have to believe they weren't—the *Quest* may not be equipped to take off. Then again, Caro can fix anything, and I trust them to be canny enough to escape some idiots on hover bikes.

Not that I was, but I assume they're better than I am.

Item three: despite the armor's compression, I'm still bleeding from my leg and if something isn't done about this, the good news may not persist for long. Item four: some Nakatomi was smart enough to divest me of my mask and concealed knife, leaving me with only the lockpicks with which to escape a heavily armed and populated military base. Item five: the same Nakatomi who removed my mask took one look at my hair and my mark of banishment and went racing out of my cell, which probably means they recognized me.

Item six: the Children were gathering more numbers in the canyon when we came back. The crowd was even bigger when we passed them, just out of range, and they no longer seemed to be having dinner. Clearly the Nakatomis aren't worried about the activity of the Children. I'm more concerned. They're working themselves up to retribution for Nakatomi's imagined slights. Rashahan doesn't seem like the sort of person to think in half measures.

Item seven: the heavy footsteps approaching from down the hall are familiar. I painfully rearrange myself until I'm propped against a wall in a carefully insouciant pose: head tilted back, eyes half-shut, injured leg stretched out in front of me like I *intended* to be bleeding profusely.

"Hey, brother." I'm proud that my voice is steady and clear. Perhaps this is what hopelessness feels like. It's not as bad as I thought it would be.

"I'm not your brother." Ever the literalist. That's what banishment is, after all. Frederick hasn't changed. Doesn't even look much older. Still a mountain of a man, shaped like a rock suddenly decided to become a person. His straight red hair is carefully combed back from his face and his brilliant green eyes glow like phosphorescence. It's not even mods. He just naturally has great eyes. Mine emerged swampy. I wonder how many more mods Frederick has now. Wonder if he's more artifice than man.

"'I'm not your brother.'" Ever the mature one, I parrot his words back to him in a stuffy man's voice.

Irritation flashes in his eyes. I have power enough for this, it seems. I never expected my greatest talent, when all others were stripped away, would be the ability to annoy my brother.

"You've been spying." He really does have a stuffy man's voice. My imitation was excellent.

"You've been striving. Staying in your lane wasn't enough for you? There's no place for Reed AI in this venture. No branding opportunity. Was destroying people's lives the old-fashioned way too simple? What the fuck are you thinking, brother?"

He grimaces minutely every time that I call him "brother," which is why I do it. Frederick is wearing plain clothes, although I thought it was a uniform earlier. It's like he's putting on the costume of the Nakatomi clan to blend in. It's probably a good strategy but he looks like a fool in his starchy little collar that's devoid of medals because slimeball executives don't usually win medals.

Seeing him is like throwing shrapnel in an open wound. I thought I'd come to terms with what happened to Nati. It's been years, after all. That numbs a person even if they never manage to work through their trauma. I was so wrong. It feels like it was just this morning that Frederick marched me by Nati's body on the way to my banishment trial. One last thing to taint my home before I lost it forever. One more reminder to others of the cost of being my friend.

To ensure I'd remain isolated.

The room was crowded with Frederick's cronies, none of them quite looking at Nati's body. That pleasure was saved for me. I looked so hard that now I can barely remember him any other way. I can still see the dark curl of his hair, threaded with gray that gleamed with every hue known to man under the light of his multicolored blown-glass chandelier. The gentle illumination kissing a bloody-teared cheek.

"Tell me who hired you, Temper. That's all you have to do. Look at you, you've been punished enough."

I'm not sure if he means my general state of being or all the blood. I'm completely sure this suddenly friendly brother act is a lie. Which means it's time for me to twist the knife a little harder. "Who hired me for what? I'm a successful planet scout. I've been hired by nearly every Family there is. Including the Nakatomi Family. How's the view from inside their ass? I didn't realize you can kiss it so hard you fall in. Is entrée to the Five worth that much to you?"

"Must you always be so crass?"

"Must you always be a fuckhead?"

He crosses his arms over his broad chest. "Who hired you?"

"Why would I tell you? I know there's no good ending for me in this story. Let me say one thing, whoever hired me, it was to scout a planet. I had no clue you'd have any part of it, or I'd have stayed away. This little reunion holds no appeal." It's best to stick as close to the truth as possible, especially if they've figured out the trick of those pale plants.

He snorts, like I've made a funny joke. "You always thought so small with your goals, Temper. Even when we were kids, your focus was scattered. You wanted to fight, you wanted to get away, you wanted to protect that imbecilic tutor, or to impress our parents. You wanted to help people." He says the word "help" like it's foreign to him . . . and primitive. "It's why you lost every fight we had. You lacked the vision to do what was necessary."

I thought I lost every fight we had because he is double my size and mean as jet fuel. Nice to know it was just my mentality that got in the way. He's still talking but I can't bring myself to care what he's trying to say.

"His name was Nati," I interrupt. "You know that because he was your tutor, too. He was our mother's friend. Kari's father. He was an artist. He was *loyal*." I'm becoming seriously concerned about my blood loss. My head is almost weightless and the lights behind him appear to be dancing.

"To you." His lip curls back in disgust. "Not to me. Never to me. I'm the head of this Family. I'm in charge and for some reason— probably because you always played the good girl—they liked you better. Like you were one of them instead of their superior."

I'm fairly certain I've never played a good girl in my life. I wonder if he really sees our past that way or if he's just told himself the story as an excuse. "Someone once told me that the sign of a true leader is stomping your foot and demanding to be in charge."

"What would you know about being in charge?" he snarls with his usual disdain. "You don't know a thing about power. You never had what it took to do something big. You never had the weight of a Family empire on your shoulders. You were the spare. All you had to do was smile and marry well and you couldn't even manage that much. You couldn't possibly conceive of something like what I'm planning."

"I'll give it to you, brother, a top-secret volcano weapon pointed at the shipping lanes is certainly big. And labyrinthine. And fucking *ridiculous*. That's how I know it's your plan, not theirs. You always had to make an elaborate show, even if you could have done the exact same thing silently and efficiently. You want to be noticed so bad that the desperation seeps out your pores."

"Who hired you, Temper? It's the last time I'll ask nicely."

Frederick was always creative with his unkindnesses. I don't want to see any new ones. I heave a sigh and shift my body to take some of the weight off my damaged knee. If he believes I'm weak, I might as well capitalize on it. "It was the Chandras. They wanted to see if there were phydium deposits near the volcano, where the readings got hazy. While we were here, they requested samples of the plants. You know them, they love a new plant."

He stares at me for a long moment, face carved from granite. He expects nothing of me. I'm his idiot younger sister and he's never bothered to consider that I might be anything else. When he finally pushes away from the bars, a cocky smile is already curving his lips. "We'll have someone take care of that leg. I'd hate to have you die from blood loss before I'm done with you."

With that ever so encouraging closing statement, he strides down the tunnel like a conquering hero, leaving me to wonder what "take care of that leg" means in this context.

. . . . .

It means an ultrarapid repair machine that combines fast phagocyte wash with blastclast in a mix that is far more excruciating than
the one Micah has because it works twice as fast and I'm about ten
times as damaged. When Frederick returns, he is accompanied
by three soldiers who point weapons at me from the front of the
cage as a medic comes in and straps the device around my damaged joint and squeezes what appears to be glue into my shoulder.
When the medic is done, she leaves the cell, and the guards leave
with her. Frederick stays, watching me with an expressionless face.

"I've been told it's like being burned alive."

It's hard to focus on his words because the device feels like being burned alive. I have a high pain threshold. You develop one
if you experience the amount of pain I have and the man on the
other side of the bars ensured I experienced a lot in my early pain-
training days. It doesn't matter. My nerves are aflame; the deep
part of the joint is a rolling ball of lava. Spikes and shards of ra-
zored fire are twisting around the knee. It is torture and he knew it
would be. That's why he's still here.

"Burned alive is nothing compared to how it feels knowing I'm
related to a priap like you."

I want to stick this device over his face and see how he likes
it. With the anguished burn of pain comes the familiar wave of
anger, clean and pure and focused in its intensity. It doesn't matter
that he's my brother: I will make this man bleed. I will scrape my
fingernail over his most delicate vulnerability and then I'll puncture it with a smile.

"The funny thing is, you think I'll believe that I'm the weak
one." I pause and gasp for breath. "I've known you all my life. Every
part of you is soft. It's why you're such a fucking bully."

I grit my teeth for as long as I can, as wave after wave of agony drowns me. "What's your plan, brother? For when they find your tech all over this base? They will find it. And then the other Families will wipe you off the chart."

He leans his forehead against the bars, a smile playing across his lips like he's just been waiting for me to ask. "I built a fail-safe. I can destroy this whole place if anyone on the outside realizes. Bring it down in rubble. And then I go public as the hero who was briefly duped by the evil Nakatomis but realized it in time to save the day."

As plans go, it's got Frederick written all over it: backstabbing, violence, and lies. His voice lowers even further, so that I can barely hear him over the blood pumping in my ears.

"The Nakatomis offered us a slot in the Five if I help them bring down the Escajedas. You know how rare it is for one of the Five to fall. And when they do, none of the others really accept the newest Family for a generation. We'd have allies. I provide Reed AI to them, to work with their adaptive optics and identify targets and trajectories and Pierce's new batteries and . . . other goodies. In exchange, we get a free ride up. It's what our parents always wanted, Temper. What we always wanted. We'll be replacing the most powerful Family there is."

I'm horrified. It is *not* what our parents wanted. Not like this. They used their AI for language, not murder. Perhaps a naive belief considering the Family system, but they weren't willing to sacrifice lives to make it to the Five. One might argue they didn't live long enough to see that their strategy couldn't work, but I have just enough of their naivete that I wish they'd had the chance to try. Frederick's never done anything but sacrifice lives. "People will die, Frederick. Innocent people. Surely you care about that, even a little. Even if all you care about is how it looks."

He rolls his eyes like I'm being childish. "Greatness breeds collateral damage. You've been in the world long enough to know that. How do you think people get to the Five?"

Does he want me to be impressed with him? The shock of that thought briefly permeates the pain. I won't break through to him with an impassioned emotional appeal. It was a mistake for me to even bring up innocent deaths. He simply does not care.

"Won't other customers realize that if you built a fail-safe into this tech, you probably built it into theirs and can use it against *them*, too?"

His fingers curl into the bars and his mouth opens. Stays open. Snaps shut.

"Didn't think of that, did you, brother?"

His knuckles pop, they're so tight around the bars. He doesn't respond, just watches me as the waves of pain crash down. Determination only fuels me for so long and then the tears escape my tightly squeezed lids.

"You have failed at everything you ever attempted." He spits the words, finally divested of all that careful control and artifice. "You were a failure at everything you did. In class. In the ring. That ridiculous attempt to help the Wolf Family when we almost had them in our grasp—to try to make me look like a fool. A betrayal of your own Family that got your only ally killed. He covered for your traitorous ways, but I won't. I know you never had our best interests at heart. Your only goal was to bring me low. You are nothing, Temperance Reed."

I laugh so hard the sound saws at the inside of my throat. The tears streaming down my face aren't even all due to the agony in my leg that's slowly gnawing its way toward my torso. "Not Reed anymore, brother; you're confusing my failures with your own. Damage done to the Reed name is yours alone. You never understood the value of diplomacy. True diplomacy when you don't stand to gain. That's when they know they can trust you. You can't be as important as you think if you have all this time to sit around watching me roll on the floor. Doesn't Kaori wonder where her little pet has wandered off to?"

"Fuck you, Temper. Fuck you and your eternally condescending attitude."

I win. I win I win I win. If he can't even craft a response, it means that, in the midst of him literally torturing me, I still win. For the first time. I laugh and laugh and laugh. And, eventually, when Fredrick finally storms away in a huff, the laughter turns to screams and the tears streak down my face.

. . . . .

Still alive. And now I have two items in my good-news column: I'm not dead and my leg is repaired. All other bad news is present, if not exacerbated. Knowing Frederick, my small victory will not go unpunished, and I'll soon be incapacitated in an exciting and new fashion. He'll do it himself this time. Which means I have very little time to plot my escape.

There's also the matter of Escajeda the junior. Pablo has been in Frederick's clutches far longer than I have. If I can get him out, I have to.

The cell door is a standard keypad, powered by an internal battery. I may not be Caro, but I know my way around that. The thing with battery-powered locks is that they require a manual fail-safe, just like the lock on Micah's collar. If your power fails, you may still need to access whatever is behind the door. The keyhole is usually somewhere inconspicuous to the aesthetic impression of the panel, meaning on the side, meaning accessible to me.

This is why you search prisoners properly before throwing them in their cells. Arcadio was right, the Nakatomis don't have their best and brightest in this base. I wonder if Kaori hasn't told her father her plan. If she's going rogue during the power transition. If so, she must have support from someone else. Someone big. Frederick implied Pierce is in on this, whatever it is. They're just smart enough to keep their logo off all the weapons.

The tunnel is empty. If a guard was assigned to me, they grew bored watching someone writhe on the ground in agony and went looking for dinner.

I feel around the edge of the lock so that it isn't quite so obvious what I'm doing. The keyhole is in the bottom center. When I rap my heel on the floor of the tunnel as hard as I can, the small insert containing my lockpicks slides out the toe.

The thing about picking a lock is that it's not much harder to do from a blind angle than it is from straight on. It isn't a visual task. The feel of the pins, the gentle pressure of the tension wrench, the slow slide of the pick, that's about feel and maybe sound. This lock is a complicated one. Obviously. They don't make prison cells with easy locks.

Then again, they don't make prison cells assuming that the prisoner is armed with lockpicks. The tension wrench is a comforting and stable presence at the bottom of the lock, cool in my fingers. The pick is fiddly as always, depressing one pin with relative ease and struggling with positioning of the next. I close my eyes and focus on the sensation. It's a relief to focus on any sensation that isn't pain.

The lock gives way with an anticlimactic spin, almost tumbling me into the tunnel outside. When I get to my feet, my new knee is tender but supports my weight. I relock the cage behind me in a moment of spite. Might as well build my mysterious reputation.

One cell over, that skinny man presses against the bars, watching me. His lips are pressed into a thin line of displeasure, barely visible through the thick growth of his beard.

"Pablo Escajeda?" I ask, hopping as I tuck the box for the picks back into my boot and keep the tension wrench and pick in my hand.

He studies me warily. Seems to decide I'm not on the Nakatomi side. All the dried blood on my clothes is probably a dead give-away. "Yes."

"I'm here to rescue you."

"Weren't you just screaming in pain a little while ago?"

I clench my jaw. "Luckily for you, I can do both. Would you prefer me to leave, and you could wait around for someone more suitably heroic to come to your rescue?"

His eyebrows go up. One slightly higher than the other. "Do you have a plan?"

I puff out a gust of air as I crouch in front of the lock on his door, picks in hand. "I swear, you fucking Escajedas. Of course you'd find a way to criticize your own rescue. Sure, I have a plan. Item one: get you out of your cell. Halfway done. Item two: escape the tunnels. Still working on that. Items three through ten: survive."

"That's a terrible plan."

"Again, I could just leave." The lock gives way under my gentle ministrations, and I swing open the cell door. "Maybe you haven't made it to the room with the giant space laser, but I have. They're eager to target your Family when they send another rescue mission. I assume you'd rather not have their deaths on your conscience."

I don't tell him that his brother isn't on the planet anymore. That he had to flee in the Quest and can't come back thanks to said giant space laser. At least, that's the best-case scenario. I'm try-ing to ignore any other possible scenarios. People like Arcadio— strong, capable, intoxicatingly, charmingly irritating—don't get killed in stupid skirmishes.

They survive.

And so, I believe that the rest of my crew has survived, being as how they are also strong, capable, and—at times—irritating.

"I made it there. I made it almost all the way back out before they caught me." His brother's faith in him was apparently warranted.

The accountant has some mettle. "I hope my Family wasn't stupid enough to send a relative to rescue me and feed right into their plans."

"Do you have a ship on-planet?" I'll ignore that last part of his statement.

"I did when I landed. It's been over a month since then. At least I think it's been that long." His eyes go vacant under his matted dark hair. Pablo's nose has a raptor slope to it. It gives him a predatory air that belies his current physical fragility.

It's also been well over *two* months.

Now that we're free, I consider next steps as we creep down the tunnel. We are alone, with few resources, in a volcanic weapons base that is run by my evil brother and a Family who is not known for mercy. I hold the tension wrench between my fingers like a claw. The dark of the tunnel wraps itself around us. This time, Frederick didn't win. This time, I'll stick in his craw.

I'm so focused on my thoughts of revenge that it takes me a while to realize the hum in the tunnel walls surrounding us isn't Nakatomi action. It's a familiar recording, just as garbled as the last time I heard it, bouncing off the walls of the canyon, spreading a message just as distorted as the recording.

"Can't go back . . . won't let us. Fight . . . fight love . . ."

Pablo and I don't need to find the Children. The Children have found the Nakatomis.

CHAPTER 20

Which means we're pretty much fucked. The Children can't help us survive outside the volcano if they're presently *in* the volcano and about to get killed by the Nakatomi Family for breaking into a top-secret weapons base.

We gingerly jog down one of the tubes. I don't know what tube it is. Not the one the Children are in, because while the sound of the ever-present Rashahan sermon continues to reverberate through the tunnels, it's still muffled and confusing.

Having been present for one of Rashahan's sermons, it would probably still be confusing if I was right next to him, but the man does have good diction. The gist I get is the same old song and dance. The big Five have banished them because the Children are special, and now the Five are out to get them, as evidenced by the two attacks—one fake and the other accidental. Why they'd banish them and then hunt them down, when they already had them in hand, is a question that doesn't appear to occur to any of the Children. I'm sure he has a pat nonsensical answer ready and waiting for if it does.

Shuffling footsteps echo out of a side passage in just enough time for me to stop my jog, snag the back of the loose-fitting tattered shirt that hangs over Pablo's shoulders, look desperately for a hiding place, and then adopt something resembling a casual pose while yanking the youngest Escajeda behind me. He has his brother's height and smells like he's been a prisoner for a long time, so there's only so much I can do to obscure him. The soldier who stumbles out of the passage is familiar, the man from the rooftop whom I nicknamed Hero.

"The fucking cult has invaded." I spit the words in authoritative Akentimogo for added authenticity. "Get to your position immediately."

He immediately throws me a salute and goes running down the tunnel without even looking at Pablo. It's amazing, the power of a well-timed show of confident authority.

I drag Pablo into the tunnel they came from, assuming it is likely unpopulated, and discover a dark alcove containing an earth borer. Fan-*fucking*-tastic. Who needs to escape down populated tunnels when she can make her own?

"This isn't a good idea. These vehicles move very slowly." Pablo tries to edge back toward the primary tunnel. I pause to stare at him. Up until now, besides the complaints, he's seemed content to let me lead the way. Then it hits me. Of course an Escajeda knows about drilling equipment. Mining is the Family business. Ina and Armando were just as diligent as my own parents in training their children in all aspects of their industry.

"I move slowly when someone shoots me in the head. At least the borer offers a bit of defensive capability and camouflage. This is part two of the plan." I lever myself into the machine and strap into the driver's seat. Pablo looks dubiously between the borer and the dark tunnel outside before following me in and wedging his skeletal body in the small space behind the seat. The flip of a switch lowers the door until we're surrounded by something like safety for the first time in quite a while.

The keys are in the ignition because when you have a top-secret volcano base, you don't really anticipate a petty thief will come in and steal your equipment. Unluckily for them, I'm the pettiest thief they'll ever find. The borer rumbles as the rotating blade powers up and the machine slowly creeps forward.

Pablo was right. We won't be making a speedy getaway. Maybe, with the cult in arms, we won't need to. What I absolutely don't want is to accidentally bore my way directly into a magma pit. When we finally reach the main lava tube, I proceed in the direction we were previously traveling until we reach a crossroad.

Periodically, movement flashes in connecting tubes as we pass them. More frequently, I feel the rumble of the earth as explosives detonate or hear the reverberative firing of an unknown weapon. The Children must be getting slaughtered in there. I think of Generosity with that gap in her teeth and her blind desire to return, and shame pools deep within. If we hadn't framed the Nakatomis, the Children wouldn't be here. My problem is with Rashahan, not with the rest of his flock.

But I'm not in a position to ride to anyone else's rescue. By the time this earth borer gets there, the fight will be over, anyway.

I assume incorrectly because, at the next gentle curve of the tunnel, we burst forth into the main fissure. The three-story memory-metal building rises ahead, the small lean-to buildings line the walls, and the constructed floor is populated by highly armed Children in military poses and Nakatomi soldiers who look scared shitless.

Let me repeat that, the *Nakatomis* are the scared ones.

After a moment, I see why. Rashahan's forces are trained surprisingly well. One is in position atop the three-story building, sniping Nakatomis with a blast-rifle of such a high intensity that it penetrates their helmets. The others are blocking the escape tubes, armed with rocket launchers and frag grenades. All the lava tubes except for mine, because I accidentally slam into the back of the Child in mine, sending him tumbling to the side as I pass, hugging the wall of the fissure and trying to think invisible thoughts.

He's fine. Probably.

I don't know who to root for. I wanted the Children to cause a fuss, but I didn't think there was a chance that they'd succeed in defeating a highly trained military force. Escajeda's words whisper through my head. *You don't assign someone to a clandestine mission if you can't afford to lose them.* You fund what you expect, and they expected science and engineering—not a well-armed cult with a vendetta. I wonder where Frederick is. Certainly not bravely defending his work.

Normally I'd celebrate this rout but the problem with the underdogs winning is that underdogs notoriously exhibit immensely poor decision-making skills when given access to giant volcanoblasters. Who knows what Rashahan's going to do with the thing? At least Kaori Nakatomi wouldn't disrupt the universal economy or target civilians. Probably. Rashahan either won't realize what he's doing or will purposefully try to sow chaos.

I think I might get lucky enough to roll all the way over to the access tunnel I recognize, one story up, when suddenly some of the combatants on the perimeter of the closest skirmish realize that I'm behind the controls of a very useful piece of equipment—carrying the Nakatomi's valuable hostage who is currently pawing at my head like he wants to trade seats.

Too bad. Part of being the rescuee is that you don't get to drive.

Pulse blasts ricochet off the chassis of the borer, and with no other option for defense, I turn the blade on. It takes a long time getting up to speed. Long enough for the blasts to almost take out the windshield. The drill whines as it turns, building momentum, and I crank the controls to the side, intending to spin the machine, cutting into the few combatants who are trying to break in.

Instead, it lumbers in a slow, lazy, easily avoidable circle.

"What are you *doing*?" Pablo's long arm reaches past my head, and I smack it out of my way.

"I have a plan!" No, I don't. My plan has failed me. It's all about staying alive now. Strategy is out the window and pure feral survival has taken precedence. "Stop distracting me."

Apparently I sound convincing because he stops poking at me. After a short startled pause on the outside—likely where they prepared to run for their lives and then realized they were in little to no danger—the fighting continues. I complete my arduous circle and creep forward, the spinning blade reflecting some blaster shots but battered by others. Just as I think this can't possibly be more excruciating, one of the Children gets the clever idea to shove a gaping Nakatomi soldier directly into the spinning drill of the borer. He explodes like overripe fruit. I shriek as a shower of blood sweeps the windshield—which has no cleaning mechanism. Pablo shrieks and clutches my head again, momentarily blinding me.

I duck out of his clutches and watch in horror as everyone nearby attempts to turn us into a murder weapon. It's not many people.

It's enough.

I've been in my share of combat. Before now, I would say that I was inured to violence. I've never seen anything like this. The borer shudders when a body hits the blade. Everyone is screaming. Threats. Pain. Anger. I'm screaming right along with them because I can't imagine much of anything worse than this exact moment. There also isn't a thing I can do about it because the second I step out of this machine I'm completely weaponless.

Another shudder reverberates through the machine. Another arc of crimson on the windshield. A dropped blaster spins off the drill and comes to a rest on the stubby hood. Three shots hit the glass as I lean forward to look—just in case I'm foolish enough to think that everyone is too busy killing each other to waste any time on us. A female Nakatomi soldier with a pretty face and steely eyes levels a dangerous-looking rifle in our direction but jerks to the side, glassy-eyed, as a headshot from the sniper takes her out.

It isn't a blaster bolt that finally explodes the windshield in a shower of glass shards, it's part of a boot, flung backward by the drill. The corresponding spray of blood from whomever was wearing the boot catches me in the face. I flatten myself in the machine, wiping frantically at my face, spitting, questioning every life choice that led me here.

Pablo grabs the boot and chucks it back out the windshield. I'm proud of this small display of mettle.

I angle myself so I can sort of see out but the blasts can't reach me, just in time for a frag grenade to soar through the window directly into my lap. With a yelp, I huck it right back out the broken windshield and it takes out the small cluster of combatants who were targeting the borer. In the momentary lull after the blast, I grab the blood-coated blaster from the hood of the borer and turn its intensity to the highest setting.

With everyone who was targeting us either in pieces or screaming about all the pieces that are covering them, we continue to creep around the edge of the battle unnoticed because we aren't actively trying to kill anyone.

The borer comes to a jarring halt as it hits the earth directly under the lava tube we spied the day before and then fails at its only purpose when it doesn't drill its way through some simple rock-hard magma. All those blaster and frag hits must have damaged the blade too much. I try to up the speed, but the drill simply can't make any headway.

"Shit!" I scream. It feels so good, I scream it again. Then I glance back at Pablo because I'm probably not being the most reassuring rescuer. He's gazing out the window behind him with a hard look on his face. Better than a nauseous look. I'm doing that one; he can't have it.

With the borer unable to drill, we're going to have to climb out the windshield, stand on the roof of the borer, and hope that gets us high enough to leap into the tube. Also hope that no one decides to shoot us. I look out the back window with Pablo. Most of the fighting seems to be focused around the tall building in the center of the fissure as the few remaining Nakatomi soldiers try to take out the sniper. In turn, the sniper is focused on the soldiers who are focused on him.

No one seems to be focused on the sad bloody borer that doesn't even serve its primary purpose. We won't get a better chance.

I drag myself over the broken glass and out to the blood-slicked hood, coating my hands with red and drenching the front of my armor. A shudder ripples through me and I try as hard as I can not to think about what I'm crawling through. A gob of my hair sticks to the side of my face, but I can't bring myself to rub more blood through it when I push it back. There isn't much space, but I awkwardly twist until I can climb to the roof.

The green but highly trained Nakatomis were clearly entirely unprepared for the Children's naked hostility and weaponry— both improvised and advanced. One Child near the central tower is swinging what appears to be a double-sided battle-axe, and another has a motherfucking *sword*. That axe cuts through the blasterproof armor like air. The actual air is thick with screams, thuds, small impact explosions when blaster fire hits, and the squish of feet on bloody ground.

I won't go into the smells. Assume there are many. None pleasant.

Pablo climbs out after me and stumbles as he gets to his feet. I might be giving him a piggyback ride before we go much farther.

Hands hook into my armpits and yank me up into the darkness of the lava tube. I kick out before I hit the ground, spinning to point the blaster at my attacker. It drops from my hand as I see Micah's familiar face through a transparent face shield, banishment tattoo twinkling under his eye. I grab his arm, just in case I'm hallucinating. Feels real. Well-filled-out armor. He slips one of the shield bracelets on my wrist and then retrieves Pablo.

"Trust you to come out of imprisonment with the upper hand." Micah glances from me to Pablo. He's being generous with his definition of the upper hand. "We had a whole rescue plan and you had to ruin it. Escajeda's right, you *are* a calamity."

Like an idiot, I wrap my arms around him. I'm just so fucking happy he's alive. "How are you—?"

"No time to talk. They said you got shot in the knee. Can you run? I have to get you back to the rest of them. They had their hands full when I left, but Caro said you needed me. Her swarm drones have been tracking you."

"I can run. Did we lose anyone?" I jog alongside Micah, knee tender but holding up for now. Pablo is just as slow as I am, so I don't look bad.

"No." Sparks flare to life within my chest at his words. They're alive. Not only are they alive, but they came back for me. It's not the smart move. The smart move would have been to hug the planet until they got out of range of the volcano weapon and then launch into space for help.

Later, I'll yell at them for not doing exactly that. Right now, my heart's so full I feel like I might explode.

"The *Quest*?" I brace myself for bad news. Bad news besides the fact that my knee is feeling more and more iffy with every step. The darkness of the tube wraps around me, although the dim red running lights are doing enough that I don't trip over my feet.

"That ship's a tank, despite Ven's boring name. They don't make them like that anymore. They hit us with a targeted EMP. Took out weapons for a bit until Caro devised a work-around. She plays around with them often enough that she put some impressive shielding in place so that she doesn't kill your ship in space.

We'll be ready to launch as soon as we get back. Along with your newest cargo."

The sparks in my chest meld into a small flame. We're alive. We're alive and we have a ship. There's a way off this awful rock.

Also, apparently Caro has been playing with EMPs in my engine room, but that's a problem for future-Temper. We run down the tunnel in silence, feet solidly hitting the rock below us, as the tube curves in a gentle arc toward the heavy iron door and the smaller secret door to the underwater tunnel.

Right as we're about to see the door, right as I hear the first voices, a piece of the magma wall detaches itself like a tear in reality, and unexpected hands yank all three of us into the darkness just before a sheet of flickeringly sheer material blocks us from the rest of the tube. A hand wraps around my mouth as I struggle.

"Stop wriggling," Caro's voice whispers from in front of me. Someone presses a coms into my ear. "It's hard enough to keep the invisibility illusion going without you ruining it by making noise."

"She can't help wriggling. It's her primary fighting strategy." Itzel. Also rude. I have lots of strategies. Wriggling is one of many. No one expects a good wriggle in a hand-to-hand fight.

"Stop talking." I almost don't recognize the voice that snaps with sharp authority. It's Generosity . . . the lost cult bunny. Except she's talking like she's a general. They found her body armor somewhere. In fact, it looks like my old suit. Fits her far better than it ever did me. "If you let them see us, we're all dead."

They're all in front of me, even Micah. It's so dark I can barely see, but my whole crew is here. Even Arcadio, shoulder pressed against his brother's, face looking at peace for the first time in a long time, which is something special considering our situation.

As the voices in the tunnel come even closer, he smiles and leans closer to me. "Did you miss me, Reed?"

That little flame in my chest becomes a roaring fire.

CHAPTER 21

All questions must wait because Rashahan struts in front of the invisibility curtain, shoulders thrown back and belly protruding out the front of his strange little uniform. Two of his toadies scuttle along behind him, consulting datapads. Rashahan doesn't waste time with things like obtaining tactical updates; instead, he mutters under his breath.

"The love they raised you on was a toxin." His brow furrows and the rest of his face scrunches up to meet it. He pauses and shakes his head slightly before proceeding. "The *love* they raised you on . . . the love they raised *you* on . . . No. That's not it. They *poisoned* you with their love—much better—until you thought you needed the poison to survive."

Fantastic. We caught the madman composing his next sermon.

Arcadio's close enough to clasp my hand, silent and reassuring in the darkness—warm and hard and alive instead of being charred specks raining down from the burning sky above. A tiny part of myself doubted him. Not because I don't believe he's capable of survival—but rather because I've lost pretty much everyone I ever had, and that sort of pattern is hard to break. My breath shallowly escapes in a slow stream as I try to remain as soundless as possible.

The poles of the planet have shifted beneath me, good news so suddenly overwhelming bad that I can barely balance. I feel like I've been punched in the face with happiness.

That must be why my eyes are watering. That deliriously violent happiness.

The youngest Escajeda shifts slightly beside his brother. If I were to interpret the movement through my own lens as a younger sibling, he's very happy to see his kin but also infuriated that his older brother gets to ride to the rescue while he's the victim.

The way I see it, Pablo's future goes one of two ways. One: he never leaves Escajeda space again. Two: he leaves Escajeda space immediately on an even more foolhardy mission to try to prove himself. In my youth, I would have gone with option two, but Pablo seems like he might be more sensible.

Caro's invisibility sheet flutters, cool as the surface of a river. Two little drones pin it to the wall of the tube above us. It's a flimsy protection against a group as well armed as this one. There's a chance that I seek comfort in the solid line of chest of the man beside me. The feeling of being held and comforted, just for a moment.

Rashahan pauses again as another Child runs toward him from the direction Micah and I just came. More than one, judging by the rushing sound of feet. Fantastic. This is the worst possible spot for them to stop and have a little confab, so of course they're going to do it here. An elbow digs into my chest as someone shifts their weight. I recognize Itzel's sharp little bones. I love them. She's allowed to elbow me in the chest any time she wants, so long as she's alive to do it.

"Supreme Rashahan!" The running man exclaims the words but he's also panting for breath, so it sounds more like "Su . . . pr . . . eme . . . [gasp] Rash . . . a . . . han [gasp]."

"Speak, Candor." Rashahan gestures in a way that he probably intends to be grandfatherly and inviting, but he actually sounds like an irritated day worker talking to their nagging pet after a long shift.

The sniper—at least I assume the running man is the sniper based on the weapon clutched in his hand—pulls himself together enough to speak without gasping too much, although his voice is still breathless. The thing about sniping is that it doesn't necessarily require much in the way of cardiovascular endurance. "We have success. There are two holdouts in the control center and several escaped down the tunnels, but the base and the attached weapon are our own."

If you've never seen a holy man have a silent yet still extremely disgusting orgasm in the middle of an underground tunnel while surrounded by his sycophantic followers, you don't really understand the look on Rashahan's face. I try that thing where I beg the universe to grant me another wish and it refuses to wipe the memory from my head, so I guess I'm stuck knowing exactly what it looks like forever.

"And the status and capabilities of the weapon?" He can barely get the words out without a little moan. Devastating explosions must really do it for this guy.

Come to think of it, they probably do it for most guys.

"Immense capabilities. Primed. It just successfully targeted a shuttle attempting to escape from the planet, but its range is much farther." Escajeda's arms tighten around me even more as the words come out. He probably knew the pilot. If he survives this, he'll have to talk to their family. To tell them their child or partner or parent died trying to convey a futile message to the rest of the stars. He'll carry that death with him.

"Per their satellite-relay mapping, what is the next available target? We cannot let this good fortune pass us by." Can the men around Rashahan not hear the gleeful thread that binds his voice or, do they hear it and agree?

"Several targets will pull into range over the next few days. A secondary Chandra on a retirement cruise, an Etienne distribution-and-supply ship, two long-range civilian transport vessels—" Candor reviews something in a datapad. His body armor shows torch marks and, where his face shield is pulled up, trails of sweat have dried on his face in salty tears.

"Which will be the first in range?" Rashahan interrupts Candor. Unlike the Child, the Supreme looks fresh as a flower. Maybe also sane as one.

Candor pauses for a beat too long. Long enough for even me to smell the blood on the water. He fidgets with the datapad. "The Chandra retirement cruise will be in range tomorrow, late in the day."

That's a carefully worded answer. Also known as a misdirection for those keeping track at home. Rashahan is apparently sane enough to recognize it as such. "Candor. A name I gave to you. A name of honesty. Of honor. Tell me the truth, Candor. Is the Chandra vessel the first ship to come in range?"

"The first viable target." Candor's face pulls tight with displeasure, those little sweat runnels cracking on his tan cheeks.

"What is the first target in range? Any target. We must not ignore opportunity when it is presented to us." Rashahan raises his arms and his voice, the sound booming in the narrow tunnel. Arcadio gives a soft grunt of displeasure that I can only hear because his mouth is near my ear. The warm air tickles in a way that shouldn't be appealing given the circumstances but is. "The system is what is broken, my Children! We are the wheel that grinds it to dust! The discarded pieces will strike back."

"There is a target presently in range. A domicile ship." Candor pauses, mouth moving like he wants to bite down on his words, to hold them inside. "It's a boarding school for children of Families."

If I thought that what Rashahan had earlier was an orgasm, right now he's having ten of them at one time. I guess I'm still capable of naive optimism because I thought something might be off-limits. Children are supposed to be, aren't they? It's clear that, to the leader of the Children, real-life children are the perfect targets for his crusade. Itzel's low groan is luckily drowned out by Rasha-han's next words. Itzel's broadly murder-positive, but she draws a line at children.

"These are not innocents, my flock. Not as you think of them. These are the scions of Families. The bleeding heart of the ones who *poisoned* you with their love until you thought you needed the poison to survive. The ones who cast you out and laughed as you struggled and floundered. And the ones who hunted you relentlessly across the stars for daring to think differently than they did! What we have fought today is only the first salvo in a war de-cades in the making."

All that practice in the tube earlier really paid off because the flock of Children in front of him break into gleeful cries of sup-port, clapping hands and stamping feet. Beside me, Arcadio is stiff with anger. His thumb plays across my bicep with the twitching grace of a cat flicking the tip of its tail.

"I could kill him right now," he breathes in my ear.

I tilt my head back until it rests against his chest and angle my mouth toward his ear. "You could try. They'd kill *you* for it."

"We will strike at this bastion of the elite, and we will make them realize we cannot be silenced!" Rashahan finishes his dia-tribe with a flourish and strides forward into the crowd. Someone in the fissure must have turned up the output volume on his re-corded sermon because his ghostly voice echoes around us all as the other Children file out of the tunnel.

When they have all moved out of range, Caro lets the invis-ibility veil fall and we stare at each other in dread. Or, rather, they stare at each other, and I try to see in the darkness with-out decent night vision now that the Children and their light sources are gone. A red light in the distance allows me to make out shapes.

The Escajeda brothers share quiet words and a quick embrace.

Arcadio holds Pablo like he's afraid his brother will break. I wish I knew more about the youngest Escajeda. He seems incongruous for the son of a Family, but months of torture can change a person.

"We have to stop him." It's a stupid thing to propose. It will probably get me killed. Maybe all of us. The smart move is to crawl out that little side tunnel and make a run for freedom while they're blasting innocent children into the vacuum of space. I almost wish I was the sort of person who could do that. I like living. A lot.

All evidence to the contrary.

"They're armed, chock full of bloodlust and battle frenzy, and have weapons in hand. It's the worst possible time to stop them," Generosity snaps, still sounding completely unlike herself. Or, at least, whom she pretended to be. Whom I assumed she was. Her arms are crossed over her chest. She looks comfortable in the armor. Who the fuck *is* this confusing creature?

"Aren't you desperate to get back to their warm, child-killing embrace?" I ask snidely before I continue. She doesn't even blink. If we survive this, she and I will be having a talk about honesty. "There are fewer of them than there were before. The Nakatomi soldiers may have lost, but they took out a lot of cultists. I understand if you don't want to do it. *I* don't want to do it. But I have to. If I can."

"Thought you hated the Families." Micah sounds dubious. He's always been the pragmatist of the crew.

"I do. But these kids aren't Families yet. Their stories haven't been written. Fuck, Micah, I went to a stellar boarding school for a few months. Escajeda did, too. Sometimes poor kids born outside of a Family get into one of them if they have enough potential. Yeah, maybe one of them will be the next Kaori Nakatomi, the next Frederick Reed." I say his name—my name—without wincing at the strange familiar feeling of it in my mouth. "But they may also be the one who stops the system as it is. Who makes it better.

"I'm not going to ask you to stay. In fact, I'm going to ask you to get the *Quest* ready to fly Pablo to safety because when I come out of here, we need to be off-planet as soon as possible."

"Is this another one of those moments where you try to sacrifice yourself to save us? Like when you tried to take on a phalanx of hover bikes by yourself when we could have helped you?" Caro's tone is scathing, and her arms are crossed over her chest stiffly.

"Maybe. Or maybe they just needed to take one of us alive and the best shot we all had for surviving was you getting to that ship." I don't think I'm wrong here. Maybe from her viewpoint, but presented with the situation again, I'd do the exact same thing.

"Then lucky us because the ship is just fine. They temporarily damaged our weapons systems with the EMP. Dented one of the cannons with blaster fire, but we're back to fully operational so you don't get to nobly sacrifice yourself for a ship full of spoiled Family children who will never thank you. Who will probably do everything they can to keep you exactly where you belong— beneath them." Yeah, she's still mad. Caro should have been a judge instead of an engineer—she certainly spends most of her time practicing for the role.

"All I'm saying is, everyone has a choice to make. And I won't judge you for making one that's different than my own." I shuffle from foot to foot, glancing down the tube. They didn't say how soon the school would be within range.

"What's your plan, Captain?" Micah asks, sounding weary. My stomach makes a little flip in my chest. I thought that he'd be gone, for sure. Micah saves himself first. Always. I may not know his whole history, but I know enough. Prior to joining Ven's crew, Micah ran with the Claws, a gang in Pierce territory. He left them the moment things got hot—although the exact source of that heat has never been explained to me.

He's willing to help others until it puts himself at risk. Which means the only reason he's staying is either a heretofore unrevealed soft spot for the children of the universe or camaraderie for the crew.

I carefully don't look at Arcadio. He has other responsibilities. I can't pressure him into this.

I want him with us. To choose us. To desire to finish this off with us, the right way. To prove that he's the man I believe he is. But it's not my job to prod him to be that man.

My job is to think of a plan. I'm the captain and I can do this. "Does the swarm flash blue? Specifically, about four hundred and fifty nanometers? That will collapse all the memory metal structures and may wreak enough havoc to delay an attack."

"Killing them will do the rest." Arcadio's voice is slick as black ice and just as perilous. It's maybe the hottest thing I've ever heard him say.

"The Nakatomis already tried a shoot-out," Itzel argues, gesturing vaguely in the direction of the fissure. "In a blaster battle, we aren't going to beat even the fraction of them who are left. If we had time, we could formulate an assassination strategy, but as it is, we don't have enough information."

"One remaining Child is enough to trigger the weapon. We have to destroy the weapon *itself*, not the Children or the Nakatomi infrastructure." I'm glad Caro is with us but she's asking for the impossible.

"How do we take out the weapon?" Micah folds Caro's invisibility fabric for her and places it in the pack that hunches on her shoulders. He said "we." I smile, even though it's not at all a smiling time.

"Frag grenades?" Itzel suggests.

"Drive a borer into it?" Arcadio's plan isn't shabby, except I may have damaged the only borer present.

"We need something bigger than that." I say the words before I even think about them. Everyone stares at me like that's apparent. Pablo drops his head into his hands. "We can't just blow up the weapon, we have to make this entire place uninhabitable."

Arcadio snorts and runs a hand through his near-black hair.

Pablo turns to his brother. "Why are you listening to this woman at all? Who is she?"

Oh, right. I forgot to introduce myself during our escape.

"That is Captain Temperance Reed." Arcadio tilts his head in my direction. "The woman who risked her life and the life of her crew to save you."

I like the sound of that. It's much nicer than "the woman who accidentally ran into you on her way out."

"What if we flood the tunnels? The underground river runs so closely we just have to connect the dots and it'll fill up the lower part of the caldera. At the same time, we take some of the Na-katomi Family's own weapons and use them to blow up the canon while everyone's distracted." As I outline my strategy, that familiar twitchy excitement of hope fueled by little more than blind opti-mism clouds my judgment until I start to think this plan is great.

"I . . . have no better plan than that. Why don't I have a better plan?" Caro spins and paces almost to the curve of the tube and then back.

"Um. Because it's a fantastic plan?" A little rude that no one seems to be as on board as I am at this moment.

"Let's go, brother." Pablo looks hopefully at Arcadio. I can't blame him. He's been imprisoned so long that a glimpse of freedom is drugging. This isn't his fight.

It isn't his brother's either. Arcadio did what he set out to do. Anything else puts them both in danger. I hold my breath.

"No." Arcadio shakes his head and runs a hand through his hair. "The more of us who try to stop them, the better all our odds."

I think the expression I give him is a beaming smile. I also sort of want to sob with relief, which probably makes the smile more quivery than beaming.

"We're all going to die." That helpful contribution comes from Pablo, who looks at his brother like a stranger.

"We might not *all* die. I might live." Micah's really helping to raise the mood. He looks around. "Fuck. Where's Generosity?"

Not here. At some point while we were planning our next move, she slunk off, whether to the Children or to freedom is unknown. Judging by her morphing personality, I'm going to assume that she isn't warning Rashahan of shit. "She made her choice. We have to make ours. Soon. Before a bunch of children are turned to withered ice sticks in the vacuum of space."

Caro shakes her head again and pulls the stylus out. "That's a lovely picture you paint. Fine. It's the plan. Do we have any equipment to help this tunnel excavation, or do we intend to just magic a water channel from the river to the center of the fissure?"

I give a sort of helpless shrug. "About that. I have good news and bad news."

CHAPTER 22

■ ■ ■ ■ ■ ■ ■ ■ ■ ■ ■ ■ ■ ■ ■ ■ ■ ■

"This is a terrible plan." Caro's still in coms range, which means I get a running commentary about how dissatisfied she is by our overall strategy, the state of the earth borer, and everything else about our current situation. "Did you drive it through a shredder?"

"It still works. Mostly. It drives and spins. All you have to do is make it bore."

"Oh. Of course. That's like telling someone with chopsticks that all they have to do is eat broth. This blade is so dull that I could do a barefoot dance on top of it."

"I don't recommend dancing on it. That might attract attention." Arcadio and I creep around the edge of the fissure, taking shelter behind the memory-metal buildings wherever we can, as we approach the weapon in the center of the volcano, washed in a cool splash of moonglow.

"I should have come with you. You might need me for the explosions."

This is an inopportune moment for Caro to decide to experiment with being frontline crew. I know that her pride was hurt when the Children took Micah, but this isn't the time to soothe that particular ego burn.

"I need you to oversee the water half of this plan." Which is true. What is also true is that probably no one will shoot at her in that half of the plan.

The Children haven't bothered to clean up the bodies of the Nakatomi soldiers, which litter the ground, the rooftops, and even the window frames. Any scattering of dead bodies seems like a lot, but there are fewer Nakatomis present than I thought initially. Nearly all look painfully young. Too young to know any better.

If you're a part of a Family, or a vassal-link to one, you don't get a vote. The head of the Family makes the call and everyone else makes it happen. I've heard a rumor that the Chandras run as a five-member governing board, but even that relates to the core Family that surrounds the head, not the hundreds of others who share the name or the billions who share alliance. These bodies may have been creating a deadly volcano weapon, but they aren't at fault. The blame rests with Kaori and Frederick.

And whoever they're working with. A plan this audacious rarely manages to maintain secrecy without someone more meticulous covering it up. Nothing about this base or the blatant territory grab we encountered on our way here screams of meticulousness. I'd bet the *Quest* that there's a third party involved. Not just Frederick; he's as sloppy and eager as Nakatomi. A Family who will probably emerge from all of this unscathed—if not better.

Then again, the *Quest* probably isn't worth its tow fee, so that isn't the generous bet it appears.

The obvious partner is still Pierce. They habitually ally with Nakatomi, and they will be absolutely destroyed by anyone finding phydium before they do. That destruction could be daunting enough that the usually circumspect Family may be motivated to do anything in its power to halt exploration, even help their ally cut off exploration lanes via territory grabs and giant space lasers.

The Children appear to be grouping in the three-story structure in the center of the fissure for a celebration. It keeps them away from most of the dead bodies (good for them) and it also keeps them away from the weapon (good for us).

On the way through the fissure, I pause to collect a battered helmet and a selection of very nice Nakatomi weapons. Yet again, this helmet doesn't fit cleanly against my armor, leaving a thin gap of vulnerability. Arcadio stares at the sliver of skin like it causes him personal offense. He hands me a strange kind of blaster.

It's heavier than a traditional blaster. Smaller, too. Barely larger than my hand. I don't see any sort of housing for a lasing crystal, and when I pop out what I think is the battery charger, a magazine loaded with pointy metal bullets slides out in its place. One of his projectile weapons.

"Thanks."

"Might give an advantage at a key moment," he says, as though he hasn't done the equivalent of presenting me his heart. In a firefight, your survival is only as good as your weaponry. You don't share weapons with someone else because that means *you* don't have as many weapons. I don't want to draw attention to it because I'm afraid he'll take it back.

I wish I had something to give him.

The last little outpost before the fissure cracks into the center of Kaiaiesto has a light on inside and only offers moderate shelter. Windows line its walls from my shoulder height up. We crouch in its shadow, peering around the corner to study the caldera of the volcano. Someone putters around inside, slamming cabinet doors and humming a jolly tune under their breath. Odious habit. Especially when one is surrounded by a sepulchre. If we move closer to the weapon, whoever is in the outpost will see us.

I press my shoulder against the corner supporting post and Arcadio settles in behind me in that familiar hovering-crowding mode. Perhaps he really doesn't comprehend how personal space works. I'll kill whoever tries to teach him. It's reassuring having someone at my back who doesn't make my skin crawl.

"How's your knee?" Gloved fingers trace the tattered and bloody body armor that used to cover the back of my leg.

"Fine." I still have a knee. It's fine in that regard. He doesn't need to know that I'm still pale-cold with the aftereffects of the forced healing and the joint feels shaky, as if I were newly birthed.

He squeezes my knee in a gesture that I peg as half reassurance and half checking to see if I'm exaggerating. I don't scream or anything, so I probably pass the test.

The caldera is less impressive than I thought it would be. I don't even know what I expected from the inside of a volcano, but this ragged tube of rock isn't that different from the cenotes over the river. Much bigger. That's about it. The sky is an indifferent blanket above, black and mysterious. The stone walls of the caldera are narrow in the base by the fissure but broaden significantly by the time they reach the inky night air. Sort of like a bowl set atop a vase. We're in the vase and the bowl spreads its ragged sides above.

In the center of the vase is the Nakatomi weapon. I'm sure they had some fancy name for it. Dragon's Breath, maybe, considering the scaled creature on their emblem. Or Fucking Big Blaster. Maybe they had a literalist on the science team. That's what it is—a fucking big blaster pointing up at the void of space.

The weapon has a long barrel, not unlike a massive telescope. The whole structure is taller than the three-story building in the fissure. The bottom half is composed of a raised scaffolding and mounting brackets that control the movement of the cannon. The ball-and-socket joint is shallow, more a dish than a true socket. It was likely designed that way to allow greater range of mobility when targeting. A projectile weapon like the one I hold in my hand must handle recoil. A light-based weapon is not subject to the same limitations. The socket has a trough through the center, which would allow the cannon to be pointed toward the floor of the caldera for maintenance and cleaning. I'd sure hate to be the technician assigned that job.

The ball part of the cannon joint probably houses most of the controlling software, adaptive optics, and lasing medium. The weakness of a light-based weapon is the dissipation of the light—something Caro's explained to me more times than I'd like to admit. For something like this, which requires the intensity to be maintained in a certain manner for a long distance, they'd need adaptive optics to help negate the effects of Herschel Two's atmosphere.

The scaffolding is on a level with the ball and a platform with waist-high wire fencing surrounds it. A broad holo fixture is adjacent to the ball, presently showing a bulky wedge-shaped ship with a multitude of view ports swimming through space. The boarding ship. The holo is surrounded by two Children and one Rashahan. They are all pointing at different parts of the ship, perhaps debating which children they should target first.

My vote is the capitalized ones. The humming person in the room next to us continues to poke about loudly.

"Why didn't you yell for help?" Arcadio's voice in the coms is so quiet I can barely hear him.

I could pretend I don't know what he's talking about, but I do. "They only needed one of us to question. If they took two, they'd use one against the other to extract information. They wouldn't bother to capture more than two. They'd kill the rest. We were outgunned. The best chance for everyone to escape was to stay quiet and let you escape."

His hand on my leg tightens. "That's not the best plan for everyone to escape. It's the best plan for everyone except *you* to escape."

Which means that maybe I actually do know what being a captain is.

"I thought . . . for a minute . . . you might have gone aboard the Escajeda ship." I blurt the admission. I didn't dare believe he was among the debris raining down on the cracked soil of Herschel Two, but I feared it. I don't want to lose him. Which is insane because

I will lose him the moment we return to the real world and he returns to his responsibilities.

Family responsibilities don't mix with a scouting crew.

"You thought I left you." He focuses on the wrong part. "I told you I wouldn't abandon you if things got bad."

He means the mission, of course. He's a good man. He won't leave us while we're still dealing with the fallout of Pablo's rescue. But for a moment, I imagine what it would be like if it were a more encompassing statement. If he chose us.

Chose me.

If I could choose him, I would. I admit that much. I want to etch his name on my ship as crew and under my skin as something more. I want a future, and I want it to look and smell and taste and sound like Arcadio Escajeda.

Which is just about the most stupid thought I've ever had, so I return to the real world and the plan that could make all of this moot because it may very well kill me. The sound of a door creaking makes me freeze, and the person who was puttering around in the outpost exits the building.

"Fuck." Arcadio's commed voice in my ear startles me. We really have ruined his language.

"What?" I see a lot of reasons to say it but I'm not sure which one is his.

"This building is their armory." He stretches his neck and peers into the windows while still covering my back like a second suit of armor.

"That sounds like good news. Do you know how 'fuck' works?"

There's a pause where I assume he's biting back any number of responses that illustrate he knows exactly how "fuck" works. I can confirm. "It's nearly empty. They used it all in the conflict with the Children."

Oh. "Fuck."

"Exactly. We don't have any explosives to blow up the cannon."

"Do you just think flooding the caldera would stop them?" Maybe short-term. Short-term is probably enough to save those kids. Not enough to save the next people they target.

"No. Maybe a delay. Maybe not even that. If they've water-proofed the cannon, which they may have done for transportation purposes, it wouldn't slow them down at all so long as a Child or two can swim."

"The plan only works if we destroy everything." I don't see many options to destroy everything . . . except . . . "You aren't going to like this."

"What am I not going to like?" He sounds resigned to my insanity. He knows me so well already.

"We explode the volcano."

"We *what* now?"

"The weapon flips on its axis to allow for maintenance. What if we commandeer the cannon and shoot down instead of up? Best-case scenario, it blasts down to magma, which then merges with the flooding water and triggers an explosion. Worst-case scenario, it just blows itself up. Either way, problem solved."

"That sounds like a very generous definition of worst-case scenario. It's also an amazing way to get dead in either scenario."

"But once you get past that part, it could work."

"There are four of them and two of us. We underestimated them before."

"One of the four is Rashahan. The sniper isn't here. They'll be focused on keeping him alive. If we strike hard and fast, leaving them egress, we can force a retreat and fire the weapon while they regroup."

"You're ignoring the fact that regrouping means that, on the way out, we probably have to fight through the remaining Children who took out a base full of Nakatomi soldiers. Oh, and potentially there will be a wall of magma spurting forth behind us."

"It's not a fully contextualized plan yet. Give me another way through that floor and we can abandon it." I really hope he has another way through because I can't just cut and run this late in the game. That ship in the holo, filled with Family kids—the ones who might have the power to make the future better—I can't let the Children use them to make a statement. I never expected the dumb sense of responsibility I've been saddled with my whole life to extend quite this far.

I cough out a breath of disgust with myself. "Please have another way."

Arcadio shifts behind me, huffing a breath of his own. "I don't. So. While you do your cannon insanity, I'll take care of the Children."

"I know you're a tough son-of-Escajeda supersoldier, but remember the part about not underestimating them?" I shuffle my various blasters, tucking them in holsters, my belt, over my shoulder. Within the armored gloves, my palms are sweaty. We're going to do this. We're really going to do this.

His hand comes over my shoulder, cupping one of Caro's drones like it's fragile as an insect. "Blue light. If I give it the right intensity profile, I can collapse the buildings. It might cause enough of a distraction to buy you time to escape."

Hinging our whole survival on something as ephemeral as light and memory metal sounds exactly like the kind of plan we usually come up with. He really is one of us. "Let's do this now, before we realize how stupid it is."

"Too late. Try to survive, Reed." He wraps an arm around me, pulling me back into his broad chest. I take a moment to lean back, fingers clenching around his forearm. We feel solid. Right.

His hand ghosts across the exposed neck seam in my armor. Of course he's still thinking about that now. "The universe wouldn't be half as calamitously interesting without you."

"Tell them I said something clever."

"You don't survive, I'm telling them you said I was the best you ever had." His voice is strained. Maybe worried. Maybe something more than that. I can't think about that right now. If I spend too much time thinking about all the reasons to be worried, I won't be able to do anything.

"That's cruel."

"Then you'd better come running out of that caldera ahead of the lava."

That was kind of my plan to begin with, but I appreciate him providing additional motivation. I'm only taking on four of the Children. He has to handle all the others. I suppress the spike of worry in my stomach. "You don't make it, I'm definitely telling them the same thing."

Before he can respond, I move forward, keeping low and sliding around the fissure corner and into the smooth vase of the caldera. I'm almost out of range when his voice murmurs into my coms.

"It'd even be the truth."

I manage to not splat on my face at that preposterous statement, and finally, I approach the cannon, blaster in one hand and the strange heavy projectile weapon in the other. Rashahan is unarmed. At least two of the other three carry blasters strapped to their hips and thighs. I can't see the third, but I assume they also carry a weapon.

Now that I'm fully in the caldera, surrounded by dim red lights, I can barely make out the swivel bracket that allows the cannon to be moved into cleaning position. Two locking pins, one on each side, block the barrel of the weapon from sliding down accidentally. I must remove both of them before I can begin. It's like a cobweb of complexity below the scaffolding. Metal supports criss-crossing in the air, connecting with metal bars, with wire, with stiff planks of something that's probably plastic.

I take a shaky breath and continue my slow creep closer. Despite the red lights, it's dark in here and the three people on the platform are focused on the holo and the projected control panel. There's a chance that they won't notice me until it's too late. For them. Arcadio's coms are quiet. I'm too far from Caro, Itzel, or Micah to hear them. Sweat trickles and pools in the thin gap between my helmet and body armor—rolls down the sturdy black material. I wish I had that invisibility nanofabric. The shield bracelet on my wrist will protect me from a few shots before the armor has to bear the brunt of it.

The scaffolding rears in front of me, much higher than my head, and I'm about to be out of sight to relative safety when Rashahan stabs a finger into a specific part of the holo—boarding school, igniting it with red light, and then activates the control panel.

I'm too late.

The cannon in front of me begins to make a humming sound. One I've heard before on a much smaller scale, every time my blaster fires. I abandon discretion and run, sprinting the last distance before I'm at the scaffolding and ducking beneath the plastic flooring—which won't do a thing to block blaster shots but might block sight lines. No one shoots at me. They must be so excited about killing kids that they didn't even notice me.

My fingers wrap around the first pin. I rip it out. The framework around the cannon groans loudly as its weight and distribution shifts to put all the force on the other pin. Movement above me stops. Just when I think they might ignore the strange noises coming from the weapon, a face peers over the edge, eyes locking with my own.

I dodge to the side, putting the cannon's mechanism between

us, forcing them to run around the scaffolding to get a better angle. It groans and creaks with their weight, listing to the side but not falling.

I try to rip out the other pin but, with all the weight of the cannon resting against it, it's stuck. Light flares, the shield bracelet taking glancing blows, disrupting others. It's like I'm a human mirror, reflecting lasers all around me. I frantically tug on the pin with my right hand, and I point the projectile weapon with my left.

I don't have that many bullets. I don't know how many. Not enough. The light of my shield bracelet fades as the two armed Children try to get a shot.

I stop counting bullets and simply return fire, punching satisfying holes through the plastic flooring above me in the vicinity of the heads that keep peering over the edge. Someone screams. Something thuds. I wrestle with the fucking pin. Finally, it gives way and I've released the cannon.

It doesn't fall.

This was all that was holding it up. Why isn't it falling? The hum is intensifying and I'm nearly out of time. It probably takes a set duration to predictive map the atmosphere and build the energy to blast through and explode a bunch of schoolkids, but not that long.

Blood drips over the edge of the platform. I climb partially up the scaffolding until I'm level with the swivel joint. Above it. I must have only hit one of the armed men because another blaster shot slams directly into me, blowing completely through the weakened shield bracelet and smacking into my armor with a scalding burn that sizzles over my hip.

I deliver a solid kick to the heavy structure of the cannon. It moves. Only about a hair's width, but movement. The hum of the mechanism as it powers up is building, shaking through my bones. I kick it again. A third time. My arms ache. Another burning shot hits my shoulder, dispelled by the armor but intense enough to hurt. More shots go wide as I swing from the scaffolding.

My boots hit the smooth metal tube of the cannon. Again. I swing back with my entire body, curling my knees to my chest, and when I fly forward, I shoot them out, hitting the cannon with everything I have. With a creak like a skyscraper collapsing, it spins on its socket joint, sliding through the open space in the scaffolding and pointing downward.

I'm so stunned that it worked, I dangle there long enough to get shot one more time, the burn traveling over my ribs. Projectiles gone, I drop to the floor, pull my other blasters and limp-run as fast as I can toward the fissure in the stone wall of the caldera. Voices yell behind me, a blaster shot hits me square in the back, and the hum of the cannon reaches an intensity that's almost a scream.

Feet beat against stone; they've abandoned the scaffolding and are racing after me. Or away from what's about to happen. The cannon delivers its payload, a handsbreadth from the floor of the caldera, and the earth shakes. A blinding flash follows me as I shoulder my way into the fissure and around the corner—just in time for a nearly as blinding blue flare to explode from a swarm of drones hovering in the air like confetti tossed in zero-g. Metal walls collapse like fabric, pooling on the floor, except the floor doesn't want anything to pool on it. It's shaking like a giant has stomped its feet.

Screams come from everywhere, hard to track so I don't try.

A crack spikes forward, right beneath my feet. I come down wrong on the edge of it, twisting my bad ankle, and manage to roll to the side as the false roadway collapses. I got the lucky side. The other falls into a new fissure, deep below, and from that pit comes a scalding breath of air. I scrabble to my feet, running as fast as I can with a bum leg and body covered with burns but maybe—just maybe—no irreversible damage.

Someone tackles me before I can get to the lava tube that is supposed to be my rendezvous with Arcadio. We tumble across the shattered earth in a tangle of thrashing limbs. A Child. A familiar one. The one Rashahan spoke with before, Candor. I head-butt him between the eyes and shove him off, but two other Children are there, large blasters pointed at me.

Two small explosions sound and both drop like their strings were cut. Arcadio appears, another large projectile weapon in hand, kicks the still-prone Candor, and grabs my arm, hoisting me to my feet. His grip is solid and strong, and I want to climb him like a tree in relief except we aren't out of the now very active volcano yet. More cracks appear around us.

"Explosives might have been a better plan," he yells, and I can hear his voice even through both of our helmets, a fraction of a moment before the coms report the same message.

"They lack style," I holler back.

"I was unaware that 'apocalypse' was a style."

CHAPTER 23

We flee through chaos. Each direction offers a different tableau of a disaster. A woman dangles from the partially collapsed third floor of the large building, clutching the corner support with only one hand while the other spins free in the air. Two other Children stretch their arms to reach, but too late; her grip slips and she plummets to the ground. I turn my head before she hits. A man is half-trapped under fallen rock, a puddle of metal sheeting draping his torso like mercury. He thrashes feebly and a growing puddle of red pools out beneath the metal. Ahead, two Children wrestle over a box of something.

Behind them, I see Generosity—clean blond braid and gap in her teeth—shoving another woman, perhaps Charity, into a lava tube. A Child grabs her by the shoulder, and in one swift economical movement, our little cult bunny flips him in the air. He lands with a crack and her boot comes down on his neck with a stomp and a twist.

She is not the shy victim we thought we rescued. I don't know what the fuck she is. I *am* happy, however, that she didn't stomp on any of our necks. We must be doing something right.

I glance over my shoulder. A bad habit. Rashahan is right on our heels, but he's not chasing us. He's running ahead of the magma currently rolling out of the collapsing caldera floor.

It turns out I can go a little bit faster. Arcadio keeps pace with me, which makes me think that either I'm much more athletically talented than I believe or he's slowing his pace to match mine.

Kaiaiesto isn't exploding—not yet—but it's far angrier than it was a few moments ago. This should give everyone time to evacuate, but besides Generosity and her undetermined companion, none of them seem to be making the right choice. That may be because we've so devastated the space that they don't know which disaster is the highest priority.

"How smooth do you think the tube floor is?"

Arcadio takes the abrupt question in stride. "Rougher than ice, smoother than gravel."

"And the slope?" My idea is going to look deeply stupid if I'm wrong.

"Down toward the metal door." He fires on two approaching Children, takes a shot in the abdomen that the armor hopefully deflects.

"That's what I thought."

"Is this idea any better than your last one?"

"Hey! My last one worked." And I'm not sure how much longer my leg is going to hold out. My limp is growing progressively more pronounced.

"We're running through a catastrophe ahead of a slow-moving wave of lava."

"Sometimes that's what working looks like!" I yell in frustration. "Now, are you going to ride one of these sheets of liquid metal down a lava tube like it's a slide with me or not?"

"*That's* your plan?"

"It's faster than running and my knee is about to break in half."

He practically throws me through the air as he boosts me into our familiar lava tube, and I roll as fast as I can to avoid him when he follows. I scramble to the edge to help but he springs up and pulls himself to the lip of the tunnel with very little effort.

"I thought you weren't modded." The words pant out of my mouth.

"All natural. Some people like to work for it." That explains why he's wasting time with me. I may be many things but "a lot of work" tops the list.

"Instead of sledding on a dubious piece of metal just because you can't admit when you need help—" He sweeps me into his arms like I'm some kind of invalid and sprints into the darkness. I yelp, arms going around his shoulders as I feel his body working with every step. I'm definitely *not* super turned on.

It's been a rough day. I'm entitled to be carried through the tunnel. Especially if he puts me down before anyone sees us.

Also, running would have been difficult because I can't see a fucking thing; the little red lights are flickering with the disruption of the volcano.

"I swear, the two of you always find a way to wind up wrapped around each other." Caro's voice rings through the coms. We've made our way back to them.

I squirm in his grip. This is my crew, after all, it doesn't send a good message about my capability that I need to be carried. Arcadio holds me one moment longer, fingers tightening against my skin, until he lowers me to my feet.

"Do you have good news for us? Because we have a slow-moving magma wave for you. Also, fairly soon, this whole tube is going to be full of screaming Children and—this may come as a shock to you—they don't seem very rational."

I don't see the borer, but there is a large hole in the wall of the tunnel. The swarm finally arrives, little drones twisting in a murmuration along the ceiling of the lava tube before darting through the hole and casting illumination into the passage with the little sucking anemone. Itzel's in the other tube, perched atop the borer with one leg pulled up under her chin. Pablo sits next to her, staring like she's a magical creature.

It's a common reaction to Itzel.

"How did you even get it into the tube?"

"Drilled ourselves a slope after moving the borer to a more secluded spot."

I look agape at the borer. It's still shot to shit. "But it didn't work. I hit the wall with the blades on and nothing happened."

Caro snickers. Micah snickers. Pablo snickers. Even Itzel snickers.

"What?"

Caro steps through the hole in the tunnel, water lapping around her waist, and reaches into the cockpit of the machine. An articulate finger gestures at one of the many levers, buttons, and toggle switches. "Counterclockwise." She flips the switch upward. "Clockwise. You were drilling in reverse. Doesn't matter so much when you're using it to pulverize enemies. Matters a lot when you're trying to bore through rock."

I tell myself this is why the world has engineers—even though this particular mistake is one that probably didn't really require a fancy degree to resolve.

"What's the plan to complete the connection to the river?"

Caro adjusts the steering mechanism, tilts the blade so it will travel on a downward trajectory, flips the "clockwise" switch, and picks up a heavy rock. She drops the rock on the accelerator and the borer lurches forward.

"I'm glad I have you here for all these complicated technical problems."

"I'm going to get even more technical. It's time to run like hells because we don't want the river sucking us back into the magma, which means we need to get to the part flowing away from us instead of the part flowing toward us."

Arcadio grabs my hand as we slosh through the waist-high water, lit only by the whirring swarm of drones above. His fingers are solid and strong around mine, a point of contact in the wet darkness.

I cling harder than is strictly necessary, until the swarm suddenly plunges into the water directly in front of us, glowing below the surface like bioluminescent fish.

"This is the connection to the river." Caro pulls up beside us, eyes snagging on our clasped hands before pointing at the glowing water. "They'll form a path like they did before."

"Arcadio, you first." Someone armed needs to come out the other end just in case we have any other nasty surprises waiting. "Take a drone with you in case you need to signal help. Let the river carry you."

Wonder of all wonders, he follows the order. After a moment of bobbing above the string of drones, I send Micah, Pablo, and Itzel.

"You've gone from 'it's temporary' to overt affection pretty quickly," Caro says as we're waiting for Itzel to clear the gap.

"It's been a busy day." I consider letting it drop there. Perhaps it's the privacy of darkness that allows me to continue. "I want to enjoy every part I can."

She gives me a look like I'm being impossibly naive. "I know you like him, Temper. And I know I encouraged you. Just . . . be careful."

"Haven't been careful a day in my life. Seem unlikely to start now." A drone flashes green to indicate there's enough space after Itzel, and Caro dives without a retort of her own. Maybe leaving the conversation is her retort.

I'm alone, floating in the darkness under a volcano that any moment now will be doused in water, potentially triggering an eruption. No matter what, we saved the kids. It's too late for them to be targeted, not with the movement of the planet and the angle of the caldera. I take a deep breath, shove my borrowed face shield up, because it won't make any kind of seal, and plunge into the water, kicking as I pass under the flashing drones.

It's harder this time. Before, the current wasn't doing much of anything directly under this tube. Now it's trying to flow into it, to push me back into the magma and the Children. To make me burn. I thrash forward, kicking and slicing the water with my injured arms, lungs burning for want of air. I'm not going to make it. It's too far and I'm not going to make it.

Like the pressure relief of an open docking bay, I suddenly pop out on the other side, past the split of the river, the new dark current pushing me away from Kaiaiesto and the Nakatomis' weapon. From ahead, behind, all around, Itzel's and Caro's whoops of exhilaration echo throughout the swift moving river. Cracks above let in slivers of early dawn light, violet in hue.

Too many things can go wrong. Like the fact that Frederick wasn't among the dead bodies scattered around, but he knows I'm on to him. Like the fact that this whole "scouting mission" went so tits up that we're going to have to flee before our mapping runs are done and without any stealthily acquired information.

But the water is cool and smooth, the flashes of dawn are soothing, and the rolling motion of the current is comforting. I let my mind drift away from our myriad problems and, for the moment, focus on the fact that we're all alive and roughly intact.

Eventually, I emerge in a cenote that would be beautiful if it wasn't so familiar. The remains of a little fire still sit on the narrow beach on the edge. A pale tree, partially denuded of branches, climbs the wall. A scuff mark on that same wall, about halfway up, shows where my leg gave out and Escajeda took over the climb.

Arcadio stands on the beach, hands braced on narrow hips as he stares up at the warm dawn sky. Itzel, Caro, and Micah crouch over Pablo, lying on the beach rather like I once did. He doesn't look injured, just exhausted. I wonder if it would seem weak if I curled up next to him for a little nap.

"I expected you to be with your brother." I keep my voice low as I approach Arcadio.

His eyes flick to the prone form on the beach. He wraps an arm around me, resting his chin on the top of my head as we catch our breath. Somehow, he still smells good, instead of like smoke and fire and blood and sweat. I wrap my own arms around his waist, leaning into him so that I can hear the words rumble in his chest as he speaks. "He's fine. Enjoys the attention, I think, after so long with only the bad kind. And he told me to back the fuck off because he can handle himself—all evidence to the contrary. I doubt he'll be doing fieldwork anymore, though."

My stomach lurches and, for a second, I think I'm going to be sick until I realize that everything is lurching. The smooth unsettling roll of an earthquake that doesn't seem to know how to stop. I tighten the hug minutely but then force myself to step away. "I think the water just hit the magma."

Everyone swears. Including Arcadio. There's captaining left to do today, and I accepted the job. "Micah, get Pablo as mobile as you can. Itzel, cover them. Caro, gather your tech. Arcadio, let's get to the ship. We can hover over and drop a bucket to pick them up."

"A bucket?" Pablo's voice is outraged.

"It's a metaphorical bucket. You'll be fine."

He grimaces.

"Are you going to need help this time?" There's a smile in Arcadio's voice, despite it all, as we face the wall.

"I'm fine." I grab a chunk of rock and mercilessly pull myself up.

"That's what you said last time. That's what you always say. Have you actually been 'fine' even one time?"

"Sure. This time. If you're that desperate to get my hands on you, it should motivate you to help us get off this fucking planet."

It's certainly motivating me. This time, I make it all the way up the cenote wall, pulling myself over the lip and into the canyon. If we ever do get some additional funds, I'm expanding the climbing wall in the *Quest*. Who knew climbing would be so important?

And now, just a quick endless run to the *Quest* on a knee that's a whisper away from collapse and then a quick launch to sweet freedom.

"I think we're going to make it." I actually let myself smile with relief.

The ground lurches again, the air goes still and silent, and Kaiaiesto erupts in a massive gout of ash.

CHAPTER 24

My knee is in better shape than I estimated because it gets me through the canyon, up the sharp switchback trail, and halfway across the mesa before it buckles. I catch myself before I tumble. Arcadio's hand wraps my arm.

"We're almost there. Can you make it?"

"I can make it." I'm talking to myself almost as much as to him. The top of the mountain is glowing red with splashes of lava that glisten against the lightening sky. Gouts of black smoke shadow the sky. My stolen face shield is down to prevent the falling flakes of ash from scalding my face. I admire that he believes me even when I'm clearly lying.

Except I'm apparently telling the truth because we make it to the plank leading up to the entrance hatch, gasping for breath. Halfway through entering the passcode to access the *Quest*, the whine of a blaster powering up freezes my fingers.

"Hello, sister. We didn't get a chance to finish our conversation." Frederick steps out from behind the landing strut closest to the ramp, blaster drawn and fully armored. His face shield is clear enough for me to see his satisfied expression.

Both Arcadio and I have been shot enough that our armor's functionality is near zero. My blaster is also near zero.

After being shot, healed, being shot again repeatedly, outrunning magma, outswimming magma, and then a jaunty little rock climb followed by a footrace over the uncertain soil of Herschel Two, I'm *personally* near zero. Despite my constant claims of being fine, I have nothing left. Certainly not the kind of energy that it would take to contend with my brother yet one more time.

Arcadio does, though. He turns in one smoothly oiled motion, his own blaster rising.

Frederick shoots him five times in the neck joint of his armor, and Arcadio falls bonelessly to the ground. Still. So still.

"Now that he's out of the way, I want to propose a deal." Frederick sounds as matter-of-fact as if he'd just asked a servant to dispose of the remains of his breakfast.

I absolutely lose my shit.

Before I realize what I'm doing, I dive off the ramp at my brother, a heedless full-body tackle that should never work considering our size disparity. I'd never attempt it in my right mind, which is why he's not expecting it. My shoulder collides with Frederick's stomach and we both crash to the sand, his blaster spinning from his grip.

Unfortunately, he's kept up his training, because when we hit the ground, he kicks me over his head, gripping my wrist as I fly through the air yet again, and spinning me so I land half-pinned by him.

Ash flutters around us and the ground grumbles. The sun glows like an angry ember. One hand is still free and I huck the empty projectile blaster at his face shield as hard as I can. The glass splinters.

As Arcadio once taught me, modern armor is far more about protecting against light than against projectiles. The blaster made a dent but my fist following it breaks through. Shards of glass drive into Frederick's cheeks. I wriggle out from under him and stumble to my feet.

"I just wanted to talk in privacy." He rises, dodging a kick. "Don't pretend you care about an Escajeda. You've made it clear you don't hold affection for any Family I deal with."

"You don't shoot him!" I screech the words in a voice I've never used before and deliver a hard front kick to his knee, grinning with feral glee as I hear the joint pop. "You don't *ever* get to hurt one of my people."

Frederick swings a meaty fist at my head, and I don't dodge it quite quickly enough. He connects with the side of my helmet and the sound booms in my ears.

I stagger back, cheek smarting with pain where the helmet cracked into it, sparks dancing across my vision. It's hard to react quickly when someone hits you in the face. I almost don't do it in time. As his next blow shoots at me, I duck under it and deliver a low hook to the side of his knee. He shifts his weight and takes another swing that I don't clock in time.

"You've never beat me in your life, Temper. What makes you think you can today? I only wanted to talk. You're all the kin I have left. You're supposed to be the nice one. I don't want to fight you, but if you force the issue, I'll knock you out and drag you somewhere that would make you more amenable to conversation."

His uppercut digs into the space under my ribs like my brother is reaching for my heart, and I gasp as all the air is propelled forcefully from my lungs. Only my monster of a brother would think that shooting the man I'm with is an opening gambit to a conversation.

Not just the man I'm with. The man I *love*.

I haven't thought it before. Barely let myself think it now because it might be too late. Imagine realizing you're in love while your brother beats the shit out of you as a way to reestablish the glory days of his youth and the object of said love lies maybe-dead in the sand. It's not an ideal moment for an epiphany.

I try to thrust my fingers at Frederick's eyes, but I'm too stunned to make more than a token effort as I sag over his fist. The armor doesn't do much to cushion the blow.

So I punch him in the nuts. It's his turn to fold in pain.

"I'm not nearly as nice as I used to be."

He whips out a knife. I withdraw the last thing I have that resembles a weapon: the tension wrench of my lockpick set, never returned to my boot with the rest of my tools after I finished with Pablo's cell door. It looks kind of pathetic in comparison with the knife. When Frederick swipes, I roll backward into a somersault and kick up, boot contacting his chin as I tumble away. Problem is that his chin is about as hard as my boot. He grabs my ankle in a mirror to the move that Arcadio tried on me in the training space. Unlike that day, I don't play around with my response. I kick him in a spot that's still bleeding from an earlier wound and escape.

He yells and falls back, hand clutching at the bloody spot. As I trip forward to restrain him, his other hand slashes out at my neck where my helmet fails to meet my armor. I jerk backward.

"Too slow, brother."

His eyes widen like he's made a mistake. His mouth opens but I'm done allowing him to have the last word. When he lunges forward, knife falling from his grip, I stab my tension wrench right into his eye.

It's only then that I realize the blood on the ground isn't all Frederick's, and the front of my armor is sticky with fluid that is slipping out of the puncture in my own neck. I drop to my knees in the ashy sand, gloved hand clutching my throat as I watch the lava splash from the mouth of Kaiaiesto. The blood pours from me even faster.

Somewhere far away, I hear a man screaming.

.   .   .   .   .

I swim in disorientation as I wake; the periodic rattle in the *Quest* is out of place, as is the bright bluish light that shines on my face. It comes back in pieces. I'm in the infirmary. Bandages swathe my body, sticky with burn ointment that smells astringent. The gauzy fabric glows almost neon orange in the light. When I reach for my neck, it's bound in a thicker layer of bandages. I swallow. It doesn't hurt nearly as bad as I thought it would.

"Temper?" Arcadio's beautiful face and gorgeously uneven nose hovers over me. His hand clutches my arm hard enough to edge on pain. For someone as controlled as Arcadio, the gesture is equivalent to dissolving into a puddle of tears. I must have been deeply fucked up.

"Everyone okay?" My voice is hoarse.

"Everyone's fine." He's still holding my arm like he thinks I'll try to escape. When I glance over, Pablo is on the other table. A holo over his body indicates that he's been put in a healing state, where the body focuses all resources on fixing what's broken. In his case, probably severe malnutrition and some light torture. Can't do anything for him psychologically, but when he wakes up, he should be in much better physical shape. "Caro told me I'm not allowed in the helm anymore. I had too many ideas for improvements to your ship that would only cost your life's savings."

"Joke's on you." I awkwardly shift my weight on the table and squint at the lights above. His grip gentles immediately and he looks at his hand like he doesn't recognize it before setting it so close that his fingers brush my wrist. "I don't have a life's savings. It's all going to debts for the ship. You were hurt. Frederick shot you."

I try to reach up to trace his skin. I fall short. Arcadio captures my hand and sets it flat against his chest. My fingers curl into his coveralls. It's anchoring. Stable.

Secure.

"Stun setting knocked me out for a bit. If Frederick had tried to kill me, I'd be dead, damaged as my armor was, but I came to just in time to see you gouge your brother's eye out and then flop over with a river of blood coming from your neck."

"And you spent my convalescence trying to change my ship?"

"I get compulsive when I'm nervous."

"Is Pablo all right?" I roll my eyes back over to Pablo. Nothing looks too alarming, but I have a high bar for alarming.

"Malnourished. Dehydrated. You were in worse shape than he was. Tried to say he was fine but then he fainted. You two have a lot in common."

"My throat was cut—better shape than me is a low bar. Caro and Itzel?"

"Busy with a new project."

"Frederick?"

"He got away." Arcadio shakes his head in disappointment. His muscles tighten beneath my fingers. I press against him, trying to soothe. "I know you wanted to bring him to justice."

I did. I do. In a month, I'll probably be upset about it. Right now, the fact that we're all alive and largely uninjured is such a miracle that I can't dwell in my fear of what Frederick will do while loose. He shot Arcadio with a stun blast. I don't understand why he'd do that, but it wasn't a mistake. Frederick didn't want to kill him, which is just enough for me to not want my brother immediately dead. The fact that he slit my throat doesn't soften me to him, but that look of panic and fear in his eyes right before I passed out makes me think that it might have been a mistake.

Frederick is a monster. I have no illusions as to my brother's humanity or lack thereof. But he's playing a game I don't completely understand, and while he was clearly happy to beat me to a pulp, he didn't want to kill me any more than he did Arcadio. I don't believe for a moment that he's still on Herschel Two. My brother would have at least two escape routes planned for any situation.

Nati taught both of us that.

I try to sit up. "We need to make a plan. . . ."

"We've got a long trip, Captain." He calls me captain, and my heart sticks in my throat. "Right now, all you need to do is rest."

So I do.

. . . . .

Somehow, in the two days I was out of commission, the *Quest's* mess has become an aquarium. Glass tanks, bowls, and even plastic trays filled with water are everywhere, each one containing several blobby anemones.

I blink. Still there. So I limp down the hall using crutches, weak leg immobilized in a torturous brace that Micah insisted upon if I want to move around under my own steam. When I get to Itzel's shared bunk, I pound on the door. No one answers. "Itzel, what have you done to our mess hall?"

I try the other bunk.

No answer. I lumber around the top level, drift into the helm, and finally down to the armory. A new sketch bedecks the wall outside the armory. It isn't based on one of Caro's previous abstractions, although I see her hand in the forms alongside Itzel's. A volcano bursts from the deck, taking over most of the wall, with lava spilling from its caldera down its side in slick rivers. Five figures ride down a lava river floating on broken pieces of space laser, grins on their faces. Me. Itzel. Caro. Micah.

Arcadio.

I press my lips together against the swell of inconvenient emotion that threatens to overwhelm me. My fingers brush against the wall.

The door slips open, and I only have time to note that the interior lights are on before a chorus of voices yell, "Surprise!"

A shower of holo-confetti sparkles over the doorway as I limp into the room. Small drones hover near the ceiling, dragging streamers, and Itzel settles a sparkling star field of a crown over my head. It's made of cheap synth foil and the holo-sparks are created by cracking a temp-battery, but it's one of the most beautiful things I've ever seen.

"This is a 'thank you,'" Itzel says, as she fluffs the foil on my head.

I do a quick catalogue of things they should be thanking me for. Wind up empty. It must show because Caro jumps in to explain. She loves to explain. "A successful first mission!"

"What's your definition of successful?"

"We're all alive. We stopped the machinations of the Nakatomis—kind of. We rescued Pablo. We definitely stopped the machinations of the Children."

"We didn't complete the mapping for phydium."

"We didn't need to!" Itzel again, jubilant grin lighting her face. "Those anemones in the tunnels expel a very specific waste. One incredibly high in phydium."

I lean hard on the crutches. "You're telling me we stumbled upon anemones that shit phydium?"

"I'm telling you we found anemones that shit phydium!" She practically sings the words. Seems appropriate that our contribution to the advancement of the human race is anemone shit.

That explains why my mess is an aquarium. "We found phydium, saved a boarding school full of children, rescued an Escajeda, destroyed a secret volcano weapons base, and uncovered a spy?" I hoot out a laugh that's nearly maniacal. "Talk about value for their investment."

"One more thing, with your approval." Caro's own grin is wide. "We all agree that *Quest* is a terrible name." Everyone nods. "In honor of our captain and her greatest descriptor, I propose that we rename the ship *Calamity*."

Everyone cheers, which tells me that this has been discussed and agreed upon by the entire crew.

Do I wish that my greatest descriptor was "majestic" or "prodigy" or even "sexy"? Yes. Yes, I do. Do I acknowledge that their word is a more apt characterization? Also yes.

And a more apt characterization of the ship herself, who is also something of a calamity.

"Who am I to argue the perfect name?" It might not be the most glamorous, but it's earned and bequeathed with love.

Arcadio hands me an aluminum cup filled with something partially cloudy. My fingers brush against his and I look into his eyes, trying to reassure myself that this isn't a dream. He is here, alive, in front of me. He taps the side of my cup with his own. "To Calamity Reed."

"Calamity Reed!" everyone choruses. I don't argue the Reed part. I let Frederick take enough from me. He won't take my name anymore. I won't let him.

When I knock back the drink, it scalds the back of my tongue.

"Ardot." I stare at the beautiful sky-field of liquid within the cup to hide the sudden tears that fill my eyes. I haven't had a taste of it in years. So many years. It tastes just like I remember. Absofucking-lutely awful and exactly like home.

I spill a little on the floor of the *Calamity*, giving her a taste of Reed space.

"Your crew mentioned how you try to find a substitute, and I happened to bring a flask of it along with me."

Arcadio remembered a passing reference and actually did something about it. My fingers tighten around the cup. When I glance up, his face is open and there's something in his eyes that I can't quite read. A tiny terrifying voice tells me that it's spelled like "goodbye."

"Good job keeping us all alive but still giving me interesting triage." Micah pats me on the back with a heavy hand. "I'm off to cook dinner. Expect something with grilled meat and vegetables. No, not people meat. You're obsessed with people meat. Sometimes it really is a lizard."

Then he leaves. I'm going to have to tell him about Generosity. As though I understand a thing about Generosity. I hope she found her way out. I wish I knew exactly what she was there for.

I celebrate with my crew until the sparks fade from my crown, the tray of food Micah eventually brings down is emptied to streaks of grease and crumbs, and the ardot flask that Arcadio propped on the weapons rack is drained. When I return to my bunk, Arcadio follows me.

"I gave Micah his private bunk back."

"Generous of you." I blink innocent eyes at him. "Wherever will you sleep?"

Probably he figured out that the room across from me is a whole empty bunk and not a storage closet.

"I have an idea." He slides the door shut behind him and advances on me. His hand traces down the arc of my cheek. It strokes featherlight over the bandage on my neck. "I thought I lost you for a moment there."

I swallow. I was certain I lost him, too. I can still hear the heavy thump of his body hitting the sand like a dropped slab of meat. I can still see the stillness in it. "I'm hard to get rid of. I should thank you. For that lifesaving thing."

"You should. It was very heroic. I screamed while holding your neck shut and then remembered you have a whole infirmary that has much better tools for wound staunching than hands." He looks at his hands like he can still see my blood on them. "I had to choose between you and Frederick. I couldn't save you and capture him."

"You screamed for me?" It's the most romantic thing I've ever heard. Never mind the fact that my brother escaped. I'll deal with that later. "And you saved the crew."

"You saved the day. It was time to do my part."

When I finally sleep, with his large form curling around my back like a blanket, I dream of something other than fear and pain for the first time in a long time.

CHAPTER 25

■ ■ ■ ■ ■ ■ ■ ■ ■ ■ ■ ■ ■ ■ ■ ■ ■

When I wake, the warm weight of an arm curls around my waist, pressing me against Arcadio's body. I freeze, momentarily struck numb by my unexpected good fortune and the knowledge that it may be about to run out. He nuzzles at the back of my ear, tongue gently tracing the sensitive skin. The hard length of him presses urgently against me.

I don't know if we're a team or a ticking time bomb set to explode when we hit the way station. Last night was something different than before, but it was in the privacy of space. Everything will change when his Family is back in play. This has been an interlude in his life. The knowledge of how little time is left finally motivates me into turning to face him. Now we're sharing air, nose to nose, breath mingling, bodies one tight knot.

I don't ask Arcadio about his Family. About what comes next. I can't bear to hear him say it out loud. Instead, I absorb his features like they're all the nourishment I need to survive. Because I want to remember them when this is over. I want to remember every moment of it.

His eyes narrow slightly, and he angles his head, tongue trailing up my nose.

It startles a chuckle from me. "Why did you do that?"

"I wanted to see what you'd do. You didn't go running the other way either."

"You have me trapped in my bunk." I dart my head forward and lick him back. It's like a gross secret language that we share.

"I know you, Temper. Nothing keeps you trapped if you don't want it to. You somehow always come out on top. You won a knife fight with a lockpick."

"That's what I keep trying to tell people. This is what the top looks like."

"I've never been anywhere higher." He pauses, eyes pinching shut. "I don't—I can't—" And then he kisses me. His fingers press along my jaw, my cheeks, cradling my face with a desperate sort of urgency. My legs tangle with his until one broad thigh rests between my own, and my lips, my tongue, my everything is focused only on him. I want nothing more. Maybe there *isn't* anything more.

This isn't banter and play, it's something deeper and borderline frenzied. Something necessary like oxygen. Like fire. And like fire, it engulfs us. I yank at his pants. He rips at my top. We are hungry for skin. Heat. More points of connection, as though if we find enough, we will be welded together permanently and the forces that wait to tear us asunder won't find a seam to exploit.

Maybe that's just me, but as his hungry mouth traces hot wet kisses down my neck, as his hand delves between my legs, fingers stroking, probing, I feel the restrained energy in his body. That same desperate charge that is running through my own, electrifying my nerves into a kind of savage joy.

When he thrusts home, I'm ready for him, body clamping hard. My head falls back. My legs wrap his waist. His fingers thread through mine.

Our gazes lock. There are universes in the gold specks of his eyes. Whole worlds that I've barely begun to explore. His thumb traces a line over my cheek. "I have to tell you something. I—"

This time, I kiss him. Smother the words in his mouth because I can't let that be goodbye. He's going to break my heart. The tension by his eyes, his mouth, in his hands where they clasp my own, says that I just might break his, too.

I don't want to. It wasn't my goal. I never thought I'd be this far gone for him. Never in a million years thought he'd be gone for me at all. But then he's moving, urgent and strong and solid. When the tension in me spikes and then releases I can't think of anything but the feel of him in and around my body. About what safety feels like. What home feels like.

About how, sometimes, you don't leave home—it leaves you.

. . . . .

This time, we don't wait outside the door for Ina Escajeda to decide whether we are worthy of entry. Arcadio offers his eye to a scanner by the door and sketches a symbol on the touch pad below. When the door closes behind us, I realize that nearly all the sounds of the station are silenced. It's creepy. Trust the Escajedas to only be surrounded by their own noises.

The Escajeda waits in his position of power, in front of the gilt-framed paintings, hands on his knees, hair in perfect order. Ina perches beside him, as before. I wonder if they just sit like this all day. If an Escajeda stands up to go get a snack, and no one sees it, did it even happen?

The holo is active on the table, a giant plume of ash pumping vigorously from the widened caldera of Kaiaiesto. Ina rushes to Pablo's side, brushing a hand over his brow, and then holds his cheeks between her palms as she looks deeply into his face, studying it for any harm. I'm pretty sure all the harm is inside.

He steps back and says something quietly. She responds in the same tone before leading him deeper into their house. He doesn't say "goodbye." Or "thank you."

"Your ally betrayed you," I say, swiping all the information on Frederick to their datapads. I don't tell the Escajeda that I suspect the Nakatomis have someone else in their corner. Someone who kept attention in a different direction. All I have is a suspicion in the shape of the Pierce Family. The Escajeda is smart enough to make his own deduction.

Arcadio makes a deeply pained sound like he thought I would handle this in a measured and sophisticated way. His father makes the exact same sound. I manage to smother a snort. It's either that or a sob. I can't think of the future. I must focus on the moment.

"Not only did Frederick plot with the Nakatomis with the express purpose of attacking your interests, but his incompetence at the endeavor also left a devastating weapon in the hands of a group of fanatics who were about to use it to target a boarding-school ship."

"You inserted yourself in my son's mission and did not complete your own assigned task. The maps submitted are incomplete." Here it comes. The moment when the Escajeda tries to worm his way out of our deal.

"My mistake." I feign innocence. It's not a tactic, it's just fun. "I thought you were interested in phydium. If all you cared about is the maps, I would have completed them, but I believed the resource took precedence."

I remove a jar of anemone from my coveralls and set it on the wood-grained holo-table, directly in the center of rotation of the projection of Herschel Two. "Your labs will confirm that these anemones excrete compounds high in phydium. There is a natural habitat on Herschel Two, but also, they are easily reproduced in a lab. You can have a station stocked to its boundaries in less than a month at the rate of reproduction if you artificially propagate them."

The Escajeda leans forward like I put a magnet on the table instead of some squishy pieces of tissue. "Is this the truth?"

"I reviewed the data myself." I expected Arcadio to sit with his Family, as he did when we negotiated the contract. He's split the difference between us, standing off to the side. It feels like he's on the other side of the station. "My report has been sent to your servers."

The Escajeda reaches through the hologram and pulls out the jar, studying the disgusting little anemones like they're more precious than his own kin. He smiles and a small chill skitters down my back. "This will do. You're dismissed."

"This location contained two missions." Arcadio takes me by surprise when he speaks. I'm so happy to have payment that I'm already creeping backward toward the entrance. "They completed both. At great risk to their own well-being. And when they had the opportunity to leave with the job done and save themselves, they put themselves at additional risk to save a ship full of children. One of whom I've subsequently learned was Cousin Yana's oldest daughter, Nyura. They're owed payment for both."

He's been doing his research since we hit the ether-stream from the station. I could kiss him, but I suspect that would weaken his negotiating position.

The Escajeda looks as uncomfortable as if he's sitting on the still-bubbling Kaiaiesto. He glares at Arcadio like his son just stabbed him in the gut. I can see the calculations flashing behind his eyes. What is payment worth? The Family might look bad if it gets out that he chose not to be generous and he knows this story won't stay quiet. "If I agree to doubling the payment, do you have more swindling in store?"

Doubling the payment. I can wipe out my debts. I can make a significant dent in Caro's wish list for the ship. I can breathe on the way station without fearing that someone will track me down and break my knees.

"No swindling here," I affirm, and head for the door because he can change his mind and take back the offer.

As I pass Arcadio, I squeeze his hand. He doesn't meet my eyes. His bag is at his feet. Something sharp and painful skewers through me. I plaster a bright smile on my face. The way his father looks right now, Arcadio's going to be shipped deep into Escajeda territory and subjected to some intense brainwashing.

A ding from my datapad indicates that funds have been transferred into my account. I swallow the lump in my throat and pass him, allowing myself one last lingering glance. Arcadio stands tall. Strong. Still as a statue like the day we met. I hadn't realized how much he had relaxed on our ship. How he came alive. How different he is now.

He keeps his eyes on his father and doesn't look back at me.

CHAPTER 26

The story has already hit the newsfeeds by the time I get to my rented room. Caro has her sources and no one in the Flores Family would pass up gossip this good. Somehow, Frederick made it off Herschel Two and to the feeds before we did. As it turns out, his plan to come off as a duped incompetent in the eventuality of discovery works. Maybe not the best business move, but no one knows his true megalomania.

We don't have enough proof to destroy him like we do for the Nakatomis. And despite it all, I can't bring myself to go out of my way to crush my own Family. It's not just about Frederick. It's about all the people who rely on him for their livelihoods.

One of the broadcasters suggests creating a holiday in my name. Although they keep calling me Calamity Reed—something I wish Caro had left out of her communication with the Flores Family—the other broadcaster points out that I'm technically missing half my name.

"After seeing where Frederick Reed's desperation for customers got him, perhaps he should consider lifting the banishment." That's the weatherman. Yes, the story is so entertaining that the weatherman has joined the newscasters around their round table. Then again, the only weather on a station is if a regulator has gone out and then the report is: deadly.

It's preposterous, of course. Banishments don't just get lifted. But what if they did? I don't even know what I'd do with myself. I'm sure I could come up with a few ideas. I'd travel first. Anywhere I wanted to go. It would be something to have the freedom to travel unrestricted. To eat fresh food that hasn't grown rotten or frostbitten in its transport to a border way station. To track down Kari in person and tell her that I'm sorry—face-to-face.

The newscasters continue to speculate, and I go to sleep. There will be other days for speculation. Days when I haven't possibly lost the man that I love. Not that I told him I love him. I know better. The scion of a Family does not dabble with a nobody.

I wish he'd said goodbye. I wish I had, too.

. . . . .

When I wake, my personal mail is so full that a red light urgently blinks on my interface tattoo. I bring up the feed and scan it. News outlets demanding interviews. Nearly everyone I've ever met renewing our acquaintance.

Caro, bragging about how good her story was. Itzel, saying the best parts were really hers. Micah, telling me to pick up more bandages while I'm off-ship because I used up most of the old ones.

Silence from Arcadio. I haven't seen him since I left his Family's rooms. If I thought that Ven's abandonment was crushing, this is devastating. Which is silly, because I knew better all along.

He said *"our"* crew. He said "we."

That was the moment when I let myself hope. It was probably the heat of the moment. I swallow the pang away and am about to close the feed when one message captures my attention.

It's from "the Reed."

Ridiculous to message your own sister as "the Reed," especially after you just cut her throat, but Frederick never was anything other than ridiculous.

I open the message and Frederick's form projects on the holo-table in the corner. A doctor has already fixed his face, and smooth flesh-colored liquid bandages mask anything yet to heal. His hair is carefully combed. A stark black patch covers his eye. When he speaks, the bandages pucker against his skin.

"That was quite the production, sister. You always did like to make a scene. I didn't mean to kill you, though. That was a mistake." He reaches up with one hand to touch the eye patch. "You can kill everyone else, but you don't kill Family. I hope we both made mistakes. Don't worry, I have a new cybernetic eye waiting for me. I'm told I'll be able to see through walls. I suppose I should thank you for that. Some new friends are ensuring that I'm well taken care of."

Fantastic; after all that, he's getting even better mods than he had before. Mods that aren't even released for the general public. And new friends. I like that even less.

He stares down the camera, intensity sparking in his eyes. Eye. "If you're done ruining everything, it's time to help me rebuild. Somehow you . . . *you* . . . became the Reed that everyone loves."

It's like he doesn't believe I could be loveable.

"It was never personal, sister. It was business. You were bad for it. Now you're good." He shrugs as though that's all that matters. To him, it probably is.

And then his lips curl at one corner like he's savoring this moment, offering me something I'm incapable of refusing. "Everyone's giving you the Reed name now anyway. I'll lift the banishment. Only if you agree to move back to Reed station as the new face of the Family. No freedom to travel at first. I need to keep you under my . . ." He pauses and looks disgusted before tapping his face. "My eye. I'll even give you a third of the Family industries to run your idiotic way. If your strategy somehow provides growth, maybe up to forty percent of the industries. Think of all the good you could do counteracting your evil big brother. You made a point about fail-safes and other customers. I know you want to be a Reed again. You never stopped. I wouldn't either. Give up on your ramshackle ship and come back home.

"We're even, sister. An eye for a neck. Come home."

My breath catches in my recently healed throat like a fist has wrapped around it. I can be Temperance Reed in truth. I can have it all back. My room on our station, fresh food, fashion, but most of all, a budget and a purpose: the power to counter Frederick's worst evils. A real future based on more than simply survival.

A position in the Ten. All hurdles between myself and Arcadio gone in an instant. We would be equals in truth, or as close as anyone can come to an equal to an Escajeda.

All I'd have to do would be to forget Nati's murder. To leave the *Calamity*. They'd survive without me. Caro or Micah would probably be a better captain than I ever was.

For a moment I let myself consider it, really consider it.

Power and influence and catered parties. The ability to go anywhere I want. To do anything I want. To change the Reed name into something like what my parents wanted. To temper Frederick when he makes his bid to replace Nakatomi, because I'm sure he will. They're going down after this little escapade, leaving a tasty little opening in the Five.

I'm embarrassed to say that it's tempting.

But then I won't see what Itzel does with the remaining anemone that she cached. I won't have Caro in my ear, reminding me that my morals need work and my plans suck. I won't have Micah to patch up my wounds.

I probably won't even get any wounds because I'll be stuck in an office somewhere.

I couldn't hire Victor or Victory for security. The twins would get bored in a moment.

But I'd have Arcadio, maybe. I'd have a real shot and I want that shot so much it hurts.

In the end, the decision isn't difficult. I know who I am and where I belong. I know what I'm worth and I won't compromise. I send the one-word reply to Frederick.

"No."

.　.　.　.　.

"Temperance?" The familiar voice roots me in place. It's late in the day. I'm tired. I managed to make it through the day without crying, which I consider a personal victory.

"Hello, Ven."

"Talked to Itzel earlier. Didn't have to, though, your crew's been busy spreading the story throughout the station. Heard you had an adventure out there that's going to go into the story streams one day. Took on a Family and turned the planet itself to your favor." He's standing right there in the lobby part of the inn, looking dirty and rumpled and familiar. Not as amazingly handsome, though. I have a new metric for that. He looks like a man holding a peace offering and expecting it to be slapped back into his face. "Things didn't work out with Oksana. She left me before we even made it off the station."

Any other day, maybe I'd already be midslap. "Too bad."

He ignores my tone. "She decided she couldn't settle down with one person. Didn't really want to scout. Didn't want to do much at all."

That's the thing about young incompetents. They don't know what they want, and when they figure it out, they probably can't pull it off.

"I'd like to come back. I can buy back my shares."

Older incompetents maybe aren't all that different. I can't believe I saw anything in him. But we don't have security anymore.

Arcadio's gone. Back to his Family's loving embrace. It's strange that after all the years I spent with Ven, I consider Arcadio our security officer. Victor and Victory are pricey, that's why we don't keep them on full-time. We do need to fill the gap.

It feels like regression.

"I'd like to pick up where we left off," he continues, looking anywhere but at me. Is he really using himself as bait to try to encourage me to hire him? He wasn't *that* good in bed.

"Where is that?" I raise a brow.

"I know better now. I've learned better. Oksana . . . she was a beautiful package, you're the gift."

Gag. Also rude. I, too, am a beautiful package.

On some days.

If I have a month to prepare.

My answer is no, but it isn't about me. It's about the crew. We need security and I can't reject a perfectly good candidate for personal reasons. "I'll get back to you."

It looks like he has something else to say, but I don't wait for it. Instead, I go to my room and finger on my coms. Casino machines jingle happily in the background as Caro joins the link. A smothered moan comes from Itzel's end. She sure didn't waste time. Expectant silence from Micah.

"Ven wants back. Oksana left him. We're out security." There, that was dispassionate.

"Fuck, no. We just got rid of him and his stupid ship name." Caro.

"Victor and Victory are ever so much more interesting." Itzel.

Silence. Micah.

"Micah?"

"They said it for me."

"He was fairly competent at security," I argue weakly, feeling like I owe him the fight even though I don't want him either.

"Oh, that's a stellar selling point. Almost competent." Caro, as usual, is scathing. She hisses something unintelligible in the background and I hear the flipping sound of cards. "What about Arcadio? He's not just competent. He's awesome. You should get him back."

"He doesn't belong with us. He's from a Family." She thinks he's awesome. I don't think she believes *I'm* awesome and I've known her for years.

"You're from a Family, too," she flatly argues. "You saw common sense, maybe he will. If you ask. He's not a mind reader, Temper. The contract was over, and you left him with his Family."

No, I don't suppose he is a mind reader. I have a tenuous grip on my emotional state as it is and getting rejected to my face may push me over the edge. I can't do it today.

"So that's a no on Ven?"

"What do you want, Temper?" Itzel asks. The soft sussation of moving sheets sweeps over the background of the call. "Do you want Ven back?"

"Who cares if she wants him back? She *shouldn't* want him back. That's what matters." Caro hiccups an excited breath. She must have good cards. Or bad cards that she's trying to turn to her favor.

Micah disconnects.

"We require security." I rub a hand across my forehead, pressing thumb and index finger into my temples. "But I don't want it to be Ven."

I chose them. I chose being a captain. I might not be completely awful at it. I don't want to share. Even if he'd just be security, Ven is the past. Like those little anemone, I've propagated whole new emotional limbs since I saw him last.

"Thank you for your input."

The mass of the last few days weighs on me; the fast healings, the sleepless nights, the uncertainty, the sudden infamy. People keep cheering when I walk by or offering to buy me a drink. It's loud on the station, but not the noise of the *Calamity*. How silly. I finally get a chance to sleep in a nice room that doesn't have a strange rattle right outside the door, and I miss the fucking rattle.

I clear my stuff out of the rented room, scan my ident to check out, and make my way out of the inn and down to the docks. On the way, I give Ven the news. There's a cargo ship unloading on the far end, but the porters don't bother me, and I don't bother them as I make my way to my familiar monstrosity. I stroke the panel around the hatch. "We're going to fix you up before we hit planet again."

She doesn't answer. Because she's an inanimate object.

Calamity suits her. Something new. Something that isn't anchored in her past. Tomorrow, or maybe the next day, we'll take off for another station. Caro will start her repairs. Itzel will probably clone anemone. Micah will yell at me because I forgot to get more bandages. Maybe at the next stop, we'll pick up Victor and Victory. We'll need security.

I'll ask Arcadio if he'll come back. Caro was right; I can't expect him to read minds. But I know what it's like to leave a Family. How it scrapes you raw inside. There's a reason no one ever does it by choice.

I swallow back the thickness in my throat. Glance back at the station behind me. He's there somewhere. I wonder if he knows that I gave up my chance to be his partner in truth. I hope he doesn't take it personally.

I can't be in a Family anymore. I've evolved beyond it.

I step inside and that hatch slides shut behind me. Some of the weight slips from my shoulders. I could complete the walk to my bunk in my sleep. When I get there, the door slides open, and I drop my bags before I realize my room is not unoccupied.

"I'm certain you have a room of your own on the station. Probably multiple rooms of your own." I lean against a bulkhead and admire Arcadio, sprawled in my bunk with his legs dangling off the side because he doesn't even fit on the bed properly. A frantic crescendo of hope sparks my nerves. "I thought you'd be with your Family."

"I told them that I'm out of the business. They can banish me if they want." He tucks his hands behind his head, a small smile on his face like maybe he's enjoying being the rebel Escajeda.

"What I'm hearing is, you're looking for a job." Those tears I've been holding back all day spring to life in my eyes and I hold them wide. I will not cry at this moment, which may be the happiest in my entire life. I smile at Arcadio Escajeda as I sit down on the bed, straddling his hips. It's the only place in my room left to sit. He's filled my space with himself. My shaking hands settle against his chest.

"I seem to recall you have a security position open." His voice rumbles over me and my fingers curl into the shirt.

"We have several applicants. I just turned one down." I feel the need to clarify.

"If it sweetens the pot, I got you a gift."

I glance around my bunk. Don't see anything. Glare suspiciously. "You'd better not be referring to your dick."

Arcadio laughs and I feel the vibrations deep in my core. "Dirty-minded. I like it. No, I am not referring to my dick." He fishes in his pockets and withdraws a slip of honest-to-goodness paper. Hands it to me.

I unfold the paper. It's an appointment. At a mod-surgeon. "You have three heartbeats to explain yourself before I punch you in the neck."

More laughter. He holds his hands up in surrender. Uses them to frame my face. His thumbs trace a line under my eyes. "Night-vision mods. Best surgeon in Landsdown, which means he must be somewhere in the top ten thousand overall."

Something warm pools within me. "Why?"

"Life with you is going to be really irritating if you have to ask why every time I get you a gift." He pauses. Studies my face. Relents. "Because you deserve to see, and I know you won't do it on your own until you've made every ship-based upgrade possible. Because live flowers don't last long, and you don't seem like the type to enjoy candy. Because I already gave you all the ardot I have and I'm about to be broke because I left my Family for you."

He chose me. I can't believe he chose me. Not knowing that I'd choose him back. It's maybe the first time in my life that someone's chosen me. My heart lodges in my throat. I manage to choke out my reply. "We're going to be resupplying and retrofitting for a while. I suppose a security expert has an important role in all that."

His hands bracket my face. Gentle. Not like I'm precious. Like I'm exceptional. "I should probably tell you that I love you."

"You already told me." He did it when he chose me. When he chose my crew. When he was here, waiting in my bunk with no guarantees.

"This is where you tell me that you love me back."

I cradle his face back and lick the lovely crooked bridge of his nose. I press a soft kiss to his lips. "I love you, too, Arcadio Escajeda. I love your courage, and your wit, your kindness, and your fantastic mind . . . and your body. I love that you didn't expect me to change for you."

"Why would I ever want you to change? You're perfect."

He must really love me because only love could blind someone that much. I laugh right into his mouth. "You're insane. I'm in love with a crazy person."

He gently tugs me down, and when our lips meet, the rest of the station falls away. I am reduced to senses: the hot slide of his skin against my hands as I push up his shirt, the low rumble of pleasure he gives as I do so, his scent—clean and fresh but with a hint of heady musk, like the earth before a storm. I am encompassed by him. Electrified.

His arms coil around my shoulders, one hand bracing the back of my head and adjusting the angle until we align perfectly. I immediately ruin it by wrestling his shirt over his head, disrupting arms and mouth and everything else. I splay my hands across his chest, nails gently digging into the strong planes of muscle.

Worth it.

"You used to be concerned that we wouldn't fit." He comes up for breath from plotting a trail of kisses along my collarbone. At some point in the last few moments, my coveralls became unzipped and one of his hands has already delved around my hip to cup my ass. The other traces a gentle line up my spine.

Not to be outpaced in the race to have each other naked, I start work on the fly of his pants. "I'm confident that your creativity exceeds our limitations. You really said no to the Escajeda? What did his face look like?"

He chose me.

He chose me. He chose *me*. It rings in my head like a bell. Glee washes over me like a sonic pulse. A solar flare that scorches to my very core and leaves me new. Reformed.

And I choose him. I choose *this*. No more stolen moments. We own them all.

"Can we not talk about my father right now?" He shoves the coveralls down over my shoulders, taking advantage of the fabric snaring my arms to band his own around me and press me to his chest, talented tongue sliding against my own until I'm squirming on his lap, semihelpless and completely desperate for more.

"Who?" I blink at him.

His lips slowly curl into the sexiest smile that I've ever seen, feral and hungry and *eager*, and he moves the coveralls the last amount, freeing my arms and shoving the fabric down around my hips. I finally make my fingers work well enough to unfasten his fly, reaching in and wrapping my hand around his scalding hot flesh.

Impatient hunger of my own flares, and I push against his chest until I can get to my feet and shimmy the coveralls all the way off. I divest myself of compression bra and shorts just as quickly and try to haul his pants down. They get caught between his butt and the bed, and instead I yank his pelvis forward until it's almost at the edge of my mattress.

"Would you like some help?" He laughs, standing long enough to shove all clothing to the floor.

I push him back to the bunk and straddle his lap, starving for the contact, completely devoid of couth, gasping as my skin meets his in a fiery line. I allow myself to be lost for a moment in the feel of his kiss, the soft sweaty slide of his skin, the blood pounding in my veins, the flare of his pulse under my fingers, my lips. Delicious molten warmth pools in my entire body.

One of his hands traces forward, dragging over my hip, drawing slow circles on the way down to my core.

"You thought you got rid of me." His voice has dropped an octave or two, rumbling like shards of gravel dragged over my skin.

I gasp a breath as his thumb rubs exactly the right spot. "I was very upset about it."

"Did it ever occur to you to ask me to stay?"

What are we talking about? I can't think about anything other than the sharp circles of his thumb, the slide of his dick between my legs. "I was going to."

His lips curve against my own. "Beat you. I win."

I rise slightly on my knees, and he slams home so fast that I

briefly lose control of my limbs and go completely limp against his
chest. I gasp a breath. Not pain. Completion. As though this is our
natural state.

I win, too.

He presses a hot kiss against my temple. I don't know what I did
to deserve this. To deserve a bold, brave, fucking emotionally open
man, willing to offer me everything he is.

I brace my palms on his broad shoulders and roll my hips, lux-
uriating in the feeling of him within me, around me. His hands
settle on my hips, allowing me to set the pace, encouraging it. Our
current position places my breasts in front of his face and he takes
advantage, sucking one nipple, then the other.

We find our rhythm, me in a downward grind, him in an up-
thrust. I clasp hands with him. Holding them to the bed—just
holding them—as my hips flex and that amazing pressure grows
and circles in the very center of me.

He's mine. Out of all the odds, all the obstacles stacked against
us, he's mine. And I'm his. That thought, in conjunction with the
pounding urgency in my blood, the reckless hedonism that spills
through my skin, the joy of Arcadio and me and this moment, is
enough to shove me over the edge.

My body shakes, control lost, and I fall against his chest, making wordless sounds that are definitely not begging, riding the
waves as he wraps his arms around me and picks up his speed,
hammering home in powerful thrusts that are enough to ricochet
me right back into another orgasm. He finally joins me, holding
me like he's falling apart and I'm all his missing pieces.

He's all mine.

We breathe in sync as we come down, so wrapped in each other
that I'm not sure where I end and he begins. Maybe it doesn't
matter. Maybe I can simply enjoy the fact that we are here. Now.
And in the future.

I nuzzle the rich dark fall of hair just behind his ear. "Are you sure you're okay leaving your Family?"

He kisses me again, a firm press of the lips as he looks so deeply in my eyes that I can count the golden flecks within the near-black. "I'm not leaving my Family. I'm coming home to them."

I am, too. At last, after years of banishment, I'm coming home to the family I've already lived with for years. The man who knows how to light every part of me on fire. Enough of a nest egg to choose work that makes a difference. It's time for the *Calamity* to take on a new kind of job. One that changes charted space instead of merely expanding it.

ACKNOWLEDGMENTS

A debut novel in a debut series is a precarious business. Without the exact right conditions, it will never see the light of day. This book had a lot of right conditions and is only in your hands (or ears!) because of many people who worked together to make it possible.

Thanks to Rebecca Zanetti, who read three chapters and then generously offered to read more. Who gave great advice and helped to open the door to her own agent. Which leads me to my fantastic agent, Caitlin Blasdell of Liza Dawson Associates, who saw the value in this story and the series and who helped it to grow.

Thanks to the entire team at Bramble/Tor. Monique Patterson, who knew exactly what the manuscript needed to be in its final form. Mal Frazier for editing and coordination and much more. MaryAnn Johanson for copy editing, and Megan Kiddoo for production editing. Caro Perny for publicity and Jordan Hanley for marketing.

Long before the book reached any of them, thanks to Frank Harris, who looked at the roughest of early drafts with thoughtful consideration. Thanks to the Blue Badgers—Allison King and Mike Meneses—the best writing group a gal could ask for. Thanks to Liz Hersh-Tucker, Sarah McIntosh, and Katie Hossepian for support, cheerleading, and constant group-chat availability. Thanks to my mother for suggesting that I should write some smut and my father for agreeing—and to both for being early readers.

And finally, thanks to anyone who picked up the book and kept reading. Welcome to the worlds of Uncharted Hearts. I hope you stay on to our next adventure.

ABOUT THE AUTHOR

CONSTANCE FAY writes space-romance novels and genre-fiction short stories. Her short fiction can be found in *The Magazine of Fantasy & Science Fiction, CatsCast* podcast, and other publications. She has a background in medical device R & D and lives in Colorado with a cat who edits all her work first.